SHARON ASHWOOD
LORI DEVOTI
MICHELE HAUF
PATTI O'SHEA

Crave The Night

Swell Cat Press

ISBN-13: 978-0615548371
ISBN-10:   0615548377

CRAVE THE NIGHT
Copyright © 2011 by Swell Cat Press, LLC.

The publisher acknowledges the copyright holders of the individual works as follows:
ONE SOUL TO SHARE
Copyright © 2011 by Lori Devoti

CRUEL ENCHANTMENT
Copyright © 2011 by Michele Hauf

HIDDEN
Copyright © 2011 by Naomi Lester

ENEMY EMBRACE
Copyright © 2011 by Patti O'Shea

This is a work of fiction. Names, characters, places and incidents are either the product of the authors' imagination or are used fictitiously, and any resemblance to actual persons, living or dead, business establishments, events or locales is entirely coincidental.

This edition published by Swell Cat Press, LLC.

For questions and comments about the quality of this book please contact swellcatpress@gmail.com

Contents

Hidden

SHARON ASHWOOD

She took me to her elfin grot,
And there she wept, and sighed full sore
And there I shut her wild wild eyes
With kisses four.

And there she lulled me asleep
And there I dreamed – Ah! woe betide!
The latest dream I ever dreamt
On the cold hill side.

I saw pale kings and princes too,
Pale warriors, death-pale were they all;
They cried—"La Belle Dame sans Merci
Hath thee in thrall!"

From "La Belle Dame sans Merci" by John Keats

Chapter One

"ENEMY CENTRAL," RAFE DEVRIES muttered under his breath. From his position crouched in the night-shadowed trees, he had a good view of the mansion's front door. He could smell the place, too, with all a werewolf's nose for detail. There were many people inside, some of them Pack. *The hostages are here.*

But who had taken eight of his kind and why they were being held on this hilltop outside of town was a big, fat question mark. There were few correlations between the missing, outside of the fact that they all came from ranching families in Wolf Creek, and they'd each left to keep an appointment and never come home.

Rafe had been gone from the Creek a while, and there'd been no time for even the most basic investigation. He only had scuttlebutt gleaned during a burger stop at Burt's Roadhouse. Most of that had been speculation about this house on top of the ridge, but there was one real fact: All the missing folks' cars had been found along this road, keys in the ignition and pointed back toward town. Someone had dumped the vehicles.

It was their only solid clue. That, and his father's voice mail. Dad had left a one-liner: *The Pack's in trouble, boy. Come home and do your duty.*

It figured. As heir to his Alpha father, he'd always been the one in the family to come running, ready for battle or just to calm everyone down. Except this time the crisis wasn't about wounded pride and rustled heifers. This time the threat was from outside, and that made the danger real.

Especially when his dad had been the next to disappear.

Which was why Rafe had brought Darak, leader of the rogue, mercenary vampires called Clan Thanatos. They'd met when he'd served two tours with the Desert Wolves, one of the few supernatural military units. If there was a fight, Darak would have his back, no questions asked.

"The house is brand new. Your villains have assets," Darak said under his breath. The vampire was crouched just behind him. The approximate size of an industrial refrigerator, he had once been a Roman gladiator, but now looked more like a biker thug. "It looks like someone just peeled off the price sticker."

Rafe scanned the hilltop mansion high above the long sweep of Timber Lake. A stone's-throw from where they crouched, the house was enormous and ultra-modern, all random angles, steel, and glass. A hot tub sat in the spot with the best view of the moonlit water and rolling foothills of the Rockies. A pool and wet bar were a little to the right of the tub. The lights from the enormous windows lit a wide driveway, where a new Lexus gleamed soft, expensive silver. Everything said elegance and hard cash.

But there was no barbecue, no toys in the yard, not even a garden hose. The vampire was right. The place was new and impressive, but it had no soul.

No hidden escape routes, either, if he remembered the landscape. North and south of the place were woods so dense a squirrel would need a machete. The east side of the hill was a sheer drop only a mountain goat could navigate. That only left the west side approach.

Rafe glanced over his shoulder. The winding path they had climbed to get near the mansion was choked in a tangle of pines and poplars, the wild growth cleared just enough that the Lexus SUV could make it up without scratching the paint. "How the hell did they get equipment up here to build?"

Darak shrugged. "Magic."

Frackin' cow farts. Magic complicated anything to a factor of ten. Rafe straightened a little to look in the front window.

The decor was completely white. *Bet no one ever eats pizza in front of that TV.* "The boys at the roadhouse swear the fey are involved. I thought they were drunk."

Darak cursed unhappily, rubbing his shaven head. "Fey. Nasty buggers."

"That's why I called you, big boy."

Rafe sat back on his heels. They could go home, get reinforcements, and storm the place. But all he really knew was that there were Pack Devries werewolves in the house—or had been recently. Scent caught at a distance was limited intel. What part of the house were they kept in? Did they need medics? More information could make the difference between a successful mission and a train wreck.

For a moment he regretted not bringing some tech toys—long distance listening equipment, for a start—but then kicked the notion out of his mind. Magic raised merry hell with technology. Eyes and ears were best. He'd been out of the service and wandering the country for the last year, but he was still sharp.

He ghosted forward on silent feet, the cold air seeping in through his open leather jacket. The summer night was clear and clean, full of rich earth scents. Above, stars jewelled the skies in a thick blanket city-dwellers never got to see.

As he moved, he kept one eye on the picture window, watching for movement. Surely there would be guards? For a bad-guy fortress, it looked completely undefended except for a single security camera covering the front door and parking pad. Apparently intruders were supposed to drive up, park, and ring the doorbell.

Then again, maybe that lone camera was a decoy. Did the fey actually use CCTV? Or just magic mirrors and dragonflies with helmet cameras? Damned if he knew.

Rafe skirted to the right, Darak on his heels. They passed the kitchen window, and Rafe took a glance inside. It looked perfectly ordinary, if expensive and maniacally clean. Stainless steel glimmered in the soft glow of recessed pot lights, granite and pristine white tile adding to the arctic wasteland color scheme.

He dove for the ground, instinct acting before his brain caught up. *Someone's in the kitchen.* Rising to a crouch, he peered over the window sill. To his left, Darak was plastered to the wall, as if anything could make his huge frame smaller.

"What is it?" the vampire mouthed.

"A woman," Rafe returned.

That description didn't cover what he saw. Not by a longshot. She was standing with her back to the window, pulling a glass down from the cupboard. Then she paused at the stainless steel refrigerator and ice chunked into the glass. Even from that angle, Rafe could tell she was a beauty, and definitely not a werewolf. His people were dark and compact. She was tall and slender, with hair so pale it was almost silver. It fell to her hips in a smooth, thick curtain that shimmered in the subdued lights. Like pretty much everyone in Wolf Creek, she wore jeans, but there all similarity ended. Rafe was no fashionisto, but even he could tell the silky white shirt would have cost a week's pay.

Then she turned toward the sink, and Rafe ducked out of sight. He only caught a glimpse, but it was enough. Her face was small and neatly sculpted, with slanting eyes beneath winged brows. Her skin was so pale, it seemed pearlescent.

One of the light fey. *I wasn't expecting that.*

He was more familiar with the trickster dark fey, who lived off human settlements like exotic parasites. Light fey kept to themselves, as far from cities as they could get. They were seldom seen by anyone outside their own tribes. Suddenly, that seemed a crime.

So the rumors of their beauty are true. Rafe actually felt shaken.

The kitchen window was open a crack, and he caught a crisp, lemony perfume that must have been the woman's scent. Then the tap shut off. He didn't hear footsteps—she moved too gracefully to make a sound— but eventually a door closed nearby in the house. Cautiously, he rose to his feet. The kitchen was empty.

"Tinker Bell got an upgrade," Darak said under his breath.

Rafe nodded, still mute with startled wonder.

The vampire gave a soft laugh. "Enjoy the view, but remember she'd as soon eat your eyeballs with a pickle fork."

The words stung, as if the fork had found tender flesh. "And you never went into the greeting card business. What a shame."

"Just call me the Anti-Cupid. And I'm not kidding. They snare their victims by some kind of hypnosis. Light fey woo their victims and then do what they want while you're knocked senseless with lust."

That could have been me two seconds ago. "Kind of like vampires."

"They make us look like rank amateurs. The most common cause of death in fey-human encounters is wasting disease. After the fey's dumped them, there's no reason to go on living."

Rafe felt a wave of nausea. "Let's just get this over with."

He led the way around the corner of the house. Halfway along was the next window, blocked by Venetian blinds.

"Interesting," said Darak. "You can see in every place else. Think they're hiding something here?"

"I'll fix that." Rafe pulled out his Leatherman pocket knife and wiggled it into the space between the window and sash.

"What about a security system?" Darak asked blandly.

After a long minute of cursing, he pried the window up until the slider lock cleared its hole. He then slid the window open with barely a sound. For a brand-new place, it had crappy locks. "No security system."

"That you know of," Darak countered. "Could be silent. Could be something other than regular technology. Could be booby-trapped with silver bullets."

Silver was one of the few things that could injure both werewolves and vampires. Rafe was taking a huge risk, but the stakes were high. He found the cord beside the blinds and slowly reeled them up, trying to be silent. The room beyond was lit by a dim floor lamp in the far corner, but it was enough for a wolf to see what was in the room.

"Fido's balls," Rafe swore under his breath, pulling his Beretta.

It was a large space, plain and sterile-looking. Thirteen single beds stood in double ranks of six, with one larger bed crosswise at the end of the rows. It looked like a hospital ward, except here there were satin comforters and mounds of snow-white pillows. Eight of the beds were occupied.

There were eight missing Pack members. The sound of soft breathing filled the room, indicating the figures in the beds were all asleep.

Were they drugged? Bespelled? Hot, prickling rage crawled up Rafe's neck, followed by the sticky paws of fear. "What the . . . ?"

Darak gripped his arm hard enough to bruise. "We found your kin. Now let's get out of fairyland. We'll go back to town and muster the cavalry."

Rafe gripped the window frame. "I need more information."

With a heave, he vaulted over the sill, his boots landing softly on the tile floor. In truth, he needed to know if his father was safe. Using his nose and ears as much as his eyes, he scanned the room, making a sweep with his weapon. With an impatient noise, the vampire joined him inside the house.

Rafe examined each slumbering face. These were the missing Pack members, and he knew them all. Some looked peaceful, others frowned, as if their dreams troubled them. Rafe approached the nearest bed, recognizing the owner of the ranch next door to his father's. He gently shook the man's shoulder, but he didn't awaken. Rafe moved to the next bed and tried again with no result. Rafe exchanged a long look with Darak, fury climbing in his veins.

The large bed at the end of the room had been reserved for the Alpha. His father, white-haired but still strong and hale, lay there like a Viking king on his bier. Stern-faced, his fingers curled into claws, as if he were battling his enemy even in his dreams.

Rafe went arctic with anger. "Dad!"

His mind flipped into a white haze, pushing away what he didn't want to feel. Instead, he sought facts. He holstered his weapon and then checked his father's skin temperature. It was warm and dry. His pulse was slow, but steady and firm.

Darak was at his side. "So let's figure out a way to save him. All of them."

Rafe gripped his father's shoulder, shaking him, but the slow breathing didn't change. An ache of frustration caught in his throat, tearing through that protective haze. *Wake up!* Rafe made a sound that wasn't a cry or a word but had something of both.

Darak touched his arm, surprisingly gentle. "Think about it. As long as your father's asleep, you're the Alpha."

And that meant he was responsible for everyone. A tremor ran through him, tension breaking like a wave. He had to be smart. Reluctantly, Rafe relaxed his grip on his father's shoulder, his fingers releasing one at a time. "How can we get eight unconscious people down the hill to the truck without being noticed?"

"Eight deadweight bodies? Even for us, it'll take a few trips. Someone's bound to see us."

Rafe's first impulse was to reject the truth, but he choked it down until it burned in his gut. He'd never left his men behind. Leaving his father was impossible. And yet, it had to be done, at least for an hour or two. Then they'd bring back half the county and rain hurt on whoever ran this place. He turned to Darak, unfinished business bitter as ash on his tongue. "Then the faster we go, the faster we can get back here and kick some fey ass."

"Why wait?" came a light voice.

Rafe spun on his heel, a snarl escaping him. The woman from the kitchen was in the doorway, the glass of ice water poised in one hand.

He'd caught a glimpse of her before. Now his gaze could linger on every curve of her features. She was exquisite. Stunning. As his awe welled up, he shoved it aside, stomping out his kindling lust. *That beauty is a trick. A poison.*

A slow smile curled her lips. "Smart wolf. Give him a cookie."

Chapter Two

HE REACHED FOR THE BERETTA, but it was gone.

"My servants disarmed you both," the woman said. "It's impolite to carry when you go visiting."

Rafe swore and checked the room for gun-toting hostiles. There was no one there.

Darak fumbled with his empty holster. "What servants?"

"Oh, you can't see them, but they're everywhere. And trust me, this way is better. They're not pleasant viewing." She held up Darak's Smith and Wesson, dangling it between the thumb and forefinger of her free hand. Fey didn't like holding anything involving iron more tightly than they had to. "Looking for this, vampire?"

"May a diseased zombie suppurate in your martini."

The woman gave a long, slow blink, sipping pointedly from her water. "Well, okay then. I think we've set the tone for the night."

She stood aside to let two men into the room. They were broad-shouldered, deep-chested werewolves burnt bronze by the sun—the kind of hard workers Wolf Creek had aplenty. Rafe recognized them as a pair of the hands from down at Bearpaw Ranch. "Tom, Wyatt, what're you doing here?"

Neither answered, as if Rafe didn't count. Both cautiously approached Darak, the heels of their boots clicking on the floor. Big as the two yahoos were, the vampire made them look like Cowboy Ken dolls. Darak cast Rafe an exasperated glance. "Seriously? I have to bash puppies?"

"Bugger this." Rafe's temper slipped. His people were in trouble. His *father* was in trouble. Why weren't these two stretched out in beds number nine and ten?

Because they're traitors. The thought oozed through him, slippery and hideous as a slug.

"Back off, boys," Rafe said, his voice flat with anger. They didn't have weapons that he could see. Then again, neither did he—anymore.

They continued to ignore Rafe, their attention fully on the vampire.

"We know what he's doing here," Tom indicated Rafe with a jerk of his thumb.

"But what's a vampire doing in our territory?" Wyatt said angrily.

Thinking about pulling your head off, you doorknob. Rafe spun Wyatt around. "Never mind him. Talk to me."

"But Miss Lila wants to know!"

Lila. The name hung in the air, uttered like an invocation. As he said it, Wyatt's eyes grew vibrant with devotion. Then, he turned back to Darak with single-minded purpose.

Rafe's stomach flopped. *He's under her influence. He might as well be drugged.* Rafe grabbed Wyatt by the collar, hauling him backward hard enough that his feet left the floor. "I said, back off."

He cast a quick glance at the woman—Lila—but she just sipped her water and looked on with the mild interest of someone watching a wildlife documentary. The cool look ignited his temper, making him jerk Wyatt that much harder.

"Hey!" The wolf pulled free and wheeled around, breaking Rafe's grip with a sweep of his arm. "What makes you think you can come in here and...."

Rafe caught a glimpse of Wyatt's fist just as it swooped toward his temple. Instinct took over. Rafe ducked, driving his shoulder into Wyatt's middle. He heard the breath leave his opponent's body in a whoosh, then the thump of flesh as Wyatt's back hit the wall. Wyatt swore, writhing to get away.

Rafe let out a wolfish snarl. "I am your next Alpha. Pay attention when I speak."

Pain sliced through him as a fist pounded into his kidneys. It was Tom, attacking from behind. Eyes watering, Rafe sidestepped and spun, using the momentum to deliver a clean cross to Tom's jaw. Tom fell into Darak's waiting arms and was lifted clear off the floor.

"Naughty, naughty," said the vampire in softly evil tones.

Apparently, the diversion was all that Wyatt needed. He launched himself at Rafe, fingernails lengthening into claws. A slash to Rafe's cheek drew blood. He roared in fury. Rafe grabbed his shirt and pulled Wyatt close, limiting his ability to strike.

Hot blood trickled down his face like tears. He could see the gleam of Wyatt's eyes, the lift of his chin as he sniffed the blood. Pulling claws like that was dirty pool, and Rafe saw guilt in the nervous twitch of Wyatt's jaw.

"You really shouldn't have done that," Rafe snarled.

Sweat gleamed on Wyatt's high forehead. "I didn't have a choice."

"You always have choices, even if some of them suck."

He backed up just enough to flip Wyatt around and smash his head into the wall. Wyatt slumped to the ground like a deboned chicken.

Tom was already unconscious. Although every second had stretched like taffy, the fight was over in a flash.

Lila cleared her throat. "Alpha, you said?"

Rafe rounded on her, temper loosening his tongue. "I am Rafe Devries. In the absence of my father, I'm in charge. Whatever you're up to, Pack Devries will fight back."

Instinct drove him to stand between his people and the beautiful enemy. The sight of her still moved him, even if the wolf inside knew they were on the brink of a fight to the death.

Her luminous green eyes narrowed slightly, but he couldn't tell if it was amusement or annoyance. He could smell her fear, but she was hiding it well.

She didn't spare a glance for the men on the floor. "So far all you've proved is that your automatic response to aggression is aggression. That makes my job easy, because I know exactly how you'll react to everything I do and say."

He filed that bit information, not letting it distract. He was in battle mode, every sense alert. He could still feel the pull of her presence, as if every atom of her body were calling to his. She took a step forward, and he felt her focus on him, pushing at the barrier of his will. Her skin looked so soft, like she might melt in his hands. Desire settled in his belly, fogging the reasons why he shouldn't do whatever she asked. Desire turned to heat, heat to something feral. Rafe's need for her incinerated his reason, leaving it burnt wisps of ash.

Or would have, except for the need to protect the Pack. That alone remained solid though every other rational idea deserted him. Rafe took a long, shuddering breath, fighting the urge to kneel before her, leap on her, worship her, grind into her. It was like clawing free of a python that crushed his lungs, except this one attacked his will.

Good thing he was one stubborn cuss. When her hold on him finally slipped, there was an almost audible snap in the air. Rafe staggered back, breathing hard. With a bolt of satisfaction, he saw her flinch, too.

She's a trickster. Beautiful, but evil. Remember the pickle fork. He chanted the words to himself a few times, using them like a talisman. *Pickle fork. Pickle fork.*

"What do you want?" he snapped. "Let's get this over with."

Her eyes flared, her expression uncertain. No doubt the failure of her spell made her nervous. Still, her voice was calm. "To acquire Wolf Creek for my employers. They want it cleared of residents."

He flicked a burst of fury aside, refusing to react. "We homesteaded that land. It's our territory."

Suddenly the choice of hostages made sense. Every one of the sleepers owned a big parcel of land.

Her cold expression didn't change. "It won't be yours for long. Not if you want your loved ones to wake."

Rafe had been braced for those words, but hearing them still made the blood rush in his ears. He barely crossed glances with Darak, and the two of them surged toward her, using speed faster than a human eye could track.

He grabbed one of her arms, forcing her to her knees. Darak grabbed her other wrist and wrenched his gun away. Her glass hit the carpet, ice cubes tumbling out to glisten against the thick white pile. Water stained a dark patch in the knee of her jeans. A noise escaped her, half cry, almost a laugh. Rafe grabbed a fistful of her thick, pale hair, holding her as gently as he could without letting her stir an inch.

Darak pressed the muzzle of his gun to her temple.

"What did you do to my people?" Rafe snarled. "What's keeping them asleep?"

"Wouldn't you like to know?" she taunted. "Not that you could hope to understand the technical points of a soporific spell."

"Are all fey this snotty?"

She didn't reply. A booming sound resonated in the house. Rafe stiffened, his heart speeding faster. "What the hell was that?"

The booming sound repeated, coming closer, and closer again. Rafe figured out what it was. Doors closing. No doubt every door in the house. Were Lila's invisible servants sealing them in?

"That is the sound of your incarceration," she said. "Not that I need more hostages. I've taken eight of your Pack for my own. A six-Pack would have been amusing. The mounting numbers are just getting tiresome."

Darak pressed the muzzle a fraction deeper into her temple. "Time to rethink, Tinker Bell."

The front door slammed, followed by the sound of metal bolts sliding home. "I think I have all the cards," Lila said coolly. "You're going to surrender to me."

Rafe caught a whiff of something burning. Darak grunted in surprise and dropped his weapon to the floor. It sizzled, blackening the white carpet. Steam hissed as the red-hot metal touched an ice cube. The vampire cursed in a language older than the Crusades.

The next instant Lila seemed to melt from Rafe's hands. One moment she was firmly in his grasp. A second later she simply—wasn't. She was on the other side of the room, her hands clenched into fists.

Electricity rippled through the room, raising the fine hairs on Rafe's arms and leaving the faint smell of ozone behind. A moment later, the two felled wolves rose to their feet, heads lolling and eyes shut. A shudder rippled along Rafe's skin. Their movements were too fluid, too boneless. They looked as if someone were behind them, lifting them like rag dolls and shaking their limbs into place. *Those damned servants again.*

Revulsion was making him sweat. Rafe pulled off his jacket, hands damp and sticky on the leather. Half of his brain was already mapping out the next fight, the other half admitting their efforts weren't getting them anywhere. He glanced at Darak. His friend's scowl said he was thinking the same thing. They needed a new plan, but what the hell did this macabre puppet show mean?

"Enough already. Leave them alone." Darak reached for Tom, his big hand engulfing the werewolf's arm.

The moment they touched, a blazing light filled the room, like a thousand cameras flashing at once.

Rafe hurtled backward, tossed over an unoccupied bed. He landed awkwardly, wrenching his shoulder as he rolled upright. His ribs ached like he'd taken a roundhouse kick.

Rafe got to his feet. He heard the sound of flesh hitting flesh, which meant Darak was already in action. He glanced around. Hope flickered when he saw Lila was no longer there. Tom and Wyatt were gone, too.

Then shock speared through him. Darak was wrestling with two creatures that had nothing to do with werewolves. So these were the servants, made visible for the fight. *Holy frackin' batwings.*

They were nearly as big as Darak and equipped with beaks, wings, and claws the length of lawnmower blades. Their skin was a dark mud color, leathery and pebbled with sharp spines sticking from each joint. Gargoyles? Godzilla wannabes? It didn't matter what they were called. Darak was covered with slashes that dripped thick, dark vampire blood. A human body wouldn't last an instant.

Good thing he had options. Rafe stripped off his clothes in seconds. It didn't take a full moon to change. That was a myth, along with the idea that being a werebeast was contagious. But it was hard work and not always a sure thing. Not so easy if a person was distracted.

Like under attack by big ugly reptiles.

He heard Darak scream. Not yell, or bellow, but a scream of pure rage, and the pungent smell of undead blood washed through the room.

Rafe's breath left his body, forcing his mind to be calm. He crouched on the floor, naked, fighting the reflex to leap up and fight.

Concentrate. The floor was cold and slightly dusty under his bare flesh, the cracks between the tiles an endless, dizzying path.

A howl, not human, not animal, twisted in the air.

Shut it out! The speckles in the tile flowed like waves on a shore, ripples of dark and light and . . .

His consciousness disappeared down the dark hole that was his inside place, the part that held his other half. Mentally, it was like folding himself inside out, like a reversible garment, and simply bringing his other side to the surface. Physically, it was just best to surrender. People saw flowing fur and wrenching bones, but that wasn't what he perceived from the inside. Changing felt like a bad charley horse, a terrible cramp that needed to stretch out.

A bad, bad cramp, like every bone in his body was sucking itself inward. Like he would splinter, folded by impossible pressure. The only relief was to pull his limbs back into shape by pulling, rolling, thrusting claws and fangs from his flesh and howling his relief with all the might of his lungs.

Then, suddenly, he was shaggy fur and sharp teeth, with a terrible need to kill and eat. Rafe sprang to his paws, his ears swiveling to catch the sounds of the fight. Now that he was armed—or pawed, as the case may be—and protected by his thick coat, he could leap into it and hope to survive.

In real time, the change was almost instant. Rafe circled the bed. Moving slowly, his broad paws made no sound. Colors had faded, but his vision was excellent. He could smell far more scents now, the traces of people who had come and gone. And magic. *Fey magic.* Rafe growled deep in his chest, unable to quell the instinct to warn off danger.

Darak was barely holding his own. The vampire swung his fist like a hammer, smashing the reptile thing in the side of its leathery head. It recoiled with a snarling scream, wings unfurling to block the faint light in the room. Darak slammed an uppercut into its beak, snapping its head back, but with a single beat of the huge, leathery wings the creature rose in the air, raising its back claws to rake down the front of the vampire's chest. Darak went over backward, the gargoyle riding him down. Both creatures jumped on him, jackals on a wounded lion.

One of the things turned to peer at Rafe over its shoulder, a curiously ordinary gesture. Rafe sprang, knocking the gargoyle aside, closing his jaws on its hideous throat. That gave the vampire the moment he needed. Darak tossed the creature to its back, twisting the snapping beak away from his bleeding wounds.

Then, suddenly, Lila was in the room again. Rafe clamped his jaws tighter on the gargoyle's neck, holding it still but waiting a moment before the kill. There was no telling what such a monstrosity might be worth to its mistress.

Tensed to rend and tear, he tracked the fey's movements from the corner of his vision. She was moving too fast to see clearly, and all he could tell was that she had something in her hand. She released it with a word, flinging it into the air. It sailed and Rafe crouched down on his prey, keeping out of the glittering object's path.

Darak wasn't so lucky. The silver net fell over the vampire, dropping him helpless to the floor. Fey-spelled silver would rob him of his extraordinary strength. He let out an angry roar, tearing at the web that tightened even as he struggled.

The next moment, Lila covered them both with Darak's Smith and Wesson.

"Get this straight, boys." Her tone cracked in the suddenly silent room. "I have millennia of magic bred into my bones. I'm fast, strong and smart and maybe just all-around better at everything than you are, so don't mess with me."

Oh, yeah? Rafe itched to prove her wrong. Everyone had an Achilles heel, he just didn't know hers yet. *But I can find out. Wait and watch to see what she hides.* He wasn't going to lose to a frackin' fairy.

Lila had other ideas. Her eyes widened with pure fury when she saw his teeth on the gargoyle's throat. She pointed the gun at the closest sleeping figure. It was Eloise Lambert, who ran Wolf Creek's credit union. "Back down, wolfman, or she dies. I'm not joking."

Rafe hesitated a moment, wondering if she'd carry out her threat. The odds were fifty-fifty, but he wasn't gambling with Eloise's life. The fey was too angry. He took his jaws from the gargoyle's throat and gave Lila his best wolfish glare. The gargoyle scuttled to hide behind its much smaller mistress. Then the gun swung from Eloise's head to point right between Rafe's eyes.

Well, that was sort of an improvement. Maybe. Now he just had to convince her to start letting people go.

He had to risk returning to human form if he was going to talk her into anything. Rafe shifted back without apology for his nakedness. "You smell like fear."

Lila's gaze roved over his body. Pink stole into her pale cheeks like the rose-pearl light before dawn. Sadly, her fingers tightening on the gun spoiled the charming effect. "Maybe, but I'm winning. I had eight hostages; now I have ten. I lured all the strong members of your Pack here, one by one. The wolves you have left in your pathetic little town will tuck their tails and run at the first sign of trouble."

Her blush contradicted her hard-boiled words. She also didn't know a thing about the citizens of Wolf Creek. They were a tough, independent bunch down to the last pup. Tinker Bell had a fight on her hands.

"Points to you," Rafe said dryly. "But you've got every member of the council here, either asleep or at gunpoint. If you're trying to deal with the wolves, who are you going to bargain with if all the Pack's leaders are here?"

"Who said anything about a bargain?"

"I don't see an army. Or are they invisible, too?"

He'd never get used to looking down the business end of a gun, much less one he knew held silver bullets. Sweat trickled along the small of his back. *We can't win this by brute force. We need to be clever. I need to know why the fey are mixed up in this.*

He put all the lust he felt into his voice. "Let's bargain, Lila."

A spark of interest crossed her face. "Are you offering to trade yourself for someone here?"

"What the hell are you doing?" Darak interjected. They both ignored him.

"Yes. For the real Alpha. My father. Let him go."

"How filial of you." Her hands shifted again on the grip of the gun. She was nervous—which could be good or bad. Her gaze kept drifting down his body, then jerking away. "At the moment, I have ten captives. If I accept, then I lose a hostage. I don't like that."

Darak muttered, but the second gargoyle was sitting on him and the sound was muffled.

"You lose two. Darak isn't a wolf, he's not involved, and I need someone to make sure Dad gets home safely. And I want Dad awake and healthy. If you want to negotiate for the town, he has to be competent."

She stalked up to Rafe, hovering just beyond his reach. Now the muzzle of the gun was pointed right at his forehead. He suddenly felt as naked as he actually was.

Her green gaze raked over him. "Your father will awake one hour after your vampire friend puts him back in his own bed. Satisfactory?"

"Yes."

"Then I agree on one condition."

"Name it."

"Give me your oath you won't try to leave the house."

"Don't!" barked Darak from beneath the gargoyle. "Never give your word to a fey. You'll always regret it. No exceptions."

The gargoyle pressed a leathery hand over the vampire's mouth and gave a rattling hiss, forked tongue flickering.

Rafe glared at Lila, but his words were for his trusted friend. "I accept the terms. Just get my father out of here."

Chapter Three

LILA WASN'T SURE WHAT TO DO with this latest wolf creature.

She marched into her office, her jeans still uncomfortably wet from the spilled ice water. At least she was more comfortable than whatshisname now chilling in the caged room in the basement.

It had been unpleasant to watch her gargoyles drag him from the room. They weren't the gentlest when it came to transporting reluctant prisoners and, despite what had just happened, Lila wasn't a fan of brute force.

The office was dark, but she fell into the chair behind her desk without switching on the lamp. There wasn't a lot to see in the white-on-white room. Desk, chairs, a couch and a TV she occasionally watched to ensure her activities hadn't hit the nightly news. So far, not a peep. She'd been both careful and lucky.

Lucky. The word echoed mockingly in her mind. She stared for a moment at the starry sky outside the large office window to her left. This side of the house faced the cliff and the view was breathtaking. So was the zillion-yard drop to a rocky death below. Unlike most fey, she couldn't fly. Tonight, that seemed as much metaphor as fact. *My luck is dropping like a stone.*

She turned away from the skyscape and planted her elbows on the desk, resting her face in her hands. *Wolves. Big, bad, bloody nuisances.* Weariness washed over her, leaving her feeling as bleached as driftwood. Ralph? Rafe. That was his name. *C'mon. You knew that. You don't forget the name of a guy with abs—and stuff—like that.*

He'd walked right into the enemy camp armed with nothing but a handgun and a vampire. Something about his defiance had broken through her studied calm. *Not good.*

She should really put him to sleep with the rest. Curiosity was a fey's greatest weakness, and Lila knew herself too well. In more carefree times, she'd been all in favor of unruly naked men. But that was then. Now was not a time when she could afford indulgence. There was oath-magic at work.

Three vows had been made, each dangerous enough on its own, but piled together they made a precarious house of cards. The first and most serious one she'd made was an oath to save her people, whatever it took.

Second, she had made a bargain with the man who threatened them. No ordinary human, he had the backing of a powerful corporation, wealth, and the law. He'd promised to leave the fey alone for a year and a day or until she gave him something he wanted even more than their annihilation.

The third vow hinged on the second. Her sisters had agreed to help her. The price for their generosity had been high, for magic never gave without taking away. In order to empower Lila, they had traded their exceptional beauty to become gargoyle servants for the term of her quest, or until her mission failed.

Three vows. One tangled web.

She'd used the energy from these three spells to do a lot of things: she'd found Wolf Creek and its riches, and then built the opulent house calculated to reassure her wolfish visitors—right before she hit them with a sleeping spell. Most of all, the triple-spell magic kept her activities cloaked in secrecy. That had been part of the bargain: Lila had to keep the whole affair out of the news and invisible to the eyes of human law.

There were too many "ifs." If she could pull it off. If her magic didn't fail. If her enemy kept to his half of the deal. If it all worked out, she could go home knowing her family would be safe. If not . . .

The phone rang and she started upright, heart racing. The backlit caller ID read "Masterson. Cell."

The boss. He who had threatened—still threatened—everything and everyone she held dear. *The enemy*.

Her pulse hammered in her ears. Every time Masterson called, she worried he would renege on his part of their deal and bring everything crashing down. Fey charms were useless on the man. She would have had to dress up like a net profit to make her seduction spells work.

Suddenly needing the comfort of light, Lila switched on the lamp before picking up the receiver. "Lila Wilding."

"Progress?"

That was how he started every call. And like every time, her tongue was suddenly sandpaper. "Um. Well, sir, I acquired a new guest tonight."

"How many does that make? What use is he?"

Lila put the situation in terms a shark like Masterson could understand. "He has the means to persuade others. He's valuable to the wolves."

"Why?"

"He's the son of their king."

"Then make it happen. You're almost out of time."

The line went dead in her hand. Lila took a deep breath, and let it out in a sigh. Masterson was right about the ticking clock. The year and a day she had to work a miracle was almost up.

Oberon's balls! Rafe Devries wasn't going to betray his Pack. Her instincts said he was far too stubborn.

But nothing was as tricky as a fey.

And no fey was as desperate as Lila.

The house had been built on a slope, leaving half the basement—mostly utility rooms—with plenty of light. In the other, windowless half were chambers equally useful but far less ordinary. At the end of a long hallway, deep under the earth, were the darkest places. Lila walked down the corridor toward her prisoner, wishing she'd thought to bring a sweater. It was cold and damp.

Lila slowed as she neared her destination. Rafe was alone in the cell. She could see everything, since the door of the room was made of bars like a cage at the zoo. He slumped on the edge of the hard single bed, pulling on his socks. Evidently, her servants had reunited him with his clothes. A pity, but she had to admit beefcake wasn't quite the same with goosepimples.

Her irreverent thought vanished as he looked up, dark eyes smoky with anger. He had the typical werewolf looks: dark springy hair, high cheekbones, narrow jaw, straight nose. He was tall for his kind, but lean. Wolves moved like coiled springs, all edgy tension that filled a room even when they were completely still. Despite their civilized facade, it paid to remember they were still wild beasts.

"What do you want?" he asked, his voice husky with resentment.

"Your co-operation, wolf."

"Try 'please.' There's an old human saying that you catch more flies with honey than vinegar." He pulled on his other sock, then started on the boot.

Irritation pricked at Lila. She'd grown used to the adoration of the males she'd held captive. His indifference chafed. "Then how do I catch wolves? Something squirmy from the pet shop, or will a raw flank steak do the trick?"

He gave her a look that made her regret her words. Attitude wasn't going to get her very far with this specimen. He finished with the boots and stood up, dusting his hands on his jeans. "You don't know a thing about us, do you?"

Not much. Then again, the wolves probably thought *she* was the villain. Secrecy had its down side. *You think you've got problems, wolfman. Try some of mine.*

She folded her arms. "So then tell me."

He paced, quick, restless steps. "What?"

"Anything. Do all your people live in Wolf Creek?"

"We're ranchers. Where else would we be?"

She shrugged. "Just asking. You don't seem the type to spend your days chasing cows."

"We're not like the urban Packs. The Devries wolves don't do appletinis and book clubs."

"Yoga?"

"Not so much." His words were clipped with impatience. "Now it's my turn to ask something. What did you do with Wyatt and Tom?"

"I sent them home with your vampire friend."

"To die of broken hearts," he snarled. "*La Belle Dame sans Merci.*"

The name meant beautiful, pitiless woman. Bloody hell, she hated that poem. "No, of course not. I took the spell off. They'll bounce back."

"How very generous of you."

"I'm not a monster." His look said otherwise, and she felt herself flush.

He raised an eyebrow. "Why did you take them in the first place?"

"To prove a point. To scare you. I have power. I can glamor the wolves whenever I please."

"Not all of us." He stalked back and forth, looking more like a caged tiger. "That's why you put the others to sleep. Those are our leaders. Those with Alpha blood. Your charm is powerful, but not enough to control a very strong will. Easier to knock them out."

He was right and by the look on his face, he enjoyed finding a weakness. She wasn't going to add to his satisfaction by telling him that the others had come far closer to surrender than he. His will was forged of an iron she could not break. *So far, anyway. I'm not out of the game yet.*

She kept her own voice ice-cold. "They might be stubborn, but not smart. They were easy enough to lure here."

He matched her chilly look with one of his own. "But once your victims arrived, you couldn't get them to sign over their land. Not even to save their friends."

When she didn't answer, he went on. "Once they knew what you were after, you couldn't let them warn the rest of Wolf Creek. So you put your victims to sleep, turning them into hostages until you're ready to make your move. Since the individual approach didn't work, you're going to force the whole town to give in. Our land for our Alphas. And you want me to be your mouthpiece in this hellish blackmail."

Lila folded her arms. He'd figured it out. *Smart wolf.* "When the time comes, your people will awaken with no ill effects."

"They're bargaining chips."

"More or less."

"What a wonderful Alpha bitch you would make."

"I assume you mean that literally."

"You've already got there metaphorically."

"I'm a quick study." She gave him a thin smile. "And I'm not going to spend all night trading insults. I have better things to do with my time. Let's get down to business."

"Fine." He whirled mid-pace, frustration contorting his features. "What can I do to end this?"

"When I get Wolf Creek, you get your people back. Your daddy gets his heir back. Like you said, you're my mouthpiece."

The muscles in his jaw twitched with anger. "That's not going to happen. I won't do it."

Lila kept her cool. As long as he was emotional and she wasn't, she had the upper hand. "I've been patient, but the clock is ticking."

"What's the rush?"

She shrugged. It wasn't any of his affair.

"Well?" he repeated.

She looked at him through the bars, still wondering how the hell she was going to persuade him to fall into line with her plans. She'd be smart to put a few cards on the table. "I represent the Masterson Group."

The name made him recoil. Well, at least they had that feeling in common.

Then a look of understanding washed over his face, as if he were connecting a whole lot of dots. His lip curled, the human version of a wolf's snarl. "They've been around here before, doing geological surveys. There's a notion Wolf Creek is sitting on an oil field."

"Your families were the original homesteaders. You still hold the mineral rights."

Rafe gave a single nod. "So let's get this part out of the way: I know oil companies lease the right to drill in return for a cut of the profits. We're not interested."

"If we can't lease the rights, then we have to force you to sell."

"Good luck with that."

Lila curled her hands around the silver bars, exasperation making her want to bang her head against them. She'd had this conversation with every one of the sleepers upstairs. Even charmed right off their paws, she couldn't make them sign their land away. "You could be rich and still keep your ranches. Be reasonable. Do it for the sake of your people."

Rafe glowered, stalking back and forth just the other side of the bars. She could feel his body heat as he passed. "Rich in human terms. We're wolves. We don't look at things the same way."

She gave the bars a shake. "Then change your perspective, Mr. Devries."

"Money isn't everything. You don't rent out your home so that some oil guys can wheel up a drilling rig and suck the life out of it. It's a violation of everything that matters to us."

Frustration grated along her nerves. She turned from him, now pacing herself as she waved a dismissive hand. "Oh, come now, I've heard of werewolves who live in downtown apartments. Their idea of a good hunt is finding a drive-through window."

Rafe kicked the bars, his heavy boot making them ring like the bell from the Tower of Doom. The sound made her flinch.

"We're good, old-fashioned, howl-at-the-moon varmints, and we like our grass green and our water pure. Each Pack member might own his or her mineral rights, but it was decided long ago, the first time the oil barons began sniffing around our land, that we'll move together. Either the whole Pack agrees to a deal, or none of us do. And we won't."

Wolves and their territory. It was starting to make a weird kind of sense. "So you say." Her bottom lip curved into what she hoped looked like a knowing smile. "I say you'll change your mind."

"And what do you get for all your efforts?" Now he stepped close to the bars, peering down at her from beneath a lock of dark, curling hair. "What's Masterson paying you to destroy us?"

She gave him a long, considering look. He was too raw, too real for games. She could feel his presence like a gathering storm. "There are a lot of us praying he keeps his word."

His brow knitted, his anger morphing to something else. "Who is 'us'? What did he promise you?"

That look undid her. It was too close to sympathy. Pain caught in her throat and she looked away, the lights suddenly too bright.

Though the touch of the silver-coated bars must have been painful, he reached between them, grasping her hand in his. "Lila, are you in trouble, too?"

Like all the wolves, he ran hot. Her fey senses swam with imagery carried in his touch—racing through the woods on all fours, the hot grit of desert sand, the notion that, despite her magic more than because of it, he thought she was beautiful.

She pulled away. The warm shadow of his grip tingled on her skin, reawakening the image of his naked body. Her mouth suddenly ran dry with unexpected desire, an electric need that pulsed through every nerve. *I want him. I must be mad.*

She looked up, seeing the same uninvited interest in the set of his mouth. His nostrils flared slightly, as if he were catching and memorizing her scent.

The moment stretched on and on. They were enemies and yet he'd reached out. That deserved a response.

If only she could give one. She lowered her gaze, staring at the toes of her shoes. When she spoke, her voice was listless, almost sad. "My business isn't yours, wolf, but I thank you for asking."

Imagery flickered through her mind, a montage of her childhood: Gilden Woods, rolling in the grass with her sisters, the snow on their house the year the elk nearly walked right through the front door.

She blinked, and she was back in the cold basement of the white-on-white prison that magic built. She was here because she was in a fight to the death—and not just for herself.

Now there was pity in the wolf's eyes. Somehow he'd caught a glimpse of the real battle.

Lila grabbed for her defenses, pulling them around her like a protective blanket. Maybe pity was the key to winning Rafe Devries over. With a sad story and some hand-wringing, maybe she could get him to convince his Pack to sell after all.

A wave of nausea caught the back of her throat. *How low are you going to stoop before this is over? Who is the real beast here?*

She turned and strode away before he saw her cry.

Chapter Four

LILA HURRIED BACK UPSTAIRS, but not to her office. She slipped out the door to the poolside patio, feeling the cool summer night through the silky fabric of her blouse. The mountain air had the same snap as a crisp apple, bright and alive with energy.

It soothed away the heat of her burning face. *How dare he?*

She wasn't even sure what she meant by the question. How dare he upset her? How dare he resist? How dare he be justified in objecting to absolutely everything she was doing?

Maybe, how dare he be so damned appealing? She'd got an eyeful of werewolf *au naturel* earlier, but he was just as good eye-candy fully dressed. Added to that, he had that smouldering aura of a male beast in his prime. There'd been moments when she'd been infinitely grateful for the silver bars between them. And yet, even when he had been wrestling her to the floor, he hadn't hurt her. Rafe Devries might be a beast, but he wasn't a brute.

Perhaps that was her, *La Belle Dame sans Merci.*

She kicked off her shoes and padded to the edge of the pool. The lights from the house reflected in ripples from the dark water, dancing in time with the breeze. She knelt by the edge, trailing her fingers through the pools of brightness. *I was so sure what I was doing was right, but every day that goes by makes me doubt more and more.*

Her vows had been hasty, made in passion. Made in front of her entire tribe of fey. She hadn't thought through the consequences, but the heart she'd poured into the act had bound her fast. Fey held their honor dear, and promises bound them tight.

Lila never did things half-way when her blood was up.

Conjure in haste, regret at leisure. One of her father's favorite lines.

But her intent had been pure. She sank both hands into the water, cupping them to catch the water. She raised the bowl of her palms, letting rivulets fall between her fingers to bubble and splash in the pool. *Show me,* she willed the water and the moonlight. *Remind me why I do this.*

Magic rushed through her like bubbles through champagne. Borrowed magic, sacrificed by her two sisters for a year and a day because Lila had forfeited her own long before.

The bubbles in the water began to multiply and seethe, taking on new colors and forming into hills and trees. The scene grew larger as more and more of the water drained into the image. The trees stretched and grew, rising high above Lila as the vision filled the pool to the very edges, floating above the rim. The deep glow of spellcraft shimmered around it, like a nimbus of starlight. Lila leaned closer to the scene, her throat aching when she recognized the familiar landscape of home. Like a camera coming into focus, every blade of grass grew clear as she watched.

People began to emerge from the shady grottoes, clad in the dark, rich shades of bark and loam. They had the same slender height, the same pale hair as Lila. Each was a face she knew and held dear. These were the light fey, going about their nightly rounds before settling down to sleep.

Two little boys chased a moth, tripping over their feet and each other in the game. She could hear their piping voices in her mind. Her sister Arabelle's sons, the eldest only four. The sight of them filled her with longing and amusement.

Lila waved a hand, turning the scene to see different parts of the forest. The fey dwellings were vibrantly painted, every surface a rainbow of colors. It was happiness that gave their magic-built houses their brilliant hues, and none were white like Lila's hilltop prison. There was the great meeting hall, a few young people dancing on the lawn before it, one of them playing a flute made of bone. Wherever there were fey, there was always music. Silence was a rare thing when there was someone to play, and someone to listen.

She turned the vision again. Ah, there was her father, standing outside his home and watching the stars. He did that for a few moments every night, with two or three of his students waiting patiently nearby. Though the king, her father was also a teacher of history and fey lore. He hadn't understood why Lila wanted to wander the bustling cities. For him, everything one could ever want was in their private forest home. And yet, he had made it possible because he loved her, even if she walked a different path.

So Lila had given up her magic for twelve years so that she could explore the human world. That had got her an education, an apartment, and everything else a young woman could desire. Most of all, it gave her a chance to find out who she was without spells and enchantments.

It also meant she was powerless when she needed her fey heritage the most. The twelve years weren't up when Masterson came on the scene ready to destroy their tribe. Lila knew the ways of human cunning and was the best equipped do battle, but she had no magic. Her sisters had come to her rescue, giving her their strength for the year and a day of the vow—and their battle for survival.

Lila wasn't sure she would have had their courage. Arabelle had left her little sons behind so that Lila could fight for their future.

They are all counting on me. Lila pressed her face into her hands. *That is why I must do this. If I don't, they will be destroyed. There will be no forest, no fey, no family.*

But it was so difficult. It wasn't as if she could zap Masterson with a spell. Magic couldn't change a person's essential nature. Change an evil man into a bug, and he would strip the leaves from every tree in the forest. Change him into a leaf, and he would carry the blight that poisons the land. Kill him, and his evil would simply be free to find another host.

But she had come up with a plan. A perfect one.

One that now depended on her wits and one stubborn werewolf. It suddenly seemed too fragile.

Lila stared at the image of her home, wishing she could walk into it, back to the secure happiness of her childhood.

The only thing missing from the conjured vision was the shadow that would end it all.

"Who's there?" Rafe demanded of the darkness.

A low, chittering laugh was the only response, followed by footsteps that sounded like claws on stone. Rafe backed away from the bars, sitting on the end of his narrow bed. It had been like that since Lila left, hours ago. Rustling wings. Whispers in a tongue he'd never heard before. Scents he'd never encountered anywhere. No doubt Lila's invisible servants were standing guard, and the two gargoyles were only part of the crew.

So what was with the creepy-assed help, anyway?

Lila was one scary babe, even though she was beautiful beyond any woman he'd ever seen. Still, it didn't take a genius to figure out that she was in trouble. He'd seen her tears, smelled the subtle change in her body chemistry that said she was afraid. When he'd touched her, she'd jerked away like a frightened bird. Her tough exterior was about as sturdy as an eggshell. For all her powers, she was terrified of Masterson. Why?

He was certain that answer was key to everything, and he had to discover it. If he could solve her problem, maybe she'd stop being his.

Something walked by his cell, footsteps shuffling like a giant sloth in mule slippers. A few seconds after that, he heard the buzz of dragonfly wings. *What the hell are those things?*

Rafe lay back on the bed, but every muscle was tensed into a hard knot. The strangeness of the situation reminded him of the desert patrols, never sure what creatures the enemy had stalking the night. The Wolves hadn't been the only non-humans who'd joined the war.

As the Alpha heir, he'd gone into the army because he knew sooner or later he'd have to look after the Pack. It was the best way to see the world and sow a few wild oats before bowing to the weight of a leader's responsibility. It also eased the inevitable tension between the Alpha and the Alpha-in-waiting. He loved his dad, but Wolf Creek was a little small for the both of them.

Rafe rubbed fatigue from his eyes, pain dragging at his limbs as he moved. Werewolves healed fast, but the gargoyle-inflicted bruises still hurt.

The Desert Wolves had been an eye-opener for Rafe. There hadn't been as much carefree oat-sowing as he'd planned. He'd led a lot of patrols and learned what being in charge—an Alpha—meant. He was responsible for every life in his care.

Those lessons had stuck. Now the Pack's future was on the line. He had to step up.

And that came back to Lila. He and Darak had already established they couldn't outmaneuver her with brute force, but maybe he could beat her through subtler means. Time to take his own advice and slather on the honey.

He'd have to keep it real. There was no way he could out-trick a fey— and to be honest, that wasn't a game he wanted to play. If Lila was backed into a corner, and he was pretty sure that was the case, the smartest thing he could do was to give her a safe exit.

Rafe surprised himself by actually falling asleep for an hour or two. When he awakened, his clothes were washed, mended, and folded neatly at the end of the bed. *Creepy.* He hadn't heard a thing.

A breakfast tray sat on the floor, still piping hot. When he lifted the domed lid, he found coffee, eggs, ham, and biscuits dripping with butter. Taking a gamble that it wasn't poisoned or enchanted, he ate hungrily.

When he had drunk the last of the coffee, the door to his cell swung open, and he smelled gargoyle. "Come," said a voice like stones grating together. "You have questions to answer."

After a long march through the mansion, the invisible creatures shoved him through the door of a large room with a view from the cliff top. Rafe stared a moment, distracted by the broad expanse of blue sky, before his guards dropped him into one of the side chairs. The touch of scaly claws withdrew. Rafe barely resisted the urge to scrub at the places where those talons had been.

Lila was sitting at a large, pale gray desk that would have looked more at home in an office building. Today she was wearing a sleeveless black dress that made her hair and skin look nearly white. The surface was clean but for a laptop computer, a lamp, and a telephone. He searched in vain for a picture or a plant, but there was nothing personal anywhere in the room. If Lila vanished, there would be no clue that she had ever existed. Maybe that was the point.

After a moment of typing, she closed the laptop and folded her hands on the dull surface of the desk. He noticed a thin, jagged scar on the inside of one bare arm, pink against the subtle blue of her veins. A knife wound. It made him curious.

"We need to talk," she said.

"You sound like my old girlfriend."

That earned him a slight lift of her brows. "I need to understand why the Pack won't bend, even to save their most respected members."

"I answered that."

"Your answer was insufficient."

Rafe let the silence stretch a beat, weighing how much he should say. How much might she use against them? "Do you have children?"

She balked, as if reluctant to give away anything about herself. "No. My sisters do."

Rafe thought he heard stirring from one of the invisible gargoyles, but then silence resumed. He hated talking when he had no idea who—or what—was in the room. "Then you know there's nothing a family won't do for the future of their kids."

The lids slowly lowered over her intense green gaze, shutting him out. One hand travelled to the scar on her arm. "I understand."

"And if you touch one of our pups I will personally end you."

Her gaze snapped back to his face. "Touch one of the . . . ?" There was anger, even offence, in her expression, but it slowly faded to her usual impassive expression. "Then I need to know how to win, because I don't dare lose."

The harsh statement didn't measure up to her shock of the moment before. She was talking tough, but she was no threat to a child. Good to know. "Losing well is no dishonor."

"It's not about honor anymore."

"Then what is this about?"

The conversation stalled until Rafe itched to leap up and pace the room. He could sense her struggle, but if he was going to figure her out, he had to let things unfold at her pace.

At last she sighed, leaning forward until the lush fall of pale hair hid her face. "I made a bargain. A vow. That's all you need to know."

"A blood oath."

She looked up sharply. "How did you know that?"

"Your scar. I wouldn't think the blood necessary for a magic user. Vows spoken in the presence of a fey, and all that."

"A blood oath is stronger." She put her hand over the scar, hiding it. "It's only used for the most important promises. I wanted to make a point."

Rafe watched her, wondering what it was she wanted to conceal. "That takes guts. Shedding your own blood takes more courage than people think."

"That depends on what's at stake." Her voice was low and husky, almost a dare.

"How much are you going to lose? Because you will lose. Wolves are stubborn."

She gave a low laugh that was surprisingly frank. "This negotiation is more complicated than you may think."

"I think the kidnapping and brainwashing is a pretty good clue how far you're willing to go."

She lifted her eyebrows. "Is that how you see my little parlor tricks?"

"Parlor tricks." He swore under his breath, and she flinched. "You meant it as far more than that. You intend coercion."

"You use teeth and claws. My powers serve the same function. Survival."

"It's not the same. Not at all."

"Glamor is a standard fey tactic. We have to show our strength, and if we do it right, it's no worse than a hypnotist making a person do the chicken dance. Embarrassing, but harmless."

"I doubt your victims would consider it harmless."

"Do you apologize to your prey?"

Rafe stewed a moment. "Are we your prey? Is that why you're tearing an entire town up by its roots?"

"Don't cry to me about that," she shot back. "At least your people will survive."

"And yours won't? Is that what's at stake?"

She gave him a hard look, but said nothing. Apparently, he'd hit the truth. She'd taken a blood oath to protect her people. He felt a sneaking respect for her, predator to predator. Under the right circumstances, he would do the same thing to protect his Pack.

Enlightening, but now he could almost see her retreating behind the thick walls of her reserve. This wasn't getting him answers.

"Why are your gargoyles invisible now?" he asked, deliberately changing directions.

"Huh?" She blinked, and then looked uncomfortably around the room. "Um. They prefer it that way."

"I've never heard of sensitive gargoyles."

Rafe heard rustling again. He'd posed the question to unsettle her, but he was truly curious. He leaned in from his side of the desk, closing the distance between them. "They usually revel in their ability to frighten the enemy. Why are these so different?"

"Don't." To Rafe's surprise, she put a hand over his. "Please, don't. I can't answer that question."

Adrenaline jolted through him at her touch. Her fingers were cold, slight tremors coursing through them. She was afraid? Disturbed? Certainly shaken enough to break with her tough-girl stance.

Unexpectedly, it moved him. "Why not?"

"I can't tell you that."

Of course not. Fey don't give straight answers. Playing to the moment, he put his other hand over hers, warming it. "What about the other servants? Are they also invisible because they're shy?"

"Yes. No. You're holding my hand, Mr. Devries."

"So I noticed."

She closed her eyes, as if refusing to look at him. "It's not necessary."

"Is it pleasant?"

"That's immaterial."

He released her, sitting back in the chair. She suddenly felt too far away. *Get serious. She's a psycho fairy.* "So what's the deal with the staff?"

"They came with me. They built this house."

"They're your people? All of them?" Rafe glanced around the deceptively empty room. "Wherever they are."

"They are light fey, like me, but we are a confederation of many sub-species. Not that it's any concern of yours." She leaned back in her turn, folding her arms. "Given the option, we'll hide ourselves rather than interact with others."

"Why so unsociable?"

For a moment, her face softened, as if she were dropping her guard a fraction. "Maybe it would be easier if you understood."

"Probably," he said dryly.

She gave him an annoyed look. "We don't *use* magic, we *are* magic. Just like your friend said, if a vow is spoken in our presence, it becomes true. That's a dangerous state of affairs unless one takes precautions. Humans never could follow the rules. Just read their so-called fairy tales. Promises, vows, enchantments, gold pieces turning into dried leaves, princes turning into frogs—it was pure chaos, and we always took the blame. So we hid for safety in the wild places. If we have to be near other species, invisibility acts like a dampening field. Far fewer accidental spells take hold."

Rafe felt like he'd been handed a puzzle piece, but wasn't sure if it was from the right jigsaw. "Must be getting harder, with so few uninhabited places to run to."

"These mountains are one of our last refuges."

Did that mean Lila was from these parts? "But you seem perfectly comfortable as a corporate type. How does that work?"

"A few of the younger generation pursued an education. I admit that even with precautions there is risk involved, but we're not as eager to hide away. We find the modern world exciting." It was the first substantial thing she'd said about herself.

She rested her hands again on the desk, near his but not touching. His fingers itched to brush against her fine, smooth skin, but knew it would be a mistake just when she'd decided to start talking. As with coaxing a wild animal, haste was his enemy.

He adopted his shooting-the-breeze voice. "Yeah, well, the wolves went through the same thing. The rural Packs like ours were the last to resist human contact. We gave in."

"Did it cause a rift among your people? Those that wanted to keep to themselves, others who did not?" It sounded like she really wanted to know.

"Oh, sure," Rafe answered, realizing that they'd found tenuous common ground. "But once we got cable TV, the naysayers shut up. There's no such thing as a werewolf who can resist the World Series."

To his utter surprise, she laughed. It was the most beautiful sound he had ever heard, and it changed everything. He'd found a way to win her confidence.

Chapter Five

"WHAT KIND OF PLACE DID you grow up in?" he asked her hours later.

They had done nothing but sit there and talk, at first about the wolves. It was all inconsequential things. Grandma Reed's wild berry pie and rose hip cordial. The old drive-in movie theater down in Blainesville. The calf that got its head stuck through the gate. His young nephew Ben's antics. He had spread himself out like a photo album, leafing through the pages of his childhood and pointing out the events and characters at a leisurely pace. As he rambled on, he could almost smell the sun-washed earth of a Wolf Creek summer afternoon.

Clearly fascinated, Lila listened to every word. She leaned forward on the desk, her chin cupped in her hands, her green eyes searching his face for every nuance of expression. This, then, was what fey liked, what they absorbed like meat and drink—stories. It didn't seem to matter much what they were about.

That suited Rafe fine. He'd always been able to spin a good tale, and if that was what moved Lila from fighting him to trusting him a little, he'd talk until he turned blue. But turnabout was fair play. Now it was her turn to share something.

"I grew up in the forest." She looked down, playing with a pen. It was the one small item on her bald, featureless desk. "We don't form a village, exactly, but scatter—sometimes with big distances between our homes. We do that so we don't have to cut down the trees. The only thing we ever built of stone was the great hall where we all meet at the quarters of the year. Those are times of celebration."

She looked up, a sudden look of mischief in her eyes. "It's a good thing we're far away from anyone else. The dancing can get a bit noisy."

Rafe imagined a forest full of drunken, frolicking gargoyles, and backed away from the image as quickly as possible. The thought of Lila dancing in the moonlight glades was quite a different prospect.

She looked out the window at vast blue sky with the air of someone making a careful decision. "Are you hungry?"

"Sure, I could eat."

She gave him a sidelong glance that was almost shy, and pushed back her chair. "Follow me."

Leading him through a different door, she went down a spiral staircase that ended in the room nearest the hot tub. Floor to ceiling windows covered one wall, showing the view of the water and the mountains in the distance. The silver ribbon of the Owl River linked the lake and the foothills like a long, sinuous leash.

"Beautiful, isn't it?" she asked, pausing near the window.

"Yes, it sure is." But Rafe was looking at her still form, as slender and tall as a rush by the riverbank. He was supposed to be getting information out of her, but he was getting dazzled in the process. Her sheer loveliness tore at him, a constant ache that had a little to do with her magic, and much to do with his natural desires. He stood next to her, barely an inch between them. He could feel each one of her breaths and see how the sunlight played on the soft architecture of her throat as she spoke.

By the way she stared at the horizon, she didn't belong indoors any more than he did. They both were creatures of the field and wood. *If only we could stop pretending and run for the wilds.* He imagined taking her in the long, waving grass of the fields. In the fall it would be as pale a gold as her hair, her skin luminous in the fading autumn sun.

But they were tied by fear and magic. The only way out was past the steel door she'd built around her reasons for being here. He'd barely caught a glance of the woman behind the triple locks.

He had to be careful. Even in the short time they had been talking, he was losing sight of the basics: he was her prisoner. He was trying to learn enough to resolve this hellish situation. Maybe there was a way they could both walk away in one piece. She seemed so damned vulnerable. *Pickle fork. Remember the pickle fork.*

And focus on what she could do—had done—to other Pack members. His mind flashed to his father, Darak, the town. What was going on while he was here, about to have lunch with the enemy? A wave of frustration and impatience mixed with his attraction, making a conflicting brew of emotions.

Stay on track and keep the information flowing. "Do your people ever have contact with the other species?"

"As I said, some of the younger fey do." She turned to look at him, squinting a little against the light. "It is a mixed blessing, the quiet of the woods. It can be isolating. I remember my first look at the human schools. They were so huge, and so filled with people. I was appalled and delighted. In a single instant, I knew I had to go there."

"And when you arrived?"

She gave a self-deprecating smile. "I was hopeless at first."

He touched her arm, keeping the gesture casual. Gaining her confidence. "You?"

This time, she didn't pull away at his advance. "I'd never seen most of the objects around me. I remember discovering highlighters and thinking they were the most beautiful, marvellous inventions ever, like exclamation points packed in a tube. I barely understood computers. I nearly failed the first term until one of the human girls took pity on me despite the mockery of her classmates. She helped me adapt."

He tried to imagine anyone mocking Lila, but couldn't.

She shrugged and turned back to the view. "It was the happiest time of my life. I learned so much from her, including the fact that there are kind people willing to share their potato chips and pizza even when they're broke."

Rafe studied Lila, trying to envision her happy. "Do you stay in touch?"

"A little. She's married now." She sounded wistful. "I loved my human friends. I wanted a part in their busy, colorful world. It was bursting with interest for me, challenging everything I knew. I hurled myself into it, awkward though I was. Though I still am."

He pondered the image for a moment. A girl who loved friends and excitement, one prepared to throw over convention and follow her own star. That's who Lila was once. How did she get to be the dangerous, frightened woman he'd found here?

"What did your family think about all this?"

"They did not understand the appeal."

"You were the rebel in the family?"

"Not the only one. My sister, Rosemund, formed a scandalous attachment to a werebear."

Despite himself, Rafe chuckled. "The girls, they do love their teddy bears."

"I had a partiality for the football team. In general." She gave him a sly smile. "But then my sister kept her trophy. I was more interested in catch and release."

Rafe felt his eyebrows rise. "Obviously, I went to the wrong college."

Her eyes twinkled, giving her fib away. *Trickster fey.*

For a moment, it was like he was looking at a different Lila. One who was alive, vibrant, and full of excitement for the future. An odd shock of recognition hit him. In another time and place, he could fall in love with this woman.

Her smile grew wider. "So there is my life story. Now you can stop asking questions and tell me what you would like for lunch."

Something squirmy from the pet store? A nice, raw flank steak? "Just a sandwich would be fine."

"Wait here," she said, heading off to yet another part of the rambling house.

Rafe looked around. The room was large and airy with a pale pine floor and large, comfortable-looking furniture grouped around a fireplace. Near the window stood a small white table and two chairs. It looked like a room people used for themselves instead of for formal entertaining. There was even a painting on one wall—the image was formless and abstract, but splashes of greens and muted reds made it stand out. It was the one thing he'd seen with some color.

Then he understood. Lila had taken him to the part of the house that was her personal space. There was even a stack of books on an end table. He'd read some of the same titles. Apparently they shared a weakness for spy thrillers.

She hadn't talked nearly as much as he had, but in other ways she was revealing herself. That meant she trusted him. The thought made his chest hurt. *What's she doing here, tangled up with Masterson?*

His exploration brought him to an open window, one of the tall kind that could be used as a doorway to the patio beyond. Through it, he could smell the warm stone and the tingling wash of pine on the breeze. There were more tables and chairs, spangled by light glittering from the pool. All it needed was people. He was used to his large family, always with kids, always with voices raised to be heard over the roar of conversation. This house was so damned quiet.

Tentatively, he raised a hand to reach through the window to the swath of sunshine beyond.

His palm touched something as hard as glass. Its temperature was the same as the air around him, but the unyielding surface was slick and solid. A thrill of fear rushed through him. He'd promised not to leave the house, but surely that didn't imprison him completely? Even from the garden?

Rafe pushed, putting all his weight, and then all his muscle against it, straining until his arms shook. It didn't budge. He was trapped, well and truly unable to touch the world beyond the bland white walls. *No, this is impossible for a wolf to stand!*

How am I going to protect my Pack? Wild panic fountained up, squeezing his ribs until his lungs refused to fill with air. Rafe paced from window to window, throwing them open and testing himself against each possible route of escape. By the time he had circled the perimeter of his invisible cage, sweat slicked his skin, cold with the need to run away.

Frustration peaked as he got back to the original window. He backed up twenty paces, eying the apparently empty space. He took a running start, piling up speed and kicking from the hip.

The force of the blow knocked him from his feet, but nothing gave.

It was no good. *You made a vow in the presence of a fey.* He'd just become another casualty of Lila's magic. Animals chewed off their own limbs to escape a trap. He didn't even have that option. He was stuck.

Rafe scrambled to his feet, almost dizzy with the need to fight back.

Calm, calm, calm. He reined in his skittering nerves, forcing them under control. *Running won't help. There's nowhere to go.*

He stood mute and stiff as Lila returned with a tray of food and coffee, arranging it all on the table by the window.

"I can't get out," he said, hearing the tremor in his voice.

"I know." She kept setting out the food and drink. "I heard you."

The weirdly domestic moment made his head hurt. He was a prisoner, but she served him with her own hands. She wanted him to coerce his people into giving up their home, but she listened with bated breath to every story of their small-town lives. He could feel her fear and loneliness, but she had all the power. Beautiful and terrible, she held him.

"Did you understand what I said?" he ventured, struggling to keep his voice light. "I'm trapped."

"You traded yourself for your father. I know you haven't forgotten that." She sat down, gesturing for him to take his chair.

His temper lurched, filling his voice with rage. "Do you have any idea what it feels like?"

"No." The look she gave him was filled with pain. "No. But my sisters have told me."

"Are they prisoners?" He forced himself to sit down, though his limbs tingled with the need to move.

"They gave up a lot to help me come here."

Her oblique answers fuelled his fury. "Like what?" he shouted.

She bowed her head, her gaze fixed on her plate. "I don't want to talk about that. We were having a pleasant conversation. Tell me more about your nephew. Tell me more about anything."

He picked up a glass, but in a twist of anger, he squeezed until it shattered in his hand. Glass and water splattered the table, a thin stream of blood dribbling from his fingers. "I can't. I tried but I can't pretend anymore. I can't eat with the woman who threatens my wolves. Who has me *caged!*"

"Look," she said, her mouth twisting down. She stared at the blood, her face turning a sickly white. "I don't want to hurt your Pack. I really don't. But I'm not going to apologize for trying everything I can to save my own family."

He wiped the blood from his hand onto his napkin. It stung like fire, the bright red feathering into the pristine fabric.

She flinched. "Here. Let me do that."

He snatched his hand away. "I can manage."

Anger flickered in her eyes, but it collapsed almost at once. "I know I've done everything possible to make me your enemy. I don't expect you to forgive me. I meddled with vows and magic when I was drowning in anger, and now . . . one way or the other, I'll be the one who pays."

Rafe tried to untangle what she was saying. Sadness poured off her like a smoky perfume. She crumpled her own napkin into a ball, unable to meet his eyes.

She cleared her throat, drawing herself up in her chair. "That doesn't mean I'm not serious about needing Wolf Creek. We can play the get-to-know-you-game, and it's lovely, but it won't change anything. I like you—a lot—and I understand your position, but I can't give up. Not yet. Not while I can still fight."

Rafe snarled with frustration, a low rumble that ripped from deep in his chest.

"I'm sorry," she said, rising from the table. "Whatever you think of me, know that's the truth."

She started toward the door, then paused, not bothering to turn around. Her spine straightened, as if she were gathering her nerve. "You can finish your lunch here. Feel free to sleep in any bedroom you like. As you can see, there's no way you can leave."

Rafe jumped up. "Lila! This doesn't solve anything."

Lila wheeled to face him. Her devastated expression ground into Rafe's soul.

His mouth went dry, his gut suddenly hollow with the hopelessness of their positions. "Lila . . ."

She took two steps toward him and then reached up to lay her hand on his cheek. Her touch was cool and gentle, feather-soft. Rafe felt it deep inside him, not simply on his skin but all the way to his core.

"I see you struggling so hard, working against such odds." When she spoke, her voice was so soft he could barely hear it. "I don't know what else I can tell you. I need what you have, and I don't know how to make you give it to me. Not without feeling worse than I already do. The only thing left is a sacrifice, and it will either be yours or mine."

With that, her hand slipped away. Rafe was left staring down at her, speechless with a wild sorrow. She was adamant, but he couldn't accept her words. He'd seen flashes of who she really was. Surely there had to be another path to follow.

He grasped her arms, pulling her to him. Her eyes flared, but she didn't pull back. His lips met hers with all the force of his outrage. She made a noise of protest, but it soon softened to something else, a low, throaty cry of hunger. The sound of it went straight to his belly, melting his body in a painful heat. She tasted like no female he had ever known, sweet and tart at once like the honey of a citrus flower. He deepened the kiss, plundering the softness of her mouth, feeling the soft sigh of her breath on his skin.

For that moment, as long as the kiss lasted, she was his. All was simple. There was no trickery or plots, no one pulling their strings.

He felt the moment she responded, leaning in, adding her own soul to the exchange. As they moved, finding new angles, her long lashes brushed his cheek. The delicacy of the touch moved him, making him fold her tighter in the circle of his arms.

When he finally broke away, they were both short of breath. Neither spoke.

Lila stroked his cheek again, her thumb tracing the sensitive skin of his lips. Then she put one forefinger to his mouth, silencing him.

"Let's leave it like this. Unspoiled." She leaned in, sealing her words with a soft, quick kiss, and left the room.

Chapter Six

SINCE WHEN HAS IT BEEN THE girl who didn't want to talk about it afterward?

Rafe's entire being felt bruised. He'd kissed her out of need and frustration, but that had only fuelled his desire for her. He felt like an engine about to burst its valves.

He'd spent the rest of the day prowling the house and avoiding Lila, who was clearly avoiding him. For a time he'd sat with the sleeping prisoners, but mostly he had to keep moving, testing every door and window like a dog whining to get out.

He adored her. He hated her. She fascinated him. Eventually he'd settled on a bedroom as far as possible from *her* corner of the house. It faced the direction of Wolf Creek.

This room had a bed and a desk. He sat in the desk chair and glared out the window, watching the azure sky turn to an indigo dusk. His watch had stopped since he entered the fey-built house but, since it was only the end of summer, the hour had to be late. He hadn't heard the servants moving around for at least an hour, though he had no illusions that there wasn't something prowling the halls. He'd firmly shut the bedroom door, jamming a second chair under the handle.

He'd come to two conclusions in the course of the day—besides the fact that Lila kissed like a teenaged wolfboy's stormiest fantasy. First, he was absolutely a prisoner and second, Lila's family history held the key to unlocking this mess. As the baby of the family, she had gone her own way until something happened. That mysterious event made her older sisters sacrifice a lot so that Lila could be here in Wolf Creek. That was what kept Lila glued to her purpose.

Family involvement wasn't entirely surprising. Few things were stronger motivators. Talking to Lila about his childhood had sharpened his need to protect his own kin. If he got out of this mess in one piece, he'd consider his wild oats sown. Maybe think about starting a family. Be there for when his Dad was ready to let a few things go.

Strange how that future—the one he'd always expected—now felt oddly incomplete. Maybe it was because he'd kissed a fey. Maybe that would make him crazy for the rest of his life. *La Belle Dame* and all that.

A rapping on the window glass snapped him out of his broodfest. The room had grown dark. Rafe blinked the night into focus, only to see Darak's battle-scarred face floating in the night sky. He pulled open the window.

"Fido's balls, talk about nightmare visions."

Darak leaned his elbows on the sill, giving him a fangy smile. He looked perfectly comfortable, clinging to the wall like a gigantic bat. "That any way to treat your good fairy?"

"Don't talk to me about fairies."

"Been having fun, eh?"

"There've been moments exactly as much fun as sticking your hand down a live garbage disposal. How's my dad?"

"Pissed off, but otherwise healthy. He's ready to tear off your tail for putting yourself in danger for his sake."

"Figures. Never could say thanks."

"He's talking all-out Pack aggression. The only question in his mind is how many allies to call in."

Rafe swore softly. "No frackin' way. Numbers don't matter against magic. There'll be too many casualties. Plus there are still hostages here."

"You're his kid. That trumps everything. He can't sit on his backside, and he can't surrender. It's just not in him."

"Tell him to wait."

Darak made a face. "I'll try. You're okay, right?"

"Sure. I'm just stuck here. Like you said, the vow became real." Rafe poked the invisible shield just inches in front of Darak's nose.

"Fascinating." Darak poked his own finger through to Rafe's chest. For him, the barrier simply didn't exist. "And kind of fun from this side of the force field."

"I need a serious Plan B."

"I figured I'd have to help save your ass, so I had a computer whiz I know do some digging."

"Who?"

"Another wolf. A computer prof from Pack Silvertail. I was out in Fairview last winter and met him and a werecougar who's a freelance reporter. They're good with the research."

"And?"

"I wanted to know what they could find on Miz Lila. Figured you wouldn't have access to much tech, being a prisoner and all."

Darak was absolutely right. They'd taken his cell and the only other phone was on Lila's desk. "What did they find?"

"My computer genius found Lila Wilding's name at a local business college. She graduated six years ago and has been working in the area since. She's volunteered her talents for a lot of environment-focussed start-ups. Then she went to work at a privately-owned corporation called the Masterson Group almost exactly a year ago. When we checked into them, things got interesting."

"How?"

"Masterson has an interest even greater than drilling in Wolf Creek. The forest at the north end of Owl River has miles and miles of old growth as far as the eye can see. They've made a move to acquire logging rights."

"Bugger that! It's pristine land." Fury clogged Rafe's throat, but he forced himself to stay on track. "Still, what's it got to do with Wolf Creek?"

"It has a lot to do with your pretty jailer. About a thousand of the light fey court live there."

Stunned, Rafe fell back in his chair. *Lila's people.* The oath. The need to protect her home. He could almost feel the connections as they snapped together in his mind. She'd thrown herself in the path of Masterson's corporate juggernaut and fought with whatever weapons she could lay her hands on. The sheer gutsiness of it stole his breath—but it hadn't been enough. The one thing the secretive fey sucked at was making allies, and this was not a fight they could win on their own.

Rafe turned the problem over, looking for a way in. "That forest is owned by the government. It's parkland, right?"

"It is, but that doesn't mean it can't be logged under the right permits. On top of that, the fey have never acknowledged the rule of human law, so their standing in the matter is very shaky, especially when the Masterson Corporation allegedly has a few politicians on the payroll. The fey were ordered to vacate a year ago."

"But they haven't."

"No. It's not like there's a lot of places for a thousand fey to go. Plus, not all of their sub-species can live near human developments. They're deadly allergic to industrial pollution. The rest, even those who could survive city living, won't leave them behind. They're big on clan loyalty."

Rafe groaned. "So what's going to happen?"

"You have heard those stories of men and women refusing to leave their cabins on the side of an erupting volcano? Those are the fey of the Owl River forest. They'll stay there until they're logged right along with the trees. It'll be genocide."

Rafe sprang to his feet and paced the room. "How come I haven't heard about this? Wolf Creek is barely a hundred miles away!"

"You've been away. It's a big forest. The fey have done everything they could to stay hidden, including using all kinds of shielding spells. It's a silent storm. The only reason my friend was able to find anything out is because a few dark fey are willing to rat out their light fey cousins."

"Still, it's weird. Normally you say "old growth" and at least twenty tree-huggers are there in five minutes. Somebody should have heard something."

"Same with your situation. I know Wolf Creek avoids publicity like the plague, but the takeover of an entire town should still be attracting attention. If nobody speaks up or drags the case to court, human law can't do squat."

Rafe rubbed his forehead. Calling in the humans made an Alpha look weak in the eyes of his Pack—and so was something his father would never do. Still, Masterson Corp was a human company. Nothing wrong with turning in their CEO and president for breaking human laws.

Darak continued. "The interesting factoid here is that the moment Lila signed on with Masterson, their attention shifted away from the forest."

"To the oil under Wolf Creek." *Which is why she needs the mineral rights. She's trading our oil for her forest.*

"Exactly."

"She's trying to save her home."

"By throwing Wolf Creek under the bus. I wouldn't waste any sympathy on her."

"I'd do anything to save the Pack. I can't blame her for doing the same for her family."

"Bloody noble of you. She could have asked for help."

"Maybe she needs to know she can." His mind was racing. "But there's still a lot that doesn't add up. For one thing, how could one employee, however talented, change the course of an industrial giant? A company used to bribing politicians to get their way? Why wouldn't they just take both the trees and the oil?"

Darak frowned. "Pretty smart questions for a dog. What do you want me to do?"

Rafe was done with secrets. "You said you have a friend in the media?"

"Errata Jones. She's a damned good investigator."

"See if you can catch her interest. Tell her to call all her reporter friends. We need to shine a good bright light on Masterson. The only reason they're getting away with any of this is because nobody knows about it. The best court in this case is public opinion."

"Are you so sure about that? You're not humans. That matters to some. Plus, oil and timber mean jobs."

"Sure, but I doubt the average taxpayer would be down with throwing entire populations out of their homes. People can be greedy and stupid, but not on that scale. Joe Average is a better guy than he gets credit for."

"It'll bring the press down on Wolf Creek like a bunch of fleas."

"I'll tell Dad not to eat them."

"And the fey are going to hate the publicity. They've been hiding out there for years."

Rafe sighed. "Frankly, that's just too bad. They can hide or they can lose their forest. If we nail Masterson, we'll be saving their backsides as well as our own."

"*Jawohl*, captain. Anything else?"

Rafe thought a moment. "I'm running out of chips in this poker game Lila and I are playing."

"So you're telling me to move my ass?"

"Yeah."

Darak raised his eyebrows in an expression of innocence. It didn't really work on the vampire's craggy face. "My friend's already on standby. Full coverage on today's late news good enough for you?"

Rafe grinned. "That's just about perfect."

"You owe me a lot of beer for this, dog breath."

"I thought the dead were patient."

"Only for revenge and foreign films, and they're kinda the same thing."

Lila had the sensation of falling, as if she'd been clinging to the edge of a balcony miles above the ground, and her hands had finally slipped. So much had spun out of control.

She played with her pen, rolling it to and fro on her desk. It was tempting to play the game of "if." If she had not left home for school, if she had not fallen in love with the human world, if she had not believed she could use her business-world experience to negotiate on behalf of her people. It had all put her on that balcony, in a position to fall. And then had come Rafe, and a whole other kind of falling.

She couldn't afford to think about that. She had spent the last hours bludgeoning her brains for a way out of the Wolf Creek mess, but Rafe's kiss had complicated everything. He'd melted her resolve when she could least afford it. When there was no time for second thoughts.

She picked up the phone and punched speed dial, her heart in her mouth.

"Masterson," grunted her boss. She could hear what sounded like a truck motor in the background.

"It's Lila."

"Progress?"

She heard a car door slamming. He was obviously on the road. She decided to skip over his opening question. "You've tried to buy this land before."

"Who told you that?"

"The wolves." It was a gamble, bringing it up. Pushing him. He could back out. She half expected it. On the other hand, she needed to take one more throw of the dice and hope against hope for a reprieve.

Masterson made an irritated sound. "So what? You said you could deliver their land. Do it."

"You said you'd told me everything. This complicates things. You owe me a penalty shot."

"You're out of time, Lila. The deadline is tomorrow."

The receiver felt slick in her hand. The vow that had bought her a year and a day was ticking down the last few hours. "Now the deadline is Friday, because I say it is. That's your price for hiding information."

"You can't worm out of the agreement."

"You bent the spirit of the rules, Masterson."

"Whatever. Your rules, your problem. No wonder you fey are going extinct. You're bad business people. You made a bad bargain."

"But not today. Today you take my terms."

She heard a babble of excited voices, some of them angry. *Where is he?* "Okay. Fine. Gotta go." The line went dead.

She hung up, sucking in a deep lungful of air. Two days. She'd bought herself two days of safety.

Is it enough, Liliana? Her sister's voice rang sweet in her mind. Even in private, her sisters stayed invisible and silent, hiding the grotesque forms and voices they'd taken for the duration of the vow. If they spoke, they used the power of their minds.

I don't know, Lila answered. *It will have to be enough time, I suppose.*

You feel sympathy for the wolf.

He is kind, Rosemund, and strong of will like your bear. That is not to be scorned.

It is his people or ours. There is no third choice for us, and certainly not for you.

Lila buried her face in her hands. Masterson was right. She'd made a bad bargain. As foolish a blunder as any human who didn't know the rules of oaths and vows. *Go to bed, Rosemund. I need to think.*

There was the rustling sound of wings, and a rush of air that surrounded her like an embrace. And then silence eddied around her. For a blissful moment, her mind was empty.

Then Rafe knocked and opened the door, not waiting for an invitation to enter. His face spoke before he even uttered the words. "I know."

Chapter Seven

THE BREATH LEFT LILA'S BODY in a single choked curse. "Know what?" She closed her mouth before she could start stammering something foolish. *How much does he know?*

"Turn on the news."

Lila was about to ask why, but his expression stopped her. She pulled the remote out of her desk drawer and clicked on the flat screen. What she saw made her gasp. It was the entrance to Gilden Forest filmed from the air, right above the spot where the main access road disappeared under the canopy of trees. The scene was dark, but the lights of the news chopper showed Masterson's machines of destruction were poised to begin chewing through the forest. *He wasn't going to give me one second longer than our deal demanded.*

The reporter was saying something, but Lila was transfixed by the images. The view had shifted to footage taken by a camera on the ground. Microphones bearing the letters of various TV stations bobbed toward a man in a yellow hard hat. She couldn't see who it was, but she recognized a crowd of fair-haired people in the distance who had to be fey.

"This can't be happening!" Lila said, her voice just above a whisper. Shy, secretive fey showing themselves on camera? Had the world gone mad?

"It's happening, Lila. It's happening as we speak."

"Sacred Titania!" She felt suddenly sick.

"I'm sorry about the press, but publicity is the one medicine Masterson can't stomach. If enough people know what he's up to, he'll be forced to do the right thing."

"You did this?" Her voice held a universe of shock.

Rafe nodded, his face grave.

Lila was silent for a long moment. When she spoke, her words were quiet. "Masterson made me swear to keep it secret. This is the last thing he wanted."

"Too bad. I didn't promise him anything."

"My father . . ." She trailed off, and buried her face in her hands. "You don't understand. It's not just Masterson who wanted secrecy. This much attention will be like death to the fey."

"They'll get over it when they get to keep their homes," Rafe said bluntly. "It's the only way to work through this. The vampires and shapeshifters came out of hiding when it became clear living off the grid just wasn't possible anymore."

"Tell me again how this will help us?" She heard the tears in her voice, and winced.

"There's such a thing as squatter's rights. With the right lawyers, the fey can get the law on their side."

"We don't have lawyers. We don't recognize human law."

Rafe shook his head. "You need to start. I'll give you the names of some legal firms. A lot of lawyers are vampires, no pun intended. They're used to working on inter-species cases."

Hope flickered to life in Lila's breast, but then died. "Maybe that will solve the legal side of things, but when the humans know where we are, they'll come hunting us. There's always some fool who wants a pot of gold or a love spell and will stop at nothing to get it."

Rafe put a gentle hand on her arm. "The wolves love the woodland as much as the fey. Let us run unharmed in your wild places, and you will have a patrol against unwanted visitors."

Lila tried to digest this, but the cameras swerved toward a fleshy man arguing at the top of his lungs, red-faced and sweating. He was casually dressed, but would have looked more comfortable in an air-conditioned boardroom. *Masterson.* So that explained the noise in the background of their phone call.

And he was screaming at her father. The king of the fey was the personification of tall, pale elegance but, by the stiff way he held himself, he was on the verge of screaming himself. *Oh, no.*

A reporter shoved her microphone into Masterson's face. "You've been accused of buying political favor that secured Masterson Corporation's logging license without the requisite environmental impact scans. Can you comment on that?"

Masterson spluttered.

The reporter turned to Lila's father, who eyed the microphone as if it might turn into an adder. "Mister, um, King, can you tell us what arrangements have been made for your people when you leave this forest?"

Her father focused intense green eyes on the camera. "None whatsoever. We were not consulted. We have no intention of leaving." He turned his face away, as if dismissing the outside world.

"What if you're forced to go?" the reporter demanded.

The king gave her a weary glance. "We don't know how."

Lila felt as much as heard her father's voice. It held profound sadness, but most of all it held resignation. The world was changing faster than the fey.

"Are you going to fight back?"

The king gave the cameras a look, but did not answer. Lila knew why. The kind of power it would take to beat Masterson's machines by force would turn Gilden Wood into a nightmare of wild magic. Lila's plan was the only way for the fey to survive.

Rafe touched her arm. "We're on the same side, Lila. Masterson's the enemy, not me."

She stood up, too agitated to sit. "You don't know the whole story."

He grabbed the remote, turning off the TV. "And I suppose you can't tell me."

Lila tried to snatch the remote, but he held it away. "Give that back!"

His brows drew together. "Tell me."

She gave up. "I made a vow to give Masterson something of equal value to the woods as a bribe for leaving us alone." She was getting a horrible headache, as if someone were driving an ice pick into her skull just above her right eye.

"I guessed that much."

"I was watching my people get thrown off their land. There's no place else for most of them to go where they'll survive. What was I supposed to do?"

Rafe said nothing. She felt hot tears leaking from beneath her lashes.

"It was a bad oath, made in haste. I should have slowed down and thought about what I was doing, about the promises I made, but I bound it in blood. I have to live with that." She snatched the remote and turned the TV back on, dreading what she might see. The sound blared, jamming the ice pick further into her head.

Masterson was raging at the cameras. "I had a bargain with these fey, but this press fiasco negates any agreement we made. The deal is off and the forest is mine!"

Bloody hell! He'd betrayed their bargain. Now she'd have to pay the price.

Lila dropped the remote. As it hit the ground, the news program switched to a comedy show. Silently, Rafe picked it up and shut off the TV. The ensuing quiet blared through the room.

Lila's vision had gone white with fright and fury. Her lips chilled to numbness. "The wolves are safe. For now at least."

"Can Masterson break his side of your deal?"

"He just did."

"There must be consequences if he backs out now."

"For me. For the fey." Her voice sounded distant in her own ears.

"But it was Darak who called the media. You didn't do anything."

Lila shook her head. "The only thing that matters is what Masterson said. The deal is off. He always had the option of backing away at any time. That was one of the flaws of the oath. I should have known better."

"What does he forfeit?"

"He cannot profit from whatever replacement deal I found for him. Wolf Creek is safe." Her voice shook, and she could feel the tremors spreading through her body.

Vows had been broken. Magic was unraveling.

Rafe swore long and foully. "That doesn't seem penalty enough."

Lila pressed her fingers to her temples. "Masterson's honor, such as it is, lies in amassing gold for himself and his supporters. His word means nothing. It's hard to penalize him for breaking something he does not value himself. The magic has nothing to stick to."

Rafe gave a low growl. "Next time let me negotiate your deals. Better yet, don't make any."

Lila managed a withering look.

A rumble came from somewhere deep in the house. Rafe looked toward the office door, shoulders tensed. "What's that?"

The pounding in her head was compounded by the harsh flicker of the overhead light. The pen on Lila's desk rolled back and forth. She grabbed it, then her cell phone, which was skittering across the desk, and stuffed them in her pockets. The world lurched again. She gripped the back of her chair, feeling the floor slide sideways for an instant. The rumble stopped as abruptly as it started.

"Earthquake." Rafe concluded. His shoulders tensed under the tight fabric of his shirt.

Lila forced the words past rising nausea. Her vision was narrowing to a dark tunnel, with unbearably bright light at the other end. "No. Everything that was created as a result of Masterson's bargain with me is breaking down."

She felt Rafe's hand on her arm. "Are you all right?"

"It doesn't feel great." She licked her lips. Fey were supposed to be light, airy beings in gossamer nighties. They weren't supposed to hurl in public. "Before it disappears, the house is going to collapse. We have to get out of here."

She could already feel the fey gathering, alarmed by the sudden drop in the field of magical power. If the humans had a technical instrument to measure such things, the needle would have been dropping to the red zone.

"I have Pack members asleep downstairs." Rafe's voice was hard as granite. "What about them?"

She could feel her sisters in the room, feel their questions crowding in on her. The vow that bound them was fading, too. *Take the wolves to safety. Get the others to help you. Then go home. You've done enough, and I've failed.*

Do you not need us any longer? Rosemund asked.

Can we do nothing for you? Arabelle chimed in.

Lila hesitated, wanting their comfort but knowing they could afford to give no more. They had families waiting in the woods who needed their protection and comfort. Their homes were under siege. *No. Go now.*

Her ending would be different.

A rush of wings told her they had gone. She felt tears slip down her cheeks. *I'm sorry I couldn't make this work.*

She cleared her throat, fighting against a lump of pain. When words came out, her voice sounded thick and odd. "My sisters will see your wolves to safety. They will wake as soon as they are outside."

The house began to shudder. Pain speared through her, lancing white-hot from jaw to tailbone. Lila cried out, groping for the chair before she fell. The huge glass windows cracked then shattered, glass raining from the frames.

"Go!" she cried, scraping together the last of the failing magic and thrusting it toward Rafe. "I release you from any and all vows. Get out of here! Save yourself!"

Her vision cleared just enough to see him glaring down at her, hands on his hips. His eyes had flared wolf-yellow, startling beneath the fall of curling dark hair. Was he going to murder her on the way out? It would be a waste of time. She was finished.

"Yeah, right," he said. She could barely hear the words through the sounds of collapse.

Cracks spidered up the wall, mirroring the agony scampering along her nerves. Lila hissed air through her teeth, digging her fingers into the slick leather of the chair. She didn't want Rafe looking at her. Not like this. "Get. Shoo."

Instead, he picked her up as if she were no more than a toddler. The motion hurt, and she couldn't stifle a cry.

"Hush." Rafe turned to the window, his expression falling as he examined the steep drop down the cliff. "Can you fly?"

"No."

"Then stairs it is."

"We'll never make it out."

"Well, aren't you a ray of sunshine."

"Promise me you'll leave me and go."

"Lady, I'm not promising you squat. That seems to backfire around you fey." He was already out of the office and onto the landing.

"But—"

"Busy now. Talk less."

The stairs gave a heave, throwing them against the wall. Lila's head bumped against something solid, but the knock barely registered. She already felt like goblins were using her for origami. Being carried was doing nothing for her lurching stomach.

Rafe stumbled, catching his footing at the last second.

"Put me down!" she wiggled out of his grasp.

"Can you run?"

"If you will."

"Okay." He grabbed her hand, dragging her out of the way as the top landing sheared away, spraying drywall and wood shards into the air. The overhead light crashed to the floor at the base of the stairs. Rafe leaped over it, swinging her past the explosion of crystal and sparks.

"This way!" Rafe shouted. They made a dead run for the front door. Jumping out a main floor window would have been faster but, with so much glass flying through the air, the door was the safest route. Somewhere deep in the house, a support beam whined as it torqued and splintered. The roof buckled to the chorus of more breaking windows.

The front hall had a cathedral ceiling, and it was raining debris. Lila felt something slam into her shoulder, sending her staggering forward. Her palms hit the floor, but she just pushed up and kept running. Rafe was heaving at the door, fighting against a frame that was losing its proper shape. In another minute, that too would fall to rubble—with them under it.

Rafe had the door open a few inches. He wrapped his fingers around the front edge of the heavy oak planks and planted his feet. Plaster coated his hair and clothes, sweat streaking his dusty face like war paint. He strained against the door, muscles bunching and feet pushing against the floor. The door moved, but only inches.

Lila scrambled to the other side, bracing her back against the frame and pushing with all her might. It probably cost her more effort than it helped Rafe, but the door moved another foot before it wedged against the buckling floor. With a massive crunch, the high ceiling of the foyer collapsed in earnest. Chunks of drywall fell like gigantic hail.

Wasting no time, she wriggled through the opening, Rafe barely squeezing through behind her. She could see at a glance the destruction had spread outside. The Lexus had disintegrated to a puddle of molten metal and plastic. The hot tub and pool were reduced to a muddy slough. Once a spell was broken, it was over—just like her dreams of saving her home.

He caught her hand, pulling her across the grassy clearing until they were well away from the house. Then he finally let her fall to the soft, springy cushion of leaves and fallen pine needles. She could see the sleepers at the other side of the clearing, where the fey had set them down. Her former prisoners were just beginning to stir.

Lila felt tears tracking down her cheeks, part sadness, part relief. At least this part of the nightmare was over. Above, she could see a twinkling blur against the stars. Those were her sisters and the other fey, flying home without her. At least now they could go home, restored to their former selves.

There had been no good-byes. It was the way they had agreed it would unfold, if things ended this way. Less pain for them all, or so she'd thought when they'd made the pact. Now she would have given anything to feel her sisters' arms around her one more time.

The last of the house finally smashed to the earth. A faint glow clung to the rubble. Lila watched, hypnotized, as bit by bit it dissolved to nothing. In an hour or two, the hilltop would be as pristine and wild as she'd found it, cleansed of her intrusion.

She suddenly realized she was alone. Rafe was gone, leaving only the sound of the breeze in the trees. The physical pain had ended, but it had left her hollow, her emotional and physical reserves pounded to nothing.

And then she heard the wolf. She twisted around to see a great grey beast standing on a rise, muzzle raised to the sky. *Rafe.* He howled, the mournful sound starting low and rising up the scale, shivering through her like all the aching solitude of the world distilled into one cry. Even as it ended, it still filled the night like a question begging answer.

And after a long moment, that answer came, first one voice, then another and another. The wolves had been close by, no doubt waiting for a moment of weakness. *Well, this is it. Come and get me.*

Her attention went back to the sleepers, who had all assumed their beast forms as the sleeping spell faded. Now they rose, shaggy gray and brown and white with eyes like molten gold and copper. They shook themselves awake and bounded forward, barking a greeting to their Pack. Lila shrank into the grass, making herself as still as she could.

The next moment the Pack boiled up from the steep, overgrown trail. In a flood of fur, they raced in a circle that ringed the grassy clearing, looping around their missing members. Lila saw nose-touching and tail-wagging, the yips and friendly bites of greeting. There must have been thirty beasts milling in a noisy, furry knot. From Lila's place in the shadows, the mob looked like a single wolf with dozens of tails.

Except one wolf was still sleeping. Lila thought it was the oldest of them, the patriarch of the land down by the elbow of Timber Lake. He was a big and burly old rancher with enough head of cattle to throw the nation a barbecue, but the sleeping spell seemed to have a special grip on him. Lila held her breath as three of the wolves gathered around, nudging him with their noses. *What have I done? Surely the old wolf will be all right?*

Her heart beat painfully as the seconds dragged on. Finally, the old wolf's tail gave a thump, startling one of his inquisitive friends into skittering sideways. Lila exhaled in a rush that was half a laugh as the werewolf clambered to his feet and shook his coat with an air of affronted disgust.

From his perch on the hilltop, Rafe sent out another howl. When it was taken up by the others, this time there was no mistaking the note of jubilant triumph. The freshly-awakened wolves joined in the romping chaos, folding into the dance of ears and tails and fur. The roiling Pack circled for a moment more, and then poured back down the rocky path, the noisy chorus floating back to Lila long after they had gone.

She let out another long, relieved breath and rose to her feet. She was safe. The wolves hadn't given her a single glance. Surely they had known she was there, known what she had done, but they had chosen to leave her alone. All except Rafe, who bounded down from his vantage point and trotted to her side.

"How come you didn't go with them?" she asked. "How come they didn't eat me?"

Even as a wolf, his expression of disbelief was perfectly clear. He bumped his head against her hand. Lila staggered slightly, not quite braced for the force of a wolf so large that his shoulders were level with her hip.

Then she understood. Somehow, he'd protected her. She sank her hand into his ruff, feeling the coarse warmth of it. It made her realize how cold she was.

"Very chivalrous of you, Mr. Devries. You are kinder than I deserve."

He grabbed the hem of her dress and gave a light tug. He clearly wanted her to follow him.

"There's nowhere to go out here. In case you haven't noticed, the house fell down. You must have huffed and puffed a little too hard."

He gave her a droll expression.

"Yeah, I know. Clichés suck."

He tugged again. Lila glanced ruefully at her expensive leather shoes, then kicked them off. She didn't have to play human anymore. "All right then. You're in charge. Lead on."

They walked down the first long stretch of the drive, Rafe padding so close to her side that she could feel the brush of his coat. They stopped, picked up the clothes he had discarded, and Lila tucked them in a bundle under her arm. The gesture felt oddly normal, as if she picked up after werewolves every day. Despite all that had happened that night, despite all that would happen soon, she felt perfectly safe.

He turned left onto a deer track that led deep into the woods. He looked back at her with a flash of golden eyes. Well used to navigating tree roots and brambles, Lila followed.

Eventually, they stopped in a clearing surrounded by trees so ancient she could nearly hear them thinking. She walked to the edge of the clearing, stroking the bark of one old, mossy trunk.

Lila felt hands touch her shoulders, gentle yet heavy and warm. She spun around, the catch of her breath loud in the still glade. Rafe was in human form again, the moonlight bathing every muscle of his body in marble whiteness. *Blessed Titania!*

Chapter Eight

HER GAZE TRAVELLED THE LENGTH of his body. She felt helpless to stop herself, as if she were the victim of a fey compulsion. Suddenly, her pulse felt too thick, the blood too hot to move normally through her body. It was pooling in her core like lava about to erupt. Every part of her tingled with the need to be connected to him, flesh to warm, hot flesh.

What did she have to lose? It was time to finally share the joy and generosity buried deep inside her, to give Rafe something bright after dragging him through her dark world. It was a small thing compared to the kindness he had shown her.

Lila leaned into him, her cheek against the hollow of his collarbone. With curious fingertips, she traced the landscape of his hard, bare chest. He laid a hand over hers, stilling her movements.

"What's this?" he asked, his low voice a husky whisper.

"An end and a beginning. You're free. The wolves are free. That part of the nightmare is over."

"And the beginning?"

"Of everything that comes after, whatever that may be." She threaded her free hand into his dark, wavy hair, noticing how similar the rough texture was to his wolf's coat. She pulled his mouth down to hers, letting the heat of his lips warm her to the core.

He didn't need a second invitation. He gathered her to him with a devouring need. His tongue found hers, seeking out deeper secrets, stealing kisses from within the kiss.

In the meantime, his fingers found the side zipper of her dress and began an exploratory mission. He had the dress off her before she quite realized what he was doing. Now, though, when the cold air hit newly exposed parts, she didn't feel chilly at all. There was ample evidence that he was quite ready to keep her warm.

He cupped her breast in his hand, caressing her through the black silk of her bra. Lila pressed into him, her fingers in his hair, then raking over the broad landscape of his shoulders. Rafe bowed his head, taking her other breast in his mouth, leaving the fabric wet and her nipple aching.

He tasted the other, the sensation spearing through her until her legs were weak and trembling. Nothing he did was by halves. His scent, musky and wild, grew stronger as they touched. He nipped her neck, the sharp pain mixing so close to pleasure it nearly pushed her over the brink.

He's marked me. She should have been affronted, but just then it seemed sexy as hell.

Lila pulled him down to the soft, mossy ground. Both of them were growing impatient. In moments, her bra and panties were discarded in the nearby ferns. But then Rafe paused, pushing the hair from her face and studying her, amber wolf-light sparking in his eyes.

"You're impossibly beautiful," he whispered. "Your hair is the color of the moonlight. Your skin shines like you've bathed in the stars."

"Mhmmm," she murmured, kissing him to coax him back into action.

Your eyes are the saddest I've ever known. But Rafe didn't say it. There were moments for conversation, and this was not one of them. He let his body do the speaking, straddling her so that she was caught in the cage of his limbs.

There was grace and refinement in her form, but he knew she possessed just as much boundless courage. She was strong and fragile in a way that moved him. *You did battle for your people. You dared the impossible out of love.* So she'd lost. So she'd taken ten years off his life. Lila Wilding had guts and a protective streak that matched his own.

He bent to kiss the mark he'd made on the pale skin of her neck, laving it with his tongue. She tasted like a meadow, spring-fresh and floral. She moaned, her neck arching to expose her throat. The beast in him rose, responding to the primal gesture of surrender. She was his.

With new urgency, he worked his way over her body, claiming the gentle mounds of her breasts, the delicate flare of her hips. Long moon-pale tresses fanned around them, gleaming softly in the diffuse light. It was like a carpet of silk.

Her thighs parted in invitation. Rafe explored the soft inner flesh, nipping, tasting, coaxing a cry from her.

"Hurry up," she gasped.

Lila felt him enter, her body straining to accept his size. She was ready, but this was—unexpected. She'd heard rumors of the generously made beast-men, whispered tales among women both human and fey. They were true. She gasped, her eyes wide and staring into his. His frank satisfaction at her astonishment was clear.

Then he began to slowly move. She gripped his shoulders, riding the earthquake with a wonderment that quickly melted to elation. Suddenly she was an elemental force, part of a vortex winding tighter and tighter. The movements increased in speed and force, and then she was responding with equal strength, a dancer adding her own steps. She cried out, losing control, every nerve dazzled. Suddenly the grove seemed filled with light, but whether it was magic or simply madness, she could not tell. It went on and on, driving her up and over again before Rafe made a final, long thrust and gave himself to her utterly.

She rolled on top of him, not willing to let him go just yet. His arms folded around her as if she had always belonged just there, her head tucked under his chin, her hair spilling over them like a cloak. She kissed him, tasting the salt on his skin. He was still breathing heavily, the rise and fall of his strong chest making her burn for him all over again. He was warmth and life, precious beyond measure. Lila closed her eyes, willing the moment to last.

In the hazy state between satisfaction and the anticipation of more, Rafe closed his eyes, triumph pulsing through his veins like a primitive drum. She was his. Beautiful, troubled, tricky, courageous and *his*. He kissed the top of her head, drinking in the perfume of her glorious hair.

"When you were a soldier," she asked softly, "were you ever afraid that you would die?"

Rafe opened his eyes, staring up at the stars. *Not the conversation I expected.* "Sometimes."

Her warm weight was here and now, the urgency of desire a breath away. He pushed a lock of hair from her eyes. "Why do you ask?"

"Rafe." She wrapped her hand around his. "The vows I made. You need to know the whole of what I promised."

Her seriousness chilled him. "What?"

"The bargain was that Masterson would give me until sundown tomorrow if I could get them Wolf Creek. Specifically, that I would, with all the secrecy Masterson wanted, find something of equal or greater value to our forest."

Rafe remained silent, waiting. He was feeling worse and worse about what was coming next. "Yeah?"

She cleared her throat. "That was only part of what I promised that day. I took a blood oath that I would save my people at any cost. The only real way was through the deal with Masterson. That didn't work out, so now I pay the penalty."

Rafe waited a heartbeat. "You would save your people at any cost?"

"Or die trying."

Rafe felt the first of Lila's hot tears fall against his skin, and suddenly the urgency of her love-making made sense. *Fido's frackin' balls!*

"I failed and the year and a day I had to pull the deal off is almost up. By this time tomorrow," she said shakily. "I'm going to be dead."

Rafe tensed with outraged surprise. Lila laid her fingertips over his mouth. "Don't say anything. There's nothing anyone can say. I did this to myself."

Now wide awake, Rafe pulled her hand away, lacing his fingers through hers. "You're a hazard. In future, I'm going to pack you in bubble wrap before I let you out the front door."

She choked a laugh that wasn't a laugh.

His words sounded calm and confident, but his mind was flattened like a bug on a windshield. *What the hell?* He felt like he was falling, his stomach dropping down an endless cliff side. He settled his arms closer around Lila, feeling her soft breath on his skin. For all her appearance of calm, he could feel her heart fluttering like a bird's.

"Hush," he whispered, stroking her hair.

None of this made any sense to him. Fey logic was upside-down and backward, no more direct than a bowl of spaghetti. For a moment he hated their convoluted rules, their secrecy, and the unpredictable magic that had driven Lila to this pass. Then Rafe took a deep breath, mentally taking a step back.

Understanding the noodle-logic didn't matter, because he wasn't fey. He was a plain old wolf, with a different task in front of him. She needed a practical solution. He was good at those.

Rafe pulled Lila to his chest. "What exactly were the words of this vow again? That you would find something of equal value to the forest?"

"Or die trying."

Rafe pushed her gently aside. "Get dressed."

She sat up, her eyes huge. "Why?"

"If the oath depends on Masterson agreeing to the deal, then we need him present to unmake the oath, right? We have to find him."

"Unless he gets what he wants, he'll never let me go."

"He'll get what he deserves."

Rafe had barely zipped up his jeans when heard what sounded like rustling wingbeats. He craned his neck, looking past the treetops at the dark sky. *Friend? Enemy?* As the sound grew a notch louder, he recognized the leathery flap of the gargoyles. "I think your sisters are here."

He could use their help, but at the same time he hated to end the time alone with Lila. Well, if he had his way, there would be plenty of quality time in their future. *Not if, when.*

Lila responded by pulling her dress over her head. "My sisters were supposed to be in the forest, protecting their homes. This is folly."

Her voice was panicked. Rafe put his arm around her shoulders. They stood side-by-side, Lila pressing into his side, and staring into the night sky. The stars were blotted out by a dark, ragged shape that grew larger and weirder-looking the closer it got. The wingbeats amplified into a racket of flapping.

Two gargoyles, dangling the furious form of Masterson between them. Rafe's chest swelled with hope. *Great minds think alike.* When the hideous creatures flapped in for a landing, they dropped the red-faced man to the ground. He landed with a grunt and a thump that made Rafe wince.

"What are you doing here?" Lila cried. "What's *he* doing here?"

The gargoyles blurred, their shapes dissolving into a halo of white light. Rafe blinked and when his vision cleared, he saw in their place two women in long white dresses. One had her hair done in an elaborate wreath of braids. The other had hers cut short, framing a face filled with mischief. Both were almost as beautiful as Lila.

Almost. They didn't strike him dumb with their beauty as Lila had. Rafe cast a quick glance at the woman nestled against his side. Lila had blinded him to anyone else.

The one with the braided hair spoke. "My sister, you didn't think we would simply abandon you?"

"We agreed."

"You agreed. We thought he needed the opportunity to release you from the last of your oath." She cast Masterson an acidic look.

Rafe couldn't stifle a grin.

Masterson raised his head. He looked windblown and frightened, but Rafe saw his jaw set in defiance. To a man like that, fear was weakness, and there was no way he'd appear weak.

Masterson glared at Lila. "I'm not releasing you from anything. You're the one who couldn't deliver."

"You didn't tell me you already had a history with Pack Devries," she shot back.

"Not material."

Lila shifted from foot to foot, clearly nervous. "My year and a day isn't up. You moved your equipment in too soon. You broke your word."

"Like you were going to accomplish anything in the next twenty-four hours." Masterson folded his arms.

The short-haired sister spoke, and her voice was dangerous. "Your desire for our land is going to kill our people, and it's going to kill her. We have played this game in a way that kept wild magic on a leash, but you make us desperate."

Masterson gave a slow shrug. "Go have another granola bar."

A moment of stunned silence blanketed the scene.

The fey blinked as if there wasn't a place in their imagination for such rudeness. Rafe opened his mouth to speak, but never had the chance.

Lila slugged Masterson. Even without fey strength, it would have been a sound shot. As it was, the man went over backward with a cartoonish thud. Leaves and fallen pine needles flew up as he landed, startling a bird from the underbrush. The man grunted with pain, massaging his jaw.

"Nice," Rafe said. "Good form. Economy of movement. A definite eight."

Lila cradled her hand, massaging the knuckles. "That felt fabulous."

Unfortunately, the moment didn't last. Masterson got to his feet unsteadily. He looked around, his belligerent expression only highlighted by the angry red mark where Lila had punched him. "You are so fired, Wilding. And I'm suing the rest of you."

Dumbass. The man was either terminally stupid or suicidal. Anger choked Rafe, cutting off his air. He cleared his throat. "My name is Rafe Devries. My father is the Alpha of Pack Devries."

Masterson occupied himself with dusting off his clothes. "So?"

Rafe felt an urge to tear out the man's throat, finish the episode wolf-style. But killing the man wouldn't help Lila, so Rafe fought down the impulse. Now was the time to get practical. Lila's mention of old fairy tales—and how often humans failed to read the fine print—had reminded him there was more than one way to look at a fair exchange.

"You had a bargain with Lila Wilding, and I'm seeing it through to a successful conclusion."

"Oh?" said Masterson, now sounding curious.

"Rafe!" Lila mouthed in a horrified whisper. "What . . .?"

He held up a finger, signaling patience. "You require a trade of something of equal or greater worth to Gilden Woods."

"Yeah."

"I'll tell you what Gilden Woods are worth. They're valuable for the shelter they give, for the scent of pine and the beauty of the sun dappling the forest glades, for the sound of the bird song and the peace they give an open heart."

Masterson scowled. "Why the hell should I care about that?"

Rafe went on, not missing a beat. "I will, on behalf of the wolves, offer Masterson Corporation the ecstasy of running through the wide open fields of Wolf Creek. The scent of new hay and warm cattle. The beauty of the frost sparkling on the gate post in winter, and the laughter of our children. We offer you the enjoyment of these freely. Come and partake of them whenever you please. I'd say that was a fair exchange."

The three fey bowed ceremonially.

"The exchange is heard and witnessed," said Rosemund. "Let the deal be fulfilled."

"Heard and witnessed," said the other sister, nodding her head gravely.

Rafe heard Lila gasp, and he grabbed her as she sagged against him. He smelled the telltale burnt-toast scent of magic. *Something* was happening.

Masterson breathed heavily, as if he'd run the hundred miles from the woods rather than taken the gargoyle express. "That's not what I meant."

"Did you specify cash value?" Rafe demanded. "Were you precise in your definition of worth?"

"No, he did not," said Lila slowly, her eyes bright as she straightened and regained her feet. "So the offer is a valid one. You think like a dark fey, werewolf. I wonder if I should be afraid."

Her sisters laughed, utterly delighted, and wrapped Lila in their arms.

"That's cheating!" Masterson roared, sounding like a child robbed of his lunch money.

Rafe gripped the man's shoulder, not hurting him but making the possibility a tangible thing. "Not unless we took something you had a right to. You don't have a right to the oil under Wolf Creek, or to the trees of Gilden Wood. Those woods are parkland. If I hear you've taken so much as a pine cone, I'll make it my personal mission to remind you wolves don't mess around with vows and bargains. When we say 'no,' that's our final answer."

Masterson released a volley of expletives and wrenched himself out of Rafe's grip. "This doesn't end here, wolf."

But his eyes held the acknowledgement of defeat. Rafe held his gaze a long moment, silently forcing him to accept that Rafe had won and he had lost and that Lila was free.

Masterson looked away first.

"I'm afraid it does end here," Rosemund said with a smile that reminded Rafe more of Darak than the Tooth Fairy. The other sister—Rafe had heard Lila call her Arabelle—had already resumed her gargoyle shape.

"Are you taking him back to his media event?" Rafe asked dryly.

"I wouldn't have him miss that for the world," Rosemund replied. "I'm astonished by the speed human communications travel. It seems word has already spread to a nest of vampires in Florida who have a bone to pick with Mr. Masterson. They are most eager to speak with him about another past real estate deal once his time in front of the cameras is done. Of course, the fey of Gilden Wood are pleased to supply transportation."

The man groaned. The fey laughed in a way that made Rafe glad he was on their side. In another moment, two gargoyles were flapping away, Masterson in tow.

Alone again, at last.

"So." He turned to Lila, cupping her face in his hands. "I guess there's no need to die anytime soon."

His words were light, but he felt solemn. They'd escaped disaster by a whisker. He kissed her gently, hoping it would blossom into more very soon.

She was crying, moonlit tears silvering her cheeks. A fine trembling had taken her, the aftermath of shock and fear and relief. "You stormed into my house, Rafe Devries, a wolf bent on defeating me. You could not best me with fang or claw, but your kind and clever heart has made me surrender. Do with me what you will."

Rafe allowed himself a lazy smile. "I just see you for who you are, and I like what I see, my *belle dame sans merci*." He kissed her lightly on the forehead. She was anything but the merciless siren of the poem. She was a champion. A woman. His lover. "You can't hide from a wolf."

"Why not?" she laughed, her green eyes filled with the light of happiness, and the beginnings of a mischievous twinkle.

"We're not afraid of pickle forks."

Her joy turned to profound bewilderment. She wrinkled her nose. "What's that supposed to mean?"

Rafe grinned. It was nice to be the one sowing confusion for a change. "I think we might have a future, Lila Wilding."

One Soul To Share

LORI DEVOTI

Chapter One

THE BAR WAS DIRTIER AND DARKER than any dive Nolan Moore had ever entered, even on a dare. Smoke clouded the air, shrouding the bar's patrons and decor, but Nolan could smell the humans, each and every one, and hear them...hear the beat of each of their hearts and the whoosh of every breath as it exited their lungs.

His nostrils flared, and his hands fisted. He didn't want to know that the man on his right, drinking beer from a chipped glass mug, had a heart valve that was close to failing. He didn't want to know that the woman that man was standing close to had slept with someone other than the man, only hours earlier.

But, damn, his vampire senses, he did.

The man with the damaged valve moved his hand to the woman's ass and whispered in her ear. She giggled and rubbed against him.

Nolan, teeth grinding together, turned away and stalked deeper into the stink, heat and sound until he wanted to spin in circles and growl, become the monster his family already thought he'd become.

"Stranger." A man standing behind the bar, a short grizzled type with weathered skin and battered features, laid a revolver onto the wooden bar in front of Nolan. On the back of the man's hand was a tattoo of an eye— the evil eye. Nolan glanced at it, unimpressed.

His fingers curling around the gun's butt, the bartender asked, "What or who are you looking for?"

Straight to business, which suited Nolan fine. The sooner he was out of the stifling stench of the bar the better.

"I need a guide, one that knows the sea. I heard this was the place to come."

The bartender's index finger twitched, less than a millimeter of movement, but the vampire didn't miss the nervous tick.

The man replied, "You're feet from the docks. Lots know the sea here. Some place in particular you're looking to find?"

"The hag." Not a place, but a person...or being. Nolan wasn't sure what the sea hag was, and he didn't care. His only concern was that the stories were true and she had what he needed.

The bartender's fingers closed tighter around the gun's butt. "You have business with her?"

"I wouldn't need a guide to find her if I didn't." Nolan leaned closer, meeting the man's gaze.

The wall behind the bar was covered with objects Nolan recognized as attempts to ward off evil. But considering they'd done nothing to stop him from entering the place, the effort was wasted.

"There's...someone who might help." The man raised one bushy brow and slid his hand forward.

Nolan dropped two bills onto the man's palm and waited.

The bartender slid his fingers over the bills, apparently checking their validity, then slipped them into his pocket.

"Talk to the mermaid. She's been coming in for months. Rumor has it she's planning a visit to the hag herself and looking for a companion."

"Mermaid? How did she come by that name?" Nolan needed a guide, one tough enough to weather whatever journey lay before him. He didn't need a female looking for help of her own.

"Not a name. It's her...breed."

"Breed?" Surely the bartender didn't believe whoever this female was that she was truly a mermaid. Mermaids were myths like dragons and Pegasus and...Nolan flicked his tongue over one canine...vampires.

He growled. "Where can I find her?"

"She was in the back earlier. Sitting alone. Can't miss her." The bartender straightened his arms, ready to push himself away from the bar, but then apparently thought better of it. He reached out and grabbed Nolan by the arm. His fingers digging into Nolan's bicep, he whispered, "You ain't the first one what went with her. She takes 'em to the docks and they never come back."

Nolan stared down at the man's fingers. The bartender loosened his hold and stepped back as if burned, but Nolan wasn't done with him. He leaned over the bar. "She's taken others to the hag?" He hadn't heard of anyone successfully making it to wherever the sea hag called home, or if they had, they'd never returned to share their stories.

The bartender shook his head, his eyes wide now and worried. "Don't think so. They weren't gone that long. She's like the rest of her kind, but with legs. She lures men out to the water and pulls them under...from there...?" His voice dropped. "There's no coming back."

❖

Sarina Neri crossed her legs at the ankle and stared toward the front of the bar. Someone new had entered, someone different from the worn-out men who usually stumbled into the place. Maybe, finally, her search was over. Maybe, finally, she would find a man capable of passing the sea hag's tests.

He was talking with the bartender and, Sarina could tell, hearing tales of her dangers. The superstitious man's gossip didn't worry her.

No man could resist the lure of a nixie, if she turned her attention his way.

After taking a drink of her beer, she uncrossed her ankles and placed her bare feet onto the filthy bar floor. She was preparing to stand, to search out this new man, when she saw him crossing the room toward her.

She smiled. This one was coming to her.

As he approached, she studied him, looking for some sign that he was different from the others. She'd tried eight so far, each younger and, from outward appearance, stronger than the last, but none had survived her test. None had lasted the quarter of an hour Sarina considered the minimum she would need to trick the sea hag into thinking she had brought the old goddess what she demanded—a man who could live out his life beside her under the sea.

This man was tall with broad shoulders that tapered to an athletic waist. Trim and fit—neither signs he possessed the talent Sarina needed. He was handsome too, with rugged features and a cleft in his chin. The hag, like all sea beings, appreciated beauty. So, his looks were a plus, but neither that, nor the confident way he prowled forward, were enough.

He had to be able to stay alive in the sea hag's home long enough for Sarina to swim away with the soul.

As he moved closer, Sarina spun in her seat to face him. "Are you looking for me?"

He paused, surprise registering on his face. Like the others, he'd probably taken her soft features and feminine form as some sign she would be submissive, an easy target for whatever caused him to search her out.

But mermaids, nixies, none of their kind, were submissive or easy targets.

She stood, sweeping her waist-length hair behind her. The long shirt she'd taken from her last failed candidate fell open over one bare shoulder and the dungarees she'd belted at her waist slipped. Annoyed with the human clothing, she undid the belt with one hand and let the pants fall to the ground.

Stepping out of them, she moved forward.

She trailed her fingers over the newcomer's chest as she walked around him, appraising. "What did the bartender tell you?" This man was the first to come to her. The others she had searched out. They had come willingly enough, of course, but they hadn't walked into the bar looking for her, as she suspected this male had.

"I need a guide," murmured.

His chest and back were layered with muscle. She paused for a second to lay her palm flat, over his heart. Its beat was slow, slower than any she had felt before. Her brows pulled forward, and confused, she took a step back to study him again.

He was not a merman come to land, or a selkie. Her fortune couldn't be that great. Or poor—another creature like herself would be harder to fool, harder to mesmerize into thinking he was in love with her, and harder to convince to accompany her on her journey to see the sea hag.

"What type of guide?" she asked, for the moment making no effort to charm him in any way. She wanted to hear the answer he intended to give, not one put into his mind by spell.

"I have business at sea." He paused, and she sighed. Nothing special after all.

"With the sea hag," he added.

Sarina's body stiffened, and she stepped back, studying him again. "You know Melusine?"

"My business is just that...business. I have no prior connection with the hag...Melusine."

Sarina tilted her head. Ordinary humans didn't know of Melusine, or if they did, thought her nothing but legend. But this man before her wasn't selkie or merman, so what could he be? What was his story?

She inhaled, checking for the scent of the sea.

Sadly, or luckily, she wasn't sure which yet, he smelled no more of the ocean than any of the unbathed seafarers seated at the tables nearby. He didn't, however, smell entirely human either. There was something different about him, but Sarina couldn't peg what it was.

"As it happens, I'm in need of a companion myself," she replied, keeping her tone neutral.

He smiled, confident, like a man used to getting his way. "So I heard. That is, then, fortunate for us both, isn't it?"

Perhaps. Sarina still didn't trust that her luck had finally changed. "Can you swim?" she asked. All said they could, but none really knew what they might expect to encounter in a journey to Melusine's home.

Like the others, he nodded his head in assent.

Tired of speculating as to whether her search was finally over, she walked past him and strode to the door.

❖

The mermaid, as the bartender had called her, said nothing to Nolan as she passed. She simply walked toward the door showing not the tiniest amount of doubt that he would follow.

And he would. In fact, he was surprised every man in the place didn't rise to his feet and rush after her.

Maybe one-hundred and twenty pounds and under five feet eight inches in height, she was slim and athletic, but also exuded femininity.

He had never encountered another woman, or creature, like her.

As he turned, his foot caught in the pants she had dropped so casually to the floor. He stared down at them, wondering if he should scoop them up and carry them along.

From the front, the bartender's gaze met his. Even through the hazy air, Nolan could read the man's face. He thought Nolan a fool, or worse a *soon-to-be-dead* fool.

Little did he know, Nolan was already the walking dead.

With a grimace, he left the pants and followed the "mermaid."

Sarina stood on the damp dock, waiting for the human. The wind had picked up, catching her hair and wrapping it around her. She could smell the water behind her; her body itched to leap into the bay that lead to the ocean. Her toes wiggled, already preparing to shift to the fin she still found so much more natural.

As the man approached, her hand wrapped around the tiny vial hanging from her neck. Feeling its pulsing warmth against her palm calmed her, assured her that what she was about to do was necessary.

Having a soul had saved her, but at times like this, it cost her too.

"Now what?" The man arched one brow and stared out over the water.

She moved toward him with all the power and grace of her kind. Humming, she grabbed fistfuls of his shirt and rose up on her toes. "You said you can swim, right?" She sang the words with no tune in mind. The notes didn't matter, any that left her throat, any mermaid's throat, would be enough to lure a human into her bidding.

He stared down at her, his gaze hooded. "I did."

"Then now...." She brushed her lips over his, and took a teasing step back. "...is the time to prove it."

With no other warning, she fell backward into the bay, taking the human with her.

Chapter Two

ICY WATER RUSHED OVER NOLAN, hitting him in the face. He closed his eyes and cursed his own stupidity. The bartender had warned him. The woman had too, in a way. She had asked him if he could swim.

Stupidly, he had expected her to take him at his word.

He held his breath and waited for her to loosen her hold on him so he could prove his claim, but as seconds ticked by, her grip remained iron strong. And he was no longer falling, he was being pulled...down...at an impossible speed.

His eyes flew open, and his upper lip pulled back, revealing his fangs—not that the woman saw them. She was too busy swimming herself, tugging him down in steady flap, after steady flap, of her undeniably aquatic tail.

The bartender hadn't been wrong.

The guide he had searched out *was* a mermaid.

And, based on the hold she had on Nolan and the speed she was traveling, her intentions were not good.

Nolan's first instinct was to lash out, to show her the timid fish she thought she'd caught was in fact a shark, sharp teeth and all, but as water slid over him and he caught sight of her hair flowing behind her and her shirt clinging to her breasts, he calmed.

He was at no risk. He was a vampire. He had no need to breathe. Let her tow him wherever she liked. It would do her no good, and he would learn more about her and her kind—the mystical mermaids no one truly believed existed.

Just as no one believed vampires existed.

Her tail slapped against his side. He closed his eyes and enjoyed the feel of being swept along. In some strange way—despite the tight grip she had on his body—it felt like freedom.

Sarina had quit singing when her back touched the water. She swam now, strong and determined to reach the bottom of the bay before the human she held came out from under the fog she had created.

She glanced at him. His eyes were closed and he looked...peaceful. Minutes had passed, five at least. By now, the need to breathe should have overcome the fog—or should soon. She flapped her tail again, sending her and the human shooting another ten feet toward the bottom.

The man moved. This was the part she hated...the part that having her own soul made hard.

For other mermaids—shells with no souls of their own—it was easy, expected even, to capture sailors and the like and tow them to the bottom of the sea. The mermaids gathered men, not even realizing what they hungered for—a soul—couldn't be harvested in this way.

But, not any soul would do. For a mermaid to be free of the hunger and the ties to the sea, she needed the soul meant for her and her alone.

Sarina glanced at the man again. His eyes were open now. She steeled herself against his panic and tightened her grip to keep him from breaking away.

Then he smiled.

Sarina's mouth opened and a bubble escaped. They were pressing against the fifteen minute mark now, and he was calm, beyond calm. He looked...pleased.

She loosened her hold and pushed him free. He didn't move; he just hung in place like seaweed attached to the bay floor.

His gaze shifted, from her face, down her borrowed shirt and finally to her tail. It clung there, making her feel uneasy and exposed.

She'd walked among the humans for two years now, knew the bartender had guessed her secret, but she had only revealed herself so thoroughly to the men she had brought to the bay for her test. And none of the others had survived.

This man, however, was different. He WAS surviving, and he would know what she was, know mermaids were real.

She pulled back further, suddenly uncertain. The idea that mermaids were myth had protected the nixies. Sure, a few storm-tossed sailors had washed to shore with tales of her kind, but that was it. There were no real photographs, and no rational accounts. No proof that other humans couldn't brush off as the rantings of some battered, most often drunk, sailor wanting for attention.

But this man...with his self-possessed gait and his confident stare...this man people would believe.

She twirled in the water and swam to the side, leaving him floating and watching her, his attention and ability to hold his breath eerie now.

It wasn't too late. She could drag him deeper, to a part of the ocean that, no matter his ability to hold his breath, he could never escape.

She rushed forward, intent on righting the mistake she'd almost made and stopped in front of him. Her hair billowed forward, forming a veil around them. He reached out with one finger and lightly touched the vial that floated upward, away from her chest. She clasped her hand around the tiny tube and jerked it back down.

His eyes met hers, and her heart thumped hard in her chest. No ordinary man this, but not selkie or merman or any other being she had ever encountered in the sea. That she knew for sure.

Whatever his magic, whatever gave him the ability to walk the earth with such confidence and stay calmly submerged under the bay too, he was the one to fulfill her plan.

A plan she had dreamed of for too long to give it up now.

And, she reminded herself, she needn't worry that he knew her secret. His part of the journey would be one way. He would meet the sea hag as he asked, but he wouldn't be coming back. There would be no one but Melusine, her kelpies and the fish for him to tell.

She grabbed the man by the front of his shirt and towed him back to the surface.

This time as the mermaid pulled him along, Nolan kept his eyes open.

The bottom of the bay was dark, too dark even for his vampire vision to make out more than murky shapes, but as they moved upward, back toward the surface, his eyes adjusted and he could see the mermaid clearly.

Her hair flowed behind her, and her body undulated with the water. Her skin, in this form, was silvery, giving way to glistening scales just below her waist. Her breasts were high and firm, the same, he imagined, as they would be in her human form. His groin tightened at the thought.

Mermaids were sirens, known for luring men to their deaths.

Staring at her, having heard her voice and felt the brush of her lips, he could understand sailors who steered their ships up onto the rocks or dove into the ocean knowing they were about to die. Death would seem a small price for a moment in the arms of such a creature.

So, despite the fact that she had pulled him to the bottom in what had to be an attempt to kill him, he had no doubt that he had found his guide.

He, like any man, would be tempted to follow her anywhere, even hell itself. Making it good fortune that she was willing to lead him where he wished to go.

Where she wished to go too, if the bartender was correct.

Why she, a creature of the sea, needed a companion was a question Nolan would at some time ask, but for the moment, it didn't matter.

He had found his guide.

Sarina popped through the surface of the water, releasing the man as she did and plunging her body immediately back down into the bay. She swam beneath the surface for a moment, assessing her plan.

She could not return to her human form until most of her body was dry of the sea. She hadn't thought to place towels on the dock and was unprepared to air dry herself here, in the human domain, as mermaids often did when sunning on the rocks.

But, if she let the human go, would he come back? The journey was too long and dangerous to swim while towing him. They would need a ship.

She returned to the surface a few yards from where the man waited, treading water.

"Do you have a name?" she asked. Humans were simple creatures, fond of being called by their own names.

He glanced toward the dock, as if questioning her choice of location for this chat, but then looked back at her and answered, "Nolan Moore, and you?"

"Sarina..." She paused. "...Neri."

"Sarina." He smiled, and a strange warmth filled Sarina. She usually found talking to humans, especially the men, frustrating. They were obvious creatures filled with base desires. No human she had ever encountered wanted her for anything other than what she could do for them, or they thought she could do—lead them to treasure, supply them with sex, or entertain them with song.

She moved her tail, swam a little to the side and then back.

"Why did you try to drown me?"

The question caught Sarina by surprise, not that the human realized that his life had been in danger, but that he was, without her doing anything to charm him, so calm.

She came to a stop, holding her body in place with tiny movements of her tail. "I wasn't trying to kill you."

"Really?" He stopped treading water for a moment, allowing his body to sink down beneath the water before bobbing back up. "Last I checked, humans need air."

"You don't." If he chose to be direct, she could be too.

Again, he smiled. "Of course, I do. I'm no different than any..." He shoved a damp chunk of dark hair off of his forehead. "...man."

Her eyes narrowed. He was lying. He had to be. He couldn't, despite his appearance, be human.

"You are...."

"What?"

"Different." She circled him, careful not to get too close. "I'm just not sure how."

"And you are a mermaid."

She flicked her tail, sending water spraying to the side. "Obviously."

"Are you dangerous?"

"Yes." Mermaids didn't lie. They had no reason to. Men would follow them even if they were told within minutes they would die.

"Should I trust you?"

"No."

Her answer seemed to please him. He smiled again. "Trust is over-rated."

It was a strange reply, and she had no answer. She waited.

"Will you take me to the sea hag?" he asked. His gaze was direct now, demanding the truth.

"Yes." She held his attention.

"Dead or alive?"

She shook her head. "Dead you do me no good." She dove under the water and swam along the docks, emerging twenty feet away. "Meet me at the ship, The Mermaid's Dream." Then, her message delivered, she disappeared under the water again.

He would follow her, not because she had charmed him; she hadn't. He would follow her because his desperation to find Melusine was as great as her own. She had seen it in his eyes.

Chapter Three

NOLAN PULLED HIMSELF UP ONTO the dock. His soaked clothing slapped against the damp wood. He ran fingers through his hair, sending water droplets flying.

The mermaid, Sarina, had said she hadn't been trying to kill him, but she had also admitted she was dangerous and not to be trusted.

Which was he to believe? Could both be true?

He supposed, but whatever the female's motive for pulling him under the surface of the bay, he was sure no other occupant of the bar would have survived the trip. Which explained the bartender's warning.

If Nolan had still been human, he wouldn't be alive now.

He was a lucky man, cheating the grim reaper like that twice in one lifetime.

He laughed, an ugly sound that had taken over any carefree noise he could make years before.

Being ostracized and cursed was not anyone's definition of lucky. Death would have been better, and Nolan might well have searched it out if he hadn't learned of another possibility, a way to reverse what had been done to him.

As he sat dripping on the dock, a new light approached, the beam of a large flashlight, dancing over the wooden dock where Nolan sat and the bay behind him.

"You survived." It was the bartender. Behind the glare of the light, Nolan couldn't see the man's face, but he could smell his fear. If the bartender had been afraid of the mermaid, it seemed now he was even more afraid of the man who had swam with her and survived.

Nolan stood, running his hands over his clothing to remove some of the water as he did.

"I was right, wasn't I? She is a nixie, a mermaid." The man's voice quivered and his flashlight's beam shook.

Nolan paused. Behind him he heard the slap of a tail against the water. He pulled off his shirt and wrung it out onto the dock. Water fell against the wood in loud splatters.

"The mermaid. Where did she go?" There was an eagerness in the bartender's voice now, his merchant mind realizing the potential draw a real mermaid might hold for his business.

Nolan slung his wet shirt over his shoulder and walked forward. "No mermaid here. Just a girl looking to play a joke with some friends. I called her bluff and she shoved me in, then ran. Her friends did too."

"A joke?" Uncertain.

"They had a camera. My guess? They were planning to upload these 'mermaid encounters' on the Internet and become the next big thing."

"A stunt?" The bartender still didn't sound as if he was buying Nolan's explanation.

The vampire shrugged. "Believe me or not, but I don't think you'll be seeing her again."

"Oh." Disappointment now.

Nolan walked past the bartender without looking back.

If the mermaid thought to dump him now, she would at least have to find another place to fish for his replacement. Of course, he had also saved her from possible pursuit by the bartender and other fortune hunters, but that had held no weight in his decision to lie about her real identity.

None at all.

They had been at sea for two weeks. Sarina had given the main cabin of the yacht she'd "borrowed" to the human, Nolan. She slept on deck or in the water, her hand pressed against the boat's side so she didn't lose it in her slumber.

The sun was fully overhead now, and she was alone on deck. Nolan, she'd soon learned, preferred night to day, disappearing into the cabin at dawn and not appearing back above deck until dusk.

He had other habits too that didn't fit with what she knew of humans. While he slept each day, she would swim and catch fish for their dinner, but he had yet to eat any of them in front of her. He drank wine and once she had seen him sipping something from a flask he'd pulled from one of his bags, but he had declined all of her offers of food.

She had quit asking, preferring to eat her fish alone in the sea anyway.

His habits, she realized, suited her...gave her privacy to be in her natural state in the sea. And, since mermaids didn't require the same amount of sleep as humans, staying awake through the night was no issue.

She was able to do what she wished in the day, even sunbathing in her mermaid form on the deck, and watch the human at night.

But still...she slapped her fin lightly against the deck...Nolan's habits added to her certainty that he wasn't what he appeared, that he wasn't human at all, but some other creature she hadn't encountered before.

A gull squawked overhead, pulling her back to the present and reminding her that they were approaching land—a small string of islands, uninhabited by humans, but the first visible sign that they were moving closer to the sea hag's home.

There would be a test soon.

Sarina had no idea in what form it would come or when, but she knew it would come.

She only hoped that whatever kept Nolan hidden in the cabin by day wouldn't prove to be their downfall.

Nolan's body rolled off the bed and slammed into a wall. His eyes flew open, and his nails scraped over the cherry boards that lined the cabin walls. He fell back onto the bed, only to be flung sideways again as the boat was catapulted sideways by some unknown force.

With a curse, he leapt to his feet and clawed at the walls to keep from falling again.

His head throbbed, telling him night had yet to fall. Since his turn, he had avoided the day. He had never been caught in the daylight to know if the horror flick images of vampires erupting into roman candles of flames were true; the general groggy feeling and aches he experienced when the sun was in the sky had been enough on their own to keep him inside.

The boat listed violently to the side again. Only Nolan's hands pressed on the walls of the tiny hall by the cabin's door, kept him from slamming into the wood.

He could, he realized, stay here and drown, or go out and hazard the sun.

Water or flames?

He chose flames.

As the boat continued to tilt side to side, Nolan struggled his way through the bedroom door and into the kitchen and living part of the cabin.

Sarina was nowhere to be seen, which meant the mermaid was above deck facing whatever threatened them alone, or she had already left—swam off to safety.

Grim but determined, Nolan flung open the main cabin door. Sun blasted into the room, hitting him in the eyes like a giant laser. Wincing, he stepped back, out of the light.

His eyes burning, he groped around the room, looking for the small desk and a pair of sunglasses he'd seen tucked into a basket.

Glasses in place, he opened the door again.

The sea hag's pet, a sea wyrm, rose over the yacht and blew steam from its nose. Sarina clung to the boat's railing and stared up at it.

The creature's tongue danced over her face, smelling her. She held still, knowing any movement on her part would only anger the dragon.

It snorted, spewing hot water over her. She shook her head, freeing the droplets from her hair and held up both hands, revealing she held no weapon. "I'm here by Melusine's invitation."

It was the right thing to say, although most likely unnecessary. If the dragon had thought the yacht and its occupants were trespassing, it would have sank the boat long before this. Still though, its job was to guard the outer perimeter of Melusine's territory, and it apparently took its job seriously.

The dragon's worm-like body curved up on both sides of the ship.

The yacht was trapped now, sandwiched.

"If you are going to sink us, get on with it." To show the creature his threat was wasted on her, Sarina lifted her head to meet his gaze and allowed her body to shift. In seconds, her human legs were replaced by her tail and only the strength of her arms holding onto the railing kept her upright.

The dragon moved its body again, sending the boat popping upward and out of the water before landing back down with a bone-jarring jolt.

Sarina lost her grip on the railing and went flying. With a roar, the dragon moved in and caught her on the bridge of its wide nose.

Stranded like a beached animal, she could do nothing but stare into the creature's over-sized amber eyes.

Holding her gaze, it pulled its tail from the water and slapped it hard against the surface of the water.

A wave washed over the yacht and the dragon, sending the boat and Sarina airborne. She closed her eyes and prepared to hit the water, but the welcome feel of the ocean embracing her never came. Instead, she was grabbed again, this time by the dragon's tail.

With a roar he held her overhead, like a human dangling a mouse by its tail.

On deck, Nolan blinked—not from the sun, but what was blocking it.

A huge gold and green dragon with fins jutting from the sides of its face and a tongue that danced out of its mouth like an excited snake's rose from the sea next to the yacht.

At Nolan's arrival, it opened its lips and roared. Hot steam coated Nolan, clouding his glasses.

He had wanted fire. It appeared the dragon might soon give him his wish.

He glanced over the deck, searching for Sarina, but the mermaid was nowhere in sight.

Free then. Swum away, leaving Nolan to face this beast on his own. Not that Nolan could blame her. He couldn't imagine a mermaid had much defense against a creature this large—no more than a lone vampire might.

But then Nolan couldn't swim, at least not like the mermaid.

Which left him with one choice—fight.

While he thought, the dragon had turned the boat, using a part of its body submerged beneath the water, Nolan guessed.

Nolan stood still as it analyzed him and his apparently hopeless situation.

"If you are going to sink me, do it now," he muttered as much to himself as the beast.

The dragon paused and for a moment leaned closer. Its tongue darted out, touching Nolan's face, chest and legs.

The boat rose and the dragon turned, another bigger section of its body appearing from beneath the waves—its tail, Nolan realized, but something more too.

Wrapped tight in the creature's tail was Sarina, her face pale and her eyes closed.

She hadn't swam away.

One simple thought, but it was enough.

The beast Nolan worked so hard to keep hidden behind a human face burst free. His fangs extended and his muscles clenched. His thick vampire blood pounded through his heart, and the pulse at his neck jumped.

He hadn't fed in two weeks, not from a living creature. And while the blood of this over-sized snake was far from what he craved, it would more than do for now.

He ran forward, leaping as he did.

His arms wrapped around the dragon's body, not far below its head and his fangs sank into its flesh.

Its scales were soft and easy to pierce, but in an anger-fueled rush, Nolan had taken no time to assess his target. His bite sank into flesh, but missed any veins the creature might have.

If it had veins.

The dragon jerked and tossed its head trying it seemed to dislodge the vampire attached to its throat, but determined, Nolan hung on. The creature roared, and steam rolled from its throat.

Nolan's clothing stuck to his skin, and his hair clung to his face. He was sticky, and his arms ached with the effort of holding the twisting, angry beast, but none of that mattered, nothing mattered but getting it to loosen its hold on the mermaid.

His lifted his face and yelled, "Drop her."

The dragon sank under the sea, beneath the boat and lower. Arms and legs wrapped around the creature now, Nolan closed his eyes and willed his mind to slow.

He was accomplishing nothing holding the creature like this. Would accomplish nothing. He was to the dragon what a mosquito might be to a bear. Annoying, but little more.

Deeper they went until sun no longer filtered through the water, until only Nolan's vampire ability allowed him to see at all. Suddenly with no apparent reason, the dragon slowed until he seemed to barely be moving at all.

Nolan pulled the sunglasses from his face and shoved them into a pocket. Then, thinking this would be his chance to let go and escape back to the surface, he looked around, but he quickly realized that he had no idea which was up and which way was down.

He could as easily swim deeper into the sea as swim to the surface.

As he pondered his choice, something slipped under his waist and curled tightly around him. Then with no other warning, he was jerked from the dragon's throat and dropped. He floated for a moment, stunned and unsure of what had happened.

With no sound and no backward look, the dragon slithered away. It was then Nolan realized the creature had done as he'd ordered. He had dropped Sarina, and Nolan too.

Unfortunately, wherever he had left the mermaid was nowhere near here.

Deciding his only choice was to take a chance and hope he swam the right direction, Nolan swept his arms through the water, pushing his body upward...or what he hoped was upward.

He had moved maybe three feet, before his body jerked to a stop. Confused, he looked down.

A long, green tendril of some plant was wrapped around his leg. Curving his body down, he tried to loosen the strands with his fingers. The plant held tight. In fact, if Nolan hadn't known better—that plants were incapable of action of their own volition—he would have sworn the vine actually tightened in protest to his pulls.

Tired of messing with the thing, he bent lower and tried to saw through the tendril with his teeth. After what felt like minutes of scraping his fangs over the plant, he pulled back again.

The plant was completely unscathed, not even a scratch to show where Nolan's fangs had touched it.

It was then he realized that the dragon's unexpected release of him might not have been unexpected at all.

He had been trapped.

Chapter Four

SARINA FLOATED TO THE SURFACE AND gasped in air. The dragon had held her too tightly, too long. The air she'd held in her lungs had been squeezed out. She'd been close to passing out when the beast had dropped her and left her floating like debris in the deep water.

Mermaids didn't die easily though, and she'd managed, despite a shooting pain in her chest, to make her way back to the surface.

She had also, however, lost sight of both the dragon and Nolan.

An image of the human flying toward the dragon shot through her mind. She'd been weak then, desperate, and the human had seemed to notice...had seemed to care.

An impossible thought, of course. Humans didn't care, not about mermaids as beings like themselves. They cared about what they thought mermaids could bring them.

But the light in Nolan's eyes; the way his face had twisted....

It had reminded Sarina of her mother, fighting the pirate who three hundred years earlier had thought to steal Sarina and her sister away. Rage so pure and intense, no creature could face it and think they would win against it.

Her mother had won, at least what she fought for. Sarina and Allera had slipped out of the pirates' net.

But Sarina and her sister had lost.

Allera had lost her soul, and their mother hadn't survived. She'd died in that net, speared by a sailor when she tried to follow her daughters through the opening she'd created with the slashing of her tail.

Her mother's tears and blood had coated them. Sarina could still feel and smell both. She'd stared at her sister and known Allera, younger and more vulnerable, was her responsibility now, and she'd sworn she would find away to get her sister's soul back.

Sarina's hand wrapped around the vial that hung from her neck.

Which brought her back to Nolan. Whether he'd attacked the dragon out of rage for Sarina as a being, or Sarina as the mermaid who could get him to the sea hag, didn't matter.

Sarina needed him.

In the distance she could see their yacht, still a float. She spun in place, scanning for the human and the dragon. There was no sign of either.

If the dragon had left, his assignment must have been completed. The boat seemed stable and Sarina, though hurt, was alive.

Which only left Nolan. Sarina couldn't imagine the sea hag would have ordered a possible mate killed, but tested? Yes.

And how would Melusine test a mate?

She'd do the same thing Sarina had done. She'd see if he could last underwater.

Ribs aching, Sarina dove deep into the sea.

❖

Sarina searched the ocean for hours, long past time any human could possibly still be alive, but despite the growing pain in her chest and all logic, she couldn't stop. She couldn't believe Nolan was truly gone, and she wouldn't until she saw his body.

She had worked in a spiral out from the boat, moving deeper into the ocean as she moved outward. She was at the bottom now and further from the boat than she had been at any other point. Once back to the yacht she would have to stop. The pain had moved past something she could describe as an ache or throb and now edged toward agonizing.

She wouldn't be able to stay under water much longer.

Her mermaid body, legendary for its ability to survive any storm and hundreds of years, was about to give out.

Her fingers trailed over the ocean's floor, touching sand and debris. She was pulling herself along now, her body too tired to even swim. She coughed and tasted metal. Her hand moved to her mouth and came back red.

Blood. She was coughing out blood.

In a sea filled with predators, that couldn't be good.

The thought was fleeting.

Her eyes closed, and she let her body drift.

Nolan smelled blood, or maybe he tasted it. He wasn't sure how he knew blood was in the water somewhere close, but he did.

Realizing he most likely was not the only predator in the sea that might be drawn by the scent, he spun in place, searching for the source and any creatures that might have been attracted by it.

At first he saw nothing.

Then something long and silver fluttered.

Nolan's gut tightened.

There had to be many things in the ocean that were silver—plants, debris, fish....

A logical thought, but one Nolan couldn't accept, not without seeing for himself.

He jerked his foot upward again. The plant that held him tightened like a seat belt activated by a sudden stop.

Nolan paused. The analogy gave him a thought. He pulled again, this time softly. Again the plant tightened, but not as quickly or as tightly.

He took a step to the side with his free foot and dragged the other behind him. The plant allowed it. He tried to swim upward. The plant objected, jerking him back down.

Another step to the side and then another. Soon Nolan, never lifting his trapped foot from the ocean's floor, was six feet from where he had originally been pinned.

He could move, in an ungainly manner, but move.

He lowered his head and concentrated on his steps and nothing more. He kept going until the smell of blood had his vampire hunger snapping to be set free.

Then he looked up.

Sarina floated six feet above the ocean floor, looking like a magician's assistant levitated for an astonished crowd.

Except most magician's assistants didn't have blood leaking from their mouths.

Nolan leapt forward, forgetting his constraints and the repercussions moving upward had. The plant's tendril tightened around his ankle, so tight it cut through Nolan's sock and skin. Now Sarina wasn't the only source of blood in the sea.

But Nolan had no time to worry about that, he lengthened his body as far and as quickly as he could, desperate to latch onto the unconscious mermaid before the plant could retaliate fully and jerk him back to where he had started.

His fingers wrapped around her hand and they both went flying backward to his starting point.

But Nolan didn't let go of Sarina; he clung to her like a child holding a prized toy.

When they stopped, they were no better off than they had been before—except they were now together, bleeding.

One arm around her waist, he used the other to pull her hair from her face. Her features were fine and her skin delicate, at least in appearance, but Nolan knew from stories that mermaids weren't delicate or easy to damage.

What had the dragon done to her and why?

It was a useless question, one, if Nolan wanted to save them before sharks or something worse arrived, he had no time to answer.

Now he needed to think—not about the dragon or its motive, not even about the beauty of the mermaid in his arms, or the arousing scent of her blood. He needed to think of how to save them, how to get his foot loose and them both back to the ship where maybe he'd think of a way to save her.

Save her. How much life did she have left? Unable to do anything until he knew, he pressed his ear against her chest.

The vial she wore around her neck, dug into his cheek. He grabbed it in his fist, his first instinct to jerk it free and release it to the sea, but something about the feel of the tiny object in his hand caused reason to return. She wore the object for some reason; it had some meaning to her. It wasn't his place, in a fit of annoyance, to steal it from her.

He brushed the vial aside instead and placed his ear back against her chest.

Her heart beat...weak, but he could hear it.

He closed his eyes for a moment, relieved and not, he realized, just because he needed the mermaid to find the sea hag.

He was relieved because he saw something in Sarina—a quiet strength and determination.

She was, in some eyes, a monster like him, but she was beautiful too. He'd seen her swimming when she didn't think he could see her. Seen her staring into the distance too.

He didn't know her purpose for coming on this trip, or for wanting a companion, but he knew it wasn't for money or personal gain. It was for someone or something she loved.

He envied her that—that she had something to love.

He lowered her body, so he could stare into her face. Her lips parted. Blood still trickled from her mouth. Unable to resist, he lowered his face and kissed her lips, tasted her blood.

His lips tingled, his body tingled, and his nostrils flared. He had never tasted anything like this mermaid's blood.

He pulled her body close to his so her face was cradled against his neck, and spun in a slow circle, thinking—resisting.

The color of her skin had lost its silvery sheen and shifted to blue green. He knew nothing of mermaids, but had to imagine this change was tied to the blood she continued to lose.

His eyes went to the trickle of red. Guilt shot through him for tasting her blood while she suffered, perhaps even died.

No. His jaw clinched. She wouldn't die. She was a mermaid, a creature even more mythic than vampires, and vampires didn't die, not this easily.

Vampires. He'd only been one a few short years, but even before his own turn, he'd heard stories of what they could do—knew at least part of what had happened to him too.

He had been close to death, at the hands of his sire, but he had survived. His sire's blood had saved him.

Could he do the same for the mermaid? What would happen to a mermaid who drank vampire blood? Would she live? Die? Become a vampire too?

Nolan had no idea, but he could think of no other options.

He jammed his fangs into his wrist and slit his skin. Then he pressed the wound to Sarina's lips and waited.

Chapter Five

WARMTH SPREAD THROUGH SARINA. She flexed her fingers and lifted her tail.

Cold. She had been so cold, colder than when she'd swum through the Arctic Ocean, colder than the first time she'd stepped onto land, naked and shivering.

Those had been a surface discomfort, but this...what she'd just felt...went past that, deeper, into her very soul.

Soul. Her hand reached to her neck and the vial that hung there. Her fingers touched the bit of glass and metal, and her body relaxed.

Safe. Her soul was safe, and so was she.

Her eyes fluttered and as she came a little further out of unconsciousness, new sensations followed. Taste first, something thick and earthy filled her mouth. She parted her lips, letting more of the substance in.

A band around her waist tightened, pulling her against a hard surface. Her hands moved up and forward, defense against whatever thought to pin her in place. But her lips and tongue kept moving, kept lapping at whatever the heady substance was making her warm and whole.

Something moved through her hair, like a caress, like...fingers.

Her eyes flew open, and she twisted her head to the side. Nolan stared down at her.

His face was pale, and his hair floated around his head, reminding her that they were underwater and had been...how long?

He moved his arm, and she stared, shocked, at the gash in his flesh. Blood oozed from the wound...she touched her lips and looked back at the human.

He gestured, brushing away the question in her eyes, as if feeding a mermaid his blood 14,000 feet underwater was an average event in his life.

She pulled away, shocked more that he'd thought to share his blood with her than that she had ingested the fluid. The mainstay of mermaids' diet was raw fish, eating cooked food had been an adjustment. Drinking blood, while not something mermaids did, held no revulsion for her, and that the blood was from a human made no difference at all.

Nolan's face hardened. Realizing he'd misinterpreted her reaction, she moved back to where she had been and placed her palm on his chest. His eyes met hers and for a moment, she couldn't move. She could feel his hurt, so intense she wanted to pull away again, but also, strangely, she wanted to comfort him, to make whatever caused the pain in his eyes to disappear forever.

Confused, she folded her fingers into her palm and busied herself by floating downward, studying what held him in place.

A plant was wrapped around his ankle. She ran her fingers over it, but knew instantly the greenery was no ordinary bit of ocean vegetation. It, like the dragon, served Melusine.

Nolan grabbed her by the arm and pulled her up so she was once again looking at his face. His head shaking, he pointed upward.

He wanted her to leave him? Sarina pulled back again, this time swimming a few feet away, far enough she could study him and think without the pressure of his gaze.

A soulless mermaid would leave him. A soulless mermaid would have dragged him under the water, then torn him apart with her hands—so desperate would she be to get at his soul.

But Sarina had her soul, and she told herself, if she hoped to get another one, she needed Nolan alive and back on the boat.

She swam back, circling him and keeping her gaze low, away from his face. If she looked at him...she pushed the thought away. She didn't need to look at him. She only needed to save him and only because she needed him to trade to Melusine.

He was just a human—nothing more.

But, as she reached for the blade of grass that had wrapped its way around his ankle, her fingers trembled.

She feared having a soul was finally catching up with her. She feared she was close to caring—for man, a human.

She bit down on her cheek and concentrated on the grass. She tugged and it tightened. She leaned closer and bit at it with her teeth. Nothing.

The grass wouldn't loosen and it couldn't be cut. What other options were there? Her brows lowered and she swam back again.

Seeing her failed efforts, Nolan pointed up again.

She ignored him. He wasn't in charge. She wouldn't leave him. The ocean was her realm. Even Melusine couldn't argue mermaids' rights to the land below the sea.

Melusine was cursed and forced to take up her under-water home. The mermaids chose to live here.

This plant, as a part of the sea, was as much Sarina's to command as it was Melusine's.

And like that it came to Sarina, she opened her mouth and began to sing.

Nolan stilled, and his eyes closed. He could feel his body drifting back and forth in the water, leaning with each sway more toward Sarina and the incredible sound that was coming from her throat.

At least he thought it was Sarina singing. He couldn't hear her song...not like he could hear on land, but he could feel her song. It vibrated through him like note after note hit on a tuning fork, except delicious and alluring in a sleepy, dream-inducing way.

A smile curved his lips. She was his and waiting for him. He couldn't wait to get to her.

She swam upward, until she was looking down at him, and held out one hand. Her hair fanned out around her face, silver and glistening. She was an angel, beckoning him to paradise.

He took a step, then bent his knees to push off of the bottom. His arms moved overhead, catapulting him upward. A band tightened around his ankle, and he jerked to a stop. He frowned and stared down. The plant.

Anger ripped through him. He bent down, ready to rip the vegetation from the seabed by its roots, to do whatever it took to escape its hold and get to the angel who called him from above.

But, as he did, the greenery loosened, fluttering through his fingers like a ribbon. The strands floated up, past his face, reaching, it seemed, for the mermaid whose song still beckoned.

Peace settled over Nolan, and he swayed in place. Then, unable to stay away from the mermaid and her song a second longer, he pushed himself off the bottom of the sea and swam upward to meet her.

Nolan's face was pale, but content as he drifted toward Sarina. She'd seen the look before, on other humans, moments before one of her kind grabbed them and sucked them to the depths of the sea.

She closed her eyes, hoping to block out the image, but it only grew stronger. She could see the mermaids' faces now, the hunger that threatened to consume them, their eagerness as they dove with their prize, swam away in search of somewhere private to rip into their human captive with their bare hands—to find the soul they so craved.

Fingers slipped into hers, and despite the horror that had engulfed her, she felt herself calm.

Her eyes open, she reached down with her other hand and pulled Nolan upward, until he was facing her.

The blind joy she'd expected to see in his eyes immediately disappeared. Concern darkened them instead. He bent his elbows toward his body and pulled her close. His arm slipped around her waist, until her hips were pressed against his.

Surprised and confused, her song died and she stared at him.

He didn't pull away, or blink or do anything to show that the spell she had woven around him had ended, but she knew it had, knew the only way to keep a human in thrall was to sing and keep singing, until he had been dragged too deep to fight.

His fingers ran over her face, and his thumb brushed over her lip.

Then he leaned forward and kissed her.

Nolan had never kissed anyone underwater. Of course, until he had met Sarina, he had never been underwater, not for longer than a few seconds.

Holding the mermaid in his arms, water and her hair swirling around them, he realized how much he had missed out on, how little he had lived when he'd been alive, or at least before he'd been declared undead.

The skin of her back was soft and smooth. His fingers kneaded their way down her back, pausing at her hips where her fish half began. Her hands grabbed onto his shirt, and she kissed him back.

There was something both desperate and sweet in the touch of her lips, like the experience was as new and surprising to her as it was to him.

The thought made his vampire heart beat a little faster, far from racing, but fast enough he could almost believe he was still human, still alive.

He kissed her harder. His fingers pressing into the back of her head, holding her mouth to his.

He realized then a plus to their shared lack of humanity, neither needed to breathe, at least not for very long periods of time. They could kiss and kiss, stay beneath the ocean, secluded and alone for hours, be together just touching each other with no thought to the outside world and the hurt it held.

Hurt.

The word jolted Nolan, reminding him that Sarina had been hurt, had only moments earlier been losing blood.

Concern wrapping around him, he pulled his face from hers and one arm still around her waist, began moving them upward toward open air and hopefully, the yacht.

❖

Nolan had stopped kissing her.

At first the realization hurt, but then Sarina realized he still held her tight and was swimming, pulling her with him as he moved toward open air.

Feeling selfish for forgetting that he was not like her, not a creature of the sea, she swam with him, flapping her tail in strong steady swipes that ate through the water.

In moments they broke through the surface, into the dark cold night.

She stared at him, uncertain. Their kiss while below water had seemed natural and right, but here in the open air she felt embarrassed and awkward.

She had never kissed a human before, not like that, not willingly and wanting more.

But she had kissed Nolan and given the chance, she would do it again...and again.

She pressed her lips together and turned in a circle, hiding her embarrassment by pretending to search for their ship. It was less than a tenth of a mile away, a quick swim, too quick for Sarina to recover from the emotions tearing her apart.

Fingers brushed over her shoulder, and knowing she couldn't avoid Nolan any longer, she turned to face him.

"You were bleeding," he said, and there was concern in his voice. "I..." He closed his lips and glanced to the side.

The blood. He'd given her his blood, and she'd taken it.

Sarina studied him, her own uncertainty gone for the moment. "I drank your blood," she replied. "It made me better. How?" He wasn't human. She'd suspected it all along, but now she was certain.

His jaw tightened. "You don't want to know."

Sarina's hand moved, as it so often did when she felt uncertain, to the vial at her throat. A cold wind blew over the water. She shivered, but Nolan seemed unmoved. His gaze was stony now, all the joy she'd seen in it earlier gone.

She bit her lip, sorry for whatever had changed and wishing she could take it back. She shifted her gaze, back to the yacht. "The boat isn't far. Can you make it on your own, or do you—"

In answer to her unfinished question, Nolan leaned forward and started to swim. His arms sliced through the water, steady and sure, and his face never rose. He didn't, she realized, need to breathe—not for long periods of time, maybe never.

What creature didn't need air? She had noticed no gills on him to allow him to breathe underwater.

Her fist still closed around the vial, she stared after him. What could he be? What secret did he hide?

And, perhaps, most important, why did she care? They were in the sea hag's territory now and he had passed her test. It wouldn't be long before she and Nolan arrived at her home, and Sarina completed her bargain—a male capable of living as the sea hag's mate for Melusine, Allera's soul for Sarina.

The pirates took her mother's life and her sister's soul, in one fell swoop stealing everything Sarina valued, but now she would get at least one of those things back.

She would save her sister, and all it would cost her was Nolan.

She turned her face to the wind, letting the chill numb her, then she dove into the water and swam toward the boat.

Chapter Six

SARINA REACHED NOLAN BEFORE HE reached the boat. She held out her hand, and after a moment, he took it.

She hadn't rejected him, hadn't turned her back on him because of what he was.

Because she didn't know, an inner voice reminded him. If she did...when she did...she would look at him with the same revulsion everyone else he'd thought he'd known, thought he could trust, had.

Still, as her fingers wrapped around his and she pulled him through the water, it was easy to get lost in the joy of the moment. He sped forward, his body surfing over the water's surface and cold air blowing over his face.

It was brisk and invigorating—exciting and like nothing he had ever experienced before.

They reached the yacht, and sensing Sarina might want privacy for her transition from water to land, Nolan climbed onto the boat on his own, then turned his back. He was curious to see the mermaid's tail out of water, but he maintained his stance through the sounds of splashing and something flapping against the boat's polished wood deck.

"Thank you." Her voice was soft and almost shy.

He shrugged, and suddenly aware of his own saturated state, began wringing out his clothing on the deck. Since his turn, cold didn't bother him, but removing the water from his clothing seemed like the expected thing to do.

"Here."

Something flew through the air toward him. Nolan spun, catching it. A towel.

He rubbed at his face and hair.

The mermaid had dried off too. Her hair was still damp, but she had donned one of the loose-fitting shirts she seemed to prefer, and a towel was wrapped around her lower body. As Nolan watched, the tip of her fin, which was visible at the end of the towel, disappeared, and she wiggled her toes.

She looked up and caught him staring. He averted his gaze, but she waved her hand and stood. "It's okay. Humans have always been curious. At least you didn't try to cut open my tail to see if legs were hidden inside."

"That's happened?"

"Not to me, but others." She looked away, and he could tell she didn't want to discuss the subject more.

He bunched the towel he'd been holding into a ball. Things felt odd between them, unanswered questions lying around, weighing them both down.

And there was the kiss too.

He didn't regret it. In fact, he would have liked nothing more than to repeat it, but after she'd mentioned the blood...he lowered his arm and looked around for a spot to deposit the towel. Seeing a basket, he walked over and dropped the wet object inside.

"It won't be long now," she murmured.

He turned to find that she'd moved. She was only a few feet away from him now. The wind caught her shirt, pushing it tight against her curves. Her breasts were full and her nipples were hard. It was easy to imagine her without the shirt, remember how she'd looked under the ocean, her hair fanning around her face.

His groin hardened. "Until what?" he asked, lost as to what she could mean, lost to everything but the pounding need to touch her that seemed to grow with each passing second.

"Melusine...the sea hag. The dragon was one of her pets. She was...testing."

"And we passed?" It hadn't occurred to him that the sea hag would be aware of their approach.

"Yes." The mermaid didn't look pleased with her answer. Her lips pressed together and her hand rose to hold the vial that hung from her neck.

Remembering how he'd been tempted to toss the piece of jewelry into the ocean's depths, he motioned to it. "Is that important?"

She stilled, and alarm shone in her eyes. She took a step back, causing him to immediately regret his question. He held up a hand to reassure her. "I shouldn't have asked. Obviously, it is important to you or you wouldn't wear it."

She licked her lips and slowly nodded. She didn't, however, relax or loosen her tight grip on the vial. "It is. My mother gave it to me when I was born."

"Really?" He made a point not to look at the vial again. Instead, he focused on the female who wore it.

The decision was a bad one. His heart thumped, and he felt his body take a step toward her. She drew him as surely as fresh blood, but knew, while he had relished the small taste of her blood that he'd had, what drew him was even more elemental than that.

There was something about the mermaid that promised peace and contentment. Something that made him think with her he could relax, go back to being who he'd been before he'd met the vampire, before he'd become a monster.

He moved toward her, pulled by some invisible string. She glanced over her shoulder, toward the sea, and for a moment he thought she would dive in and leave him standing alone on the yacht.

But then she looked back.

She sighed and her shoulders lowered. Her expression changed from alarm to resigned surrender, as if she was as incapable of fighting whatever pulled them together as he was.

Relieved, he closed the space between them, slipped his fingers into her hair and pulled her mouth to his.

❖

She was kissing a human, again.

Sarina closed her eyes, closing out the sight of the ocean and the eyes she imagined staring at her from its depths.

Mermaids used humans. They didn't mate with them, or have feelings for them.

But Sarina could feel that she was on the verge of doing both. She wanted Nolan's touch, wanted to feel his lips on hers, wanted his arms around her.

She wanted him.

His hands moved from her hair, down her body, over her shoulders and arms, to her hips. His thumbs caressed the curve of her waist through her gauzy shirt. The tips of her breasts were hard and sensitive, and as the material grazed them, she wiggled. Desire was building deep inside her.

She knew how humans mated, but had never thought of how it would feel, how she would feel.

Nolan's hand moved upward, and she found herself arching toward him. Her breasts felt heavy and ached with the need to be touched. His fingers lifted and caressed and a moan fell from her lips.

She stepped closer, until her pelvis pressed against his thigh. His sex was hard and strangely, she found that exciting. She moaned again. A song was building inside her.

She murmured a few words, unable to keep it inside.

His hands moved again, cupping her butt, kneading the flesh there and pulling her even tighter against him.

Unable to resist touching him, she placed her hands on his chest and pulled at his water-soaked clothes. His shirt fell to the ground with a slap and she was free to move her fingers over his skin—still cold and damp from the water. She ran her lips over his skin. He tasted of salt and the ocean. A new thrill ran through her. He smelled of the sea too.

She ran her nose from his neck to his chest, inhaling the scent of sea and man and knowing she would never smell or taste anything more intoxicating.

Giddy with desire and new sensations, she bent and trailed her tongue down his chest to the hard planes of his stomach. His abdomen was flat and muscled, nothing like the sailors she'd seen in the past. They had been wiry, almost emaciated, not muscled and strong. And their smell...of sweat and ale...had soured her stomach, not drawn her like a bee to a flower.

"You're beautiful," Nolan murmured

Others had said the words, but they had always been laced with an unspoken "what can I get from you." Sailors believing the tales of mermaid treasure, or hunting mermaids for fame and the fortune they thought would come in selling the females to circus side-shows.

Those men had all died for their words and intentions.

But Nolan's voice held no hint of ulterior motive. He believed what he said, and simply reveled in her beauty.

Sarina felt a flush of pride flow over her body. She moved her hands again, running them over his chest and back, memorizing each plane and muscular ridge. "You are too," she whispered.

And he was. She would never have thought it possible, but this human, or whatever creature he was, was beautiful...irresistible.

As he leaned down and captured her lips with his, she suspected she knew how those sailors drawn by mermaids' songs felt. Caught as if wrapped in a net, but filled with joy that the net had chosen her to ensnare.

Nolan's heart beat so fast, he could for that moment almost believe he was still alive. Sarina's magic was that real, her touch that intoxicating. Being with her made him forget what he'd become, forget everything but the thrill of being with another being, touched...accepted.

He ran his hands, the palms flat, down her shoulders and arms. The gauzy material of her shirt clung to her skin. He could see through it, see her dark nipples as they rose and fell with each of her breaths, and see the outline of her waist giving way to the curve of her hips.

He bit his lip and tasted his own blood, closed his eyes for a second and listened to the beat of his heart.

Then he listened to hers. Steady and sure, alluring.

Sarina's tongue moved over his lip, licking up the bit of blood his fang had drawn. He froze, wondering if she would solve the puzzle—realize what he was, then run, repulsed.

But she only moved closer, her arms winding around his waist and pulling him so tight against her, he found himself matching his breaths to hers. She licked his lip again. Her tongue dragged across his fang. She inhaled sharply, surprised, and he stiffened, again prepared for rejection, but she only murmured something under her breath and continued to kiss him.

Her tongue's contact with his fang had left a mark though ...blood, hers, sweet and almost...fizzy...flavored her kiss.

His body tightened; his mind tightened. The world changed, became sharper and more alive.

"Vampire," she murmured. "I thought you were myths."

"Monsters," he replied, his world turning dark. Resolved, he closed his eyes again, this time to shut the image of her reaction out of his view.

She laughed, a strange sound that made him open his eyes. Hers, clear and green, stared back at him. "Fangs don't make a monster; actions do." Then she wove her finger into his hair and pulled his mouth to hers.

Her kiss was strong and sweet. As if the knowledge that he was a vampire encouraged and empowered her. Her hands moved to his pants. She undid the snap and shoved the wet material aside.

"I've never been with a human. Never mated as one," she said, her voice soft as if confessing. "Mermaids don't do that, not lightly."

He understood then. She was telling him this...what they were about to do...was no small act for her.

But it wasn't for Nolan either.

He stepped out of his pants and pulled her against his naked form. "What I am doesn't bother you?" He needed to hear the words.

She laughed again and tossed her hair away from her face. "Does what I am bother you?"

It was a ridiculous question, but then so was their situation—a vampire and a mermaid, two creatures most of the world didn't believe existed making love in the sea hag's realm.

"No," he replied, then he slipped his thigh between hers and lowered his mouth to her throat.

His fangs pierced her skin, clean and sudden. Her body jerked, and her fingers dug into his arms. She moaned and arched her back, pushing her sex more tightly against his thigh.

Her blood flowed slow and thick, almost as thick as his own. Sweet and effervescent, like dense sparkling wine.

She leaned back against the railing, and he lifted her up, so her buttocks perched on the polished metal. She opened her thighs, and he stepped between them, his mouth never leaving her neck.

He moved his hands down and lifted her shirt, baring her breasts to the night air. Her they were full and heavy. His sex hardened, and he knew he couldn't wait any longer.

He pulled his fangs from her throat, lapping at the wound to close it before leaning back to catch her gaze with his. "Are you—"

She leaned forward, shifting her weight from the railing to his waist. Her arms on his shoulders, she stared down at him and started to sing.

This song was different from the one she'd sung before, sad, but also happy. As if she was mourning something that had gone on before, while rejoicing in the changes that loss had brought.

And suddenly he was happy too. He was a vampire, and he'd lost his family because of it, but he had found Sarina, a creature he would never have believed existed.

Her lips touched his, and he opened his mouth for her. Her breasts slid over his chest and her legs down his back. She was wrapped around him, clinging to him as if she would never let go.

He clung to her too. His hands under her buttocks, he lowered her more, until his erection pressed against her sex and his heart almost leapt from his chest.

Her song slowed and died. There was no sound at all except the beat of their hearts and the water lapping against the hull.

Nolan stepped forward, and Sarina pressed down. They were one, moving together and blocking out everything else around them.

Sarina moved up and down, her legs squeezing Nolan's waist and her hands clutching at his shoulders. Her body tightened and her breasts tingled. She wanted to arch her back and scream, wanted to sing in a voice that would reach the seven seas and more. Knew if she opened her mouth, she would. She couldn't help it, couldn't stop the song that was building, threatening to erupt.

Her body tightened more, and her world began to swirl, as if she were caught in a whirlpool, moving, losing control. She gripped Nolan tighter. Beneath her, he thrust harder and deeper, faster and stronger.

The whirlpool's pace quickened. She spun and spun, until she lost control, until the song flew from her throat and her world whirled around in a flash of lights and smells, and sensations of freedom and warmth made her smile and sing and then sing some more.

Chapter Seven

SARINA'S SONG WRAPPED AROUND Nolan, lifting him up even as his body collapsed, exhausted, against hers.

His eyes closed, he titled back his head and let the notes fall over him like a warm rain.

He had never felt more content, or more sure of his place and the person he was with. He was, for the first time, whole.

Water lapped against the side of the boat, at first so softly, Nolan barely noticed the sound, but then, as Sarina's song continued, it wasn't just a noise, but a movement too. The yacht was tilting side to side as if swaying in pace with the mermaid's voice.

Nolan opened his eyes and looked out over her shoulder and onto the sea. Except there was no sign of the sea, no sign of the water. The space around the yacht was packed shoulder to shoulder with strange horse-shaped creatures he had never seen before.

"Sarina..." he murmured, afraid to speak louder for fear of startling the beasts and starting a stampede, or other mass movement that might end in the boat and its occupants being tossed about or crushed.

Slowly, Sarina's song died and with an expression of complete peace on her face, she shifted her gaze from the sky to Nolan. Then she looked behind him and froze.

"Kelpies," she muttered. All color drained from her face until her lips looked aqua against her skin. "The sea hag it seems has sent us an escort."

She looked back at Nolan. Her hand moved to his chest and regret was clear in her eyes.

For their lost moment of privacy? Nolan regretted that too, but the kelpies arrival, if they were, as Sarina guessed, sent by the sea hag, had to be good news.

The creatures, all horse-shaped, showed no sign of aggression. They varied in size from that of a miniature horse, no bigger than a good-sized dog, to a massive Percheron. Their color varied widely too, from black to pale green and even a few that seemed translucent.

As Nolan stared at them, they sank into the ocean, like alligators with just their ears, eyes and nostrils above water.

Somehow this made them seem even more intimidating. The kelpies surrounded them from all sides. He placed an arm in front of Sarina, to push her behind him, before realizing the worthlessness of such a move. As a fellow creature of the sea, chances were good that the mermaid would be far more equipped to deal with the animals than a once-human vampire.

Still, he placed a hand on her waist. His gaze on as many of the creatures as he could keep in sight, asked, "Are they a threat?"

Sarina hesitated. "They can be, but I don't think they are. At least not yet."

As she finished the sentence, the boat began to shift, in short jerky movements.

The water horses it seemed were now directing their travel. The kelpies rose and sank in the water as they swam. A few closest to the yacht blew air from their noses in loud watery snorts.

"So, our journey is almost over." Nolan glanced at the mermaid.

She pulled her shirt closed over her breasts and stepped to the side, toward the yacht's railing and away from Nolan's touch.

His hand fell back to his side, and his spirits dropped along with it.

A night breeze blew over him, reminding him he was naked...and cold. He'd been cold since his turn. He'd forgotten what it was like to be warm until he'd tasted Sarina's blood and held her in his arms.

He didn't move to follow her and didn't call out for her to come back to him. He just stood watching as she clasped the vial in her hand and stared out over the ever-shifting bodies of the kelpies.

He was cold, and this time, he feared it was for good.

The kelpies' arrival had brought Sarina back to reality—shattered the dream she'd allowed to form around her like delicate glass.

Melusine had accepted her offer. The kelpies' calm escort assured Sarina of that. If the sea hag had rejected Nolan or, worse, been angered by him, the kelpies would have attacked, climbed onto the deck of the boat like fleas scrambling onto a leaf until they sank the yacht and took Nolan and Sarina with it.

And sank they would have. Sarina could hold her own with one kelpie, maybe two, but thousands? No single creature aside from Melusine herself would stand a chance against that.

The boat moved side to side now, the rhythm peaceful and lulling, but Sarina was anything but relaxed. With each sway she knew they moved closer to Melusine and the conclusion of her deal.

She should be happy. Soon she would have what she'd been searching and fighting for for over one hundred years.

Her fingers wrapped around her vial, she closed her eyes and tried to focus on why she was here, tried to picture her sister's face, calm and sweet, intelligent and knowing—just as it had been before the pirates ripped her soul from around her neck.

"Sarina?"

She opened her eyes to find Nolan standing a few feet away, dressed now and with a look of such complete care and concern on his face she wanted to throw herself over the side of the yacht and hide at the bottom of the sea.

But it was too late for that.

He held up one hand.

Moving toward them, carried on the backs of two of the most massive kelpies Sarina had ever encountered, was a giant shell. Seated inside was Melusine.

The woman lounging in what appeared to be a giant oyster shell was exotic and beautiful. Perhaps, aside from Sarina, the most beautiful woman Nolan had ever seen. Moss green hair flowed down her back and over her body, covering all but her bare arms. On her wrists, fingers, and around her neck were loops of pearls, and a crown of coral perched on her head.

She waved delicate fingers at the kelpies, directing them closer to the yacht, but her focus was on Nolan. He could feel her attention like twin beams of light, burning into him.

He stood straight, meeting her gaze and resisting the urge to reach for Sarina's hand, to assure the mermaid and himself that what had passed between them before the kelpies' arrival was real. Their duty to each other was about to end, but their future had, he hoped, just begun.

As Melusine drew closer, her attention became almost unbearable. Nolan wanted to turn from her, grab Sarina and leave, but he couldn't.

The sea hag had a soul, a soul Nolan needed to be human again, and the vampire had planned to get it, anyway he could.

But that was before he'd met Sarina. With her acceptance, his family's didn't seem as important.

Still, though, he'd come too far, risked too much to leave as he'd come. His gaze locked on the sea hag's, he stood straight and confident.

Melusine smiled and a predatory, possessive glint appeared in her eyes. She stood, or prepared to, using her arms to help her rise as if her legs were incapable of holding her weight. Her hair fell back and her lower body, that of a snake, was revealed.

Beside him, Sarina touched his arm, warning him not to react, and Nolan didn't. He held his smile, and his stance.

And waited for the half-snake beauty to come aboard so the bargaining could begin.

Melusine slithered forward, her massive tail moving up and down while her human upper body stayed level and still. If Sarina hadn't known the sea hag's secret before and not seen the snake half for herself now, she wouldn't have guessed that the exiled female was anything except human. Of course, sailors said the same of mermaids.

With their tails submerged they looked human. On land, they became human—outward appearance at least, but Melusine wasn't a mermaid. She was a water spirit cursed, doomed to staying as Sarina saw her now until she could find a man who would love her as she was, her ugly inner-self fully visible in her serpent tail.

Melusine circled around Nolan, her gaze moving over him as if she was appraising a catch. "He passed the test." Her tongue flickered out of her mouth when she spoke, a hint that her shift to snake was still progressing.

Sarina felt Nolan stiffen, but he gave no other sign that he'd heard the sea hag's comment.

"He did," Sarina replied. The words felt like dry sand in her mouth. Nolan's indisputable success at living underwater was also his guaranteed doom. There was no way Melusine would let such a prize escape her realm.

"And he's handsome, not...." Melusine slithered a bit to one side and looked past Nolan at Sarina. "...a must, but a definite plus."

Sarina inclined her head. She'd known Nolan's looks would please the spirit. Now she wished he was disfigured and fat, so unappealing even his ability to live under the sea would make him an unwanted catch.

But then Allera, her sister, would be lost.

"Yes, this one, I think, will do nicely." Melusine leaned back to the other side. Her head tilted, and she reached to her throat. It was then Sarina saw it—her sister's soul tucked into a vial just like the one Sarina wore around her own neck.

"She—" Nolan started. His eyes moved from the vial hanging from Melusine's throat to the one hanging from Sarina's.

"Pretty, isn't it?" Melusine swung Allera's soul back and forth, like it was a worthless piece of coral, easily replaced. "You've heard the stories, haven't you? Of the things mermaids will do for a soul?" She slithered closer. Her hand cupped Nolan's face. "Well, my pretty human. They are all true, but how lucky are you..." She tapped on his chest with her finger. "...that this mermaid wanted one soul in particular and had no interest in harvesting one of her own." She inhaled, loudly and her back stiffened. Brows raised, she turned back to Sarina. "Is this a trick? This is no human. This body...." She tapped on Nolan again. "Has no soul."

Fear and elation rose inside Sarina. Elation at Melusine's tone. She had found Nolan wanting. She would reject him, but Sarina feared that too. She would fail her sister, lose her soul, again.

Torn and confused, Sarina wrapped her fingers around her vial and bit down on her lip, as if the pain would bring clarity and focus.

"I'm a vampire." Nolan spoke with power and determination.

"Vampire?" Melusine raised a brow. Then, surprise clear on her face, she turned to Sarina. "You brought me a vampire?"

"She didn't bring me. I came on my own. Sarina is my..." Nolan hesitated. "...guide."

"Your guide?" The water spirit laughed. "Mermaids are better tricksters than I realized if she convinced you of that." Looking back at Sarina, she asked, "Is it true, daughter of Ianthe, did you convince this...male...that he was coming to me of his own free will? That you were serving him?"

The air seemed to chill even further. Sarina couldn't breathe, and she couldn't look at Nolan. She didn't have to, though, to know his reaction. She could feel shock, disbelief, and hurt rolling off of him, like living things reaching out and slapping her.

"We...." Sarina began.

Nolan interrupted. "We had an agreement. I knew Sarina had her own reasons for coming to this place. I didn't ask what they were." His voice was cold.

Behind him, the sun was beginning to rise. A line of pink shone on the horizon. Sarina placed her hands on her upper arms, hugging herself against the shame building inside her.

"So, you had reasons too?" Melusine's attention returned to Nolan. "Tell me, vampire, devourer of your own kind, what reasons might those be?"

The water spirit cocked her hip and twitched her tail. Her face took on a new, provocative expression. Sarina's jaw tightened.

But if Nolan noticed Melusine's interest, he showed no sign. "Vampires don't devour their own kind." His eyes flashed.

"No?" The tip of Melusine's tail flicked up and brushed over Nolan's chest. "Do tell. What do they devour?" She enunciated the word, making it sound sensual and forbidden.

"Blood. We drink blood." Nolan's gaze slid to Sarina. She flushed.

"And is that what you hoped to find here? Blood? Surely, there is blood aplenty in the human realm."

"A soul. I heard you had a soul. I came to bargain for it."

Melusine's eyes widened. She twisted on her tail, seeming to address the herd of kelpies that still surrounded them. "How rich! Did you hear that? He came for a soul." With another laugh, she turned back. "It seems we have two bidders, but only one soul to sell. Tell me, vampire, what do you think to trade me for this soul?" She held Allera's vial out so it glistened in the rising sun.

Nolan blinked, and his eyes began to water. Sarina's palms itched. Allera's soul was so close, but her heart ached too.

"Anything I have to give." Nolan held out both arms, opening himself to the spirit. She drew closer, her tail wrapping around him.

"Anything?" Melusine whispered.

Nolan hesitated, and his gaze moved briefly to Sarina.

Nolan stared at the mermaid, looking for some sign the conclusions he'd drawn from the sea hag's conversation were false, but Sarina didn't look at him. Instead, her fingers wrapped tightly around the vial at her throat, she averted her gaze.

Would he give anything to have a soul again?

No. He wouldn't, but would Sarina? Was the soul so important to her, she would give anything to have it? If so, how could he deny her?

His heart heavy and his stomach sick, he looked back at Melusine's. "I thought I would, but I was wrong. If the soul is important to Sarina, give it to her."

So, his family wouldn't accept him? So, he would continue as a monster? At least this time the choice was his.

"Oh." The sea hag's disappointment was palpable. "No fight? No disagreement?" She looked from Nolan to Sarina and then back. Finally, she sighed, her human shoulders rising an exaggerated height.

"Just as well, I suppose, since I had already decided on the victor." The half-snake, half-human female spun. The vial she'd held up to the rising sun dangled from her fingertips. "You did well, mermaid, bringing me this mate. Better than I ever dreamed." Then, her lips curving into a smile, she tossed the vial into the sea.

Sarina gasped, and Nolan stiffened. He stepped forward, ready to dive into the ocean to recover the vial he sensed the mermaid wanted so desperately, but the sea hag's tail tightened around his waist and thighs, making it impossible for him to move.

The mermaid's gaze locked onto him, her eyes huge and sad. Then she dove into the ocean and disappeared.

Chapter Eight

NOLAN'S HEART SEEMED TO GO with Sarina. He waited, tense, expecting her to return, expecting...he didn't know what.

"You didn't expect her to give up her quest for YOU, did you? Mermaids are tricksters of the highest form, especially where men are concerned." The sea hag slithered closer, until her bare breasts brushed against Nolan's arm. "She did do well, though." Her tongue flickered out, over his face. She was, he realized, smelling him. "Of course, you aren't a man, are you. Perhaps you thought you were immune to her tricks."

"And I'm not looking for a mate." He held the sea hag's gaze, his own hard. With each additional second that Sarina was gone, his heart cracked a bit more, but he wouldn't show his pain.

"Really?" Melusine glanced over her shoulder, to the place in the ocean that Sarina had disappeared. "Or does the mermaid's thrall still lay claim to you?"

"I'm under no thrall." Nolan was familiar with the term and the concept. Vampires used thrall to lure in their victims. When the human awoke from the hypnotized state, they were confused and lacking a clear memory of what had happened before.

Nolan's memory, however, was painfully clear.

"I don't know what she did for you, or promised you, but she tricked you—used you." The sea hag ran one hand over Nolan's arm. Her touch was light and seductive. So much so that another man might have forgotten her snake-half, but Nolan wasn't another man. He wasn't a man at all, not any longer, and he was immune to any touch...except the mermaid's. He swallowed, fighting again to hide his hurt.

Minutes had passed. Sarina wasn't returning. Perhaps, the sea hag was right. Perhaps Sarina had tricked him.

"What will she do with the soul?" he asked. He needed to know. Needed a reason for her desertion.

Melusine curled her fingers into her hand and pulled her body back. She studied him from under lowered brows. "I can't lie to you. Did you know that? You have to love me without tricks, with my tail visible, with all truths laid out." She muttered to herself, cursing, he guessed.

When she looked back at him, her expression was as hard and cold as the marble floors in his family home. "So, when I say the mermaid tricked you, that she brought you here fully intending to give you to me as she might hand off a shell or other worthless trinket, you know I speak the truth." Her tongue darted out again, forked and in strange opposition to her claims that she had to speak truth.

But, despite that, Nolan believed her. He'd known all along the mermaid had reasons of her own for agreeing to be his guide, and he'd known those reasons went beyond the payment he'd offered her. She had, after all, already been looking for a male companion, testing them...and now he knew for what.

His stomach clenched, and he had to fight to keep his gaze on the sea hag. He wanted to look away and hide the emotions he was afraid she could read on his face.

"Ah, I see you already knew that. Good." She smiled and swayed back and forth a bit on her tail. Then sucking in a breath, which caused her breasts to rise and fall, she replied, "The soul is her sister's. Mermaids and their souls are separated at birth. Most spend their lives looking for a replacement."

"But Sarina has hers." He knew now why the vial was so important to the mermaid.

Melusine inclined her head. "Her mother was...unusual. Ianthe had the love of Poseidon. He granted her one wish. She asked that any daughters she bore be able to keep their souls. He agreed. In fact, he threw in a bonus, he gave Ianthe hers too."

"But her sister lost hers?" Nolan asked. The tale sounded impossible, but what about mermaids could sound possible?

"It was taken from her, by pirates, over one hundred years ago. Ianthe fought them, and while she saved her daughters' lives, she lost her own life and Allera's soul."

"And you found it?"

Melusine smiled, a slow, wicked tilt of her lips. "Mermaids attract men, and I needed a man."

"You stole the soul?" Any sympathy Nolan might have felt for the creature before him dissipated.

"I told you, pirates did. I just saw an opportunity and took it." She snapped her tail against the yacht's deck. "You would judge me for that?" Her eyes narrowed. "Mermaids are no better than I am. They're half-fish, yet men flock to them, declare their love, give up their lives—for one kiss." Her tongue appeared again. Nolan ignored it and her tirade. He was watching the kelpies. *Water horses.*

If he could reach one, could he force it to take him back to shore and hopefully, Sarina? He'd grown up in his family's stables; he'd been riding horses since he was three. He had never met an equine he couldn't handle.

How different could a water horse be?

And what options did he have? Stay here with the sea hag?

It wasn't an option he chose to take. When she turned again, he bolted to the side and leapt, targeting one of the largest kelpies, a silver Percheron-sized animal that nipped when another of its kind got too close.

The creature had spirit. Hopefully, enough to break away from the others and get Nolan back to shore. Once there, he'd...he didn't know what he'd do and he didn't have time to think about it further. As his chest and legs hit the kelpie's back, the creature reared up and screamed. Then it lowered its head and plunged into the sea.

Water rushed past Nolan so quickly he couldn't believe he wasn't washed from the kelpie's back. He clutched at the creature's mane, determined to stay on its back and ride until the animal's energy was spent.

Then he would direct it back to the surface and somehow find land.

The kelpie raced to the sea floor. Once there, its pace slowed to a trot. Confident he could control the creature now, Nolan pulled on its mane and kneed it in the side. The kelpie tossed its head, but ignored his urgings.

It was then he realized the animal was headed somewhere—its home or stable, he guessed. Somewhere the sea hag would be sure to find them.

Nolan kneed the creature again and jerked hard on its mane, but for the second time the kelpie ignored him. It continued its trot in steady even strides.

There was no moving the kelpie off course. Nolan had to choose between continuing on its chosen path or leave the creature behind and risk the open sea on his own.

Confident the kelpie's choice would insure the sea hag's discovery, Nolan loosened his hold on the animal's mane and tried to push himself off of its back.

His legs clung to the creature as if glued, and not just Nolan's pants, which he would willingly have shredded to secure his freedom. The muscles of Nolan's legs clung to the animal. Rock hard and unyielding.

He had lost control of his own body, and despite all efforts—striking his thighs, attempting to pry his hands under his legs—he couldn't gain that control back.

He was, it seemed, stuck.

The kelpie, still trotting, lifted its head and neighed...laughed.

Her sister's soul in her fist, Sarina swam in circles.

She had seen Nolan's face when she jumped.

He knew she had used him. Knew she had brought him here with every intention of leaving him behind.

Guilt lanced through her. More than guilt—pain.

She needed Nolan...loved him.

Admitting that truth hurt almost as much as seeing the disbelief on his face when she jumped.

But her choices weren't good. If she tried to save him now, it would be Sarina against an army of kelpies, water dragons and any number of other creatures the sea hag might have enlisted to serve her.

One mermaid stood no chance against such an army, but still, Sarina couldn't force herself to swim away. Couldn't force herself to look at Nolan as she knew she should—an expendable human who had served his purpose in her quest to retrieve her sister's soul.

She spun in another circle, swimming away and then swimming back twenty times before reality truly sank in.

What was done, was done. Now that Melusine had met Nolan, she wouldn't give him up—not willingly.

And Sarina had made a promise, to herself, her sister and her dying mother.

Allera's soul gripped tight in her hand and her heart dying, she swam away.

Outside a large metal cage the kelpie stopped, falling forward onto its knees as it did. Nolan flew over the creature's head and landed inside the cage with a thud.

He leapt to his feet, but it was too late. The door had already slammed shut.

His hands wrapped around the cold bars, he hissed, or tried to. Air gurgled from his lips.

A few yards away, the sea hag appeared on a kelpie of her own. Her snake-tail draped like pearl strands over the creature's sides, and her fingers wove into its mane. With a shake of her head, she guided the kelpie closer.

"Fighting will do you no good. Why not accept your fate and give love a chance?" She tossed her hair over one shoulder, revealing one perfectly formed breast. "I assure you, I have every charm the mermaid offered." Looking like some twisted version of Lady Godiva, she leaned forward. "Love me and I will set you free."

A globe appeared in her hand. She tossed it toward his cage. He tried to move, but the bubble burst, coating him in some invisible liquid.

"Speak now," she ordered, impatient.

Realizing her voice sounded clearer now, he did. Water didn't rush into his mouth and his words came out with ease. "You can't order love delivered like milk to your door." Disgust and disbelief warred for control of Nolan's emotions.

Her eyes narrowed. "Perhaps not, but I can and did order a man, and I can order more. Would you like to see your predecessors?" She waved her hand and the water around Nolan lightened, as if illuminated from below. Twenty cages were anchored to the sea floor.

"They're empty," he replied, unimpressed.

Melusine smiled. "Look again." She motioned to two kelpies. The creatures walked toward him, pulling one of the cages with them.

Bones littered the bottom of the cage—human bones.

Nolan's stomach clenched, but he held his gaze steady. "That won't happen to me. I'm a vampire."

Again, Melusine smiled. "All the better. You have eternity to realize our love. In the meanwhile, I have more suitors to gather." She flicked her tail against the kelpie's side, but then, as the creature started to move, pulled back on its mane. "If you have a breakthrough, simply tell your guard. He will be happy to find me so you can declare your love."

The dragon swam toward them, knocking against the empty cages and jostling the bones inside. The kelpies parted and pulled back; then after a signal from the sea hag, bolted as one upward and out of sight.

The dragon curled around Nolan's cage. Its head propped onto its body, it watched him with one slitted green eye open.

Finding the dragon's regard unnerving, Nolan closed his eyes and allowed his body to drift upward to the top of the cage. Once there he floated, feigning sleep and wishing for the millionth time he wasn't a vampire. Wishing he could die.

Chapter Nine

NOLAN FLOATED AT THE TOP OF the cage like a dead fish for days. The sea hag returned regularly to tempt him with promises of sex, riches and everything her twisted mind could imagine that a human turned vampire might desire.

The first day into what Nolan calculated was his second week trapped underwater, she arrived on the back of a kelpie, a dagger in her hand.

"What about blood, vampire? Would you love me for blood?" She held out one smooth green-tinged arm.

The need for blood had been growing in Nolan for days. He closed his eyes, but could feel his body shake.

"Ah...you do need blood...." The sea hag reined her kelpie closer. She hovered above his cage, looking down at him.

"What kind of blood do you crave, vampire? Mermaid? Kelpie? Dragon? Tell me you love me and it will be yours."

The herd of kelpies that always accompanied Melusine on her visits blew air softly out of their noses, and the dragon stirred.

Eyes still closed, Nolan replied. "Will a lie break your curse, hag?"

Melusine slapped her tail against her kelpie's side, causing the animal to shriek. "Don't call me that."

"What?" Nolan opened one eye. Melusine had never shown emotion before. "Hag? The world calls you hag. Didn't you know that?"

"No!" Melusine lowered her tail and whacked it against Nolan's cage, sending it, and the dragon still curled around it, flying. The chain anchoring the cage in place tightened, and the cage jerked to a stop. Nolan slammed into the bars, releasing a grunt as he did.

Holding onto the bars, he forced his body into a vertical position and stared at his captor. "Outbursts won't change the truth anymore than a lie. The world knows you as a hag and a monster, and it appears they are right. Melusine, whoever she was, is dead. This is what you are now."

"No!" Melusine dropped onto his cage, her tail wrapping around it and her hands reaching inside to grab him.

"Truth," he yelled. "You will never find a man to love you and break your curse. No man could love what you have become."

"Then more men will die," she muttered, her hands groping for Nolan, while her tail continued to squeeze the cage.

The kelpies and the dragon had backed away. They floated at a distance now, watching as Melusine raged and clawed, trying to reach Nolan to silence him.

Metal creaked, and Melusine smiled. "I will crush you in this cage, vampire."

"And you will still be alone," he replied, his gaze shifting to the corners of the cage and the metal that was beginning to bend...to weaken.

If the cage broke, he could get free, but could he escape? He hadn't fed in a week.

The tip of Melusine's tail poked through the bars, jabbing the water, searching for Nolan.

Blood. He needed blood.

Not allowing himself to think further, he kicked his legs and propelled himself forward. Wrapping his arms and legs around the sea hag's tail, he sank his fangs into her flesh.

Her blood was cold and thick, and tasted of salt and oil. Nolan's first instinct was to spit out the vile liquid, and pull away, but something told him to hang on and drink as he had never drank before.

He did, guzzling until he thought he would be sick.

Melusine screamed and thrashed, trying to free her tail from his fangs. She slammed his body against the bars, but the more he drank, the stronger he felt. Until he looked out at the sea and saw things differently.

The kelpies morphed, not horses, but women, bound in chains of seaweed with their mouths gagged. And the dragon, was a merman, tied in the same bonds as the kelpies but his entire body wrapped in the stuff so his arms were pinned down and he had no choice but to undulate his body like a snake's.

She's trapped you, he thought. And the dragon lifted his head. A new understanding...hope shone in his eyes. The kelpies moved too, their eyes wide and filled with fear.

Re-energized, Nolan kicked his legs against the bars. They creaked and bent. He kicked again. He felt them give, but Melusine did too. She reached inside the broken cage and grabbed him with her tail.

Then she squeezed and squeezed some more until Nolan heard a new noise...his ribs and spine breaking. His heart would be next—not pierced, but crushed. It would have to have the same effect.

Blood dribbled from his mouth and his senses dulled.

Wishes do come true, he thought. I'm dying.

Allera swam by Sarina's side as they returned to the sea hag's home. Sarina had told her sister how she got the soul, but she hadn't told her everything. She hadn't admitted that she loved a human, or what the mermaids would see as a human.

"Why are we returning?" Allera asked as she brushed aside a school of fish that had surrounded them. "Does Melusine have more souls?"

"Perhaps." It had occurred to Sarina that if the sea hag had found Allera's soul she might have found others too, but that wasn't why Sarina was swimming until her arms and tail ached, why she hadn't stopped to sleep or eat since leaving the sea hag's realm.

She was going back to find Nolan—to save him.

She knew their love was lost, knew there was no way he could forgive her for what she had done to him, but she also knew she couldn't leave him to the fate the sea hag had planned for him.

"We should have brought the others," Allera added.

"They wouldn't come."

"For the promise of souls they would have."

Perhaps, but soulless mermaids were too undependable and unstable. They could have been captured by the sea hag and turned into man-hunting monsters in her quest for the love that would free her from her curse.

"We can take the souls to them," Sarina said. She'd tried to get her sister to stay behind, but Allera had insisted on following. At some point she would learn Sarina's true reason for returning to the sea hag's world, but not until Sarina had Nolan in her sights—when it would be too late for Allera to fight her.

It took them another hour to reach the area where the dragon had attacked them. Sarina slowed her frantic pace to a steady flip of her tail.

Allera slowed too. "Something is...off," she murmured.

Sarina nodded and slowed to a stop. "I smell...blood," she said.

Without waiting for her sister to reply, she dove forward, following the scent as quickly as she could—three times their previous speed.

"Sarina!" Allera called, but Sarina had already left her sister behind, and her focus had already shifted—to a scene of mass destruction such that she could never have imagined.

Cages were strewn over the floor of the sea like broken toys. Bones occupied most, or fell from them onto the sandy floor.

Sarina's hands fisted as she tried to stay calm. The bones couldn't be Nolan's. She hadn't been gone that long. He'd survived her test, survived the dragon's too. He wouldn't have drowned, and Melusine wouldn't have killed him. He was too valuable to her; he held too much potential.

"Your vampire wasn't up to par. I want a new human or my soul back." Melusine wove her way through the wreckage. She was alone, no sign of her kelpies, the dragon or any other creatures she might have enslaved to her service.

"Where is he?" Sarina asked, pulling herself upright to face the water spirit face to face.

"Gone." Melusine fluttered her hand. There were gashes in her tail and the human part of her body bore bruises.

"It's your blood I smell." Sarina lifted her eyes and stared the sea hag in the face. "He fought you."

"He insulted me." Melusine's eyes narrowed, and her tongue flitted out of her mouth. Then her gaze shifted, and a smile curved her lips. "My soul. You brought it back to me."

She raised her hand and kelpies surged forward, like green water pouring from a tap.

"Get the soul!" Melusine yelled.

"No!" Sarina threw herself toward the sea hag, but the kelpies flowed between them separating them.

"The dragon has your man."

Sarina spun, unsure where the words had come from.

A blue-green kelpie raised its head to catch her gaze. "The sea hag has us bound so we can't shift or speak, but your man weakened her hold." The horse-shifter glanced over its shoulder, toward Melusine. "She doesn't realize her power over us has weakened."

"He weakened her?" Sarina didn't realize it was possible to weaken a water spirit as old and powerful as Melusine.

"Bled her and ingested some of her magic," the kelpie replied, but Sarina could tell talking with her was making the creature nervous. It shook its head, nudging her with its nose. "Go to the dragon."

"But my sister—"

"Her soul is safe." The kelpie whinnied then and reared up on its hind legs. As one the herd began to move, and Sarina was swept along with them. Afraid of being crushed or left behind, she grabbed hold of the nearest kelpie's mane and hung on. A few yards away, Allera did the same.

The kelpies cut through the water faster than the fastest ship, or even the fastest mermaid. Sarina closed her eyes and hung on, praying she was doing the right thing, praying the kelpies weren't leading her astray.

Outside a massive sea cave, still within the sea hag's realm, the kelpies slowed.

Sarina loosened her hold on the mane she'd held and floated to a stop.

"The dragon," the kelpie who had spoke to her said, then whinnied to the others and turned to leave.

Allera swam up to her looking dazed and uncertain. "What happened?" she asked.

Sarina shook her head. "I don't know. One told me—" She broke off her response. She hadn't told her sister about Nolan. "One told me, the sea hag had bound them so they can't shift or speak."

"But they took us away from her."

"And she won't be happy." Sarina hoped the kelpies could handle Melusine, but the creatures had given her and Allera their assistance of their own free will. She had to believe they knew what they were doing when they did. And now she had other issues.

She turned to Allera. "I have to tell you something."

"Do you?" Her sister's eyebrows lifted.

"There's a man...a vampire...I traded him to Melusine to get your soul. And now I have to get him back."

"A vampire? They are real?"

"Yes." Sarina was surprised Allera knew of vampires, but, she realized, she hadn't seen her sister in a very long time. They hardly knew each other anymore.

"And you are risking yourself to save him?"

There was no censure in the question, just curiosity, but still Sarina looked away. "I have to."

"I see."

And maybe Allera did. The young mermaid she'd been when the pirates stole her soul couldn't possibly have understood, but this Allera was older...changed.

And so was Sarina.

She placed a grateful hand on her sister's arm and swam into the cave.

The place was dark, darker even than the deeper part of the ocean where Melusine's cages had been. Sarina sensed the rock formations that jutted from all sides of the cave. She swam around them instinctively while her other senses stayed alert for other living presences.

She quickly sensed one...a large one...the dragon.

It was curled into a spiral at the back of the cave.

"Mermaid," he said. "You've come for my treasure."

"Treasure?" Sarina paused. "No. The kelpies said you have the vampire." Her eyes roamed the area around the dragon, but there was no sign of Nolan, no sense of him either.

"Treasure." The dragon lifted one loop of his body. Nolan lay tucked against him like a baby. "He's dead."

"Dead? No. That can't be." Sarina rushed forward.

The dragon's tongue darted out of his mouth, brushing against her chest. "He gave me the strength to swim away."

"You too?" Sarina edged sideways, wondering if she could call Allera, wondering more what good it would do. Two mermaids against a dragon that equaled fifty of their kind in weight.

"But I'm not free, not completely. I thought if I brought him here, I could save him—so he could finish what he began."

"Finish?" Sarina paused. The dragon didn't want Nolan dead. It wanted the vampire alive. She moved forward a foot. The tongue pressed against her chest again. "I can save him." Her hand moved to her vial.

Nolan wanted a soul. She couldn't give him Allera's because it wasn't hers to give, but she could give her own.

"A mermaid soul," the dragon muttered, causing Sarina to hesitate. Dragons were dumb creatures motivated by base needs and greed. They didn't know about souls or mermaids.

This dragon wasn't what it appeared.

Before she could ponder the thought more and think of how she might use the realization, a voice called out behind her.

"Stop!"

Allera stood in the opening of the cave. Realizing her sister had figured out her plan, Sarina spun.

"You can't understand. I have to save him."

"Because you used him to save me."

Sarina shook her head. Her hair streamed up and outward. "Because...because I love him."

"Love?" Shock was clear on Allera's face.

Sarina bit her lip and turned back to the dragon. Allera could judge her, would judge her, but it didn't matter, because soon, without her soul, Sarina would be like every other soulless mermaid—an unfeeling shell devoured by hunger and knowing nothing else.

Chapter Ten

AGAIN SARINA REACHED FOR her soul.

Allera raced forward. Arms outstretched, she knocked into Sarina, sending the mermaid flying into the cave's wall.

"Allera, I—"

Allera stood in front of her, her hand raised in a stop gesture. "You'll kill him."

"No, I...." Sarina glanced from her sister to Nolan.

"You said he's a vampire. Vampires are immortal, or close to it. If you give him a soul in the state he's in, he will be human. He will die."

Sarina rose onto her arms, then slowly, pushed herself upright. She swam forward, closer to the dragon. This time the creature, its attention shifting between the two sisters, allowed her to approach. She lowered her body into a kneel and placed her hand on Nolan's chest. No heart beat, but there was something else....

"He's alive," she murmured, to the dragon, her sister, herself. She just needed to say the words, but she couldn't keep from admitting the truth either. "Barely."

Allera blew air out of rounded lips. "He needs land. Just surviving here has to be draining him—too much for him to heal."

Land. It was an idea. Nolan wasn't a creature of the sea, and despite the fact that he'd been able to tolerate staying so long beneath the water's surface, it made sense that he would fare better on land.

She looked at the dragon.

The creature's tail closed back over Nolan, hiding him.

Holding very still, Sarina waited. The dragon had said he wanted to save Nolan, but he had also called him a treasure. Dragon's didn't hand over their treasures lightly.

"Let me try," she murmured.

The dragon stared at her. His tongue flicked out again, but this time didn't touch her. "You'll bring him back to me?"

Sarina couldn't promise that. She froze, but Allera saved her. She swam forward and placed her hand on Sarina's shoulder. "If he won't come, I will and I'll bring the mermaids. We'll figure a way out of your enchantment."

Surprised again by her sister, Sarina's eyes widened. Allera seemed to have knowledge and instinct that Sarina lacked.

"Enchantment?" she asked.

"He's a merman," Allera replied. "The sea hag trapped him six decades ago. Whatever your vampire did, broke the bonds, but not the enchantment. He's still stuck in this realm and this state."

The dragon lifted his head. "If Melusine finds me before you return...."

Allera folded her arms over her chest. "I know, but I won't forget or forsake my promise."

The two had lost Sarina, but that didn't matter. What did, was getting Nolan to land. While the dragon stared at her sister, Sarina leaned forward and carefully pulled Nolan free.

Then, with his body wedged under her arm, she swam for the surface.

❖

Days later...

Nolan gagged and began to cough. Rolling over, his body began to heave until the contents of his stomach, nothing it seemed but sea water, flooded onto the ground beside him.

Ground. He was on solid ground.

He coughed some more, his hands gripping the rough wooden deck he lay on. His fingernails dug into the planks, tearing them to the quick. His skin felt shriveled, and his clothes were heavy and wet.

He coughed again, expelling more sea water until his throat burned and his stomach ached.

A foot nudged him in the side, shoving him onto his back. "What are you? That you survived her tricks?"

He looked up. The bartender stood above him. The moon shone at his back, clearly illuminating the pistol in his hand.

"Are you part fish? A witch?" The bartender cocked the gun and held it up, his hands and the weapon shaking.

"Where is she?" Nolan rasped. His voice was rough, and it hurt to speak.

"Gone. She dumped you here and left. With luck, she won't be coming back."

But she had to come back. Nolan had to get her back. He pushed his body to a sit, the world shifted as he moved and his head ached. He clasped it in his hands.

"I should ignore her threats, and kill you now," the man beside him muttered.

Nolan glanced at him again. "Threats?"

The man's lips thinned and his hand moved to a pocket. "If I give it to you, will you leave? Never come back?"

"Give me what?" Nolan couldn't imagine what the bartender could have for him.

"I wouldn't...but she was different this time...hard...cold. I could see she didn't care, meant every word she spoke. She'd have eaten my liver and fed my brains to the birds, then sent her sisters to hunt down all I've loved." The man's thumb caressed the gun's hammer. "I ain't got much, but I've fought for what I have. I don't fancy losing it to the mermaids."

Nolan staggered to his feet and threw his body against the bartender. His hands, still stiff from their time under water, gripped the man by his shirt. "What did she leave for me?"

For a moment the bartender hesitated, and Nolan could see the decision revolving behind his eyes. Then he pulled his hand from his pocket and shoved it toward Nolan. "This. She left you this. Take it and leave!"

The vial Sarina had worn around her neck fell from his fingers and onto Nolan's palm. With a harried glance, the man shoved his gun into his pants and scurried for the safety of his bar.

Nolan didn't watch him leave; he barely noticed that he had. He just stared at the vial and wondered at what it meant.

A soul. Sarina had given him a soul. Elation and warmth shot through him. Then he closed his fingers around the glass, and his emotion changed.

Not a soul...her soul.

Sarina had sacrificed her soul for him.

❖

Dawn was approaching. Nolan had been at sea for six days. This sunrise would mark his seventh. His eyes burned from sleeping on deck in the day, and his skin itched from the salt still coating his body after his time under the sea with Sarina.

After he'd realized what the mermaid had given him, he had forced his body to stand and follow the bartender. Then he'd used his built up hunger and exhaustion to show the man how intimidating a preternatural creature could be.

The bartender hadn't even reached for his gun. Instead, eyes wide and face pale, he'd babbled every bit of trivia and lore he'd collected about mermaids, including how to find them.

In the distance, silhouetted by the rising sun, Nolan could see the island he sought. The bit of land was covered in rocks, no sign of a sandy beach or a tree, but jutting from the water around it were hulls and masts of ships long ago wrecked and their sailors taken.

Taken by mermaids, harvested, according to the bartender in the mermaids' never-ending quest for souls.

Sarina's soul safe in a silver box, Nolan walked to the front of his small vessel and waited.

Slowly, as he approached, the mermaids came. Only a few at first, brunettes and blondes, red-heads and a few with silver or green hair that glistened like some exotic precious metal in the gathering light.

All were attractive, but none were as beautiful as Sarina.

The mermaids circled his boat, confused, he guessed, by his presence but obvious lack of a soul.

As more mermaids appeared, the water beneath the boat shifted. Nolan widened his stance to maintain his balance and continued to scan the growing group of mermaids.

According to the bartender, the mermaids couldn't touch him or his vessel, like vampires they had to be invited aboard—more than that—invited to touch him. And there was only one mermaid he would give that permission.

Another half an hour he waited. The sun was up now and strong enough Nolan was forced to pull sunglasses and a hat from a duffel.

She wasn't coming. His presence alone wasn't enough. A bit of him died, but he wouldn't give up hope; he couldn't.

Kneeling, he dug into the duffel again, pulled two softened chunks of wax from inside and placed them into his ears.

Then he opened the box.

Immediately, the mermaids began to rise out of the water and sing. They bared their breasts, held out their arms and tossed their hair. It was enough to get any male of any species to step off the boat and into the water, to give up his life...his soul...for just the brush of one mermaid's finger.

Enough, that is, for most, but not Nolan. With his ears plugged and his heart taken, he looked over the alluring bodies with the cold clinical eye of a computer tech searching for a missing piece of code.

And then he saw her.

She rose out of the water like the others, her hair flowing over her shoulders and her lips curved in a smile.

Only, Nolan, knowing the real Sarina, could see the cold death behind her eyes and the robotic lack of caring in her movements.

Still, his pulse jumped, and it took all his self-control to keep from jumping overboard into the mass of undulating mermaid forms.

His eyes never leaving Sarina's, he pulled the chain that held her soul from the box and held the precious piece over his head. "Sarina!" he called. "Come for me."

And she did. She pushed the mermaids closest to her out of her path, then sliced through the water with her arms. At the boat, she looked up at him. Water slicked back her hair and glistened on her breasts.

"Human," she whispered.

"Nolan," he replied. "Say my name, Sarina."

Her hand reached up to take his, but he stepped back. "My name."

Her brows lowered and confusion flitted across her face. "You called me."

"My name. Say it." He didn't know why he needed her to say his name. Perhaps it was to prove that even minus her soul, she could remember him, love him as deeply as he loved her.

To prove that neither of them—soul or no soul—was a monster.

"Nolan," she whispered, then placing her hands onto the boat's edge, she lifted her body up. As she rose, her face changed; her mouth opened and her teeth sharpened. Not just fangs, teeth...like a piranha's.

He didn't pull back. He didn't feel any horror. She was still his, still everything he loved. "Sarina. Say it again," he ordered, stepping back again and hiding the soul behind his back.

She shook her head as if trying to dislodge some thought or nightmare. "Nolan," she muttered. "Nolan...the vampire...the man I...."

Her face crumpled, and she fell limp into the boat. She curled into a ball, shaking.

A trick. It's what the bartender would have claimed, but Nolan knew better. *She remembered him.*

He rushed forward and pulled her close. Her face was hers again; the monster was gone. Her fingers tightened on his arm, but her eyes remained closed, screwed tight as if she was afraid to open them.

Carefully, he slipped the necklace over her neck and let her soul fall down against her heart. Then he tipped her face up to his and stared into her now open, beautiful sea-green eyes.

"I don't need to be what I was. I don't need a soul," he murmured. "Not if you can love me as I am."

"But..." Her fingers went to the vial. "I would have killed you, dragged you to the bottom of the sea and torn out your heart. I...wanted to."

"But you didn't."

"But—"

"You didn't." It was enough. He didn't expect perfection, didn't expect the impossible. Her loving him at all, accepting him, was miracle enough.

"The sea hag has more souls," he told her. "Enough for all the mermaids here."

"You would go back? Risk being captured again?"

"I would." For Sarina he would risk anything...everything.

"I love you," she whispered. "I shouldn't, but I do."

"And I love you."

Then he pulled her close, and he kissed her.

One soul, one life, one love—nothing could be better than what they had, together.

Cruel Enchantment

MICHELE HAUF

Chapter One

BREE KICKED AND SCREAMED and clawed. The powerful men wrangling her added their own share of hissing and swearing as they moved her from a van toward a dark building. One cried out at the pain she inflicted with slashing fingernails.

Kidnapped from the back lot of the strip club where she worked, Sabrina Kriss hadn't seen the three men coming until it was too late. Normally, she got along with werewolves. These bruisers were trying that relationship. Whatever they wanted her for, she wasn't about to make it easy.

Aware they were moving her into a dark room, she kicked blindly. Something tender crunched under her spike heel. She hoped it was a pair of gonads. Fingernails cutting through her captor's flesh, she shouted and spat, and—

Suddenly, she was free. Shoved, stumbling forward across a hard cement floor. The door slammed shut. Utter darkness surrounded her.

Bree spun and beat her fists against the metal door. Not iron but some kind of cheap tin. Iron would weaken her. Stupid werewolves.

"Let me out! What the hell is going on?"

She pounded the door until her fists ached. Pressing her forehead to the dented metal, she huffed. Heartbeats pounded faster than a heavy metal guitar solo. Nasty-smelling wolf blood coated her fingertips.

This was not happening. She would not allow a bunch of werewolves to harm her. Squeezing her eyes shut, she fought against releasing a mournful cry. She was tougher than that. Besides, crying would get her nowhere.

A *clink* disturbed the air behind her.

Bree swung about, slapping her palms against the door behind her. "Who's there?"

The metallic noise had sounded distinctly like chains. Now they clattered as if being pulled through a heavy ring. A deep male groan accompanied the commotion.

Impossible to press her shoulders any tighter to the door. She couldn't see who or what was chained, but sensed it was male by the baritone groan.

Did her captors think to feed her to a hungry wolf? Made little sense. For the most part, wolves got along with her kind. Werewolves didn't eat faeries, nor did they drink their blood—though they were partial to fresh rabbit.

Another growl rumbled from the man's throat. She didn't know what was chained perhaps twenty feet from her. He wasn't human, for she perceived his distinctive aura of something *other*. Humans did not give out such peculiar vibes.

Her sensory perception bounced off the walls, determining the room was small, perhaps the size of the huge kitchen in her St. Paul loft. The air was stifling, and the smell—

For the love of Herne, now that her anxiety had begun to settle the scent crept into her nostrils unbidden. Blood, and lots of it. Neither fresh, nor stale. She wiped her fingers over her dress, but there was little werewolf blood. She wanted to sneeze from the acrid pinch the odor delivered her sinuses. And punctuating that odor, a salty male scent she recognized as exertion, perspiration—and heightened arousal.

Overhead, an electronic buzz preceded a blinding flash. Ultraviolet lights whitened the room painfully. Bree squinted, but didn't take her eyes from the creature before her.

He strained against the chains, using his shoulders, as his wrists were bound before him by manacles. Tight, rock hard muscles pulsed his abs as he struggled to get closer to her. Jaw tense and neck thick with strain, he groaned, sweat dribbling along his limbs.

His eyes were bloodshot. His mouth was open, stretched wide to reveal—

"Fangs. Oh hell." Bree's leg muscles gave out. Her body slumped against the door. "A vampire."

She didn't fear vampires. And she had a habit of getting along with most in the paranormal nations because she believed in treating others the way she wished to be treated in return. But seeing the man's fangs now clued her to where she'd been taken.

Some werewolf packs practiced the macabre sport of pitting blood-starved vampires against one another. For weeks, they kept their unfortunate charges chained under UV lights, which rendered them sick and weak. Later, when put into a cage with another vampire, the opponents fought to the death, desperate for the healing blood.

This vampire didn't look weak. But he didn't look eager for a friendly chat, either.

Why had they brought her here?

Another growl and he gnashed his teeth. The chained vampire rasped, "Hungry."

"This must be some kind of sick joke."

Bree slid along the wall, palms flat against the cool cinder blocks. The position anchored her, and, for the moment, enhanced a feeling of safety. But it was a false feeling, not a tangible guarantee. The chained vampire could get to her if he tugged those bolts from the steel plates secured to the floor.

"Come to me," he growled.

The vampire lowered his head, yet looked up at her. Eyes dark as hell entreated, but instead of making her feel warm and sensual, a shiver traced Bree's neck. A shiver of...recognition?

Her heart stopped for so long she noticed it. Bree slapped a palm over her chest. Then her pulse started rampaging. Something in the vampire's gaze...

"Can't be. No. No way."

Her mother had told her that some day she would find her Intended, the one man meant for her, and that her heart would recognize him before she did. She'd given up on ever finding that man in Faery and had left for the mortal realm years ago, only to be further disappointed by the male offerings this realm put forth.

"No. Not a vampire. That would be so wrong."

But her heart stuttered. It spoke to her in a whisper, *He is yours.*

A vampire, her Intended? A ridiculous match to comprehend.

A vampire bite wasn't awful. She'd been bitten once. Never saw the creep again. So much for one night stands. But faeries and vampires did not mix for one reason—her ichor would prove addictive to the vampire. And if this guy didn't know what she was, she didn't want to be the one to spring on him that his snack could do more nasty to him than another UV sickened vampire could.

Nor must she tell him she suspected he was her Intended. She had to be wrong. What she saw in his eyes was hunger.

So why did your heart stop beating? And why are your shoulders tingling right now? As if preparing to unloose her wings.

Bree rubbed her shoulder against the wall, attempting to distract the tingle with a new sensation. The wolves must have put her here to further torment the poor creature with the possibility of a wicked addiction.

"Chill." She held out a hand before her to placate.

The vampire snarled, revealing bold white fangs.

"Listen, buddy, you don't think that razor charm is going to win you a bite, do you?"

The chains clanked. The manacles about his wrists were medieval, thick enough to contain him. But, oh, his wrists bled. He'd been straining at the cuffs too long.

Bree bit her lip. She would not succumb to the frustrating inner desire to protect and make better. But a homeless man nestled in an alleyway or a woman standing by a car with a flat tire? She was all over the situation. And what if he really was her Intended? She couldn't allow him to suffer.

"So...hungry." His voice was hoarse. He must have been here a while. It took weeks for a vampire to crave blood, to starve from it. But if the wolves kept him under UV lights, that sped the process. "Please."

"What's your name?"

Keeping one eye on the vampire, Bree stretched her gaze along the ceiling. In the far corner a green LED blinked. They were watching.

"Listen, buddy, how long have you been in here? If you give me a name, I'll tell you mine."

Yeah, make nice. Food wasn't as appealing if you knew its name, right?

"Too long." He swung about and lunged against the wall. Bloody palms slapped the cinder blocks, leaving smeared tracks. He beat the ungiving surface and pounded his shoulder against it.

"Stop it!" She couldn't bear to watch him hurt himself. Maybe he'd settle if she talked to him. And hopefully a chat would distract her from the pining ache between her shoulder blades. "Listen to me."

Like she expected to cure him of horrible torture through talk? Oh, Bree.

"My name's Sabrina. Bree. Those bastards kidnapped me and tossed me in here. Yeah, you guys." She flipped the camera the bird. "They must be waiting for a show. Which, they won't get. I work for real solid cash," she commented again to the camera. "No freebie here, boys."

Oh, Sabrina, don't make them angry. For all she knew there was a release button for the chains. If she pissed off the wrong werewolf, they'd set the longtooth free to devour her.

Could he recognize what she was to him? No, the sidhe were able to recognize their Intended, but it generally did not work in tandem, since the Intended could be anyone, sidhe, paranormal, or even mortal.

"Need blood!" He lunged for her, fingers clawed. The chains stopped him short and he landed on his knees and slipped in his own blood. Sprawled, he shouted. "The light!" Tucking his head down, his whole body arced into a protective fetal curve.

She scanned the walls. No light switch. Hands to her hips, Bree approached the camera and spoke to the silent watchers. "What the hell? Are you all insane? What did I ever do to you? And for that matter, what's his crime?"

The rush of air at her back clued her she'd stepped too close to danger. The vampire groped in the air, straining. Spinning about, she settled at the wall beneath the camera.

The lights went out. The brilliant afterglow danced on her retinas. The scramble of chains and limbs alerted her. Emboldened by darkness, he lunged, and she could feel his hot breath upon her ankles.

She wouldn't move. The last thing she wanted to do was treat him like a thing or show him that she was frightened. He needed compassion.

"Rev," he said, panting.

"Your name? Thanks. I hate seeing you in pain, Rev. More so, I hate to give those bastard werewolves the sick show they're jonesing for." She softened her voice, unsure if the wolves could also hear them. "But you have to know something. Even if I were willing, you wouldn't want to bite me. Oh no..."

Her wings shivered, pulling at her shoulder muscles. Must be some sort of involuntary reaction to her Intended. She did not want this to happen...

"Yes. Blood," he gasped. "Need it. Won't...harm you."

He was going to learn the truth, whether she liked it or not.

"Rev, I don't have any blood to give you. I've ichor in my veins."

Her wings sprang free at her back, unfurling and fluttering to their full length.

Chapter Two

THE LIGHTS FLASHED BACK ON and Rev coiled forward, protecting his eyes. But the flash of the woman he'd gotten before he'd recoiled had not been good. Wings?

They'd tossed a freaking ichor-laced faery in with him. That was worse than the UV light that burned his eyes and made his skin crawl with a million insects. Worse than two weeks of starvation—if it had been two weeks. Rev thought so, but had lost count after day seven or eight.

Straining at the manacles, he no longer winced at the pain of iron tearing through his flesh. The throbbing had become a distraction from the light, replacing one agony with another.

And now this delicious new distraction he wanted to bite. And suck. And drink. To ease his pain. To regain strength.

To afford escape.

Please, let her step closer.

A warm, pulsing, sexy female who shot off pheromones that screamed to both his tormented lust and hunger. He could hear her heartbeats, proud and strong. A trace of fear laced the strangely confident gush of gorgeous blood. Perfect. He could taste her already. She would be as sweet as those wide violet eyes of hers.

But blood did not run through her veins. *Get it right.* It was ichor, the faery version of blood. And those wings were so...not what he wanted.

Damn, damn, damn!

Ichor could sustain a vampire much like blood. It could also rock the vampire's world, because ichor—naturally laced with faery dust—worked like a hallucinogenic drug, to the tenth power. But there was one caveat to the high: Faery dust was addictive. One taste and the vampire became like those human junkies who lived, breathed and sacrificed sanity for the crack pipe.

Rev didn't want that. He was stronger than that. Nothing could take him down. Not even a sip of faery dust.

He needed blood. Rivers of hot, flowing crimson elixir. His body craved it. He'd licked his abraded wrists, but that only disgusted. His own blood did not satisfy.

"Bree," he groaned, not recognizing his voice after days of mindless shouting, and then the parching effects of lacking blood. "Put them away. Your wings."

"I can't. Sorry, it's—I can't control it right now. I recognize—uh, I can't say. You wouldn't understand. I want to help you, but one bite from me and you'll become enchanted."

What an exquisite word—enchanted. It spoke of faery tales and tender things, brilliant colors, and of daylight he could never again view.

"Enchanted doesn't sound half bad," he murmured, sinking in the delicious fantasy of it all. Luscious sparkling ichor spilling down his throat, launching him on a loopy brightness he never wanted to abandon. Maybe her wings didn't look so bad, kinda pretty, actually.

"You think?" she said. "You ever see a vampire on dust?"

"Yes." His kind called them dust freaks. They were pitiful shells who were better off dead. "Not what I want."

"That's what I hoped you'd say. Cheer up, Rev. It could be worse."

He snatched the chain and lunged, his body forcing him toward what it craved. "Give me!"

"Sorry. Maybe this is your worse."

Close to it. Rev couldn't imagine anything worse than being chained and treated like an animal. Bloody werewolves.

Then again, addiction would be worse.

The light crackled under his skin and burned in his eyes and mouth. Yet it would not kill him. Nothing but a beheading and/or removal of his heart would bring final death—or a battle against another blood-starved vamp who would rip out his veins to get the last precious drops that sluiced through his system.

So what if she was a faery. He wouldn't become addicted. How could he? One taste? He could handle it.

"Please," he tried in a low tone. It didn't sound as gentle as he wanted it to. He knew he was a bloody, sweaty mess. Not an appealing sight. He didn't want to speak the words. He had never spoken surrender. But he no longer owned rationale. Desperation overwhelmed. "Help me."

The faery shot a glance to the camera over his shoulder. He'd tried to take it out with a kick days ago—or had it been weeks?

"They want a show," she said softly so if the wolves were listening they would not hear. As it was, Rev strained against the pounding blood in his ears to focus on her voice. Sweet sparkling tones. *Enchant me.* "I know you need something, Rev. But I won't be responsible for your addiction."

"Please. Better than this torture."

"Just breathe. Relax. We can get through this."

He lunged again, straining at the chains, pushing out his chest, but he got no closer to her. The faery stood with shoulders straight and breasts high. Gorgeous. Sensual. Full lips battled for attention against bright, curious eyes. Violet wings glowed red around the filmy, feathery edges, but she held them down and back as if ashamed to release them in their full glory. In any other situation, he'd make a pass at her—and only retreat when he learned her truth.

The only other option was starvation, and the eventual bloody fight he'd be forced to endure. The wolves starved vampires for weeks, then put them in cages, two at a time, and sold tickets and made bets on which vampire would kill the other first to get the blood he so desperately needed.

He did not want to go out that way. Hell, he had been working tactical for the Rescue Project. His job had been to get into the warehouses where wolves kept vampires and rescue them. What an idiot to get captured!

If the lights were turned off, and he could drink the faery's ichor, he may gain enough strength to break the chains from the floor bolts.

"You're messed up, Rev. I believe in the power of mind over matter, but no amount of Zen focus is going to help you. I'll do it," she suddenly said. "But on my terms."

Yes.

"Anything." He panted, hating his vulnerable position. And yet, he could still overpower her.

"Step back against the wall. And keep your arms down. You want this? I need to put myself close to you at my own pace."

Sounded reasonable. *Not really.* And who was she to call the shots? Could he fight his own mad desire for blood? Hell, he'd do what he had to for a taste of her.

Rev slammed his body backward. Shoulders slapped the wall, as did his palms. The chains clanked against his thighs.

"Promise me, vampire. I don't want to die."

"W-won't kill you," he growled. *Get on with it already!*

"Promise?"

"Don't need...your death. Just your life."

She flinched at that statement. The faery slid her palms over her slender hips, her wings shuddered, and again she glanced at the camera. Pale white-blonde hair dusted her bare shoulders. She wore a violet sundress tied with thin straps about her neck. The short skirt revealed gorgeous legs that could wrap around his hips for the ride.

Don't care. Feed me.

Rev's thigh muscles tensed. He forced himself to remain at the wall. *Let it happen. The food will come to you.*

She took a step forward. His fangs tingled expectantly. Anticipation coursed through his veins. Soon he'd taste sweet ichor to quench his parched throat.

"Can you get us out of here?" she whispered. Another step forward. Close enough to grab. But she was thinking beyond their situation. Not a stupid faery, by any means.

Rev clung to the wall. He nodded once. Escape was at the top of his list—just below sustenance.

"I can remember the layout," she said. "I can dust the wolves if given a moment."

Whatever that meant. He didn't care what she thought she could do. All focus remained on her sliding foot. Move another few inches closer. Sweet flower scent, like meadows. Too pure. Dripping with aching desire.

Rev bowed his head, opening his mouth. Twisting his neck, he fought the urge to lunge.

"A bite won't bond us," she said. "Only one thing can do that. If I'm right about my Intended."

What was she talking about? *Come closer!*

One delicate hand reached out. Thin fingers tested the air between them. She would dare touch a ravaged vampire?

Cowed by the remarkable bravery of this delicate woman, Rev forgot his restraints. His body remained against the wall. Suddenly, he wanted to know that redeeming touch. Enchantment would be a gift.

Her violet eyes scanned his. What was she looking for? Why couldn't he simply grab her and sink his teeth into her flesh? Was it enchantment? Did her eyes hypnotize him to submit as only the vampire could work persuasion on a mortal?

Chains clinked as he slashed a hand, ready to grab—then stopped abruptly. He would not. But he could. He just had to know it was possible.

When she took a step away from him he said, "Won't move again." Twisting his head, he winced at the utter control required not to take her swiftly.

The tender flutter of a feather stroked his cheek. He tilted his head into the touch. Not a feather. Flesh on flesh. Stroking, touching, exploring. So warm. Devastating.

What was she doing? Did she not understand the tremendous control required was making him weaker?

Rev moaned as the touch skated along his stubbled jaw. Felt great. Heady. Enchanting. As she glided closer to his mouth, he sensed she would do what he could barely tolerate while not crazed and blood hungry.

Don't touch my teeth. It will frenzy me.

"I trust you," whispered softly. "I want to help you. Together we can do this. Go ahead. Drink, vampire. Take what you need."

Not an invitation to disregard.

Rev gripped the woman's body, one hand at her back, the other shoving up her chin to expose her throat. Teeth sunk into flesh. Her body melded against his as he clutched her delicate form against his aching, bruised muscles. A sweep of wing dusted his cheek.

She did not cry out. But he did.

The first trickle of warm ichor across his tongue answered the ravenous thirst that had made him bang his head against the wall for days. Madness scurried to the dark corners of his brain, fleeing the glittering salvation. Instantly, his flesh heated as the faery's ichor permeated his veins and pores and infused his entire body.

The burning UV lights faded to background annoyance. Sucking at the twin holes he'd pricked into her neck, Rev drew in life. Sweeter than blood. More dangerous than holy water.

But oh, the delirious joy of shimmering light infusing his veins. Was this enchantment, then? Why had he never drank from a faery before? He could sup this elixir all day. All night. Endlessly.

Beware the enchantment.

Rev pushed Bree away. She tumbled to the floor, gripping her neck and moaning. The swoon had begun, an orgasmic reaction to having her ichor taken. The victim always got that bonus thrill from the bite.

Rev licked his lips. Damn, she was good. Already he felt strength returning to his tense muscles.

And he smelled...smoke?

Now his surroundings faded in to reality. The UV light flickered, and popped, reducing the room to blackness.

Rev smashed a fist through the air, pulling at the chains. The bolt gave free. He followed the momentum of freedom and landed the floor on one palm next to Bree's head.

An alarm sounded, beeping systematically.

"Smoke alarm," he said. "Must be a fire."

He felt her body roll against his. She lingered in the swoon, and was weak from all he had taken from her.

Standing, he did not sway or falter. His mind felt clear after days of starvation. He wasn't sated by any means, but he had grown capable.

Ripping his other bound hand through the air, he felt the floor bolts skim his ankle as they were jolted from the cement. Kicking each foot successively snapped the ankle manacles from the floor chain.

A spume of smoke poured through the ceiling ventilation duct. If a fire raged, smoke inhalation would blur their senses and make escape difficult.

The door he'd stared at endlessly, knowing he could punch a fist through the hollow core aluminum, gave as easily as he'd dreamed it would. Hinges bent and he tore it from the frame. A gush of smoke assaulted his tired lungs.

Stepping outside the cell where he'd thought to spend his final days, he pounded a wrist against the wall. The steel manacles would not break. He'd have to flee with chains still attached.

The hall was dark. Red emergency lights flickered, but smoke muted the glow to tiny specks. Sprinklers did not activate.

A moan from inside the cell stopped him. "Bree."

She'd helped him. More so, she'd *touched* him.

Rev ducked inside the smoky room and found the faery lying on the floor. She weighed little, and he easily swung her over a shoulder, aware her wings did not sweep his skin. She must have retracted them.

Escape through the murky darkness was difficult, but he encountered no werewolves as he fled the premises and into the surrounding forest. Not sure exactly where this particular sporting den was located, he assumed he tread the Twin Cities outskirts.

He ran for an hour with Bree over his shoulder, until finally he gained a suburb, and the back lot of a closed bar. The blue neon sign beamed bright and bold against the midnight sky.

Setting Bree on her feet, she then clung to the dumpster where they stood. She no longer coughed and could stand without swaying.

"You okay?" Rev asked. He bent and brushed the long white hair from her eyes.

She nodded and sucked in fresh air. "You should go. I can find my way home. Thank you for not leaving me to die."

"You saved my life. I saved yours. We're even, yes?"

"Works for me. I don't think we should see each other again, even though you're my— Like I said, I won't be responsible for bringing a good vampire down."

"I'll be fine," he said.

He was too strong to succumb to addiction. Though one last bite would be the thing.

She slapped a hand to his chest as he leaned in toward her neck. "No more, Rev. The enchantment is strong. Go find a human and feast upon blood. You must do that to rid your system of my ichor."

He nodded, knowing she was right, but regretting he'd never taste such heaven again.

Chapter Three

Three months after Revin Parker went cold turkey...

REV EYED THE METAL STAIRCASE hugging the three-story brick apartment building. Set at the end of a block of nightclubs, the side of the building was dark, no lights in the windows directly below the roof. He took the stairs two at a time.

Fernando Degas was the vamp who had been working the blood sport case for the Rescue Project in Rev's absence. The vampire had been reassigned to tactical—which had been Rev's job *before* he'd been taken by the werewolves. It was humiliating, the demotion to field work, but Rev knew he had to work his way back up the ladder to earn his tribe's respect.

Before his reassignment, Fernando had lost their best informant. Or rather, the informant had clammed up, and was no longer willing to provide information on the wolves. This informant had successfully led them to closing down two blood sport warehouses. The Rescue Project leader, Creed Saint-Pierre, was adamant they win the informant's renewed trust.

Now Rev was on the case. He didn't have the informant's name, only an address. Much as he considered Fernando a friend, the vampire's records had been shoddy, at best. Rev only knew the informant was faery. Odd for a faery to inform on wolves; the two species were usually pretty tight. Whatever had happened to shut up the informant had to be due to threats from the wolves. If they had found him or her out, he might have fled the neighborhood, or moved deeper into the city where wolves rarely tread.

He knocked on the bleached wood door and tried to see through the curtains. Inside, the third-story flat was dark.

Halfway down the block, techno music thumped out from a nightclub and neon lights flashed designs on the wet tarmac. The rain had stopped and the silver moon lightened the sky. Tonight the wolves were out in the countryside, shifting and answering their mistress Luna's call. Rare was the wolf that risked visiting populated areas while in werewolf shape.

After his capture, Rev held no love for the wolves. Not that he had possessed any before, but pre-capture he'd been on the fence about the species. He wasn't a hater. He enjoyed the physical work involved in tracking the offenders and the satisfaction of rescuing ravaged vampires, but really, he'd had a few werewolf friends even then, lone wolves who did not associate with a pack.

All that had changed.

He knocked again, careful to keep his coat sleeve tugged over his fist. The nasty addiction had taught him to be wary around faeries, and cautious of everything they touched, lived within or passed by. He'd suffered agonizing months thanks to their ichor and wasn't prepared to go through that hell again. So long as he didn't bite one of them, he should be fine.

Fine, but always craving. A damned monkey with thorned wings would never completely scramble off his back. He was handling it now, but knew it would be a lifelong challenge to avoid falling back to addiction.

What better way to face the monkey head-on than by tracking the informant?

If Creed knew about his addiction, he would not have sent Rev on this assignment. And yet, the Rescue Project supervisor presented a double standard to his employees. Wolves and vamps simply did not mix, let alone, pick out china patterns. Creed Saint-Pierre, former Nava tribe leader, was actually married to a werewolf. Rev recalled attending their wedding. Blu Masterson was one sexy werewolf princess with freaky green hair. She had no ties to the packs now, save the dwindling members of the Northern pack headed by Ridge Addison. Rev counted Ridge as a friend. That wolf was honorable, and had slain the former Northern pack leader who had been a first-class asshole.

Banging a fist again, Rev decided to kick. The door flew inward and clattered against the interior brick wall. He entered the dark loft, sensitive to motion or heartbeats.

The place was one long stretch of room, walled in open wood framing and high, exposed rafters. A twisting stairway climbed to a loft where a computer and desk must serve as an office.

He strolled the flat's length. A king-size bed sat at the far end before a glass block wall. The bed was neatly made with silky violet fabric and beadwork that sparkled from the moonlight shining through the glass blocks.

Actually, the bedspread glittered.

Rev retracted before touching the fabric. Could be faery dust.

"The informant is a woman," he decided from the décor.

Three mismatched bar stools queued before the kitchen counter. He rounded the counter and examined the cabinets, none of which had doors, leaving all contents exposed. A few plates and glasses, a couple wine goblets, and some ceramic containers for whatnots.

He tugged open the fridge and bent to inspect. "Strawberries and tofu?"

Faeries were big into the organic and natural stuff. But seriously? What *was* tofu? It didn't resemble anything natural he had seen, unless it was something he'd peeled off the bottom of his boot after a hike through the woods.

The sudden snap of pain across his back plunged Rev forward. He caught himself against the top of the fridge. Reaching inside his coat, he palmed the SIG Sauer he carried, loaded with silver bullets, and swung about. Arm out straight, he aimed at the offender's head.

A broom handle rallied for another fierce strike. "Who the hell are you? And what the bloody stones are you doing in my home?"

Angling the pistol so the barrel did not block view of his attacker's face, Rev choked back a swallow. "Sabrina?" Sight of her averted his attention from his tense muscles to the sudden tightness in his heart.

Broom handle swinging for another strike, she lifted it high. It was enough to grant her view of his face. "Rev? What are you doing in my fridge?"

"Certainly not eating the tofu." He dropped the gun to his side and put up a palm. "Put the weapon down, please. We need to talk."

"Talk? You broke into my home." She swung the broom handle around, tipping his chin up. "How did you find me? *Why* did you find me?"

"You look great, Bree." He lifted his hands near his shoulders to show compliance. "I'm not here to harm you. Gun's put on safety. I just want to talk."

"We have nothing to talk about. What happened was half a year ago. I don't think about you much— I thought we were even?"

"We were. We are. You saved my life, I saved yours."

"Right, so that means you'll be leaving, and I'll be shopping for a new door."

"I'll pay for a replacement."

No longer patient, he gripped the broom handle and wrenched it from Bree's grip. He tossed it over the counter to land on the floor with a clatter. She backed against the counter. Those wide violet eyes looked as fearful as they had in the warehouse months earlier. And just as enticing.

Often, when floating in an ichor haze, he'd fallen into her arms. Soft, sexy, and smelling like a meadow, she'd always catch him, and kiss him, and that word she'd muttered, *intended*, repeated over and over. He could never stop guessing what it had meant. Intended for what? For her? Him?

"You've been informing on the wolves," he said. "I've taken over Fernando Degas's case. You'll be working with me now."

"I don't work for anyone. And I told Degas I hadn't more info to give." She lifted her chin. Wary. "Put the gun on the counter where I can see it."

"No. A man never leaves his weapon out in the open for anyone to claim. Listen, Bree, this is important. I know the wolves must have got to you. If they've threatened you in any way—"

"That's not it." She swung out of the kitchen and paced to the center of the flat. "Just leave, Rev. It's not good you're here. With me." She turned to him, a delicate brow lifting. "Is it?"

He sensed the worry in her tone, and knew what she was thinking. The last time they'd seen one another, she had allowed him to drink her ichor. She'd been worried he'd become addicted—for good reason.

"I'm clean, Bree." He cautiously approached. "No longer a dust freak."

"But you were?" She stepped away, arms wrapping protectively across her chest. "After we parted?"

He didn't want to get into this. Talking about it dredged the dark emotions and desperation to the surface.

"You want to know something?" He dared to broach the distance between them. She smelled as he had dreamed, as sweet as a sun-drenched meadow. What he wouldn't give to stand in a meadow under full sunlight now. The UV sickness had made his eyes ultra-sensitive to sun. "Not a day has passed since that night that I haven't thought about you."

Her inhale cautioned him. Rev did not touch her. He wanted to. To reignite the sensation of tenderness contact with her had given him.

"I've thought of you, too," she said in the softest tone.

"You have?"

"Just wondering if you were okay. You know." She rubbed an arm nervously. "You are okay? You look much better. Not..."

"Crazed?"

"Healthier. Calm. Still...so handsome. Oh, I think you should go. Please. I can't do this. Not right now. You're the last person I expected to see again. Much as I wanted to see you..."

She was distraught. He'd get nowhere by forcing information from her. And since he did know her, and had a sort of connection to her, Rev decided he would play this one carefully, gain back her trust, to finally get the information he needed.

"Can we get together?" he tossed out to test her resistance. "Tomorrow night. Just to chat. I won't bring up business. I want to get to know you better. To talk to the woman who has been on my mind for half a year."

"Do you think that's wise?"

Still thinking she might enchant him against his will. Which she could do—but only if he dropped his guard and tasted her ichor. "Very wise. Just friends, yes? How about Shadows down the street?"

"The restaurant on top of the building?"

"Yes, dinner under the moonlight. Safest place to be when the werewolves are out prowling the countryside, far from the busyness of the city."

She shrugged. "I could do that. Tomorrow night." She extended a hand. "Just friends."

Rev stared at her waiting hand. A peace offering between two who must never again touch. A first *hello, how do you do*, between two who had already shared so much. And a deadly invitation to a brush with enchantment he could no longer risk.

"Tomorrow," he said, and shoved his hand in a pocket to avoid further contact.

Chapter Four

SABRINA SKIPPED UP THE STAIRS to the rooftop of Shadows. Club music from the dance floor on the lower level thumped in her veins, yet despite an innate urge to groove, she had no desire to dance. Her thoughts were erratic. Cautious.

Rev hadn't shaken her hand last evening. That meant he was leery.

A vampire couldn't become enchanted—and thus addicted—to faery dust unless he actually drank the faery's ichor. Merely touching the faery, which sometimes resulted in rubbing faery dust onto the skin, would do little harm.

Yet if a dust freak were to get dust on his skin it would be like mainlining ichor directly through his pores. A small high, but a high all the same.

Was Rev in denial about his addiction? Why would he risk approaching her if he were? The dude had to be some kind of devoted to his job to do so. Unless he was merely angling for a means to get close to her—and her ichor—by using the job as a front.

Bree discarded the notion. Though she barely knew Rev, she trusted him. He could have killed her at the warehouse, or taken her with him and enslaved her for the dust. He had been honorable at a moment when he had struggled to stay sane.

Besides, he was her Intended. She'd confirmed with her aunt in Faery the sudden pulsing in her heart and being unable to control her wings unfurling. Her sidhe soul had recognized her destined mate.

The universe was definitely playing a joke on her. Try as she might, she'd not been able to come up with a time when she'd put out negative karma, and thus, deserved the karmic backhand of a vampire as her Intended.

But it didn't pay to lament the issue. Now she had to figure if it was worth pursuing. To win her mate, they must bond sexually. But how to do that when her dust drove him mad? And did she really want to bond with a vampire?

She couldn't deny he was one sexy vampire. The hurt glossing Rev's dark eyes had been more attractive than warning. And what a sensual mouth. If she didn't recall his lips sucking at her vein, she could entirely go there with the fantasy of kissing him. Besides, fangs didn't bother her. They were an added thrill when making out.

Rev had already claimed a table near the rooftop corner. The view was spectacular, looking across the west side of St. Paul and Lake Harriet. Stars pinpricked the sky and a dazzling moon stamped the black sky.

As she approached, Bree extended a hand to Rev, but slid it down her hip before he could consider the offer. She wouldn't force him to make contact. That would be cruel.

"I took the liberty of ordering mead," he said. "I know it's all the rage with your kind."

"It is." She sipped the sweet drink a few in-the-know local restaurants stocked for their paranormal clientele. "This stuff is awesome. You try it?"

"Not bad." He tilted his goblet to hers. "You look gorgeous, Bree."

She smoothed a hand over her short green dress, the floaty silk kissing her bare skin sensuously. Everything she owned was risqué due to her former profession as a stripper, and her love for fun and sexy. But she'd vacillated tonight before leaving her apartment: to show some skin, or run out and buy a jacket that covered everything?

"I'm glad you came. Wasn't sure you would."

"Let's skip the small talk and get straight to confession time," Bree dared. "I've spent a lot of time thinking about the vampire who, even in his weakest and most dire time, was kind and honorable toward me. You've been on my mind."

Though she wouldn't bring up the part about him being her Intended. Wasn't necessary when they both knew so little about one another.

"As you've been in my thoughts."

She set the goblet on the table and leaned forward. "Why are we really here, Rev? Please be truthful. Are you looking for a hit?"

He gripped her hand so quickly she knocked the silverware in a clatter. "No." Then, realizing he'd touched her, he retracted and she noticed he slyly wiped his hand along his pants leg. "Sorry. I'm not an addict, Bree. Trust me."

"But you said you were?"

He rolled his head on his neck, easing at the tension she could sense without looking for it. His aura reeked of unease. She wanted everything to be right for him because her heart ached to see him like this.

So long as her wings stayed concealed tonight, she felt safe. Them popping out in the warehouse had been a visceral reaction to seeing her Intended for the first time.

"Truth?" He leaned forward, resting his elbows on the table. He touched her hands, and she turned them upward to clasp within his. It always surprised her vampires were warm and not cold. They weren't dead, but popular literature tended to distort the truth. "Yes, I can touch you," he said to her wondering gaze. "But not for too long."

He lifted her hands and kissed the backs of them. The second kiss he lingered at, and Bree wondered how safe she really was. Rather, how safe *he* was. She did not fear the desire he aroused in her. Goddess, but she craved intimacy from him.

"I was a dust freak for three months," he said, setting her hands on the table. "The moment after I left you following our escape I began the search for dust. I succumbed immediately and fell hard and deep."

"I'm so sorry."

He shrugged. "I never believed it could happen so quickly or be so devastating. I secluded myself from the world, alone with a constant supply of dust."

"Live?"

The addict could obtain the dust directly from the vein, via ichor, or from dust dealers, who extracted faery ichor—usually without the faery's permission—and sold it like crack cocaine in small vials to either be snorted or injected.

"Both," he said. "Though initially I preferred live for the skin on skin contact. Enhances the high. Eventually it didn't matter. I just needed the fix." He looked aside, his gaze fleeing hers. "I didn't come here to confess like that. I don't know why I just did."

"Maybe you feel a connection to me. Thank you." She reached across the table, but he did not move toward her. "For the truth. I needed that. But you're clean now?"

"For three months. But it is a daily battle to stay sober. I never expected the informant would be you. If I had known..."

"Would you have turned down the assignment?"

"No. I wanted to see you again, Bree. Those eyes of yours. So trusting. And yes, I do feel a connection to you, though it baffles me why I should from one bite. I needed to know you were all right."

"I'm fine. A little bite never hurt me."

Dinner was served and Bree picked at her fruit plate. She was more fascinated with Rev and he answered her questions freely while he ignored the salad he'd ordered for show.

Revin Parker had been vampire for only twenty years, which made him a youngster amongst his breed. He'd been a science teacher at a Minneapolis school for two years when he'd been bitten and forced to alter his mortal dreams and desires. Now he was a member of tribe Nava, unbaptized and not fearful of holy objects, yet he did have a healthy respect for faery dust. He could fall into enchantment in an instant.

The best thing for him would be to walk away from her and never look back. But the unasked question—he'd been true to his word about not discussing work—remained: he needed her to track the blood sport warehouses.

And she needed him in ways she'd yet to comprehend.

Rev had mentioned he and Fernando Degas were friends. She should really warn him about the guy. And yet, Degas's duplicitous truth presented an even bigger risk to Rev's habit. She'd keep that information tucked close until she was sure what to do with it.

"A science teacher, eh?"

He nodded and smiled proudly. "I loved watching young minds muddle over scientific formulas and puzzles. I taught in a small town, but moved to the Twin Cities after I was transformed. Too many people know me in my hometown. I'm not keen on hiding what I've become. Too much work. If you adjust to the world as a vampire, the world walks along beside you, never aware of what you really are, and I'm better for it."

"I can imagine what your classroom was like. All the girls jockeying for the front desks so they could swoon over Mr. Parker."

If vampires could blush, Rev did. Bree guessed it was probably the neon club lights across the street falling over his face. The divot above his upper lip was firm and deep and she wanted to touch it. Play with his lips. Maybe even kiss him.

"And you?"

She startled from her admiration of his mouth. His smirk indicated he realized she had gotten lost.

"You mean what do I do?" she asked.

"Yes, that is, when you're not informing on the werewolves."

"You have to know I've always been on good terms with the wolves. At least until, well..."

"Until they kidnapped you and tried to feed you to a hungry vampire?"

"Yeah. Changes things, you know? I quit my job after that. Rearranged my priorities. I used to dance strip at the Goddess."

That got a lifted brow. Bree liked that she could throw the vampire off his game a bit.

"We faeries are very comfortable with nudity."

"That I do know."

Of course he did. But had all that nudity appealed to him as a lusty man when he'd been in an ichor haze? Probably not. She hoped it hadn't attracted him.

"I like dancing. It worked for me at the time. But since reflecting on the reasons I initially decided to live in the mortal realm, I realized I've been off course. Lately I've been working on a new business venture. It's all about recycling, and home delivery and pickup. I'm calling it Zen Sidhe."

"So it's like you then?"

She smiled. "My girlfriend Blu calls me Zen sidhe because I'm always calm in the face of a storm."

"Or when faced down by an angry, hungry vampire."

"We got through it together."

He took her hand and kissed it again. "We did."

After the bill was paid, Rev offered to walk her home. Bree lived four blocks away and had never felt scared to walk home alone at night. She accepted his offer because walking away from Rev would never again be easy.

She invited him inside her flat, and Rev crossed the threshold without reluctance. How he had initially gotten into her home puzzled him now. Vampires did need the proverbial invitation to enter private places.

Standing in this woman's atmosphere was too much to bear. The presence of her, her very *being* surrounded him, brushing his skin and whispering at his ears.

He could not take his eyes from Bree's face. Her wide bright eyes saw all of him—good, bad and ugly. Her full mouth was so expressive when she smiled or smirked or gasped in surprise. He wondered about touching her thick lower lip with his tongue, tracing, testing. Falling into enchantment.

Gorgeous white hair flowed like the sea across her shoulders and down her narrow back. It was unnatural, beyond the mortal realm, and made him wonder how easily she could blend in with humans. But then he knew humans accepted all guises and costume and never really knew when a paranormal passed in their presence.

"I've chamomile tea," she offered.

"No alcohol?"

"I'm not into the hard stuff."

That ruled out him. Because he was getting hard. Every sniff of her essence, every wonder over her sensual anatomy sent his blood rushing south. And what was wrong with that besides everything?

Danger, Rev, don't forget that.

But he could touch her; he'd done so in the restaurant without developing the urge to bite her. Hell, he could even kiss her. He had to actually drink her ichor to get a high. Or imbibe in large amounts of dust through skin contact.

Should have worn gloves, tonight, buddy.

"What are you thinking about?" She leaned against the counter, the angle of her hips thrusting her breasts high, and a tilt of her head sweeping her hair across those tempting hard nipples.

"Kissing you," he offered easily. "I never got to kiss you in the warehouse."

"You think intimate contact is wise?"

He closed their distance, putting a hand to either side of her on the counter. By some monumental feat, he did not touch her. Yet.

"I wish you'd leave the struggle between wisdom and futility to someone else, Bree. Are you afraid of me?"

"No. I've seen you at your worst." She tore her gaze from his and studied the floor. "But I won't be the one responsible for returning you to that worst. What was your bottom, exactly?"

"You think I was huddled in some dark corner with the shakes, jonesing for dust?"

She shrugged. "I don't even want to imagine."

"Dust brings up my Hyde. It makes me volatile. I think I can run the world and kick everyone else off it. But don't worry, it's not going to happen again."

He leaned in closer. The fringes of his bangs tickled across her lush white curls. The sweetness of Bree blossomed like a meadow thick with honeybees and pollen.

"I'm too smart for that," he said. "And even were I not, I know you're one smart faery."

"Smart enough to entertain kissing a dangerous man?"

"I'm not dangerous to you."

She exhaled. "You don't know that, Rev. Right now? My heart is racing for you. And my wings are tingling. You fascinate me. You attract me. I want to know the touch of your mouth against mine. And that feels so dangerous."

"Exciting," he corrected, whispering it against her soft cheek, and loving her confession. "Exhilarating."

"I don't want to get hurt."

He paused, and looked into her searching eyes. "I would never, I swear it to you."

Her fingers glanced across his cheek, finding the same path they'd taken half a year earlier, searing heat into his flesh and marking him in its wake.

"Bree, I've dreamed of your touch," he said. "You touched me like this then. I've wanted it again. The memory of it is what kept me sane in my darkest moments, and made me want to get clean."

"Really?"

He nodded, and pressed his forehead to hers. Still she stroked his face, exploring the rough stubble darkening the hard line of his jaw and tracing under his chin as if to map out his sensual zones.

"Promise this isn't a trick to get me to spill, to start informing again?"

"This has nothing to do with business. Us, right now, this is what I want and need." He wanted to tug up his shirt and feel her hot and pulsing against his skin. Not yet. Slowly. He would make this moment right. "Kiss me, Bree. Give me your touch again."

Her mouth landed on his. He stood a head higher than her and he liked that she was small, yet unafraid of his brawn. Her lips crushed against his, warm, seeking. The tip of her tongue skated his lower lip, then dashed to trace the indent marking his upper lip.

He had never tasted a woman so exquisite, one so unabashedly curious and unafraid to explore what she claimed dangerous. Her courage quickened him.

He lifted her and she wrapped her slender legs about his hips. This one was his. He felt it in his heart, he felt it all over his skin as she glittered into his pores and captured his nerve endings in a riot of desire.

"Bree, can this be as good as it feels?"

"It can never be right."

"Right is boring. But this, this is interesting. Forbidden. And yes, dangerous. I won't ever bite you. That will keep you safe."

"You may not want to now, but the more you touch me..."

Neither wanted to finish the sentence. Both knew it ended with a monkey clawing deep into Rev's shoulders. A renewed plunge into devastation.

It wasn't worth the risk.

But risk meant nothing when holding Sabrina Kriss in his arms. She belonged to him; his body screamed for that ownership. And he would have her.

"I won't let that happen. Let's take this as it wants to go." He scanned her gaze. "Can we do that?"

"Fooling around with me won't interfere with your job?"

"I have to get the information, Bree."

"So you're seducing me to help the vampires?"

"I said I would not. I know it's a conflict of interest, but I think I can work the business around the pleasure. Right now I just want to hold you. To kiss you. You were made for my mouth."

She kissed him full and lush and deep. The faery in his arms, light and clinging, brightened his senses with wonder and marvel. Rev pushed down the dress strap to kiss her shoulder. There her skin sparkled with the dust innate to her kind. Sweet on his tongue, the minute taste reignited a familiar craving.

He tensed. *You're stronger than that.* No more tasting.

Carrying her across the room, he laid her on the bed beneath the moonlight and crawled over her.

"Not so fast, vampire." She lifted a knee to keep him from snuggling the length of her body. "You want to make love?"

He nodded.

"You're moving too fast. I'm not that kind of girl."

"Sorry." Right. What was he thinking? He'd stepped beyond a boundary he'd imposed not a few minutes ago. "Just kissing. In more places than here?" He kissed her mouth. She giggled as he tugged down the other dress strap. "Maybe here?"

"Mmm." She purred as he nudged his nose along her skin, tracking toward the small, perfect breasts that had earlier hugged his chest.

He tongued a hard nipple and followed by laving at it hungrily. Bree's body arched against his chest and hips. Her arms stretched out and fingers clung at the bedspread. He couldn't get enough of her skin, her soft flesh, and the hard tight buds crowning her breasts.

"Goddess, that's good." Her fingers slid through his hair and she grasped at the back of his head, encouraging him. "No teeth, vampire."

He willed his fangs up. *Bad, vampire.*

But you're tasting her again. Watch it, Rev.

He paused over her breasts. Looking up, he found her mouth open, her sigh dusting the air. Dust? It wasn't visible, but he knew when faeries became aroused it seeped from their pores in a fine sheen.

He pulled his hands from her body as if burned. Studying his palms, he searched for a glint of dust.

"Why are you stopping? Rev?"

Why was he stopping? He wanted all of her. In his mouth, at his tongue, beneath his body. He wanted to be encompassed by her, to be inside her.

"You're right, this is too fast," he finally said.

He pushed off the bed and paced away. Easing a palm over his erection he cursed his body's insistent and greedy needs. Behind him, Bree tugged up her dress straps and licked her lips. An abandoned innocent, she sat in the middle of the big bed. Delicate.

And sinister.

"I've some work to do with the project," he summoned the lie. "Can only be done at night. I promised you I wouldn't mix business with pleasure. This was stupid. I'm sorry to leave like this."

"I understand."

She did. And that understanding tore out his heart and smashed it against the wall. Did she suspect he wasn't as strong as he thought he was?

"Tomorrow," he said, and rushed for the door.

Shoes clattering down the metal stairs, Rev turned into the alleyway with no destination to mind. It wasn't long before he found himself inside a club pulsating with the scent of desire, desperation and temptation. Music thundered in his brain and the sensory overkill made him wince. Darkness shrouded his sweating skin. He could sense when he rubbed against another vampire, for the telling shimmer tickled his veins.

When a thin woman in red dress with matching red hair skimmed his hand with her thigh, he stiffened. *Faery.* His pores opened in anticipation of the fix.

Rev slammed a fist into the wall. The faery flinched and shoved her girlfriend into the crowd to get away from him.

Clenching his jaw, and closing his eyes, he fought the mental desire to succumb. "You don't need it," he growled. "You want it, but you don't need it."

Get out of here. He had to remove himself from temptation as he'd done by swiftly exiting Bree's home.

Rev fled into the night, and when the darkness overwhelmed, his footsteps sped to a run. Run away from temptation. It was all he could do.

Chapter Five

THE BEST WAY TO AVOID temptation?

Rev counted three-hundred-fifty as he lifted his upper body from the workout bench. Sit-ups at a forty-five degree incline always worked up a sweat and cleared his thoughts. It was something he'd learned he couldn't *not* do. If he skipped a workout, his idle muscles would go wandering in search of a fix.

He needed this workout now to get her from his brain. Sabrina Kriss. Her last name sounded too much like *kiss* not to conjure images of them kissing.

"Kissing the faery," he grunted as he sat up for another excruciating hold. Feet tucked under a padded bar, he kept his knees bent to increase the pull at his hamstrings. "Idiot vampire."

Dropping backward, he didn't allow rest, and strained to pull up his body weight again.

Sweating cleansed his pores of any latent faery dust he might have rubbed into his skin while touching Bree. He felt it on him, scurrying beneath his epidermis like heat-seeking missiles.

Or was it merely the former addiction tickling at his nerve endings, laughing as it waited for his next fall?

"Won't happen." He blew out. Abs strained as he held the punishing crunch. "Can't."

Blowing out a lungful of air, he dropped and slid off the bench. He paced the floor, working his muscles by swinging his arms to ease his strained deltoids back and forth.

Twenty years ago he could have never imagined this life for himself. But he was living it. And not hating it. This crazy world tossed him something new every day. And what it tossed at him was always paranormal or beyond mortal man's belief. Made the scientist in him cringe, and then titter with glee. The dark denizens of imagination did exist. And faeries fluttered—nix that. He'd never seen a faery fly, though a few years ago he had once glimpsed a trio of faeries at a rave with wings exposed. Knowing the dangers of dust, he'd not given them a second glance then.

And when he'd been a freak for dust, he couldn't remember their faces let alone if they'd had their wings out or not.

"So why can't I stay away from this one little faery?"

After what he'd been through, Bree should be the furthest thing from his thoughts. Was it that she had literally gotten inside him? How to completely purge her?

"Do I want to?"

No. Honestly, he wanted to pursue this woman. Kiss her again. Find out for certain if the attraction was heartfelt or merely a deadly tease.

❖

"Another fight last night?" Bree chatted with her girlfriend Blu Masterson on the phone, the only werewolf Bree truly loved and cared about. Blu told her about a blood fight the werewolves had organized. Blu's husband had been too late to rescue the enslaved vampires, and both captives had died during the match. "This has got to stop."

"I thought you were informing the vampires?" Blu said.

"I don't know anything, Blu, all right?" When she'd been working at the strip club, one of the strippers had dated a wolf who worked the blood games. Bree could not stand back and allow it to happen, so she'd begun informing. "Just...don't ask me anymore."

"Who has scared you, Bree?"

Friends always knew better.

"No one," she lied. "And since when do you work with the Rescue Project? Your hubby sic you on me since the other guy doesn't seem to be working?"

"What other guy? I thought you'd told me you made a break with the vampire you were informing to."

"I did."

The bastard Degas had threatened to hand her over to the werewolves—or worse. And yet, had her abduction something to do with Degas? She'd thought it merely idiot wolves looking to torture the vampire with faery dust. She needed to learn the truth. From Degas.

"The Rescue Project sent a new vampire after me. Someone I know."

Suddenly she gasped and a teardrop plopped onto her ankle.

"Bree? What in heck?"

"It's him, Blu. The vamp I told you about from that awful night in the sporting warehouse."

"The one you think is your Intended?"

"Yes. Rev Parker is his name. He's been here twice and I kissed him last night, and I can't stop thinking about kissing him again, but I don't want to hurt him."

"Whoa. Slow down, sweetie. The vampire you let bite you is on your case now to continue informing? Wow. You were really attracted to him."

"Are, not were. He's amazing, Blu. So sexy. And he's got these intense dark eyes that focus directly on me. It's like he sees through me. It makes my wings shiver."

"A reaction to him being the one for you?"

"Yes. Maybe. Oh, Blu, when a sidhe finds her Intended it should be exciting, not crazy fearful. The last guy I ever expected to be the one for me is a vampire."

"Hey, don't knock vampires."

Blu, a werewolf, had been forced to marry a vampire recently to bring together the werewolf and vampire nations. She hadn't expected to fall in love, but she had, and now she and her husband Creed were closer than close.

Despite her tears, Bree smiled. "I'm not knocking them. And you know I have nothing at all against vampires. It's just...we are so wrong for each other."

"Did you tell Rev he's your Intended?"

"Don't know how to. It's not like I'm the best thing for him. If he doesn't know, then he won't feel obligated toward me."

"Oh, sweetie, I wonder if there's a way you two could ever be together?"

"If we have sex and bond maybe that would overwhelm the addiction."

"Then what's stopping you? Oh, wait. Sorry. The fact your dust sends him into a dust freak stupor is stopping you. Poor girl."

"He's cautious. We were making out, and he stopped before it went too far. He's like no man I've ever known, Blu. The kindness in his eyes... But I see pain there, too. I want to hold him and make it all better."

"You can't always be the one to make things better, Bree. Think about yourself. What's best for you?"

"What's best is some intimacy. I haven't had a man for months. Is it so wrong to crave affection? To want to claim the one man put on this earth just for me?"

"Not at all. But you can date other men. What happened to the three day sex rule?"

The rule they considered gospel between girlfriends. One should never go longer than three days without sex. It just wasn't right.

"I know, I've been having a bit of a dry spell lately. But, Blu, the bonding between a sidhe and their Intended is supposed to be amazing. If we could get together as lovers we'd never desire another. How can I not want that? If we could have sex," Bree suggested, teasing a strand of hair across her lips, "then I think he'd move beyond the desire for dust."

"You sure about that?"

"No. Maybe. What better way to lead a man from addiction than to offer him a greater high?"

"Sounds possible. We do love to make our men happy with sex. But be careful. And don't forget my party next weekend."

"Right. BYOB?"

"Yep, that's Bring Your Own Boy. And if he's a vampire then he'd better not be strung out on dust. Got that?"

"Got it. See you soon. And don't worry, I'll be careful." Bree hung up and sighed. "Mostly."

Life wasn't worth the spin unless it was dangerous. She knew what she was doing. Having some fun with a man who made her wings curl. And if he decided to have sex with her, then yes, baby, yes.

"Do I need to put another agent on the informant?" Creed Saint-Pierre stalked before Rev, fists to his hips. The nine centuries-plus vampire wore his years well on his face, and always wore Armani on his body. "We lost another man last night during that damned blood match!"

"I'm sorry, Saint-Pierre. I've made contact with the informant. She's...skittish."

"Fernando's reports weren't thorough. He never did explain why she stopped talking to him. Who the hell got to her?"

"I'll find out. Give me another day or two. I'm getting closer to her." But not the kind of close his leader wanted to know about. "I will bring you results."

"You'd better." Creed marched off, leaving Rev to let himself out of the man's estate.

With his capture, he'd almost become a statistic himself. And to succumb to the dust? He'd kept those months hidden from the tribe, claiming he'd needed time after his imprisonment to recover, get his head on target. He'd wanted to be in top form to help the Rescue Project.

In reality, Rev had been gorging himself on mortal blood in an attempt to purge his system of dust. Hadn't been pretty. But he took heart in the fact he never killed mortals, and never would.

Now he was more determined than ever to come back strong and to prove himself. He was an asset to the Rescue Project. He'd once worked tactical, charging into the fray with a rescue team to extract the victims. He knew the interior workings of the sporting warehouses. Now he needed to learn the warehouse locations that moved constantly.

Bree was the only one who could help him with that.

He followed her, keeping a half block distance between them. She'd exited the Goddess strip club and was walking home. She said she'd stopped working there after the incident. Wonder what she'd been doing inside just now?

The faery carried herself with confidence, and winked at the passing cars that slowed to give a cat call or hoot at her. Mortal men wouldn't know what hit them if they were to indulge in her enchantments. Faery dust wasn't as addictive to mortals, but it could be wielded like a weapon to either enchant or disenchant them. That vampires were so susceptible killed Rev.

Truly, he'd discovered his kryptonite.

And now he would have to face that sinister delicacy if he wanted to prove himself to his tribe members.

She passed through the wooden gate surrounding the parking grounds below her building. Moments later, Rev passed through the gate and was slammed against the fence.

"Why are you following me?" she said. "Why not catch up and walk with me? We know each other. No reason for the spy games."

He lifted his palms, and she relented her not-so-weak grasp about his collar. Faery glamour gave great strength. "Tonight's business, Bree, not pleasure."

"Oh." She stepped back.

Clad in body-hugging white jersey, she looked a winter princess crowned by pale tresses, and sparkled like a century celebration cake. Club goers would suspect it was store-bought glitter. Rev knew better.

"You wanted honesty," he said. He nodded down the street where the pink neon flashed. "You still working at the club?"

"No. What's it to you?"

"Nothing. Something. It makes me want to punch someone to imagine you taking off your clothes before a crowd of leering men."

"Yeah?" She didn't hide a small smile. "I was visiting a girlfriend, helping with her routine. Only time I do the naked now is in the privacy of my own home."

"I'd like to see that sometime."

"It's okay for you to leer but not others?"

"I wouldn't leer, Bree. I'd—" Worship. "Hell, I'm being rude." He walked toward the stairs leading up to her flat. "Can we talk?"

"Business? Nope, nadda, nein."

"We can either talk or I can rough you up."

Her jaw dropped.

"I'm kidding. A little. Do you consider kisses rough stuff?" He smiled, trying to rescue the moment, and only failed a little.

The faery softened, grinning, and gesturing he lead the way up. "I don't know why I keep inviting you in but I'm doing it again."

Once inside she offered him blackberry tea, which he politely refused. Bree plopped onto the bed, which was the only furniture, save the bar stools. She sat cross-legged and patted the bed for him to join her.

Rev remained standing, shoulders to the brick wall. She wasn't being suggestive, but sharing the huge silk-covered bed with her was a no-man's land he couldn't explore. Not yet.

"Right," she said, and took a sip of tea before setting the cup on the floor. "Business."

"Whatever it is you've been threatened with, I promise you safety, Bree. No wolf is going to bully you around and get away with it. I promise you that not because I'm working on the case, but because I care about you. You have my word."

"How can you care about someone you've known but a few days?"

"You've been on my mind for months."

She glanced aside, conceding the point. "If we're all about honesty, then do you care about me or crave me?"

He lifted a brow. *Not so easy to answer, is it, tough vampire who is fighting the urge to lick the faery's skin clean of any dust he can find?* He'd never understood the meaning of *crave* until after biting Bree and consuming her luscious ichor.

"Give me a name," he said. Shoving his hands in his pockets he looked high, scanning the rafters. Anything to keep from admiring her soft, sparkly glow and those pale pink lips that pouted for a kiss. "Or even just a pack."

"It's not that easy, Rev."

"Of course it is!" He lunged into her space, prepared to grip her shoulder and give her a swift shake. "You have to want to make it easy. Please, Bree." He squatted before her. "Would it matter if I told you my reputation depends on your cooperation?"

He shouldn't have brought it to such a level—his desperation—but he didn't know what else to do without breaching his self-imposed rules not to get involved with her.

"Won't they just send another vampire after me if you fail?"

"Yes, they will. And the next one might not be so nice. He might like to rough you up and maybe get in a few punches if he thinks that'll loosen your lips."

She stroked the tip of her tongue along her lower lip and cast a slow, sensual gaze at him. Teasing him when he was trying to interrogate her? The faery certainly wielded the tricks.

Rev grabbed her by the shoulders and kissed her hard and long. She wrapped herself about him, and moaned into his mouth as he matched her wanting pace.

"Bree, you're killing me."

"You don't like kissing me?"

"Love it. Need more. Deeper. All of you."

He lifted her in his arms and sat without breaking the kiss. Shifting her body, she straddled him, snugging her groin against his stomach. He slid his fingers along the slight curves of her body. Lithe and lean, the faery was more toned muscle than voluptuous curves. He liked that just fine.

"Kissing me won't get me to talk," she murmured against his mouth. "In fact, it'll keep my lips so busy I'll never be able to say anything important."

"Bree, you steal my concentration. All I can do when I'm with you is think about how good it feels to touch you." He slipped a hand under her dress and glided it along her thigh. Bad business practice, but impossible to resist. "Tell me to stop."

She arched her spine and her breasts brushed his chest. "I'm sorry, handsome, but...keep going."

Not what he needed to hear. Definitely what he wanted to hear.

Rev kissed her through the white jersey, using his teeth to pull the neckline low and bite softly at the mounds of her breasts. So sweet, ever sweet and giving. She never tried to stop his advances when she knew they could be dangerous. How dare she?

The same way he dared.

Licking her skin, he tasted the essence of her, the dark menace of Faery and the macabre pleasure of its glittering seduction. Tingling on his tongue, dancing icy then hot against the back of his throat. Permeating his body and bones and shimmering into his heart.

The puncture, teeth into flesh, happened instinctually. He bit shallow upon the mound of her breast, and licked at the flowing ichor. Bree cried out softly, a moan of delight as he sucked at her, and drew her into the giddy swoon a vampire's bite always delivered.

Flooded with her hot, pulsing life, he moaned deep in his throat. Crushing her body against his, he ground his hips to hers. Falling backward onto the bed, he rolled her to her back and moved on top, pinning one delicate wrist to the silk spread. Kneading her breast with his fingers, he tended the other with tongue and mouth, suckling, drinking, devastating.

"Oh, goddess, Rev, no."

"You can't tell me no when you were the one to start this."

She pulled at his hair, shoved his shoulder, but he did not relent. It wasn't really a fight. She was just going through the motions. Pulling him closer, she settled, slipping into the swoon, surrendering not peacefully, but feisty, as any faery would.

And when he'd taken a long draft and his head swam with sparkling things of wild and mystic oddity, Rev pushed away and slid from the bed, his back banging against the mattress. He caught his head in his palms and swayed forward, following the swoon's sinister tease and the high only faery ichor could promise.

Returning. Descending.

Swallowed once again by the addiction.

Chapter Six

SWIMMING IN A SEA OF PLEASURE, submission and outright shock, Bree clung to the side of the bed. Eyelids fluttering, she could not see Rev, but she could hear him moaning—with pleasure.

She touched her breast where he'd bitten her. It was sore, yet had already healed. He'd taken a lot of ichor. So good. So wrong. Her heart sank.

"He couldn't help himself. And I encouraged him." Hell, she'd seduced him when he'd been set on business. "What have I done?"

She scrambled off the bed and stumbled against the glass block wall. Didn't want to get too close to him. Wasn't sure how to react. What to do? Rush over and hold him? Or push him out the door and lock it behind him?

"This is all my fault. Why did I let this happen?"

She'd been following her heart, not her better judgment. She'd wanted to bond with her Intended.

Rev sat on the floor, head hung forward and legs stretched out. He worked his fingers through his hair and tossed his head back to rest on the bed. Dark eyes searching his surroundings, they landed her face. He smiled a drunken grin and a low guttural chuckle tainted the air.

Bree's heart dropped to her gut. She'd stupidly slaked her own greedy desires to seduce a former dust freak.

"I'm so sorry." She shut up. Apologizing? Like it was going to do any good now.

Rev pulled himself up by the bed and, wobbling, sat the end of it. He smiled widely, like a junkie knowing his next fix stood two steps away. "Bree, Bree. Apologies are not necessary. God, I feel great. It's been a while. Come here."

She pressed her back against the cool glass. What had happened to her plan to have sex with him in hopes it would entice him with more than her ichor? She hadn't a chance, that is what happened. The vampire had been too fast, too eager for the fix. So seductive. Or had that been she as the seducer? She'd wanted him as much as he had wanted her. Maybe even more.

She should have never dallied with his unstable condition. Once an addict; always an addict.

You risked a silly infatuation and now you've created a monster.

It wasn't an infatuation, it had been a desire to claim her mate, risks be damned.

"Do you want me to call a friend for you?" Stupid, Bree. Make him feel like a leper, will you? "I mean, someone to take you home? Rev, are you okay?"

He moved swiftly, his body fitted to hers and pinned her against the wall. She felt every hard surface on Rev Parker. Great Herne, his body was a sculpted masterpiece and every movement flexed a different muscle against her slender frame. The dark gaze searing hers melted her silly worries. He was gorgeous. A man she desired. A man she'd wanted to lure into her bed.

"You want to be rid of me so quickly?"

"You bit me, Rev."

"I know." He dipped his head to lick her breast, using a fang to drag down her dress.

Bree tensed, but his hot tongue worked wicked pleasure through her body in irresistible waves. She stood on tiptoe to keep the connection. Difficult to push away what she wanted so desperately.

"Didn't mean to," he muttered as he glided his tongue under her chin and along her neck. "But you taste like heaven, Bree. No one passes up a bite of heaven."

"Heaven is closed to you and I."

"Then the closest I'll ever get is you. Let me have it again."

"No." She pressed two fingers over his mouth as it moved to parallel hers. "You can't do this, Rev. Don't lie to me and tell me you're not jonesing for more ichor."

"Jonesing?" He smirked. The man stretched back his shoulders as if to display his brawn, and she did not miss the pulse of his muscles. His confident chuckle echoed in her core. "Not even."

"But why not? That was—"

"The best bite I've ever had. And I want another. You going to deny me?"

He must not realize he was in the throes of the dust. A wicked enchantment wanted to pull him under again. *Her* wicked enchantment. Or maybe he did, and didn't care. What junkie did care about anything but their next fix?

Curse her for wanting to be his next fix, for wondering what another bite would feel like. Wicked good. Like an orgasm stretching inside her veins and endlessly shuddering from head to toe. Could a faery become addicted to the bite?

Yes, she'd heard of those sidhe who sought vampires for the pleasure of their bite. They left dust freaks in their wake, and were shunned by their kind for working their cruel enchantments to fulfill a twisted desire. And that was exactly why vampires and faeries did not mix.

"One more bite and I promise I'll leave," Rev cooed against her ear.

His breath tickled her skin and pricked her nerve endings. His smile revealed a gorgeous white fang, sharp and promising exquisite pain.

Want more.

He slid up her skirt. His warm hand cupped her derriere and glided over the dimples at the base of her spine, testing their concave shape. "You've captured me again." He blinked and shook his head, and found a moment of clarity. "Christ, this shouldn't be happening."

Yes, he was finding reality. And she should, too.

Another blink spread the sexy grin across his face and he cupped her chin firmly. "But if I'm going to fall, what better person than with the only woman I desire. I want you, Bree."

Fall? This man was no angel, and neither was she for allowing this to happen. Perhaps she could yet rescue him. Steer his desires toward safer territory. It wouldn't be easy, and would take all her strength, but if she could enchant him sexually it would overwhelm the dust coursing through his system.

"Make love to me?" she wondered softly. "Yes, let's make love. I have something better than ichor to offer you, Rev."

"Nothing better than dust, pretty, sparkly faery mine." He nuzzled into her neck. The sharp slash of teeth made her shiver.

She didn't feel the intrusion of fang through flesh, only realized when he sucked at her skin and the ichor pulled within her.

This was wrong.

It felt too right. It had to be right. Why else would he be her Intended?

Rev's mouth seduced her body to melt against his hard ridges and firm muscles as if a flower softening against stone under the sun. She wanted to be under his touch, within his embrace, mastered by his hold upon her.

This time the swoon attacked him first. The powerful vampire shuddered against her body, his erection hard and angry against her thigh. Yes, angry, for he was unwilling or unable to join with her, for the ichor high was greater. It overwhelmed all.

Slapping his palms against the wall above her head, he groaned with pleasure, and tugged her into an embrace with one arm. Bree's feet left the floor. He held her to him, rocking her, smothering her, bleeding her pores of dust and thriving on the high of it all.

Don't let him fall. Save him.

"No!" She kicked at him and managed a heel to his thigh.

Dropping her, the vampire stumbled backward. A growl flashed ichor-dripping fangs.

"Think clearly, Rev." Bree ran to the door and opened it. A cool evening breeze gushed in, clearing her head. "Leave, please. I'd never forgive myself if—"

"So it's all about you, then?" He staggered forward, more a swagger, actually. Aggression tightened his jaw. Bree remembered him saying the dust brought out his Hyde as opposed to sinking him into oblivion. Would he hurt her? Trash her place? "The faery gives and the faery takes away."

He slapped his palms to the door frame, standing over her. The wood frame cracked, giving credence to her suspicion he'd take out his aggressions on her home.

Until he leaned down and licked her aside the temple. Oh, sweet hot touch of her lover's tongue. Could she really make him leave? She didn't want to leave him alone when this was all her fault.

Rev growled at her. "Fine. You want to play this game?"

"No, Rev, I didn't mean—"

"Next time we meet, faery, you'd better have some information for me. Or it won't go well for you." He grabbed her wrist and before she could struggle, his fangs tore along her vein. Rev licked her oozing ichor and smiled behind the wicked act. "Love it when a woman pushes me away. Makes it a kick to push back. And this time no chains to keep me off you. Heh. See you later, Bree."

He jumped over the stairway landing, accomplishing the three-story drop with ease. Bree didn't look. Didn't want to watch him slip away. Because he wasn't gone. She'd opened a connection tonight that shouldn't have been unlocked.

The vampire would return. To push, as he'd put it. And while she should be fearful, regretful, she teased the idea of meeting his push with as much shove as she could muster—and perhaps, a little pull.

Chapter Seven

REV STALKED THE SHADOWS tracing the alley behind the nightclub.
Fists tight at his sides and jaw clenched he fought the shudders
threatening to tremor through his body and steal his control.

He was in control. Dust heightened his senses and made him
stronger. He just had to keep this new strength. He would maintain...

Lunging, he punched the brick wall. The skin on his knuckles,
already bloodied from previous punches, opened and bled, yet healed
moments after. He growled with pain, but even more so from lack of
dust. His insides were losing their grasp on her enchanting ichor.
Everything was gradually becoming...less.

He needed a fix.

Slapping a palm against the wall he closed his eyes and pressed a cheek
to the rough brick. "What have I done?"

She'd trusted him.

He had trusted her.

Both had allowed it to happen last night.

Now here he stood, trembling like a junkie, with an eye out for the
first faery he could spy. Hell, it had happened so quickly. He couldn't
have stopped it if he'd wanted to.

She could have stopped him. Had she wanted this to happen to him? Why would she be so cruel?

He could return to Bree's flat. It was just down the street. Salvation loomed close. He growled and kicked at a curious alley cat.

He would not go to the fickle faery who had trapped him in the addiction with but a curve of her gorgeous mouth and a bat of lash.

He wanted, he needed, he devoured dust. He would have it. By any means. But a small part of him still recognized his respect and admiration for Bree. He couldn't harm her. He'd promised.

Because betraying Bree would betray his heart. Their connection was more than friends, more than a means to get his job done. She was a part of him for reasons he couldn't quite figure, and he valued that trusting sacrifice.

A trio of women crossed the street at the end of the alley, giggling and chatting about their clothes. Two mortals and a cat-shifting familiar, to judge by her feline mien. No faeries out tonight. Damn it!

Clamping his arms across his chest to fight the urge to again punch the brick, Rev beat the back of his skull against the wall. Teeth chattering, he exhaled and bent double. Need worked at his gut. He could remember that kind of visceral hunger, yet had never starved or gone hungry. It was but a shadow of the pain he felt now. Pain mixed with craving. And the craving promised bliss.

He had to find more ichor.

Stumbling forward, he broached the end of the alley. Red and blue neon bar signs flashed on the sidewalk. Cars cruised slowly by, looking for a hookup, dropping off partiers in clouds of laughter and hoots.

So many sexy women clad in barely-there clothing and the sound of spike high heels that clicked in his brain like bats navigating the world with sonar. Mortals to feed his cravings. Blood would pale in comparison to ichor. He didn't want to risk watering down the high by taking blood. He'd suffer longer to finally ease the need with the spectacular high ichor offered.

A black Escalade rolling the street boomed with hip-hop music. The driver's head bobbed and he chatted on a cell phone. In the same instant Rev saw a woman in pink step off the curb onto the street, unaware of the oncoming vehicle as her attention was on texting.

Without thought, he raced into the street, hooked an arm about her waist and slammed her against a parked car. The Escalade drove by, missing them by a hands-width.

"Holy crap." The woman shook in Rev's arms. "You saved my life."

And she smelled like cherries and blood. He hissed at the delicious concoction and dashed to the right, increasing his pace away from the woman's call of thanks.

Perched on the building roof opposite the bar, Bree watched Rev flee the scene. He'd saved the bimbo from becoming roadkill.

"If she'd been sidhe he wouldn't have left her behind," she muttered. And then she admonished herself for her cynicism. The man had saved a mortal's life, even as he'd fought the relentless cravings.

At his core, Rev Parker was a good man, who should never have to deal with the addiction. She'd followed him a few blocks and had witnessed his struggles. He was jonesing. And she guessed he was headed toward her place.

She'd like to stand in his arms right now. And she would not. It wouldn't be because he was interested in her sparkling personality or her deep thoughts or her physical attraction—or even that he was meant for her. It could only be for more of her ichor.

Bree entertained the thought of having a virile, sexy man clamoring for her attention, for her regard. To be worshipped. What woman didn't desire that? But Rev's worship would never quite reach her heart or be honest while he swam in a haze of dust.

There was where she needed his touch. Not on the surface. Not even a deep gaze into her eyes. She wanted to feel a man in her heart—and she had felt him. The intense thundering had told her he was the one. Everything about him made her heart swell and her wings tingle. Except seeing him in the throes of addiction hurt her heart, and she knew it was all her fault.

"I should tell him he is my Intended. He might be willing to bond if he knew."

Or it could devastate him that a faery—his worst nightmare—was inextricably tied to him.

"Better keep that information to myself."

Bree skipped across the roof, taking a leap to the neighboring building, and alighted down the metal stairs. She'd considered stopping by the club to see how Nicole was coming with her pole work, but the night was too bright and gorgeous and a nearby park edged in frothy-leaved sugar maples called to her instinctual need for nature.

It neared midnight, the moon was waning, and there were no children out this late. Bree had the whole park to herself. She leaped onto the spinning merry-go-round, and gripping one of the bent steel poles, riding it a few rotations. She dropped her glamour, confident the lacking park lights would keep her secret hidden from mortals out on a midnight jog.

The tank top she wore tugged at her shoulder blades as her wings unfurled and stretched through the air. A shimmer of dust dispersed across the wet grass blades. Fluttering her wings, she took a moment to honor her truth.

Most faeries preferred to live in Faery, where they never had to put on glamour to hide from mortals. Bree had become enchanted with the mortal realm the first time she'd visited, and hadn't looked back. She truly believed that by helping mortals to care for their planet the effects would reverberate to Faery. And her quest for her Intended had led her here.

A cat mewled and, obviously angry at whatever had disturbed it, took off across the park like the devil had bitten its tail. Bree knew better. Himself paid very little mind toward cats.

She spun and searched the shadows at park's edge and scented another creature. Dog? There was a dog park a few blocks east.

Before she could ascertain her musings, she landed the ground on her back. A wolf crouched over her, its paws to her shoulders. Dust glittered in the air from the impact. The beast snarled and snapped at her, revealing a deadly maw of teeth.

Even though it looked like one, it wasn't a normal wolf. Behind her a man called and the wolf jumped off her.

Coming to her feet, she stood but was unable to avoid being wrangled as the man's arms banded like iron about her body. His shoulders were broad and his coat seams torn. Mid-shift, the werewolf was in half human shape with his arms and shoulders taking werewolf form.

"Sabrina Kriss," the man hissed. "You've been a naughty faery."

He squeezed her so tightly she couldn't find breath. "Let me go, dog."

"Fernando Degas said you've been keeping him informed on where we've been sporting. That's not very nice of the chick who should be our friend."

"Friend?" She gasped when he squeezed her again. The wolf on all four legs snarled. "Is that how you treat your friends? Feed them to vampires?"

"He didn't eat you. Besides, we were just playing."

"Playing with our lives, you bastards. That was it? You shoved me in the cell with the vampire for play?" These wolves and their blood games; they really were twisted.

The thick scent of blood suddenly swarmed the air. Something warm splattered Bree's face. Her body dropped and she landed in the wet grass in a sprawl.

The werewolf who had been holding her grasped for his head. It wobbled on his neck. He'd been slashed deeply from the side.

Chapter Eight

AN ANIMAL YELP ECHOED IN the night. The wolf was tossed aside. Its jaw had been ripped wide open. The half-shifted werewolf, still gripping his head, swung around, slashing a clawed hand that began to shift and elongate.

Bree scrambled across the grass until her back hit the merry-go-round. Glamour instinctually camouflaged her wings.

Rev wielded a pistol that sported a deadly blade along the barrel, and aimed at the wolf with the broken jaw. He fired. Silver dust shimmered upon impact. The silver bullets the vampires used against werewolves were deadly. They merely had to enter the bloodstream, and the wolf would drop dead.

The werewolf howled and tore off its shirt. Bree cringed, for surely someone in the neighborhood would hear.

Rev moved sinuously, striding toward the werewolf as he fired off two rounds. Didn't look like the same dust-addled, unfocused vampire she'd followed earlier. The bullets hit target at the wolf's neck and heart. But the yowling beast didn't go down.

Instead, the wolf leapt, soaring toward Rev. Werewolf and vampire collided. The pistol spun through the darkness. Bree did not see where it landed. Blood scent infused the grass and adrenaline-tainted air. The werewolf slashed Rev's chest—the beast stiffened, clutching its gut. Falling backward, it landed on the ground not far from Bree's foot.

She ran for Rev and plunged to the ground near his body.

"My phone," he muttered.

"What?" She patted his chest in the dark but instead of finding a cell phone, her fingers slipped through blood. The wolf's talons had cut deep. "You're hurt."

"Phone in my back pocket. Must call for cleanup immediately or mortals will see."

"Right." He thought only of protecting their kind. Smart guy—smart, bleeding-out guy.

Bree patted down his torso, and Rev groaned. She tugged out the phone from his back jeans pocket and clicked it on.

"Speed dial six," he said. "Hand me the phone."

As she looked over the carnage, he gave orders to whomever she had dialed.

One dead wolf, still furred and in animal shape. One dead werewolf, now shifting to its were, or man shape. It was naked, and the neck was slashed to expose the spine. Rev must have initially attacked with the blade. The bullet entry points steamed as the silver worked at flesh and bone.

She scanned the perimeter. No house lights on. Could they be so lucky no one had witnessed?

"Five minutes for the cleaners to arrive."

She startled when Rev touched her shoulder. Must not be too wounded because he stood fairly straight and steady. "Are you okay?" he asked. "Did he hurt you?" She'd forgotten she was the one initially in danger.

"I'm fine. Maybe a few cracked ribs," she decided. "Were you following me?"

"Yes."

To the point. He was no longer high on dust, couldn't be. The fresh air must have cleared his senses, but if so, that would prove remarkable.

"Thanks," she said. "What about you? You...okay?"

"Couldn't be better."

"You don't look..."

"Strung out? You were following me."

"I was curious."

"Thought so. Spying isn't very nice."

"I'm—" She stopped herself from apologizing. Who was Rev to tell her what to do? "You must have found some dust."

"Not tonight. Blood. A poor substitute for what I crave, but it cleared my head. Least until I can find another hit." He scanned across the park and Bree's heart fell. He was already looking for his next score. "So what was with the dogs? Didn't look like a friendly conversation."

"He knew I was informing on the packs." Bree nudged the dead werewolf's foot. "He said Fernando Degas told him."

Rev's mouth tightened. "Degas? Talking to the wolves? Hell. What's up with that guy?"

If Fernando found out she'd tattled he could make things rough for Rev, because he had a secret weapon that could spin Rev into darkness forever. It was bad enough Bree had gotten him addicted again, she had better not lose his job as well. She wanted to blurt out what she knew was up with the vampire. She didn't know how to.

"Let's get you home," he offered, and spread an arm across her back.

Bree slipped from his grasp. "Me? What about you? You're bleeding from new orifices, buddy."

"I'll have healed by the time I get you to your door. Come on, the cleanup crew doesn't need us to wait around. And I'd prefer to get out of sight in case there are curious mortals observing."

"Does cleanup take care of mortal bystanders?"

"Yes."

"Oh." She glanced around the perimeter of the park, hoping no unsuspecting mortals had witnessed the attack.

"Persuasion, Bree. We don't kill mortals."

Relieved, she blew out a breath. "You saved my life, Rev. Again. You're some kind of hero."

"Far from it."

She knew better. The man had the ability to think beyond his own cruel cravings and care about others, even mortals. He was good.

He clutched her hand and tugged her into the darkness lacing the park. They walked under a thick canopy of maples on the sidewalk. "You in the market for a hero?"

"I could be."

"What about one whose armor is dented and he sold his horse to get a fix?"

"A few dents and bruises make the man, don't you know?"

"What about a vampire who wants to bite you?"

He would take her home, and then she'd enchant him again and the whole vicious cycle would start over. She had to be smart. If she really wanted this man, from here on she had to do things right.

Bree stopped at the park edge. Rev tugged her hand, but she held her ground. She bowed her head and sighed. "I care about you, Rev. I think I could love you."

He smirked and chuckled but cut his forced mirth off short. "Never had anyone tell me that before."

"Seriously? You've never been in love?"

"A few high school infatuations when I was mortal, but nothing serious. I could love you too, Bree. My heart tells me that. It aches for you. I don't know how to make it work though, because there's this thing between us determined to make it impossible."

She stroked a finger along his jacket collar, careful not to touch his skin, but close enough to feel the heat of him. He became so aroused under her touch. She must stand by the conviction that she could make things right.

"There are ways to move beyond the craving," she said. "Finding more addictive things than dust, for example."

"Trade one addiction for another? Doesn't sound good. Besides, nothing's better than an ichor high, Bree. Trust me."

Alone in the darkness, the twosome dallied with an embrace but didn't move closer. Bree lifted her head and Rev tilted his to meet her expectant mouth. They did not kiss.

"You could make love to me," she whispered across his lips.

"I stand corrected. That would be better than dust. You'd let me? I mean, you trust me?"

"It's more risky for you than me."

"Right. But I can't seem to get beyond biting you. Hell, I'd give the world to go beyond, to take you in my arms and make love to you. To put myself inside you and fall into that oblivion."

"I want to try. I want us to bond. It would take a lot of control."

"I have control. But what's this about bonding?"

"Have you heard about certain sidhe races who have one particular mate for them in a lifetime? They're called their Intended. We believe the universe gives us the exact person we need to have a whole and fulfilling life."

"Yeah? So who is your intended? Wait." He tilted his head, eyeing her narrowly in the darkness. "Are you and I...?"

She nodded. "I knew it the moment I looked into your eyes when you were chained to the wall. It's why my wings came out without volition."

"That makes little sense. We're the worst thing for one another."

She hung her head, not sure what to say now. If he truly felt that way, she had no right to try change his mind.

"I mean... Hell, Bree, I'm attracted to you. Never been more attracted to a woman, but I don't know if that's because of the dust. You mean it? We two? Meant for one another?"

"I know, it feels like a karmic punishment, but maybe we could be good for one another. If we made love, we would bond, and maybe you could get beyond your addiction to dust, and instead simply crave me for...me."

"With all my heart and soul I wish I could make love to you. But when I get your dust on my skin..." He moaned and nudged his nose along her neck. "You smell so good. Step away from me, Bree, please."

The desperation in his plea startled her. She stepped away, but her heart remained at his side, clinging to the connection they had dared to forge. And wanting. "Come home with me," she whispered.

"You're torturing me."

"I know. I can't believe I'm doing this, but Rev, you're like no man I've ever known. I want to feel you on me. Inside me."

"Bree."

Now she stood in his arms, falling into his cruel enchantment. His gentle embrace was edged with a tension she wanted to crush into and lose herself against. He was brave, kind, compassionate, and made her feel protected. Loved. Even though neither of them could truly know the meaning of that word. Faeries didn't fall in love. They laughed at love. And vampires, well...she couldn't imagine a vampire lost in a dust haze could fathom the meaning of love.

"Make love to me, Rev. Let's see if we can go beyond your addiction and find love."

"I want that. So I'm your guy?"

She tilted up and kissed his mouth, their lips barely touching, and his sigh imprinted her with his desire. "Yes, you're my guy."

Chapter Nine

A day later...

MOONLIGHT SPILLED THROUGH the glass block wall behind the head of the bed. The advantage to having but a bed for furniture was the expanse of floor stretching from said bed to the kitchen. It made for a perfect dance floor.

Held against Rev's body, her hand in his near his shoulder, her other hand straying around to stroke the small of his back through his shirt, Bree felt sure this was the heaven of which all sidhe were denied entrance.

The rhythm of Rev pulsing against her body, his heartbeats, his slow breaths, even the step of his bare feet, surrounded her as if a comforting symphony.

She wore his windbreaker jacket. He'd suggested she cover her bare arms and back if they were going to be close. Less skin contact meant less danger for him. Worked for her. Mostly. What she wanted was to pull off her dress and open his shirt and press her breasts against his strength, his very being.

Rev's inhale lifted his chest against hers. There was no music, only their heartbeats.

"Your wings were out in the park the other night," he said softly. "It was dark, but I noticed their sheen. And when I was chained up, they glowed red around the edges. They seemed brighter than the faery wings I've seen."

Because he had likely spent time in ichor dens populated by faeries who were literally dying to feed their vampire patrons.

"I'm accustomed to glamourizing around mortals. And yes, they are bright because I don't eat processed mortal foods and try to live clean and healthy. A red glow means...desire." She looked into his intense eyes. "You're shivering."

He was fighting the need for her right now.

And when he dipped his mouth to her neck, Bree allowed the vampire to bite her for what must have been the third or fourth time in the past day. Because she didn't want him to leave. Because she wanted to feel him on her always. Because she wasn't thinking rationally.

And because she thought she knew better.

Never had she felt so inadequate. So ineffectual. And yet, it was as though she had *become* Rev Parker's world.

He'd not left her home for three days. And she didn't know what to do about it. Bree fought the weakness loss of ichor threatened by eating five small meals a day and drinking lots of water and mead.

Rev, on the other hand, had not gone out in search of blood, or another faery to provide ichor. He didn't need it. He had her. He functioned well enough, padding about her home and dancing with her in the moonlight. Wearing clothing as protection against her dust? They were both fooling themselves. When in the dregs of an ichor high, Rev became aggressive and she let him stomp about, punching walls until he'd worked the edge off. Mornings he slept, the sheets pulled over his body and head to keep out the sunlight.

She wondered, as he slept through the rising sun, if she should peel away the spread and expose him to the light. But then she remembered his captivity. The harsh lights had induced UV sickness and a permanent sun aversion. The sun would burn him, as it did with some vampires who were in tribes who didn't have a high immunity to the sun, but much faster.

If she did let in the light he'd be angry with her. Would it make him angry enough to leave?

She didn't want him to leave. She had allowed this to happen. She'd stood back and watched a heroic man succumb to something she had given him, to fall into her cruel enchantment.

They'd yet to make love.

She knew he resisted, for a while at least. He said he wanted to prolong the foreplay, to know her completely. Truth was, the nasty addiction would not allow it, not let him see beyond the immediate and forceful desire for satiation.

It had taken him months to get clean after biting her once. He'd been biting her many times a day.

She'd done this for love, to claim her Intended. Love wasn't supposed to hurt or be wicked. Love should feel good. And she'd never felt more terrible. Zen sidhe, she was not. It was as if her Intended was a pre-payment for the bad karma she indulged now.

Her phone jingled and Rev nudged her away so she could answer. He wandered over to the bed and lay back, stretching out his arms. Lost in a haze.

Bree vacillated on answering—all she wanted to do was make Rev's world right—and then when she saw Blu's name on the screen, she answered, "Hey."

"What's up? Party in a few days. You ready?"

"Uh…"

"Bree? What's the deal? I'm sensing your Zen sidhe vibes have fallen off the scale. You still seeing that vampire?"

She would never lie to her best friend. "He's here right now. Blu, I…have a problem."

"He's bitten you."

She wouldn't bother asking how Blu knew that. "I let it happen."

"And he hasn't left since?"

"He saved me from the wolves again. He was brave and injured so he needed a fix. How do I save him? I care about him, Blu. I…I think I could love him."

"You can't love someone who uses you to feed his addiction."

"It's not his fault. It's the dust in his system. It won't relent. It makes him feed upon me like—"

"Like some kind of longtooth tic. Oh, Bree, this is not good for you."

"Or him! Listen, Blu, he's a good man. I want him to have the information I have on the blood sport and Fernando Degas. I want to make it right with him and help him with his tribe."

"Give me the info and we'll act on it."

"No, it's got to come from Rev. He needs the credit for this."

"Sounds like he's too fucked up to do his job."

"Don't tell anyone, most especially, not your husband because he's Rev's boss. If he knew Rev was in a bad way he might kick him out of the tribe, or at the least, lose all respect for him."

"Creed's an understanding man," Blu said.

"I know. He's the best. You two were meant for one another. But I don't want to get Rev in trouble. Please, Blu, you gotta help me."

"I don't know what you can do beyond getting him out of your home, and now. He needs to dry out."

"Maybe you know some vampires who can come get him? Someone who wouldn't tell?"

"It can't be anyone from his tribe. They'll narc on Rev to gain position in the tribe. What about some faery thugs? Didn't you used to have an elf walk you home nights when you were being stalked by a hunter?"

"Yeah, Erte. That's a good idea, Blu. If he can get Rev out of my home—"

"And freaking chain him up until he can come down. He needs mortal blood, and lots of it. He also needs a keeper to watch he doesn't sneak out to an ichor den. You know it's gotta happen, Bree."

"I hate myself for this. I just...oh Blu, I love him. He really is the man I want to spend my life with."

"A tragic coupling destined for further tragedy." Blu said it dramatically, but without any judgment. "You really buying into this Intended thing?"

"You are always the one to wax about the joys of vampire love."

"I am, aren't I? And I used to hate bloodsuckers with a passion. Still don't care for a couple in the hubby's tribe. Okay, so my girl's in love with the very last man on earth she should love. Tell me that you're sure?"

"I am."

"Then we gotta figure things out. You call your elf. I'll see what I can find out about vampire detoxification methods. And pray my hubby doesn't ask what I'm up to. Bree, you're testing me on this one."

"Sorry. You still love me?"

"Always. Talk soon."

Bree hung up and wandered over to the bed to slip into the vampire's embrace. His hair was tousled and the stubble on his cheeks and jaw had grown thick. He looked like he'd been on a bender, which was dreadfully true.

"Talking about me?" he wondered softly. His touch, so gentle, always belied his true intentions. The addiction's attentions. "Missed you."

"Me too, but I gotta get out of here for a while. I need my daily vitamin D to survive. It's a faery thing. I've some errands to run."

He tugged her into an iron embrace. Indeed the Hyde side of him acted out when coming down from the high. He was a little bit rougher, a little less caring. "You don't want me?"

"Rev, I want you. I want to make love with you. To bond with you. But you don't want to do anything more than bite me."

"Biting's good. You taste good. Love my pretty sparkly faery mine."

She kissed his chin. "*You're* good, Rev. A good man who should have never gotten involved with this faery."

"Faeries taste good. Thought I was yours?" He grazed his tooth along her jaw. Bree pressed carefully against his mouth, for to struggle would only make him more forceful. "Just a little bite?"

"Rev, I need to get groceries. Can you wait until I get home?"

"Who needs to eat?"

"I do. I can't survive on a liquid diet like you."

"No, need you now."

As his grip tightened, she managed to slip from his arms and rushed to the door. He followed closely and slammed a palm against the open door, but Bree got half her body outside before he could close it. Bright sunlight beamed in. The vampire blinked and shuffled away.

"Don't leave me," he moaned. "I won't hurt you. Bree!"

The agony in his voice made her want to hug him close and swear they would be good forever. But not like this. Not when the dust made him less than the man she knew he was.

"I'll be back soon," she promised, and slammed the door shut on the man she wanted to love, but needed to push away.

The faery bitch had gone out in the daylight knowing he couldn't follow. What was she doing? Denying him? Damn it.

Rev swiped a hand across the sheets, seeking to imbue his palms with lingering faery dust. Anything to bring on the loopy tingle. It took so much now. And he needed more.

Growling, he ripped the pillow apart. Feathers scattered. He kicked the bed and paced the floor.

"What the hell is wrong with me!" he shouted to the walls. "I'm stronger than this."

He knew what was going on. Faery dust infected his veins like a monster gnawing at his bones. It ate at him, starving him and increasing his hunger for more.

Yet he'd overcome once. He could do it again. But that would mean denying himself Bree.

Bree was everything. She was the light in his darkness. The soft in his steely hard world. Her voice glided across his aches and soothed them away. She giggled like the only sunshine he could ever know.

He'd been forceful with her. So cruel. And she had given him what he'd demanded because—well, because she feared he'd rip her apart if she refused.

He would not. But he couldn't know if the desire for dust would force him to such an unsavory act.

"I have to get away from here." How long had he been here? Days surely. Weeks? What was he doing? He should be working the case. Getting the information needed— "She keeps denying me. What she won't give me is my freedom."

He bashed a fist into the wall, but the rough bricks did not give. Blood dripped from his knuckles. Rev kicked the wall and shouted.

It's what he needed. To drown himself in mortal blood and wash away the faery dust. To not think about the delicious enchantment eddying through his system, making him warm and woozy, and wondering where she had gone.

When would she return?

Had it been hours? Days?

He rushed to the door but winced at the bright daylight. It could have only been minutes.

His mind was no longer his own. He had to leave, and now, before he lost and brought Bree down with him. There was only one way to go about during the day. He'd need protection from the sun.

❖

Erte Medalknyght would give the vampire credit. He was making an effort to put distance between himself and Bree. Not the greatest effort. Walking about with a sheet pulled over his head and sunglasses wasn't going to get him far. And his rambling gate stumbled him against the building wall so many times the vampire had taken to beating the brick and shouting at it.

Erte sighed. "Idiot dust freak."

Bree was a good friend and he did owe her one for the time she'd fixed him up with the stripper. She'd been hot, and they'd had a fabulous time of it before they'd both gotten utterly sick of the other and had mutually ended their sixty-day sex fest.

Hey, an elf took it when he could get it. And Erte got it a lot.

Smirking, he pulled the SUV over to the curb behind the vampire. The vehicle had been specially designed, all steel replaced with titanium and no iron at all. If a sidhe wanted to exist in this mortal realm, everything he owned had to be modified.

He palmed a titanium pistol loaded with wooden bullets. They wouldn't kill the vampire, but if he could plug him in a major artery, it'd slow him down enough to nab the creature and dump him in the back of the car.

The vampire was a big one. Broad of shoulder and tall. Not exactly Bree's type. But then Erte realized he didn't know her type. Chicks were always attracted to the big, studly, and the forbidden.

"Man, is that guy forbidden," he muttered. "Bree really got herself in deep this time."

The vampire punched the wall again, taking out a section of brick.

"Should have brought Silver along," Erte muttered, thinking the seven-foot troll would have loved this mission. He cocked the gun and stepped out of the vehicle.

Another body along to help would have only exposed Bree's mistake. She wanted this kept quiet. Didn't want the vampires to learn one of their own was addicted. Weird that she cared, but Erte didn't question. Sabrina Kriss was good stuff.

"Hey, buddy!"

The vampire wobbled along the wall, a blood smear from his knuckles leaving a trail. Not cool for this neighborhood. He swore at Erte, suggesting he do something nasty with his mother.

Erte aimed for the neck, and fired. The vampire swung about, the sheet falling from his head. He groped for the bullet stuck in his throat. With his other hand he tried to block the sun from his eyes.

Not the nicest way to be put down, but necessary.

He approached the vampire and kicked high, landing under the jaw. The move rocked the vampire's head on his spinal column, which successfully knocked him out cold. He fell forward, which Erte appreciated. He had merely to bend and catch the big guy over a shoulder.

Ten minutes later, he secured the vampire in his own home, chained in the concrete basement. Mortals would be brought in daily. The longtooth could feed until the dust had cleared from his system. If not, Erte would have to bring out the saber and slice off his head. He hated dust freaks.

Chapter Ten

"YOU CHAINED HIM UP? But he needs to go to work. His leader will wonder what's become of him."

"Bree." Erte laid a hand on her shoulder. The poor thing shivered and the skin around her eyes was dark. She looked as crazed as the dust freak. That happened when a faery enslaved a vampire with her enchantment. In turn, the swoon from the bite was a powerful seducer. "Stay away from Rev Parker. I'll double the mortals to three or four a day. He'll be over this in no time."

"But he needs to get important information to his superiors. I have to give it to him."

"Bree, if you go to the vampire now, don't come begging to me when he attacks and kills you. On second thought, I won't have to worry about that, because you'll be dead."

She nodded, accepting, but the shiver in her shoulders made Erte shake his head. Poor girl, she was as addicted as the longtooth.

He knew what was happening. It was all good. And it sucked like no amount of dead dog could ever suck.

Bree must have hired the elf to kidnap him and take him home. Chained in his own basement. How humiliating. Yet, the mortals were serving a purpose by purging his system of dust.

And of Bree.

He could feel his pretty, sparkly faery slip further from him with every drop of mortal blood he consumed. He hated it. He was losing her. But rationally, he knew it had to be like this.

Could he ever have a real, honest relationship with Bree?

He wanted that. He needed that.

No, you don't need it, that's the addiction talking. You would like it. That's all.

No, he genuinely wanted to be the man for her. Intended? He was in for the ride because he did love her. At least he thought he did. Hell, he needed to think beyond the dust!

A third mortal woman was escorted down the stairs. Rev strained at the chains. Her initial reaction was to scream, but he was skilled at persuasion and it took less than a minute to settle and entice the woman into his arms.

That he was being kept like an animal reminded of his imprisonment in the sporting warehouse. He'd brought this upon himself this time. No one to blame but himself.

"Bree," he murmured as he sunk in his fangs. "Come back to me."

❖

Slammed against the wall below her loft, Bree's teeth chattered from impact. The vampire Fernando Degas had returned to torment her. Not only did he collude with the wolves, he also pimped the sidhe into selling him their ichor. He, in turn, sold the dust to addicted vamps.

Why hadn't she the courage to tell Rev about this immediately?

Because she'd thought with that information, Rev might try to buy some of the dust from Degas. That she would be leading him back to his *worst*. She'd been stupid not to believe Rev was stronger than that.

Besides, she had led him to his worst.

"You are pissing me off, faery."

"Yeah? Doesn't take much, obviously."

He slammed her again. "You've been talking to my people, stepping over the line."

"So drain my ichor like you do all the other faeries and be done with me."

He hissed and snarled, revealing fangs.

"Go on, dust dealer, I know you want a bite."

"I'm not an idiot like your boyfriend. I wouldn't let a drop of ichor down my throat. This ends right now." He released her and stepped back.

Bree wasn't sure why he wasn't pummeling her, or stabbing her with iron, but when the tall figures behind Fernando walked into view, she let out a groan, guessing the man wasn't about to get his hands dirty. He'd leave that for the two hulking werewolves.

Unchained felt good.

Rev's head was clear. It had only taken five days of intensive blood donations. But it would take a lifetime to stay clean. Rev wondered why a paranormal sort of AA didn't exist. They could call if DFA—Dust Freaks Anonymous. He'd be the poster boy for possibilities since he'd now beat the addiction twice.

He knew well enough that was a crock. He'd never actually beat the addiction the first time around. He'd risen above it. Now, if he wished to stay sane he must remain vigilant about staying away from the dust.

If being dust-free meant feeling powerful and clear again, that was a great start.

Time to focus on bringing down the sporting warehouses. He'd called Fernando, hoping to convince him to go to Bree and try to get the information from her, but the guy wasn't picking up. Too late he remembered something Bree had said about Fernando. He was involved with the wolves? It didn't make sense, because he'd thought Fernando an honorable man, but he was inclined to put more trust in Bree.

Yes, even after she had swept him into her enchantment. He couldn't blame her for that. He should have been stronger.

So it was up to Rev. Two donors this evening had only temporarily assuaged the blood cravings. He knew well the hunger would remain strong until he got into a routine.

"I can do this."

He knocked on Bree's door, but it swung inside; the latch hadn't been secured.

That wasn't good.

Stepping inside, he scented the acrid odor of dust. It smelled off, not sweet and attractive like he was accustomed to. It didn't appeal at all. That was either very good or—

"What the hell?"

He raced across the flat to Bree's bed. Sprawled upon the rumpled purple silk, lay a tattered faery. Her wrists were encircled with iron manacles yet she was not chained to anything.

"Oh, Bree."

He couldn't touch.

He had to touch.

His fingers shook over the scatter of tangled pale hair that sparkled with her innate dust.

He couldn't do this alone so he tugged out his cell phone. Searching the phone's call list, Rev found a name he had recently added. They'd chatted daily since he'd been chained up to dry out and Rev had gained respect for the elf. He cared about Bree as much as Rev did.

He hit the call button and Erte answered on the first ring. "It's Bree," Rev said. "The wolves have been here. She's been shackled—hell, it looks like iron. Her body, it's stiff and her veins are purple."

"Holy Herne in a hand basket, sounds like iron poisoning. Get those shackles off her right now."

"All right. Hold on."

He dropped the phone and lifted the cold iron banding her ankle. It was heavy and her flesh was dark, nearing necrosis. A twist of the lock mechanism gave free. Too easily. Rev decided the shackles hadn't been designed *not* to be torn off, but more to intimidate and steal her power.

He made quick work of the other three shackles, tossing them to the floor. Bree didn't stir at all from the commotion. He picked up the phone.

Erte said, "If her skin is blackening the iron must have entered her bloodstream. If you don't get her ichor flowing quickly, she'll die."

"How do I do that?"

"You high on dust, buddy?"

"No. No, I'm clean right now. I can't think to get high with Bree like this. Help me, man! I don't want her to die. But I can't touch her. I...I just can't."

"Dude, you're going to have to. Get over yourself."

"It's not something I can control—"

"You can if you love her as much as I think you do. I heard you moaning her name the entire time you were chained in the basement. You got it bad, buddy."

"I do. So how do I help her?"

"Unless you drink her ichor the dust should be a mere nuisance. The craving will be a bitch, but which is more valuable? Your high or Bree's life?"

The elf wasn't stupid. Nor was Rev. This was all mental. Of course the dust was a mere facsimile of mainlined ichor. It tingled and pricked at the craving, but it wasn't the master of his addiction.

He thought he had so much control? Now it would be put to the test.

"You're right, I can do this. Bree's life is top priority. What do I do? A warm bath? Will that do it?"

"No," the elf said, "don't submerge her in mortal water. It could be tainted with chemicals, which includes iron. Strip off her clothes, then start massaging every inch of her body. You've got to get the ichor flowing. Work slowly, methodically, and not so hard you bruise her. And when she starts to rouse, do her wings."

"Her wings?" Now Rev saw they were exposed, crushed beneath her body. "They're dry and so lifeless."

"Her body first, then her wings, vampire. Got that?"

"Yes."

"You know about faeries and their wings, right?"

"Uh, they can fly?"

Erte chuckled. "You'll learn soon enough that touching a faery's wings is a sexual thing. That is, if you can bring her back."

"But I'm afraid to touch her, man. The dust."

"You got any oranges?"

"I'm not sure. Why?"

"Ancient secret of my ancestors—citric acid on your skin. Rub some on, let it dry. Repels the dust, at least until the juice rubs off. Now stop talking to me, and get to it, man. I'll come after you myself if you let Bree die."

Rev clicked off and tossed the phone. It clattered onto the floor. He tugged off his coat and crossed the room to close the door, heartbeats frantically hammering his ribs. He beelined to the fridge and let out a, "Thank you, Herne," when he saw the oranges. Taking all three, he found a knife in a drawer and cut them in half.

This was all his fault. He should have dealt with Fernando and been more intent on tracking the blood sport warehouses. Now the wolves were using Bree to retaliate against him. This wasn't her fight.

He hated that her involvement with him had led to this.

Oranges in hand, he stopped before the bed and exhaled. Fingers working in and out of tight fists, he growled in frustration. Tilting his head side to side loosened his tense muscles as he prepped for his greatest challenge yet. He worked the juice into his exposed skin on hands and face.

"Chill out, Rev. Focus. It's up to you. You can do this. And you won't get high in the process."

Maybe. The elf didn't know everything. How long would the orange juice last? And what if it only worked on elves? Too much skin contact with dust would eventually work its way into his system, and then? Watch out.

But Bree was worth another plunge into oblivion.

"Massage?" He looked at his big, calloused hands, dripping with juice. The touch of her skin had communicated with his very soul when he'd been imprisoned in the warehouse. Even swimming in the depths of addiction, he'd used that memory. It had spoken to him.

And it had killed him.

If he took too much dust into his flesh would he lose focus and bite her?

"She has no dust right now," he muttered. "Her ichor is turning solid."

And even if there was a little dust, it was poisoned by iron. It wouldn't have the same effect on him. He had to count on that being true. He wasn't her Intended by mistake. They were meant for one another, and he wouldn't let her down.

He stripped the dress from her body, taking care at the back, though the neckline swept under her fragile wings. He didn't want to touch them for fear of tearing the parchment-like webbing.

Bowing over her, he kissed her forehead and smoothed away the hair from her cheeks. "I love you, Bree. It shouldn't have come to this. Hell, we're the worst thing for one another. And the best. I'll make it right."

Hands shaking as he held them over her bare body, he decided to start over her heart. Wouldn't that be the most important area to get the ichor flowing? Softly he stroked her skin, cringing at the coolness of it. As if lifeless. Damn those wolves. He'd rip the heads from each and every—

No. He had to focus on Bree. Anger wouldn't make his touch gentle. He kneaded over her heart and under her breast, not too hard, as Erte had cautioned. The air sweetened with the smell of oranges and his nervous anxiety. After minutes he felt Bree's flesh warm beneath his touch. He couldn't be sure if it was merely from contact with his skin or if his motions were affecting the flow of her ichor.

He continued over her shoulders and down her arms. Every portion of her flesh was lifeless, so cold. And yet, the shimmy of dust came to his palms now and one of her fingers moved.

"Bree?"

No reply. He quickened his efforts, working methodically down her other arm and then rubbing down her torso and belly. The juice, warmed by their contact, worked like massage oil, and made his movements slick and smooth. He kissed her stomach, testing the warmth of her skin. Faint, but yes, he did sense she was warming. Rising from a darkness he wished she had never had to experience.

Down each leg he worked, massaging gently around her feet and ankles and her slender thighs. That he'd never had the fortitude to resist her dust, and instead make love to her, killed him now. They should have been lovers. He should have indulged in her body and passion instead of feeding his greedy hunger. He kissed her toes, each one of them, making it a blessing he prayed she could accept.

Bree moaned. Her fingers trembled.

"Good girl," he whispered.

An hour passed. He feared rubbing her skin dry and abrading it, but it did not grow rough, only warmer and moist with the subtle oils from his skin and the oranges.

"I love you, Bree. Damn it, you're the best thing that's ever happened to me. Come back to me, and I promise I'll never bite you again. I can do that. I will do that."

The moon had risen in the sky, and it bathed her pale skin and revealed her gorgeous sparkle. His palms, now dry of the last drops of juice he'd forced from the orange rinds, sparkled with dust, and they tingled, but he resisted the urge to lick them clean.

Don't need that danger. You need her alive, those bright violet eyes smiling up at you.

Easy enough to resist the temptation when the promise of Bree's smile waited. He lifted her limp body to hug to his chest, her head wobbling against his shoulder. Drawing his palms down her back he worked slowly along her spine, testing each knobby bone until he touched the base of her wings.

Save her wings for last. You'll learn soon enough, vampire.

Erte had said something about it being sexual. So had Bree. Yes, he recalled a few times when he'd taken a faery for the dust and she'd begged him to touch her wings. He never had, because then the dust had been all that he'd craved.

He tucked his head into her hair and kissed the tip of her ear.

"Rev," she whispered. "Oranges?"

"Don't speak. Your ichor stopped flowing from iron poison. You're getting better. Let me touch you everywhere."

"My arms...cold."

He moved his gently massaging grasp along her arm. Dust had permeated his skin and entered his bloodstream. He was getting a contact high now that the juice had dissipated. That meant the iron must be purging from her system. Great for her; not so good for him.

Focus, Rev. It's all about her. You've endured worse. Let it ride through you. Use it.

Use it? Hmm... The sensations the dust produced lightened his body and made him think he could fly. It softened his strokes and made them longer, more sweeping.

Bree moaned appreciatively. He must be doing something right.

She curled up a leg and snuggled closer to him. That she was moving and making sounds meant his clumsy touches were actually improving her condition.

He stroked his lips across her temple. Warm there. Sweet, like flower-stormed meadows. Her fingers clung to his shirt, pulling, grasping for strength.

She tilted her head to meet his mouth and he brushed his lips across hers like wings softly dusting the air. He touched her breathy gasp and moved away, and touched again. The teasing appeal of it redirected his intentions. He stroked a hand, exploring the base of her wings.

"They're so dry," he murmured. "Roll onto your stomach and let me see if I can bring them to life."

She coiled onto her side and violet eyes flashed up at his. "Do you know what you're doing, vampire?"

"No. But if it restores the sparkle to your eyes, it'll be worth discovering, eh?"

She smiled. "Sparkle. Mm, yes."

Kissing her mouth, longer this time, tasting her weakness yet, he then straddled her hips and glided his fingers along the delicate architecture of her wings. Pale violet and blue, they were scaled like a butterfly's wings, and yet, the slightest breath from him moved through the gossamer fabric of them and they appeared liquid.

Seeing his breath warmed the color brighter on her wings, Rev bent and hushed an exhale across her wing, following with a careful trace of his forefinger. Touching lightly he broke contact, but never for more than a microsecond.

Bree curled her fingers into the pillow and murmured in satisfaction. It reminded him of a woman in the throes of passion, but that couldn't be right. She was still so weak.

He'd never give up on her.

To trace the many striations of color moving beneath his breaths fascinated him. And there, around the edges of the violet and blue wings, they glowed red.

To touch her, a slight tickle from his smallest finger, stirred her spine to arch. Wings curled backward and the fine filaments edging the curves tickled his cheek as if a kiss. He was dazzled by the sensation.

Spanning his hand out across a brilliant violet wing, he then laid his head between them and drew in the delicious scent of Bree. Captivating. Free. Decadent. Wondrous.

"Mine," he whispered. "I want you to be mine. I don't deserve you, though. What can I do to deserve you?"

"Rev," she sighed deeply, and followed with a desirous moan. "Yes."

And he realized his touch aroused her as if she were going to climax.

"This turns you on?"

"Touching my wings... It's the most intimate touch of all. We can bond. You've never touched a faery's wings when you...?"

"No. I've only bitten your kind. Really? This feels good?"

"Oh, Rev, that's amazing. Don't stop."

"What about the iron poisoning? You're weak yet."

"My ichor flows freely now. You massaged all the iron away. I'm weak, but your touch makes me stronger. You make me want... Need. Oh..."

Sitting upright in a languorous glide, Bree slowly tugged Rev's shirt off and unbuttoned his jeans. She wanted him desperately, be damned the dangers. He'd brought her back to life, now she wanted to give him a life beyond addiction to dust.

Spreading out her wings behind her, she bent to tickle her tongue down his chin, his neck, over the hard ridges of his chest and down the slope of his abdomen. Pushing him back across the bed, she mounted him and teased her tongue from hip to hip, then dashed lower and slicked along the length of his shaft. Solid, rigid and heavy in her hands, she slid up and played the head of his erection against her moist folds.

Rev groaned and clutched the sheets. When he met her gaze, she saw something in them she wanted to know forever. Trust. And love.

"Yes," he murmured desperately. "Put me inside you."

She swept forward a wing and stroked it along his cheek and he nuzzled into the sheer fabric of it. She could feel his heart beats in that touch, and in the pulse of his hard shaft begging for entrance. They belonged to one another, for good or for ill.

Everything would be good from here on; she felt it to her very wingtips.

Settling onto his shaft, she took his thickness inside her, clutching his arms as the heady sweet torture of joining filled her with a brightness she wanted to own.

He rocked his hips, working in and out of her, and she moved in tandem to increase their rhythm. The vampire and the faery had finally come together, and this night they would form an everlasting bond. Her body shuddered above him. Rev sat up and held her against him as she slid up and down, increasing the friction, working them both toward an edge.

So close, she would not resist the fall into bliss. A burst of red violet light shimmered out from Bree's wings and she closed them about her lover's body. Wrapped within her gossamer embrace, Rev surrendered to an orgasm of dust, touch and sensation. They two, together, fell. Deeply, endlessly, flailing through time and belief and everything else that complicated this realm. This climax was pure and bright and like nothing she had ever known. They bonded, skin to skin, pulse to pulse, trust to trust.

They both cried out and then wrapped themselves tight about the other. The world fell away. Two heartbeats reigned.

"I didn't know that would happen," he said. "The elf implied, but didn't explain. Hell, Bree, that was better than…"

"If you had a choice," she whispered against his mouth, "would you rather get your high from dust, or from making love to me?"

"You have to ask? Bree, I love you. I want to make love to you every day. But touching your wings? Who would have thought?"

She wrapped her wings about his shoulders. "Thanks for bringing me back, lover." She kissed him deep and long and forever. "We've got to stop doing this."

"Rescuing each other?"

"Seriously. It could get old after a while."

"Not if it means coming back to life to be in your arms. It's like you pulled me through the craving and beyond to something so amazing."

"We've only begun, lover."

"Does that mean we bonded? That I'm yours?"

"If you'll have me."

"You don't even have to ask."

"Maybe when a vampire bonds with a faery he loses the vicious addiction to dust? It has to be. The world would not give me my Intended if he were bad for me. I have to believe that."

"So I could touch you and not...? I'd give anything for that."

"I'm not sure about you drinking my ichor though."

"I'll be good," he said and kissed her neck. "Mortal blood from here on out. I promise. So long as you take me in your arms every day and make love with me."

"That's an easy promise to make. I love you, Rev."

"I love you. We did it. Together."

Rev entered Creed Saint-Pierre's office. Fernando Degas stood beside the desk, arms crossed high over his chest. Tension spiked up Rev's neck at Fernando's castigating glance.

"Glad you could make it," Creed said. "The informant has been useless?"

"On the contrary," Rev stated.

Fernando fixed him with a steely stare.

"Though some may find her more useful than most." He shot daggers back at Fernando. "She's was compromised by one of our own. Was attacked by werewolves as a result. But I'm afraid the reason she stopped informing wasn't because of the werewolves but because of one of the Rescue Project's agents. Care to tell us about it, Degas?"

"He's a dust freak," Fernando said. "He doesn't know what he's saying. The faery refused information—"

"So you threatened her with your own brand of torture—dust removal by force."

Creed shot Degas a castigating stare.

"How many faeries do you destroy, Degas, to get the dust you sell to the freaks like me?"

"You took the assignment," Creed said to Rev, "knowing you were incapable? Under the influence of dust?"

Rev wasn't surprised Creed did not understand. "Truth? Those months I needed to recover from captivity? I was stoned out of my brain on dust. I've been clean now, for..." Less than a few hours. "I struggle with the addiction daily."

"And we sent you to interrogate a faery? Revin, you should have said something sooner. You were no man to be put on this case."

"Fact remains, the faery didn't stop talking because of the wolves. Degas wanted to drain her dry as he's done to dozens of other faeries."

"They're worthless rabble," Fernando argued. "What's one dead faery now and then?"

"You're dealing dust?" Creed beat the desk with a fist. "Fernando, I expected better of you. You've compromised this mission and the integrity of tribe Nava. Now we'll never get a lead into the sporting matches."

"Don't worry," Rev said. "The faery talked. She gave me all the info she has. I dispatched a team to a warehouse in Bloomington an hour ago. We should be hearing back soon."

"Excellent." Creed gestured Fernando leave them. "Wait for me outside the door; this is not over. Close the door on your way out."

Expecting admonishment, Rev crossed his hands before him and bowed his head.

"It was foolish of you to take the assignment knowing how susceptible a former addict can be to the faery persuasion."

"Not former," Rev said softly. "As I've said, I fight the addiction daily."

"You in trouble with this faery?"

"Nothing I can't handle. She's good, Saint-Pierre. I want her designated safe from harm."

Creed crossed his arms and hooked a leg on the desk. "Sabrina Kriss has always been under my protection. She is best friends with my wife, after all."

His werewolf wife.

"Is it difficult adjusting your life to encompass a breed you'd rather not deal with?" Rev asked.

"I love my wife, Parker. Doesn't mean I have to love all the other werewolves."

He nodded. And completely agreed.

"You and the faery, you are...involved?"

"I admire her. She is unlike any other woman I've known. I love her."

"At the risk to your sanity?"

"It's a risk I'm willing to take because without Bree, well, she's the sunshine that was taken away from me with the UV sickness. She gives me new hope, a reason to want to be good."

"Never doubt you are a good man, Parker."

Bree had said the same. He'd always toe the line between addict and functioning vampire, but he preferred goodness over another plunge into dark.

Creed crossed his arms and eyed him warily. "Will you be able to function in your role to the project?"

"I will. Sabrina and I...we've come to an accord. She doesn't want to do me harm and I don't want her enchantment. We're working it out."

"How is that possible?"

"There are some things more wondrous in this world than faery dust. That's all I can say."

"See the relationship does not interfere with your job, and I promise I can use you, Parker. You're an excellent soldier for the project."

"Thank you. I will not let you down."

❖

The Saint-Pierre mansion was decorated with red and silver streamers and balloons. Outside, partiers lingered around the pool, dancing, chattering and drinking. Bree nursed a goblet of orange juice because alcohol did weird things to her brain, and the juice had become a very useful item in her life of late. She'd never heard of the ancient secret, but was glad Erte had given it to Rev. She spied a sexy woman in bright red wig and dashed over to hug her friend, Blu.

"It's been weeks," Bree whispered in Blu's ear. "I missed you. And goddess, do you know how to work the leather."

Blu tilted out a hip and slid her fingers over the black leather micro-mini skirt. Thigh-high black stockings stopped just above her knees with red bows to draw the eye up. Red lace stripper heels finished the look. "These are your shoes. Remember when you gave them to me?"

"Those shoes served me well when I used to strip. Bet Creed loves them."

"He adores it when I poke him with them." Blu flashed a sassy wink, then scanned the crowd over the rim of her vodka martini. "So you here alone? Don't tell me things didn't work out with you and your Intention?"

"Intended. Actually...he's here somewhere—oh!" Embraced from behind, Bree tilted her head against her lover's cheek and he playfully nipped the corner of her mouth. "Blu, this is Revin Parker."

Her friend gave Rev a long and desirous once over, and with a flirtatious flutter of her long lashes nodded. "I can see why this one was worth the struggle. Nice to meet you, Rev. I think we've run into each other once or twice before."

"Yes, but your husband never properly introduced us. That wig is hot."

Blu, the biggest flirt Bree knew, took the compliment with a mock curtsey and another wink.

"I'll see you two in a bit," Blu said, excusing herself with a hug to Bree. "Does he know about the three day sex rule?" she whispered and walked off.

"What rule is that and why don't I know about it?" Rev asked, as he circled her waist from behind and hugged her against his warm body. A slide of fang along her neck stirred Bree to an expectant tingle, but he'd never bite her again, and that was one rule they both intended to keep.

"It's a girlfriend's rule. One should never go longer than three days without sex, if at all possible."

"Sounds too lenient to me. How about three hours? When did we leave the house? It's been a few hours, yes?"

She cooed and turned into his embrace to kiss him. "There are guest bedrooms upstairs."

"I don't think anyone will miss us." He swept her into his arms and carried her away. Easy enough, when he'd already won her heart, soul and forever.

Enemy Embrace

PATTI O'SHEA

Chapter One

THE FARTHER SHE GOT FROM the Tiki-A-Go-Go, the more uneasy Nicole became. This late at night, the warehouse district appeared deserted. She didn't understand why there were no deliveries...unless it had something to do with the twenty-foot tall chain-link fences topped with razor wire that surrounded the buildings. She scanned continually while she walked, but it wasn't the area near the nightclub that had her on edge. There was a much bigger reason for her tautness.

She was trailing the vampire who'd destroyed everything, every*one* who had ever mattered to her.

And Nicole had lost her quarry.

That didn't happen. She wasn't just a vampire hunter, she was a psi tracker. It was her job to follow vampires and discover where they holed up during the day, so that they could be slain while the sun was up. There was always a risk of confrontation while she followed one, but even at night, Nicole had been able to defeat them.

But this female vampire might be the oldest Nicole had ever hunted and they gained power with age.

She didn't have much information. That bothered her. All she knew was that the vampire was using the name Mary Beth Danner, that she'd recently returned to Los Angeles, and that she was a cold-blooded killer. The other questions remained unanswered.

Location of lair—unknown. Associates and allies—unknown. Vampire clan allegiance—unknown.

She stopped short. Ahead, a gate hung open on the side of one of the warehouses. A closer look showed that the chain and padlock that had kept it shut were broken. They dangled, nearly brushing the sidewalk.

Reaching under her black leather jacket, she touched her knives—one wooden, one metal—to reassure herself. It might be a trap, but Nicole had the ability to conceal her presence, making herself invisible for all intents and purposes, and she'd been using it since she'd found her target earlier tonight.

Besides, the vampire had left the nightclub with a human male and that meant Nicole didn't have much time to think things through. Even now, Mary Beth could be killing the guy.

The thought of the vampire taking another life made Nicole's stomach roll over, and pulling her metal dagger, she slipped through the gate.

Bright lights lit up the side of the building, the loading dock, and the concrete that filled the space between the fence and the warehouse, but there were still plenty of shadows. Tightening her hold on the hilt, Nicole continued forward. She reached the edge of the structure, hesitated, and then turned the corner.

Nothing. Where the hell was the vampire?

"Behind you." The feminine voice came soft and slow and laced with sarcasm.

Stiffening, Nicole pivoted. And looked at the monster from a million nightmares. The human stood beside the vampire, staring sightlessly off into the distance. "You can see me," Nicole said and immediately felt stupid.

Mary Beth's smile made her appear angelic and that was such a lie. "How astute. You're not powerful enough to conceal yourself from me."

Nicole's jaw tightened. *How astute* must be the old fashioned way of saying *duh*. "You knew I was outside the club—the human was a lure," she said as realization dawned.

Mary Beth's grin widened and she gave a toss of her blond hair. "Waiting for you to gather courage grew tedious. I have better things to do."

Nicole opened her mouth and shut it without saying anything. This entire conversation was surreal. She was being insulted by a vampire wearing salmon-colored jeans and a white tank top, and Nicole couldn't seem to take action. Maybe it was some kind of delayed shock to finally confronting this killer, but it—

The vampire sighed and gazed heavenward. Then she looked Nicole dead in the eye, extended her fangs and talons, and turned toward the guy standing passively next to her.

Damn it to hell. Her choices were gone. Nicole pulled her second dagger and charged. So much for strategy or finesse.

Mary Beth pushed the man aside. Her claws slashed downward as soon as Nicole was in range and she had to duck to avoid taking a hit.

She came up, wooden dagger in her left hand, metal blade in her right and looked for an opening. There wasn't one.

Nicole jumped back, avoiding another strike. Before she could balance her weight, the vampire was in her face and Nicole spun away to avoid taking a talon to her neck.

Mary Beth was fast. Faster than any vampire Nicole had faced before and she—

Air touched her cheek as Nicole dove to the ground. She rolled to her feet, but couldn't find the other woman. Quickly, she whirled.

Just in time. The claw left a six-inch scar on the sleeve of her leather jacket.

She hated being on the defensive. Nicole ran again at Mary Beth, but the vampire seemed to disappear as Nicole stabbed downward with the metal knife. With the strength she'd used, hitting empty space left her unsteady.

Before she could regain her equilibrium, two hands shoved at her back. Nicole flailed her arms, trying to keep from falling.

She stumbled into the loading dock with enough force to drive the air from her lungs, but Nicole didn't wait until she could breathe. Spinning, she kicked out and connected with a knee.

Not hard enough. But it bought Nicole time to regroup and regain some air.

Mary Beth didn't have her fangs down.

Nicole barely registered that when she was dodging again. Why would a vampire halve its arsenal? Nicole kicked out, but this time the maneuver was expected and finding nothing except air threw her off-balance.

Mary Beth grabbed her and tossed her.

Even as she went airborne, Nicole knew the landing was not going to be pretty. She tried to keep her body from tensing and tightened her hold on her daggers.

It didn't help. The impact was enough to jar both knives loose. Her head connected with the cement and left her dazed. Her brain ordered her to move and tried to prod her body into motion, but her muscles couldn't obey the command.

Her vision was hazy when Mary Beth sat on her chest, pinning Nicole's wrists to the ground above her head with one hand. Nicole tried to shake the other woman off. Tried and failed.

Adrenaline drove the world into sharp focus.

Mary Beth's eyes glowed blue-white as she smiled—no fangs—and drew back her arm. The talons lengthened farther.

Oh, God. Nicole fought harder, but all she could manage to do was twist and buck. It wasn't enough to dislodge the vampire or for Nicole to get her arms free.

Damn it, she had unfinished business. She couldn't die yet. She couldn't die.

Chapter Two

NICOLE CONTINUED TO STRUGGLE while her mind raced to find a solution. In her peripheral vision, she saw a blur of motion.

Mary Beth was yanked off her.

Nicole didn't hesitate, she scrambled upright in time to see the vampire tumble to the ground nearly twenty feet away. With an audible gulp, Nicole turned to confront the latest threat.

Demon. A damn powerful one.

This had just gone from bad to worse and she was unarmed. Nicole braced herself, but he didn't make any kind of threatening gesture. Instead, he ran his gaze over her from head to foot and back again. "Are you hurt?" he asked.

She stared, nonplussed by the question.

"I asked—"

"I'm fine." Maybe she was having some kind of dream. First the surreal conversation with a vampire, now a demon saving her life and checking to see if she was okay. Yeah, she had to be sleeping or something.

He looked away from her and cursed. She followed his gaze and saw Mary Beth was gone. Extending her senses as far as possible, Nicole scanned for the other woman, but came up empty.

"Where she'd go?" she demanded.

"I don't know."

Every cell in her body began to tingle. His voice was deep, slightly raspy, and so freaking sexy her nipples peaked. The reaction pissed her off. Demons were every bit as much an enemy to humans as vampires were.

But her anger derailed when she looked at him. This time she didn't only see demon, she saw male.

He was at least six feet tall with broad shoulders, muscular legs, and shaggy, dark hair. His clothes were casual—a pair of faded jeans, banged up running shoes, a gray T-shirt, and a black leather jacket. It was his eyes, though, that captured her attention. Not the dim red glow—Nicole had seen that particular demon trait enough so that it wasn't novel—but something else. Something that was...him.

Her heart pounded faster, her breathing became shallow. She wanted to trace her fingers over his high cheekbones, to run her tongue over his lips and taste him, she wanted to see his body and discover if he was as muscular as he looked. She gazed at his hands and imagined them stroking her skin. Teasing her breasts. Sliding between her legs.

Arousal shuddered through her, more intense than anything she'd ever experienced. Nicole took a step forward, the urge to press her mouth to his shoulder and bite was so strong, she couldn't stop herself.

He moved back, maintaining the distance between them. It was the growl of complaint she made that halted Nicole in her tracks and shook her out of the daze.

What was she thinking? Biting him?

"Why are you here?" she demanded, using anger in an attempt to hide her reaction.

"You're welcome."

Nicole nearly snarled again, but cursed instead. "I didn't need help. I can take down a vampire."

The demon scowled and the red flared brighter in his eyes. "You shouldn't have needed help, but you did. She would have killed you in a few more seconds."

True, but he was *a demon*. She didn't want to owe him and she hated that he saw her as weak, as someone in need of rescue. Nicole wanted him to think of her as his equal, but she wasn't sure why she cared. "I'd have come up with something and gotten free," she said, but there wasn't much conviction in her voice.

His frown deepened. "You should never have been pinned at all. You're stronger than—" Some of the ferocity left his face. "You do know what you are, right?"

It was Nicole's turn to glower. He didn't have to bring it up. "Yes."

His brows rose. "Really?" Skepticism was plain. "You know you're half demon?"

"Yes." Nicole noticed his hair had fallen into his eyes, and unable to stop herself, she stepped forward with the intention of brushing it aside. She didn't make it two feet before he backed up, keeping her more than an arm's length away. "What? I'm not going to bite."

"But you want to," he said sounding grim.

Nicole opened her mouth to rip him for his arrogance, but then she remembered. She *had* wanted to bite him.

Looking for a diversion, anything to get off this topic, her gaze fell on the human standing frozen where Mary Beth had left him. "He should be coming around. The vampire has to be too far away by now to hold the mind control."

The demon shrugged, the movement of his shoulders making heat rise again. An image flashed through her mind, both of them on top of the loading dock. Naked. Her teeth sinking into skin where his neck and shoulder met. She could imagine how his eyes would flare brighter, the red glow becoming dominant over the light-colored irises. And Nicole could picture him biting her in return. The fantasy alone was enough to make her shift, trying to find relief.

"If you know you're demon," he said, his voice yanking her from her sexual daydream, "why didn't you use your powers? Why did you make me rush in to save you?"

"Half demon," Nicole corrected testily. She was human in every way that mattered, but while she'd love to be able to deny her demon genes, she couldn't. "I didn't know you were there, so how the hell could I make you *rush in to save me?*" It irked her to say that, damn it. "And I don't have any powers except the ability to track."

For a long moment, he stared at her and she couldn't read anything on his face. She cleared her throat and put her hands in the pockets of her jeans. Maybe this way she could keep from reaching for him. "Why *are* you here?"

His lips tightened and Nicole didn't think he would answer this time either, but he surprised her. "I'm hunting the vampire."

That stunned her into silence. She knew demons and vampires weren't on the best of terms, but from what she'd seen, they worked to avoid each other rather than risk conflict. "Is it personal or do you just want to kill some vamp?"

This time he growled. The sound was soft, but it made her nipples go taut. She closed her eyes and counted to ten. When she opened them, she noticed he was staring at her breasts and his eyes were a brighter red.

Her breathing quickened and her body reacted to the intensity of his gaze. He raised his head until they looked each other in the eye. It wasn't one-sided, this desire. He wanted her just as much. This time he moved toward her and her lips parted. Finally she was going to—

The demon stopped short, muttered something in a language she didn't understand, and retreated. He had his jaw clenched tightly enough to make a muscle tic, and heaven help her, Nicole wanted to go to him. She wanted to soothe him.

She was in huge trouble here and she should be grateful that he managed restraint. If he didn't, they'd probably be having sex on the warehouse loading dock right now. When that idea turned her on, Nicole forcibly brought her mind back from fantasyland. "Well?" She cleared her throat, trying to get rid of the huskiness. "Are you after the vampire for some personal grudge or do you kill them for sport?"

"I'm not indiscriminately killing vampires." He sounded peeved. "But no, it's not personal. It's my job."

"What do you—"

"That's all I'm saying."

"Fine. Since killing Mary Beth is a job to you, you can back the hell off. She's mine and it *is* personal for me. Got it, demon?"

"Mary Beth is what you're calling the vampire?"

There was a note of laughter in his voice, enough for Nicole to yank her hands out of her pockets and take a step toward him. Not to touch him this time, but so she could let him know she didn't appreciate his humor. But, of course, he maintained the distance separating them. "Mary Beth," she bit out the words, "is what she's calling herself."

He shrugged. "Mary Beth is better than Mabilia, I suppose."

"Mab—" Nicole stopped short. The bastard had diverted her. On purpose. "Nice try. It almost worked. I want your promise to stay away from the vampire. I'm killing her."

His face went hard. "No."

That one word and the tone he used told Nicole there was no compromising with him. She'd just have to find Mary Beth first, but she had to make sure that she wouldn't be at a disadvantage. "Why did you ask me why I didn't use my powers? Not every half demon has them. Do they?"

He seemed suspicious, but lowered his arms to his sides and went along with the change in topic. "Yes, they do. Your powers might be weakened by your human blood, but you belong to one of the strongest branches and that makes you more than a match for any vampire."

Nicole was aware of the tiers of demons. "So my father was from one of the more powerful castes, huh?"

He nodded, but didn't add anything and disappointment stabbed through her. She'd never met her father; he hadn't been part of her life. All she knew was what her mother had told her—that she'd been fathered by a demon and that she'd share more with Nicole when she was older. That day hadn't come.

Curiosity surged and she tamped it down. Asking about her father would reveal a vulnerability, and she knew better than to open herself up like that. Demons couldn't be trusted. They lied and manipulated and used any leverage they were given.

She'd already handed him too many weapons to use against her. Nicole grimaced briefly. There was nothing she could do about it and she was going to open herself up with her next question anyway. "Can—"

The human moved and Nicole shut up to watch him warily. What did he recall? Depending on what kind of mind control the vampire had wielded, he might be aware of everything that had gone on or he might know nothing. Or anywhere in between. He appeared groggy as he looked around, but his gaze sharpened when he spotted the two of them. "Dude, where's Mary Beth?"

The demon held up his right hand, palm facing the human. "Mary Beth received a phone call and had to leave, remember?"

For an instant, the guy appeared confused, but that cleared quickly. "Oh, right. Her brother got arrested and she had to bail him out."

Nicole shot a quick glance at the demon and caught his smirk. A smart ass—she might end up liking him despite what he was.

"I'm not sure where we're at," the human said. "Which way's the Tiki?"

The demon gave him directions and the guy took off. Nicole did a quick scan, but there was only a stray person or two and no human gangs. He should make it back to the club safely.

She turned to the demon. He had his arms crossed over his chest again and was watching her. Nicole couldn't read his expression or guess what he was thinking and that should have made her uneasy, but it didn't.

"What's your name?" he asked.

"Nicole Ruiz." She cursed herself immediately. It wasn't that names had power—that was an old wives' tale—but giving information to some unknown demon was stupid. Even if he was so sexy she'd probably go up in flames if he let her get within touching distance. "What's yours?"

"Daktan, but I prefer Dak," he said.

She could hear reluctance and displeasure in his voice. That made them even and it improved Nicole's mood.

"Do you go by Nikki?"

The growl was low, and because she made no attempt at disguise, it came out sounding very demon-like. He was treading on sacred ground, and while it was inadvertent, it still made her mad. Her mom had called her by that nickname; she wouldn't allow anyone else to use it. "No. Nicole. Always and forever Nicole. Got it?"

Dak nodded. "You hate being called Nikki. I got it."

"Great. Now you're going to use it just to rile me, aren't you? I should have kept my mouth shut."

"I won't." He sounded as solemn as if he were making a vow. "It's not my intention to irritate you."

Something about the way he said that made heat flare deep inside her again. This time she didn't realize she'd moved forward until he stepped away. Nicole fisted her hands at her sides. Why did she have this need to touch him? And that's what she wanted—to feel the heat of his skin against hers.

Get back to business. She'd been at a disadvantage against the vampire and that was unacceptable. Maybe she hated her demon heritage, but Nicole wanted revenge more than anything else in the world and she'd do whatever it took to kill Mary Beth. Maybe she didn't know Dak, but there was no one else she could ask and he *had* saved her tonight.

"Can you teach me how to use my demon powers?" Her question came out quietly.

"Can I? Yes. Will I? No. The vampire's mine, Nicole. Stay clear." Dak turned and walked away.

Chapter Three

DAK FUCKING HATED WIZARDS. Humans with power were bad enough in general, but when one of them used his magic to interfere with Dak's job, it really pissed him off.

With a scowl, he sidestepped the person talking on his cell phone. The streets were crowded on a Saturday night, but the throng didn't interfere with his ability to track Nicole. Nothing could. It wasn't a matter of energy imprints. He and Nicole had something more than that, a connection that would allow them to find each other anywhere at any time. Their own personal homing beacon.

Dak's frown deepened. He'd planned to avoid Nicole, to stay as far away from her as possible, but Mabilia—Mary Beth—had destroyed that intention.

At some point between when the vampire had disappeared last night and when Dak had begun his search tonight, Mary Beth had hired a wizard. Those bastards didn't work cheap, and it had probably cost her an arm and a leg. But then a spell that concealed her from demons took a ton of power to pull off and was worth a lot.

But it wasn't absolute. Maybe *he* couldn't locate the vampire, but the wizard's spell hadn't blocked half demons. That left Dak with two choices, either stick close to Nicole or concede defeat. The second option wasn't one he'd entertained long.

A gap opened in the crowd just long enough for him to see the sway of Nicole's hips as she walked ahead of him. Heat surged through him so fast and so strongly, there was no way to stop it.

He could go to her, put an arm around her waist, and pull her against him. She might be surprised, but Nicole wouldn't fight him, not the way she'd looked at him last night, not the way she'd reacted to him. Feeling her body pressed to his, finding someplace where he could strip her, explore her, taste her, and yeah, bite her— Dak shuddered with need.

Nicole stopped abruptly and looked over her shoulder, her eyes scanning faces.

Damn, she'd probably picked up his arousal. She might not know exactly what she'd sensed yet, but she'd figure it out quickly. Dak worked to get his desire under control before she zeroed in on him. He wasn't sure how successful he'd been until she resumed walking.

Shaking his head, Dak followed. One conversation. One conversation while he'd kept her more than five feet away and he was already dealing with the repercussions.

If this assignment hadn't come from his king...

But it had and Dak was stuck until he killed the vampire. He'd just have to finish the job tonight.

No problem.

He pushed his fingers through his hair, driving it off his face, before lowering his arms to his sides and blowing out a long breath. The mission should have been over and done with last night. He'd had his hands on the vampire, it would have been an easy thing to kill her in that moment.

Except he'd been running on instinct, not intellect.

Nicole came to a sudden halt again. He knew the instant her awareness sharpened and followed her gaze. There were too many people in his way to see anything and he was forced to extend out beyond his body. He only needed a moment to spot the vampire.

Dak came back to earth with a lurch. The situation got better and better. Mary Beth had fed recently. If the vampire—

Nicole went from standing to threading her way quickly through the crowd. He followed. Mary Beth must be on the move again and he hadn't known. *Fucking wizards.*

Something played at the periphery of his senses, something that made him edgy. His skin tingled and not in a good way. Dak looked around, but nothing seemed off. What was he getting? There was a feeling of energy and his brain raced, searching for answers.

Blast amulet. Mary Beth had bought a blast amulet from the wizard and that gave her the power to direct an invisible current—

The burst hit him hard. Dak stumbled into the side of a building and clutched at the brick, trying to stay upright. His nerve endings screamed, his body spasmed as it fought the magic. His vision went black, but he wasn't unconscious. He just wished he was because it wouldn't hurt this badly if his brain shut off.

He wasn't sure how much time passed before he regained awareness of his surroundings. Dak didn't think he'd been out too long, not with tremors continuing to shudder through him. His shield was down, making him visible, and humans were giving him a wide berth as they walked past.

The wizard Mary Beth had hired was good. And damn powerful. He had to be or the energy wouldn't have hit with as much force as it had.

Dak made an attempt to push himself away from the building, but his arms gave out and he collapsed back against the structure, the brick abrading his cheek. A couple more minutes and he'd try again.

How the hell had the vampire known he was there? His concealment hadn't slipped until the energy had slammed into him, yet somehow she'd known. It gave her another advantage. All he had on his side was Nicole's ability to track and the time it would take for the amulet to recharge before Mary Beth could wield it again.

Dak's eyes opened fast as a thought struck. The energy block might be on full demons only, but that didn't mean the amulet hadn't been tuned to affect anyone with demon blood.

Had Nicole been hurt?

His sluggish senses refused to work, but Dak willed them into compliance. It took a minute for his mind to find her—unharmed. And she was far enough away to tell him that he'd been out of it for more than a couple of minutes.

Pushing off from the wall, he locked his knees to stay upright. As soon as he could walk, Dak moved.

Within a couple of blocks, he'd healed enough to stop swaying and for his brain to start working again. The wizard-for-hire was strong and that meant the amulet was going to recharge faster than he'd originally thought. If Mary Beth sent out another blast before he had time to fully recover from the first, she'd put him on the ground.

Dak increased his speed and ignored his body's protest. Everything ached, even his hair, but there wasn't time to wait.

Nicole was in pursuit, and as long as she didn't know how to use her abilities, she was an easy target for the vampire. He might be slow, but he'd figured it out. Mary Beth hadn't realized he was there—there was absolutely no way for her to sense him—and there were no other demons in the vicinity.

Except Nicole.

He'd bet big the blast had been meant for her, and he was simply collateral damage.

Wizards were bastards, but Dak had to appreciate that in this case. Sure, it was possible there'd merely been a misunderstanding, but he doubted it. The human had cheated Mary Beth. She thought she had an amulet geared for anyone of demon blood and she was wrong.

Deciding he was in no shape to consider what kind of games the wizards were playing, Dak cloaked himself and concentrated on Nicole. Her accelerated heart rate and adrenaline buzz made his own speed up. He broke into a jog.

The neighborhood, which hadn't been great to begin with, went downhill rapidly, and she was stationary now. Dak dug for more speed.

Nicole's turmoil buffeted him. The side effects of their link were unexpected and unwelcome. He worked to limit the connection, keeping a line on her, but nothing more.

As the bond began to narrow, Dak felt Nicole reach for him, trying to hold it fully open. Dissonance rose. She didn't know what she was doing, but it made it hard for him to shut her out. He did it anyway and ran faster.

The entrance to the park registered seconds after he passed it. Dak screeched to a halt. Yes, here. He felt Nicole. Cautiously, he walked through the opening, fighting the instinct that urged him to rush to her side and damn the consequences. He had the element of surprise, and he wasn't giving that up.

Silently, Dak wended through the playground equipment. He found Nicole at the back of the park. Mary Beth was stalking her, forcing Nicole to retreat, and with a chain-link fence maybe twenty feet behind her, it wouldn't take long before she was cornered.

He ran his gaze over Nicole. Blood trickled down her neck.

A growl began low in his throat, but he stopped it before it became audible. He couldn't contain the red haze that filled his brain.

A burst of preternatural speed put him between Nicole and the vampire. He chanced a quick glance at Nicole's injury. She'd taken a slash over an artery, but it wasn't deep and it was already mostly healed.

Dak raised his gaze to meet Nicole's and became lost in her brown eyes. He started to reach out, wanting to trail his fingers over the wound and finish its healing. Hell, he wanted to feel the warmth of her skin against his fingers and reassure himself that she was well.

The blow to his back sent him stumbling, but his leather jacket prevented injury. He scowled, pissed at himself for letting his mind shut down. For fucking forgetting the enemy was there and dangerous.

Whirling, he faced the vampire. She snarled at him—no fangs, but he didn't expect to see them—and the rest of her arsenal was on full display. Hoping it would hide the fact he was too depleted to risk a battle, Dak did his own posturing. He'd been born to the strongest branch of demon and there were some visual cues—like the intensity of the red burning in his eyes as well as the length and strength of his own talons.

If Mary Beth was intimidated, he saw no sign of it, but she didn't launch another assault. "This is the second time you've interfered."

"I won't let you hurt her," he said. Unbidden, and despite his effort to sound unconcerned, there was a growl underlying his words. Dak hated not being in perfect command of himself especially when he needed to be. A vampire would know demons had trouble thinking clearly with emotion running hot and he'd revealed his weakness to this one. She didn't miss it either, not judging by the way her lips curved.

"I've been minding my own business," Mary Beth said conversationally. "She continues to hunt me."

Dak shifted when Nicole moved, keeping her securely behind his back. He wanted the two of them out of here ASAP. If he didn't get Nicole safe before the vampire's amulet recharged, they were both in deep shit. Mary Beth would be able to kill him while he was down and Nicole didn't have the skills to fight off the other woman.

Stay put, he sent to Nicole. It wasn't until he felt her shock that he realized what he'd done. Mistake number two in less than five minutes.

"Did you just talk in my head?" Nicole poked his shoulder, but Dak didn't turn.

Mary Beth smiled. "Well, isn't this interesting?"

Fucking great. Bluffing would get him nowhere—vampires knew too much about demons—but he tried anyway. If he didn't, it would be the same as an admission. "What's interesting about telepathy?" Dak asked, trying to sound bored. "Your kind use it as easily as mine."

He battled within himself. The instinct to protect Nicole urged him to attack the vampire. His brain whispered warnings that he was in no shape to engage Mary Beth until he healed from the blast he'd taken earlier.

"That is true, but she's not exactly a demon, is she?" Mary Beth's talons flexed as she gestured to where Nicole stood. "Not when she's without awareness of how to use her powers. Since she's not much more than a human, only one thing would allow you to communicate with her mentally."

"What's she talking about?" Nicole whispered. It didn't matter. Mary Beth heard.

"Didn't you tell her?" the vampire asked with mock surprise.

Dak took a step forward before he could stop himself. Sweat chilled his skin, adding to the sickening dread. There was nothing he could do to prevent the words that were coming. It didn't take a genius to guess that Nicole wasn't going to be any happier about the situation than he was.

"Shame on you," Mary Beth said and tsked softly. "Don't you think this psi tracker should know you're her mate?"

Chapter Four

NICOLE SAGGED AS TENSION LEFT her muscles. She'd expected some kind of bombshell from the vampire and had warned herself to show no reaction, but this? Totally anticlimactic.

Except Dak remained rigid.

If what Mary Beth had said meant nothing, wouldn't he have relaxed, too? Wouldn't he be laughing at the feeble attempt to stir up trouble? But he wasn't and Nicole stiffened again. What did this mate thing mean? Was it something she'd be concerned about if she understood it?

She almost jerked when she felt Dak brush against her mind and then she heard him talking in her head.

We need to leave as soon as we can.

Nicole nearly answered aloud, but stopped herself and tried sending her reply. *Why?*

What she got from him next didn't come in words, it was more like she suddenly had what he wanted her to know. She quashed her satisfaction at communicating telepathically and paid attention to what he transmitted. It took less than an instant to understand the vampire had zapped him with some sort of weapon, one that was recharging as they spoke, and could take him out of the fight completely if she fired it again before he recovered.

Nicole didn't want to care. She could kill the enemy and they'd both be fine. Except she didn't believe she could win against Mary Beth, not after the past two nights, and simply imagining anything happening to Dak made her hurt.

"Nice try, but Nicole's not upset," Dak said. "No points for you, Mabilia."

The vampire bared her fangs at the sarcasm. It was a fearsome expression, but Nicole sensed Dak's amusement. Maybe his face gave away his humor—she couldn't see from behind his back—but Mary Beth snarled and retracted her canines.

It left Nicole confused. A vampire's teeth were formidable weapons. Why pull them back in? It wasn't only tonight either. Last night had been the same. No fangs.

Demon blood is poisonous to vampires, Dak sent.

This time he hadn't given her advance warning and Nicole had to suppress a flinch. Her relief at not reacting didn't last long. He'd read her mind and that didn't make her feel warm inside. Especially when she remembered the things she'd fantasized about doing with him.

"But then it hasn't been a good night for you on any front," Dak said to Mary Beth with a shrug. "That wizard really screwed you over. I hope you didn't pay him too much."

"The wizard didn't—"

"Didn't he?" Dak interrupted. "Then why are Nicole and I standing here when you wanted to be invisible to us?"

Last night had been weird and tonight was turning out to be every bit as bizarre. Wizards? Wizards were fictional—or at least she'd always believed that—but Dak and the vampire were throwing the word around as if it was a given that they were real. What else didn't she know?

Humans are coming. We'll use them as a diversion to get away, Dak told her.

After sending him an acknowledgment, she tuned out the exchange. Mary Beth and Dak were just snarking at each other anyway. Instead, Nicole scanned until she found normal people. Judging by the number and what she felt from their energy, she suspected a group of gang members was headed this way.

She focused back on the conversation fast when Mary Beth said, "The wizard might not have blocked half demons, but he prevented you from tracking me, didn't he? You're using her—" the vampire gestured again with her talons "—to find me. And the amulet worked on you. You're weak, demon, and as soon as the stone recharges, you're dead."

Whatever Dak would have said was lost when a burst of laughter intruded. The instant Mary Beth turned her head, Dak grabbed Nicole's hand and then he moved. Fast. The world around her blurred, but to her surprise, she could keep up with him. She'd never realized... But then she didn't know a lot, it seemed.

First things first, though. "Is she chasing us?"

"No," Dak said, not bothering to glance over his shoulder. "We're both cloaked."

Nicole wasn't ready to assume that meant they were invisible. "She's an old vampire and they're more powerful than average."

Dak's hand tightened around hers. "Not old enough, not when we're both strong demons."

"She knew I was there last night while I had my energy concealed."

His grimness washed over her, and a heartbeat later, he extended his own cloak, wrapping her inside with him. Physically, they were no closer than before, but it ratcheted up the intimacy enough to make Nicole shiver. Hoping he hadn't picked up on that, she asked, "Why are we running if she can't sense us now?"

"Because we need to be out of range of the amulet."

"*We* need to be out of range or *you* do?"

He didn't reply and Nicole decided that meant it was him. The world continued to rush by and she tried to assimilate that. Sure, she'd run before. She'd even run to save her life, but she'd never attained this kind of speed. Amazing. It reminded her that there were many potential talents she didn't know about, but that Dak could teach her. Looking at his profile, she decided to bring that up later—there were other things on the agenda.

The mate thing for one, but that made her uneasy and Nicole wasn't ready to face it yet. "There are really wizards around? In Los Angeles?"

"Yes."

She needed more than a one-word confirmation. Nicole scowled. "Why didn't I know about them?"

"Maybe because they're more secretive than demons."

More secretive? That was hard to believe because demons—and vampires, too—did their best to make sure humans didn't believe in them. Neither group was above using mind control to ensure they remained under the radar, either. "Are wizards aligned with vampires?"

Dak glanced over briefly. "Wizards aren't aligned with anyone. They're out for themselves first, last, and always. Remember that."

A demon telling her not to trust a wizard definitely fell under the heading of irony. Demons lied easily, manipulated for fun, and cheated whenever they could. It was their nature. And yet she'd put her faith in Dak anyway. Nicole grimaced, but she tightened her hold on his hand. No doubt she was an idiot, but she believed in *this* demon.

She just hoped it wasn't lust overcoming her common sense.

Lust, yeah. Nicole's scowl deepened. As much as she didn't want to ask, she had better. Squaring her shoulders, she took a deep breath and said, "Explain this mate thing to me."

Dak flinched. It wasn't physical—the reaction was purely mental and she'd felt it. Nicole wasn't sure what she thought of that, but it did put them on more even ground. "Well?" she prompted.

"It isn't the best time for this discussion." He took another corner fast enough to leave her dizzy.

"It's as good as any," she disagreed when her head stopped swimming. "Mary Beth clearly expected to cause trouble between us when she said that. I want to know why."

"What sane demon can understand a vampire's motives?"

Nicole stared at him, counting on him to safely maneuver them both through the streets. Dak had evaded the question, but he hadn't lied. He could have made up some story, and if it were plausible, she'd have believed him. Yeah, desire had left her stupid, but maybe not as dumb as she'd feared.

He hadn't lied to her.

And his evasion hadn't been all that slick either. "Come on, Dak, give."

"You humans are always a pain," he muttered with disgust.

The tone made her grind her teeth in an effort to rein in her temper. "I'm not human, remember?" And it galled her to admit that.

"You might as well be. Only a human would want to have a conversation like this now."

Her jaw clenched as she struggled to contain the torrent of words she wanted to hurl at him. If she said anything, he'd take advantage of an argument to distract her and Nicole wouldn't make things that simple for him. When she had control, she said, "We've been running at mach speed forever and you have us cloaked. The vampire shouldn't be any danger to us."

She sensed his intention to stop an instant before he did it and Nicole thought he'd given her the information to save her from a hard yank. He'd interceded twice to protect her, so she was pretty sure it wasn't her hormones ascribing honorable motives to him.

Dak's eyes met hers, the red glow nearly bright enough to obscure the amber of his irises. "If I answer your question, you'll accuse me of lying. I'll cite proof. You won't believe it, and unable to stop myself, I'll try to convince you I'm telling the truth. This is a fairly busy street."

"Yeah, so? What does that have to do with anything?"

With a gentle tug, he pulled her against him and then turned her until her back pressed into the side of a building. His body was hard and Nicole couldn't stop herself from putting her hands on his shoulders and arching her hips more firmly into him. She wanted Dak. Now. Standing up. On the street.

Voice intense, Dak said, "Yes, just like that. I could have you here, but if you think I can keep us cloaked when I have my cock deep inside you, you're greatly overestimating my control."

Nicole wanted to be furious. Never mind the crudeness, the assumption that she'd be that easy galled her—especially since it was true. At least it was true *with him*. Only, no matter how hard she tried, she couldn't manage to become angry. She couldn't even hang on to her pride.

"If we went far enough down the alley, no one would see us."

The red in his eyes eclipsed the amber now. Nicole had no doubt her own eyes were glowing, too, but she wanted him every bit as much as he appeared to want her. She angled her head and leaned in to kiss him.

"Stop."

Her lips nearly brushed his. "Why?"

"This lust, it's part of our being mates."

Dak's words came out thick and husky and the rasp was so damn sexy, Nicole shivered. "This is a problem because?"

"Because once we have sex, there'll be no one else for either of us. We'll be mated, tied to each other exclusively until death, and Nicole, demons live thousands of years."

Chapter Five

DAK STEPPED PAST NICOLE WHEN she gestured him into her apartment and looked around, curious about the insights her home would give him. The walls were a neutral off-white shade, but nothing else in the room was bland. One couch was pink, the other an oddly shaped orange thing, and a third had straight lines and wild, mixed up colors. A pink lamp reached toward the ceiling and a glass coffee table stood in the center of it all.

He heard Nicole close the door and moved deeper into the room. That's when he detected her wards. Dak scowled. They needed to be strengthened.

Heading to the corner of the living room, he picked up the crystal there, closed his eyes, and quietly intoned the spell to bolster its power. The next ward was in the kitchen. This space was plain and had no signs of any personality. Even the dish towels were white.

She trailed after him, not saying anything, but he was aware of her with every step he took. They needed to talk, but he shouldn't be here. Dak knew that being alone together could lead to things between him and Nicole exploding out of control before he could stop it. Hell, he'd been on the edge on the street. Coming to her home was definitely a bad idea.

The third crystal was in the bathroom. More color—a shower curtain with some unusual dark pink, gold, and black swirls and dark pink towels.

In contrast, her bedroom was nearly colorless. The silver bedspread was only slightly darker than the off-white walls, and while there was a colorful acrylic hanging above the bed, it was small and not enough to liven up the space. Dak considered Nicole. Who was this woman? Two rooms a riot of color and shapes; two rooms boring to an extreme.

Shaking his head, Dak went to the last crystal. As soon as he finished the spell, he returned the ward to the corner, straightened and turned. Nicole was right there and he sucked in a harsh breath as desire rushed through him.

The wall was at his back, there was nowhere for him to go to put space between them, and Nicole wasn't moving.

Two steps and he could have her on the bed, his body over hers. Two short steps.

He drank her in. Her dark hair was pulled back, away from her face and the brown of her eyes was nearly overpowered by the red glow, proof he wasn't the only one aroused. High cheekbones tempted him to run his thumbs across them, a gently elfin chin had a slight indent that he wanted to kiss, and those incredibly full lips... He remembered how close her mouth had been to his not that long ago, remembered how much he wanted to explore her.

She'd taken off her leather jacket, leaving her in a black tank top and jeans. The clothing was practical, but on this woman, it was so fucking sexy, Dak felt his self-command slip.

Would she be passive in bed like the bland bedroom or would Nicole be wild like her colorful living room? Dak's money was on wild, and the desire to confirm it burned through him. "Step back," he warned her, voice low. She didn't. "Step back, because if you don't, we'll be mated in less than ten minutes and I'll be pissed about that."

Her gaze jerked up to his and that's when Dak realized she'd been staring at his erection. A feeling of inevitability washed over him and tightened around his throat like a noose.

He wasn't sure he cared. Not at the moment.

Docile or wanton, Nicole would make him come hard. Eying the distance to the bed, he decided he could get his jeans unzipped before they reached it. It would be easier if she were wearing a skirt, but Dak guessed less than a minute to get her pants open and pushed down to her thighs. He could strip her naked for round two.

Nicole's eyes widened and she took a giant stride away from him. Wise woman.

"We should go sit down in the living room," she suggested and didn't waste any time getting away from him.

Dak watched her go. He needed a minute—maybe more—to regain some calm. That had been close. Too close. As much as he wanted to blame Nicole for his near-loss of control, he couldn't. She was as helpless against the onslaught as he was, maybe more so since she didn't understand exactly what was happening.

If he'd been smart, he never would have come here. Hell, if he had even one brain cell that wasn't overloaded with desire, he'd walk out the door right now.

Since he remained stationary, Dak figured his mind was toast. What a mess. He drove both hands into his hair and tugged, but it didn't make his head start working any better. Shit, hell, and damn. And the reason he'd agreed to come here to begin with needed to be discussed. Nicole wanted explanations about demon mates and he owed it to her. It wasn't as if he could drop a bomb like that without having to deal with the fallout.

With a soundless growl, Dak returned to the living room. Nicole stood next to the coffee table, and when she sensed his presence, her chin came up. Her glare didn't intimidate him, but it did cause the desire he'd barely contained to surge again.

"What has you pissed off?" he asked. "The fact I assumed you wouldn't tell me no if I took you down to the bed? Given the way your thoughts have run since we met and the mate connection, it's not arrogance."

The red in her eyes flared brighter. "Why do you act as if being mated to me is a fate worse than death? It's insulting."

For an instant, Dak could only stare. *That's* what had her furious? "You're taking offense and you don't even know what mating entails. It's not only sexual exclusivity, it's a merging on all levels. It means we'll be in each other's minds—sharing thoughts and reading emotions will be effortless. Do you want me to have that kind of tie with you? It's damn intimate and I'm not thrilled with the idea of giving you that much of me."

She strode toward him, temper hot. He almost didn't move, but at the last minute, self-preservation kicked in and Dak backed up. Nicole stopped in her tracks. "That's why you wouldn't let me close to you yesterday, this mate thing. But I don't get it; what's the big deal about distance?"

At least her anger was gone. "Proximity affects the bond. The more time we spend together, the stronger it gets. The closer we are to each other physically, the more powerful the lure becomes. If we have sex, the bond locks into place and lasts until death. Thousands of years with no one else."

That reignited her temper. "And you want others."

Shit, he was fucked on this question and it was one for which he wasn't prepared. He'd expected her ask how it could happen or deny such a thing existed. Dak should have realized, though, that Nicole would feel the same possessiveness toward him that he felt for her. Maybe she'd been raised human, but she was a female demon with the instincts to match.

Sticking his hands into the pockets of his leather jacket to keep from reaching for her, to keep from soothing her ire with touches and kisses, he said, "I'm twenty-nine. Not two hundred and twenty-nine, not two thousand and twenty-nine—only twenty-nine. I'm not ready to be tied to anyone. A thousand years from now, I'm sure I'd be thrilled to find you, but we're both too young to be bonded to each other for life."

"You assume thousands of years, but I'm half human. My life span is around eighty years. You'd be free in no time."

He ignored her sarcasm and answered seriously. "I don't care what you think you know about half demons, it's wrong. Those who died at some normal human age? They're the ones who never accessed their full powers. Believe me, if we mate, you'll be connected to your magic."

Nicole smirked. "Right. I have sex with you and I become damn near immortal."

His own temper began to burn. "I'm the one trying to prevent us from becoming lovers. With next to no help from you." That made her angrier yet which pissed Dak off even more. "You keep wanting to touch me, to kiss me, to bite me. I know it, Nicole. You can't lie to me. You pictured us doing it on the loading dock last night and tonight it was against the side of a building."

She went white.

"You don't like me reading your mind? Well, good luck keeping me out once we're mated."

"How much can you see?" She sounded appalled.

"Right now I'm mostly picking up thoughts and emotions from you that are sexual in nature. It'll expand the more time we spend together whether we're mated or not. Do you understand now why I'm fighting to stay away?"

She shrugged, but her pallor suggested she was beginning to get an inkling of the closeness of the connection.

"Stand aside," he asked quietly, "and let me have the vampire. I'll bring you her dead body if you need proof I've killed her, but stay out of my way."

Nicole shook her head vehemently before he finished speaking. "No, I made a vow—" She scowled. "I'm killing the vampire. You stand aside."

"A vow to what? To who?" Dak asked, but she only glared at him and he dropped it. "If I could walk away and avoid seeing you, don't you think I'd already be gone? This assignment came from my king and no one tells the demon king, *sorry, I can't do it.*"

"Then we have a problem, don't we?"

Oh, yeah, wild. With an attitude like hers, Dak would bet everything he had that she'd be fierce when they were in bed together. The image of her riding him, head thrown back filled his mind and he forcibly pushed it aside. "I'm better suited to killing her. You haven't held your own against Mary Beth yet."

"Maybe not, but you can't find her without me."

Dak scowled. The last thing he wanted to do was admit the truth of that statement, and after tonight, he wouldn't be able to follow Nicole covertly. He'd let her inside his shield, and the instant he got within sensing range in the future, she'd know he was there.

"Show me how to use my powers, Dak."

The entreaty on her face, in her voice, nearly compelled him to say yes because it would make her happy. He fought the urge. Instinct, the one that demanded he protect his mate at all costs, rose to save him. If Nicole fought the vampire even with demon powers, she would probably lose. Mary Beth was old and no doubt battle tested from the vampire wars. Nicole would be wielding talents she'd hardly learned to use.

"No."

Her anger hit him like a nuclear blast and he cursed silently. Their bond had expanded already. He was doomed unless he got out of here immediately and stayed away. Dak eyed the door.

"I won't let you follow me to the vampire," Nicole said. There was no sign she was mad in her voice or on her face, but he felt the emotion. "And if you can't find her, you can't kill her."

"You can't kill her either."

"That doesn't mean I'm going to quit trying. Mary Beth dies or I die, but I'm not walking away."

She was serious. Unable to stand still, Dak strode around the living room. Nicole was demon to the core. Only a demon developed that kind of obstinate obsessiveness. If she were human, he could probably reason with her, make her see how foolhardy the decision was. But a demon on a mission? Nothing would change her mind.

That damn protectiveness which had saved him earlier reared up, only this time it was like an anchor around his waist, dragging him so far beneath the surface, he had no hope of reaching air before he drowned. He fought against it anyway and fought hard.

He lost.

Dak stopped pacing and turned to glare. Damn her, he couldn't allow her to die. That meant sticking close to ensure Mary Beth didn't kill her. It meant training Nicole in her magic to give her a fighting chance if he went down, and to do that, he'd have to spend a lot of time with her.

It was a foregone conclusion they'd wind up chained to each other before they were finished.

His voice was choked, but then he was trying to strangle back the words. They escaped anyway. "I'll teach you how to be a demon. I just hope you don't regret our becoming mated as much as I will."

Chapter Six

NICOLE BALLED HER HANDS INTO fists and took a stride toward Dak before she regained control. Why the hell was she getting mad about his aversion to being mated? It wasn't as if *she* wanted it either. Demons were an enemy for crying out loud. And it wasn't as if he were rejecting *her*. Not really.

Even if it felt that way.

She quashed the irrational anger and focused on what mattered. "We're adults. Just because we want each other—mate thing or no mate thing—doesn't mean we have to give into the need." Dak didn't say anything, but his expression was so patronizing, Nicole felt her temper slip. "We can say no, damn it."

"For a time." His tone matched his expression.

When she realized she was grinding her teeth, Nicole forced herself to unclench her jaw. "Why do you have to be such an ass?"

"Why do you insist that human actions and reactions apply to demons, too? We're not human and this *mate thing* is very real. The repercussions are lifelong whether you're ready to accept that or not."

A chill went through her, but she ignored it. "The only thing that matters is learning how to use my powers in order to kill the vampire. We can start my lessons now."

Resignation and frustration washed over her. His emotions. Nicole shifted and tried to quell the uneasiness. She'd always been a fairly empathic person, but this was more than that. "Well?" she prompted when he didn't speak.

"We can run through the basics, but more than that will have to wait."

Nicole's jaw went tight again. "I won't allow you to stall." He muttered something she couldn't quite make out and pivoted abruptly. She waited until he made a circle around her living room. "There's no reason why you can't spend the rest of the night teaching me, and since sunlight has no impact on demons, we can keep going past dawn."

"Do you think a single lesson is going to teach you enough to kill a vampire who's at least a thousand years old?" Dak shook his head. "Even if that were possible, I can't do it."

Her eyes narrowed. "Don't—"

Dak scowled fiercely enough to stop her words. Not because he worried her—he didn't—but because she suddenly found herself wondering if that was the expression he wore when he came. She wanted to know. Nicole struggled to put aside the image of him rocking between her legs and listen to what he was saying.

"I told you I took a blast that left me weakened. My powers are maybe a fraction of what they should be. I'll need hours of sleep before they return to normal."

"You strengthened my wards," she argued and hoped he didn't pick up on the breathlessness in her voice.

"That's not the same thing."

Did he expect her to buy that? "Sure it is."

"It isn't. The draw is shallower." Maybe he read her lack of comprehension because he sighed. Loudly. "I'll show you what I'm talking about tomorrow when I've recovered. Once you experience it for yourself, you'll understand what I'm saying." He took a step toward the door.

Nicole glared. If he thought he was walking away that easily, Dak could think again. Before she could stop him, though, some strange energy raised the hair on her arms. His entire body went rigid. "What the hell is that?" she asked in a whisper.

"Get your coat."

She didn't argue. Nicole shrugged into her leather jacket, checked to make sure her two knives were tucked in their sheaths, and moved to Dak's side. They were going to run. He hadn't sent that, but it was as if he'd allowed her to slide into his head and share a few very limited thoughts. It only weirded her out a little.

Dak took her hand, his warm fingers linking with hers, and he tugged her to the front door. *Dak?*

Mary Beth is nearby. She fired the amulet; that's the energy you perceived.

Nicole hadn't picked up the vampire and she should have. As Dak opened the door and wrapped his energy cloak around her, she searched for Mary Beth, but came up empty. He was supposed to be unable to sense the vampire. Was she really there?

She's there, Dak told her. *Maybe out of range, but I know what I felt, and since it's unlikely there are two amulets, it must be her.*

He opened the door and waited impatiently while Nicole locked it. As soon as she put away her keys, Dak caught her hand and pulled her to the stairwell. For a big man, he managed to move silently and she tried to do the same. But a question lingered. *If Mary Beth fired the amulet, why weren't you affected? I thought you said another shot would take you out of the picture?*

Sure, wards offered some protection from magical attacks, but that was limited and they did nothing to stop physical incursions. Their main function was to conceal and even that was imperfect.

The energy only partially penetrated the wards, Dak sent.

Was there an edge of hurt to his frustration this time? Nicole wasn't sure and he bottled up his emotions so fast, she didn't have more than a split second before they were gone. Okay, so she felt as if she could trust him, but could she?

They reached the lobby level and Dak took the turn to the next flight, the one that led to the parking garage.

Call her skeptical, but everything seemed too convenient. Dak claimed he needed time to recover from the blast earlier tonight, but a second shot from Mary Beth—a vampire Nicole should have been able to sense if she were in the area and couldn't—hadn't injured him. And instead of asking questions, she'd put on her jacket and followed him as if she didn't have a clue about demons.

Abruptly, Dak stopped, pressed her back against the wall of the stairwell, and caged her in with his body. His eyes were glowing red, a sure sign of high emotion. Nicole guessed anger.

"You're my mate." His voice was soft, but there was so much growl to it, that she upgraded his mood from angry to royally pissed off. "That means something whether I like it or not. There are two things that you need to know right this moment—one, I won't lie to you even to make things easier for myself. Got that?"

"Yes." He opened himself more, letting her feel his emotions and leaving her no room to doubt his veracity. "And the second?"

There was an infinitesimal hesitation, then, "A demon male will die if that's what it takes to protect his mate. It's biological, instinctual—there is no choice about it. Remember that before you do anything stupid."

Nicole gasped, but he didn't allow time for that to sink in before he was moving again, tugging her in his wake. She wanted to be furious at his belief that she'd do something dumb because getting mad would make everything easier. Too bad she couldn't manage it, not when she knew he wasn't lying or exaggerating about giving up his life to defend her.

Her hand tightened around his and a need to keep Dak safe welled up—her own instincts at work? Nicole wasn't sure.

They reached the door to the parking garage, but while Dak put his hand on the handle, he didn't open it. Instead, he tipped his head, as if listening.

The vampire must have believed her amulet could take him out at a distance, leaving Nicole on her own. Only that hadn't happened and she'd wasted the shot. There were things Nicole couldn't figure out, though, like how had they been found and why the attack?

Nicole didn't realize Dak continued to be tapped into her head until he said softly, "This is an ideal time. I'm not much of a threat at the moment and she's confident she can beat you. We got lucky, though. The amulet is dead for a while, long enough for us to get out of range."

He eased the door to the garage open and hurried them through it. When they were away from the entry and deep into the shadows created by the cement pillars, he carefully studied their surroundings.

The intent look on his face made her catch her breath. It wasn't the time for sexual fantasy, she knew that, knew they were at risk, but Nicole couldn't suppress the desire. He'd have that same intensity in bed, and she could see him, naked and over her. Simply imagining how good he'd feel inside her made her shudder.

"Don't do this to me," he warned her. "Not now."

His voice was choked and Nicole blinked, focusing on Dak's face again. Instead of bringing her back to earth, the heat in his eyes sent her spiraling deeper into lust.

"A demon's greatest weakness is how easily emotion overcomes our intellect, but you're half human." Dak's hand tightened around hers. "Use that part of yourself to contain the desire. We're too tied together for me to disconnect from you and neither of us can afford to be distracted in this situation."

At first, she was lost in the raspiness of his voice, the way his lips moved when he spoke. Then what Dak said registered. That should have been enough to snap her out of it.

It wasn't.

"Come on. Help me here, Nikki."

"I knew you'd use that nickname!" One corner of his mouth quirked up and Nicole yanked her hand free. Maybe he wouldn't lie to her, but he clearly wasn't above pushing her buttons. "Asshole."

"It worked, didn't it? Let's get out of here."

Yeah, it had worked. Mostly. The desire was there, simmering beneath the surface, but the spike of anger had gotten her to regain control. With his head, he gestured to his left. Nicole followed on his heels, so close that when he came to an abrupt halt, she bumped into his back. Going up on her toes, she peered over his shoulder.

"Leaving so soon?" a feminine voice asked.

Nicole cursed under her breath. She'd forgotten to monitor the vampire's whereabouts.

Chapter Seven

SON OF A FUCKING BITCH. Dak clamped down on his emotions fast, but not quickly enough to prevent the vampire from catching the burst. Smugness emanated from her.

This late at night, the parking garage was filled with cars, limiting his ability to maneuver. How the hell had she zoomed in on them? No, he and Nicole hadn't been paying attention, but Mary Beth had been out of Nicole's range the last time she'd checked and they shouldn't have found themselves cornered.

Nicole moved and Dak shifted, keeping her safely behind him. He'd warned her about instinct, but the strength of his reaction rattled him.

"This should be fun," Mary Beth said. "You have all the disadvantages of being mated."

Dak fought to remain impassive, but he didn't like that the vampire could read him so clearly, and he hated that she was aware that she could use his need to defend Nicole as a weapon against him.

With an icy smile, the vampire splayed her fingers at her side and extended her talons one at a time. Those claws were long enough, strong enough to sever his head from his body.

There were no exits behind them—that meant they had to go through her to get away—and Dak extended his own talons. His were as long and sharp as the vampire's, but he'd never used them in battle. He checked his power level. Maybe enough for one magical blast, but nothing more than that. Hell.

With casual deliberation, Mary Beth strolled toward them. The talons on her other hand came down without the theatrics.

Dak moved forward, cutting off the vampire's angle to Nicole. This wasn't good. The only thing he could think about was keeping his mate safe and he wasn't planning strategies or countermeasures against his opponent.

The idea of dying because he couldn't contain some damn demon trait pissed him off.

With a sudden burst of speed, Mary Beth surged right, as if to go around him to reach Nicole, and Dak intercepted her. He growled before he could stop it. The sound was low, it was dangerous, and it was filled with anger.

Control. He'd been trained to lock down his emotions and do his job, but he couldn't find the off switch tonight. Dak felt wild, raw, and more like an animal than a demon.

The vampire went the opposite direction and Dak stopped her again.

Mary Beth's laugh grated. "I believe I'll incapacitate you first," she told him. "You'll watch me kill her before I end your life, too."

Nicole moved, trying to reach his side, and using his shoulder, he blocked her. *Stay put,* he sent.

I'm a vampire hunter; I can help you.

He knew that, damn it, and he knew they had a better chance if they worked together, but it meant exposing Nicole. Everything inside him balked at the thought.

The vampire lunged and Dak brought his arm up, blocking a strike. Mary Beth's claws ripped at the leather sleeve on his jacket, but she didn't reach skin.

Damn, they were in a bad position, hemmed in by cars and pillars. He needed to go on the offensive, because even without his magic, attacking was better than reacting to the enemy, but Dak couldn't take those few steps away from Nicole.

Mary Beth came at him again. In other circumstances, he would have spun out of her reach, but not this time.

Not when his body protected his mate.

The talons scored his jacket, hitting the left chest and trailing down. A finger reached his T-shirt, shredded the cotton, and drew blood.

He retreated slightly to end contact and bumped into Nicole. She backed up to give him room. Dak didn't think the wound was too deep—it stung more than hurt—but he could feel warmth trickling down his chest.

"I killed your kind in the demon wars," Mary Beth told him, her eyes glowing that freaky white-blue that vampires exhibited sometimes. "I'll kill you, too. You're delaying the inevitable."

"Right." Dak had no doubt she'd killed demons, but did she seriously expect him to concede so that she could murder him and Nicole without expending more effort? "You know that even a weak demon is stronger than a vampire and you know that I'm not a weak demon, right? Do you seriously think I'm going to surrender?"

And why was she tossing out an inanity like that anyway instead of striking? If she knew enough to realize he'd do whatever he had to in order to protect Nicole, the vampire also had to be aware that he'd never give up. So—

The amulet.

She was trying to delay until it recharged enough to blast him again. The vampire might not be able to use fangs, but that damn wizard's charm was enough weapon to bring him down without risking any injury herself.

Desperation rose and Dak wrestled with yet another emotion. He already had too many to contend with; he didn't need more.

He forced himself to take one step away from Nicole, but before he could think about attacking, Mary Beth whirled and kicked out with her foot. It caught him in his midsection, doubling him over. The claws raked his back.

Coming up, he slashed out with his own talons, but he was clumsy and the vampire easily evaded him. She jumped on the hood of a car and leaped to the next, working to get around him.

Trying to get to his mate.

Dak shifted, nudging Nicole back a few steps. One good thing about the parking garage—the ceiling was low, preventing Mary Beth from going airborne. He had enough trouble without that.

The damn vampire knew exactly what to do to keep his brain out of this fight. Part of him could see her tactics, observe his own reaction to them, but he couldn't overcome his automatic response.

Mary Beth jumped onto the roof of a SUV, crouching to avoid hitting the cement beam above her. Dak stepped back again, keeping Nicole behind him.

His mate huffed out a breath and he didn't have to be connected to her to realize she was annoyed. "I'm armed," she said quietly next to his ear, "and I know how to fight vampires. This is stupid."

Frustration rose. Didn't she think he knew that? What he couldn't figure out was how to stop acting like an untrained fool.

With a laugh, Mary Beth hopped off the SUV, landing on the pavement near him. Dak stepped away, shifting to keep himself between Nicole and the vampire. His elbow hit a cement wall.

They were fucked. Mary Beth had forced them to retreat until there was nowhere else to go. Cars to the left, cars to the right and the vampire in front of them. If he didn't overcome this need to shield his mate, they were both going to die.

Nicole might be overmatched on her own, but if they worked together, they could protect each other and go on the offensive. If he could manage to allow her out from behind his back.

Now that she had them trapped, Mary Beth slashed out with her talons once more. As he blocked one blow, her other arm came out. The tip sliced along his jaw line, but he wasn't the target. Nicole's body jerked against his as the claws connected.

Her gasp of pain should have driven him into a rage. Instead, it cooled his emotions.

Dak struck out. His blow merely grazed the vampire, but it was enough to drive her back and buy them some breathing room. She hissed at him, her fangs dropping momentarily, but he ignored the posturing.

She moved forward quickly and he came out far enough to block this attack. Mary Beth sliced open the leather over his biceps and more blood flowed.

Dak, let me help. Nicole touched his shoulder lightly.

Yeah. There was no other choice. Without giving himself time to second guess, Dak lowered the mental and emotional walls between him and Nicole. He felt naked, but he ignored that and reached out psychically for his mate. She didn't have the barriers in place that he had and they were linked in seconds. He sent his plan to her.

She went left. He went right.

Mary Beth tried to claw both of them, but failed. Dak got a blow in with his own talons, but the vampire wore leather, too.

She connected with the side of his head and his vision went dark. As he staggered, Dak blinked hard, trying to shake off the dizziness. He succeeded in time to see Mary Beth knock Nicole's knives from her grip and move in for the kill. Damn it, he should have known this would happen.

With a curse, Dak dove into the fray. By the time he turned the vampire's attention onto him, Nicole was bleeding. White-hot fury threatened to swamp him and he fought it as fiercely as he fought Mary Beth.

He disengaged and broke away to assess the situation. The good news was that his berserker assault had gotten him and Nicole out of the corner. On the bad news side, he'd taken more hits from the vampire and some were gashes. His body had already begun to heal them, but he couldn't afford to fight much longer.

This time when Dak reached mentally for Nicole, he anchored his mind to hers. She'd retrieved her weapons and she wasn't badly hurt. That helped him clear his head further.

Mary Beth looked dazed. Now was the best time to use the bit of magic he had and get the hell out of here.

Calling on every last scrap of energy he possessed, Dak powered up and let loose with a lightning bolt. Without waiting to see the results, he grabbed Nicole's hand and ran.

He was breathing hard within a couple of blocks. Damn, he couldn't remember the last time he'd been this weakened. He needed to go to ground and recover. Looking to the east, he saw the sky had started to lighten—only a touch. It wasn't dawn yet, but it was close enough that Mary Beth would have to think twice about pursuing them.

Dak, are we just going to run or do we have somewhere to go?

He could have answered her mentally, their mind link remained in place, but he spoke aloud. Maybe to assure himself that he could maintain that small amount of distance with her. "I thought we'd go to my place."

"I'm not entering the demon world."

Obstinate. Unfortunately, that got him hot. Although anything she did would have that effect on him—she was his mate and adrenaline needed an outlet. "That's not where I live."

Surprise and confusion from Nicole, but her voice revealed none of that when she asked, "Where is your home then?"

Looking over his shoulder, he said, "Los Angeles. I live in LA."

Chapter Eight

NICOLE COULD BARELY SEE STRAIGHT by the time they reached Dak's home. If she'd ever been this aroused before, she had no memory of it. He hadn't kissed her yet, had done nothing but hold her hand, and she was so freaking ready for him that it would be embarrassing if she didn't know he was every bit as primed.

She shifted from foot to foot, impatiently waiting for him to unlock the door. As soon as he got it open, she shot inside. And stopped short.

The converted warehouse had an open floor plan, gleaming hardwood floors, marble counters in the kitchen, floor to ceiling windows that showed an incredible view of the city, and a curving staircase up to a loft. Nicole wasn't sure what she'd expected, but something this expensive wasn't it.

He closed the door and her thoughts derailed. She turned to face him and saw Dak's eyes burning red. For a moment, he studied her, then one side of his mouth quirked up as he headed toward her. His stride seemed predatory and that made her hotter.

Dak shrugged out of his jacket and tossed it to the floor. She could see the slashes in his T-shirt where the vampire's claws had torn him, but the flesh underneath had already healed.

By the time he stopped in front of her, she was breathing fast and her heart was pounding. There was no doubt in her mind that her own eyes glowed as brightly as his did. Nicole lowered her gaze, but instead of helping her regain control, she zeroed in on his erection.

Reminding herself that he was supposed to be an enemy didn't cool her off. Dak felt like her best friend, like someone she could trust. He'd saved her more than once and protected her at his own expense. She couldn't hate him.

"Look at me," he ordered, voice harsh.

She raised her eyes and nearly moaned at the absolute inferno she saw in his gaze.

"The first time, it's gonna be hard and fast. I don't have much control. Are you as ready for me as I'm sensing?"

Nicole gulped and tried to speak, but she couldn't manage to form words. Instead, she sent him her response. *Oh, yeah. Oh, hell, yeah.*

He didn't grab her like she expected. Dak reached out and trailed the tips of his fingers lightly across her cheekbone. "Everything's going to be different afterward—for both of us. There's no going back, so be sure."

I'm sure. I want you, Dak, more than I want my next breath.

"Yeah, me, too." He cupped her cheek with his hand and leaned in. Despite his claim of having no control, the kiss was tender, a mere brush of his lips over hers.

His gentleness crumbled the last wall she'd held between them, and she clutched at his waist, trying to anchor herself as the whole world turned upside down. As that barrier fell, she could feel the restraint Dak was using to take it slow. She leaned back, looked in his eyes, and with a soft growl, Nicole tore open the snap of his jeans.

She started to lower the tab of the zipper, but that was as far as she got. Dak moved her hands aside. Her complaint was cut short when she realized he was trying to get her jacket off. She twisted, helping him push it away.

Their hands became tangled up as they both reached out at the same time. She won and stripped him out of his shirt. Nicole's mouth went dry. He was incredible.

Broad shoulders, narrow waist, so many perfectly defined muscles all begging for her touch. She barely grazed his chest when Dak took her wrists, moved her arms to her sides, and anchored them there. A muscle spasmed in his jaw and that's when she remembered. "You don't want this." Her voice was thick, hardly intelligible.

"I want you, don't doubt that."

Considering the hard-on he had going, she didn't question his wanting her, but there was more than sex at stake. "You said you'd be pissed if we ended up mated."

His lips quirked. "And I will be, but not with you. Should I stop?"

"No!" Nicole was sure of that. "If you leave me hanging—"

Dak released her and reached for the hem of her tank top. Before it hit the floor, he had her bra unhooked. That followed her shirt. For an endless moment, he did nothing except stare, then with a guttural groan, he tugged her against him. Just the feel of his chest hair against her nipples was enough to make her eyes close and her head fall back.

It aroused her further to feel him shudder against her. She wasn't the only one who loved this. He did, too.

Her hands went back to his zipper, trying to get the damn thing down so she could curl her hand around him. Nicole needed to feel his heat. Had to feel it.

He nudged her aside, lowered it himself. The instant it was down, she had her fingers at the waistband, pushing his jeans and briefs to his thighs. She was barely aware of him stripping them off. She was mesmerized—his erection was as gorgeous as the rest of him. Nicole licked her lips and started to sink to her knees. She wanted him in her mouth.

Dak pulled her upright and she moaned a protest.

If you give me head, I'll come in about two seconds.

"Later?" she asked.

His eyes sparked a brighter red, but that was his only answer. Dak's mouth covered hers, plundered wildly and Nicole wrapped her arms around his neck, holding on tight as the universe spun madly.

Cool air touched her thighs. She hadn't realized he'd gotten her jeans down until then. Nicole stepped on the backs of her shoes to get them off and wiggled until she could kick free of the pants. Her panties went next and she gasped as his fingers slid between her folds. She was so damn wet already and he just made her wetter.

I warned you—hard and fast.

He didn't break their kiss and Nicole decided she could get used to this mind-talk stuff if it had benefits like this. But there was the slightest hesitation in how Dak stroked her, as if he was waiting for her to give him an okay.

Nicole moved back, wrapped her hand around his hard-on, and caressed him. He dampened her palm and she smiled. She wasn't the only one at fever pitch. The urge to bite him came on suddenly, and before she could stop herself, she leaned forward and sank her teeth into his skin where his shoulder and neck met.

Dak jerked in her hand.

Nicole started to apologize until realization dawned. The biting meant something. It meant that she'd claimed Dak as hers. Only hers, forever hers, and she wanted him—all of him—now.

With seemingly no effort, he lifted her. *Wrap your legs around me.*

It took a second for the request to register, then Nicole did as he wanted. She could feel his hard shaft between them and she tried to rock, but he held her too firmly.

Nicole leaned down for a kiss and this time she was the plunderer, exploring every part of his mouth. Dak started walking, but she didn't care where he was going. She'd take this male anywhere, anytime, any way she could get him.

She gasped against his lips as cold stone met her bare bottom. Leaning back, she looked around. He'd put her on the kitchen counter. Nicole tensed her leg muscles, pulling him in closer.

Dak had moved away slightly and Nicole reached for him, guiding his head to her entrance. The feel of him sliding into her made parts of her tighten while other parts went liquid and melty. She tried to hurry him up, but he ignored her. If this was his idea of hard and fast, she wasn't sure she'd survive slow and gentle.

Their eyes met as he filled her. Clenching her inner muscles around him, she brushed his dark hair off his forehead. *Nothing in my life has ever felt as good as this,* she told him.

Let's see if I can make it better.

The thrust was short, measured, and not nearly enough. Before she could complain, he began to move. He slid almost all the way out of her before he stroked back in. Dak watched her, his gaze intense, and Nicole read his worry; he wondered if she could take him the way he needed her.

She couldn't find the right combination of words to make him relinquish the last of his self-command. Instead, she projected the jumble in her head and sent, *More!*

He moved. Like he'd promised, it was hard and fast. And oh, so good. Nicole closed her eyes and hung on to Dak. Every thrust pushed her higher. Her own control disappeared and she clung tighter as sensations rushed in. Not only hers, but his, too.

She was sharing his pleasure. Sharing hers with him.

The groan felt torn from her soul and Nicole arched harder into Dak's next stroke. She wanted him as deep as she could get him. She wanted him joined to her for always.

Orgasm roared closer and Nicole craved it. She didn't have to tell him—Dak knew. He knew and he shifted slightly, his fingers coming out to tease the nipple of one breast. She hadn't gotten his mouth there yet. She wanted that. Needed it.

Her eyes popped open when she felt his tongue trace around her areola. She looked down, saw his dark head bent to her breast, and clenched.

And then she started coming. Nicole couldn't prevent her eyes from closing, couldn't keep her head from falling back.

So good. So freaking good.

He lightly bit her nipple and the orgasm intensified. Dak clutched her hips harder, pulled her into him with each stroke, and she knew he was getting ready to come, too. She wanted that. Wanted him to find the pleasure he was giving her.

Dak nipped at her collarbone, her throat. Her orgasm began to ease up. And then he did it.

He bit her neck where it met her shoulder.

The same place she'd bitten him when she'd claimed him. Her orgasm screamed back. Dak started coming, she could feel it, feel him, and it was even better. Even better.

She reached out psychically for Dak. There was a pool of energy shimmering there between them. He was already anchored in it, and Nicole did the same, sending herself deep into the sea. There was a rumble in her ears, as if there were an earthquake inside the core of who she was.

Nicole wasn't sure how long it took before the world came back into focus, but Dak was still inside her, still partially hard, and she was still vibrating from her orgasms. Her forehead was on his shoulder and his hands lightly stroked her back.

She felt...good. Content. Not alone. For the first time since she lost her family, she had someone with whom she belonged. Her mate.

That thought evaporated some of her satisfaction. She was beginning to understand what Dak had meant when he'd said everything would be different between them afterward. It was. Before it had been a conscious effort to send thoughts to him, but not any longer.

Her eyes opened. For a second, the sight of him partially inside her eliminated her ability to think. Nicole shook it off. "It's opposite now, isn't it?" she asked and raised her head from his shoulder. "Instead of working to send information to you, now I have to work to stop thoughts and emotions from flowing to you."

"I warned you that this would change things." Dak didn't reveal what he thought, not mentally, not in tone of voice, and not in expression. "I also told you that if we had sex you'd access your powers. You have."

Dak had changed the subject deliberately, but while Nicole realized it, she didn't care. She was too interested in what she'd just figured out. That shimmering pool she'd seen, the one in which she'd anchored herself, was power.

She wasn't skimming along the edge of what she was any longer. Nicole had always seen herself as a human whose senses were enhanced by her mixed heritage, but nothing more. Everything had shifted tonight. She couldn't lie to herself any longer, couldn't evade or qualify her abilities.

When she'd mated with Dak, she'd embraced her demon side.

Chapter Nine

FROM THE BEDROOM LOFT, Nicole could hear Dak moving in the condo below. She hadn't been surprised to wake up alone—she'd expected that. It hadn't shocked her either to discover he'd blocked her from his thoughts. Even while they'd been making love, he'd kept part of himself private.

What had taken her off guard was when she'd walked into the bathroom and discovered his thoughtfulness. Dak had put out a new toothbrush for her, a set of fresh towels with a wrapped bar of soap on top of them, and he'd left her one of his T-shirts to wear. The slogan on the front made her smile—*Rogue demon slayer*. There was more than one way to interpret that.

The shirt was long enough to hit her at mid-thigh, but Nicole tugged it down anyway before heading to the stairs. With the open floor plan, she spotted Dak immediately and she watched him as she descended. He was barefoot in faded, frayed blue jeans and wearing a white T-shirt with some kind of logo on the left chest. Damn, he was almost as gorgeous in clothes as he was out of them.

When she reached the bottom, his eyes met hers and she caught the sparks of red. Arousal, not anger. Nicole relaxed.

"Did you think I'd be mad after having the best sex of my life?" Dak crossed to a panel and pressed a button to raise the blinds. "I washed your clothes. They're on the back of the couch."

Washed, dried, and folded. "Wow, a demon who does laundry. I'm impressed."

It was an attempt to hide how much his small kindnesses meant to her, but Nicole doubted she'd blocked him thoroughly enough to pull it off. Sharing emotions while they were driving for orgasm was one thing, but outside of bed? Not so cool.

"A demon taking care of his mate," Dak corrected. "And I'd like to say you'll get used to the mental connection, but I'm struggling with that myself."

"You can keep me out."

He grinned. "Good to know."

"What does that mean?"

Dak headed toward the kitchen. "I'll start breakfast while you get dressed. There's a bathroom down here—" he pointed to his left "—if you don't want to go back upstairs."

Nicole thought about pressing him, decided it wasn't worth it, and scooped up her clothes. The bathroom was down a short hallway, and while smaller than the one upstairs, was every bit as elegant as the rest of the condo. She left the door open. Why bother to close it when he'd seen everything already? And touched her in those places. Kissed her there, too.

A flush of warmth shot through her as she remembered the different ways they'd made love.

When she was dressed in her jeans and bra, Nicole leaned forward and studied herself in the mirror. She didn't look different, but everything had changed. With trembling fingers, she traced the spot on her shoulder where Dak had bitten her. The mark was healed, leaving it completely undetectable, but she swore it emitted some kind of energy.

She'd bitten—claimed—him first. He hadn't stopped her, but he hadn't reciprocated either. Not immediately.

But then he'd told her he didn't want to be mated.

Instead of putting on her tank top, Nicole pulled the black demon slayer T-shirt over her head and tucked it into her jeans. The smell of cooking food made her stomach growl, but she didn't move. What now?

Oh, sure, there were things to do. Dak needed to show her how to use her powers, and she had a vampire to kill, but after that? Then what? For all the intimacies they'd shared, she didn't know much about him. Why did he live in LA and not the demon world? And what about *them?*

He hadn't kissed her this morning and the oversight seemed significant. Would they live together since they were mated? Or would they just hook up when one of them wanted sex?

"One thing at a time," Dak said.

She looked over to find him leaning in the doorway, a shoulder propped against the jamb. "You eavesdropped."

"You were thinking loudly enough that I couldn't help but hear." His lips quirked up in that half smile she found incredibly sexy. "The food is ready. You can quiz me while we eat, but some of your questions—" he shook his head "—we'll have to come up with the answers together."

Nicole walked to the door, but he didn't move aside. She looked at him and waited. Simply gazing at him was enough to for her heart to pick up speed and she had to clench her hands to stop herself from reaching for him.

After an eternity, he brushed a finger from her ear, down her jaw to her chin, and tipped her face up to his. His mouth moved slowly over hers and lingered.

By the time he lifted his head, she clutched his forearms, trying to steady herself. It didn't help. She wanted him. Bad. Again.

"That's why I didn't kiss you earlier." Dak's voice had gone raspy. "Not because our morning in bed meant nothing. We can't afford to lose the rest of the day to pleasure and we would. You know it as well as I do."

Her nod was reluctant, but he was right. "Is it always like this between demon mates? Does it stay this...urgent?"

He shrugged. "That's what they say." Dak stepped away, put a hand at the small of her back, and steered her down the hall.

Just that simple touch was enough to send shivers through her. Control was gone when it came to him and Nicole wanted it to return. "I'm not sure I like this."

"Tell me about it."

Dak pulled out a chair for her at the table. By the time she settled herself comfortably, he was back with two plates from the warming oven. Omelets stuffed with cheese and mushrooms and bell peppers. Not what she'd expected.

And it reminded her that despite how well she knew his body, she didn't know the man.

Looking up from his food, Dak said, "You know me, just like I know you. Maybe you can't name the bands I listen to and I don't know what kind of movies you like, but it wasn't only our bodies we shared. I know who you are at your core—the rest is details."

She paused with her fork in midair. He had a point. While he'd held back part of himself, he hadn't been able to conceal what kind of person he was. It wasn't only some nebulous, psychic communication they'd shared either. They'd talked, too. Nothing deep or profound, but he'd made her laugh and he'd made her forget about vampires and wizards.

Maybe that was why she had such a hard time not thinking about the future. She liked Dak. He could be tough when he needed to be and gentle when it mattered. He preferred to be in charge, but he'd also been able to step back and let her be in control sometimes while they'd made love. And last night, he'd protected her from the vampire, but at the same time, he didn't want her as his mate.

His sigh brought her head up. "What?" she demanded.

"I want you, trust me on that one."

"Only for sex."

Frustration. His. He wasn't sending, but it slammed into her and she couldn't tune it out. What Dak had said earlier about her thinking too loudly suddenly made more sense, but it wasn't along the path they'd communicated over before they'd mated.

Curious, Nicole followed the trail of emotion. And then she "heard" him.

Why the hell is she worrying about this? The odds of us both surviving another fight with the vampire aren't good. She needs to stay focused on the enemy.

Nicole gaped at him. That's how he was reading her so easily. They had a second link to each other, a line that nobody else could use. He had lots of practice blocking the main communication channel, probably because he'd been doing that his entire life, but he couldn't close her out on *their* connection.

"You're right," she said. "We should focus on the vampire first. I just— This morning with you— It was earthshaking, and I think that's why I'm stuck in the relationship loop."

"Damn. You figured it out." He sounded resigned.

"Yes." She was aware of *exactly* what he was talking about without having to ask. "You could have told me we had a private line."

Dak snorted and she distinctly got, *Yeah, right.*

She grinned; she couldn't help it, but it faded fast. "Do you really believe we'll be killed if we don't defeat Mary Beth? So far we've been able to escape when things have gone south."

Putting down his fork, he pushed the plate away and leaned back. For a few seconds, he simply considered her. Nicole couldn't read anything from him, not clearly. His emotions were a chaotic snarl and she couldn't untangle them.

After a quick grimace, he said, "She would have killed us last night if we hadn't had some luck on our side."

"The luck being that she tried to neutralize you from a distance and couldn't do it through the wards I have around my apartment." Dak nodded, but Nicole sensed his agreement before she saw the motion. "Is there some way to turn off the amulet so she can't use it?"

"Only if I know the exact incantation, and not only are there dozens of possibilities, wizards almost always put their own stamp on the spells they use."

Dak sounded so grim, Nicole couldn't think of a response. Instead, she moved his plate until it was in front of him again. He'd only eaten half the omelet and he needed food to keep his powers maximized. She froze for a second when she realized she shouldn't know that, then gave a shrug and took a bite of her eggs.

"After breakfast, I'll show you the basics you need to use your talents." Dak reached for his orange juice. "I hope you're a fast learner."

"I always have been. And thanks. I know it's not easy for you to stand back and let me have Mary Beth, but I appreciate it."

He went still. "I'm not teaching you these things because I want you to make the kill. What I'd like is for you to stand behind me as you did last night and let me handle things."

The growl that escaped her was pure demon. "The only reason I stayed in back of you was because I was worried about you doing something stupid if I didn't. Once I can use my powers, I'm in the fight." She leaned forward to glare into his eyes. "I mean it, Dak; the vampire is mine."

If she thought the frustration she'd felt from him earlier was intense, that was nothing compared to what hit her now.

"The fight probably will be yours, whether I like it or not." His voice was rough. "The amulet will weaken me, and last night it left me dazed for around fifteen minutes. Until I can come up with some way to evade the blast, there's nothing I can do about it. But why the hell are you so stubborn? Why the fucking crusade against Mary Beth?"

Nicole began to shake and she couldn't stop. She put down her fork to hide how badly she was trembling. It surprised her that Dak didn't know, but maybe all he got from her on this subject was the same tangle of strong emotion she'd gotten from him earlier. It didn't matter and he needed to understand.

"Because when I was ten years old, she came into my house. She ripped open my stepfather's throat and she did the same to my mom, but that wasn't enough for her. Next she murdered my half brothers—they were four and two. Then she came after me."

Dak's hand covered hers and his thumb rubbed circles on her palm. It calmed her enough to finish.

"I swore that if I survived, I'd avenge my family. I lived, and now it's time to settle the debt or die trying."

Chapter Ten

DAK STOPPED IN HIS TRACKS WHEN he heard Nicole growl. Her frustration had been roiling for a while now, but she'd doggedly persisted in trying to harness her powers.

She glared at him, eyes sparking red, and demanded, "Why the hell is this so hard?"

It wasn't, not really. Demon children could access part of their magic from the time they were toddlers, but he carefully shielded that thought from his mate. She wasn't pissed at him. Yet. And he wanted to keep it that way. "Maybe you didn't have a good teacher."

That earned him a reluctant smile and he winked at her before closing the gap between them. Her hair was loose and he smoothed an errant strand off her cheek before cupping her chin in his palm. Damn, she was beautiful and not only in appearance.

Nicole got to him in so many ways, he'd lost count.

She had a sense of humor. That was important and the fact she could smile at his weak joke while she was this aggravated boded well.

He liked her courage. It could be exasperating, like when she insisted she be the one to kill the vampire, but Dak knew himself and he'd have little patience for timidity. His job could be difficult, and he needed a mate up to living with the danger he faced regularly.

Then there was her honor. He could believe in her if she made a promise. Nicole thought that demons were dishonest—and they frequently were with humans—but they were mostly trustworthy when it came to dealings with their own people.

The stubbornness? That was a major irritation, but she'd need that trait to deal with him. He could admit it.

And he was glad Nicole was too focused on her powers to be listening in on his thoughts. As a strong demon, he was accustomed to blocking everyone unless he specifically wanted to share something. With her, it took a lot more work and was only successful about half the time. Maybe less. He'd liked it better when she hadn't realized they had a separate connection.

Unable to resist, he ran his thumb across her lips. Her tongue licked the pad and Dak felt heat rise. Leaning forward, he brushed his mouth over hers.

Sweet. So fucking sweet. He could lose himself in her, wanted to lose himself in her. Dak waited for the disquiet to rise, but it didn't and that rattled him. His defenses against her were crumbling faster than a sand castle on the beach during a hurricane. That didn't shake him up either. Hell.

With one last kiss, he eased back. "Turn around, Nic."

She gave him a quizzical look, but didn't argue. He liked her faith in him, too, and Dak grimaced. Make that a sand castle on the beach in a force five hurricane.

He wrapped his arms around her from behind, froze when she wiggled her ass against his groin, and muttered, "Stop that. We're trying to get you to use your powers, not see how fast you can arouse me."

"How does this help?"

"Just a sec. And don't move around," he tacked on. Dak tugged her closer, trying to envelop Nicole as much as possible in his natural field of energy. When he had her situated, he said, "Now mentally mesh yourself with me as tightly as possible."

Dropping the last line of defense around his mind didn't make him happy. This was why he hadn't used this teaching method to begin with, but he opened himself to her, helping to interlace her consciousness with his. He needed Nicole to be able to fight the vampire if he was taken out of the picture, and as it stood, she couldn't, not yet. He remained quiet until they were in complete unison. *Follow what I do, Nicole. Feel how I draw my power, how I wield it. Be one with me.*

Dak made a shallow draw and used it to turn on the lights in his condo. *Now you try. Flip the lights off again.*

She wasn't successful this time either, but now he knew what the problem was. "The power is part of you," Dak said softly against her ear. "You're treating it like a lake and you're trying to scoop up the water in a bucket without getting wet. If you need that imagery, picture your legs as straws and draw the water in through them to your core."

Show me again.

He did, using the power to lower the blinds. *Your turn.*

Her agreement came without words, the acceptance simply there. Dak ignored how normal that was beginning to feel and concentrated on what his mate was doing. The energy flowed into her in fits and starts. Nicole lost her hold on it over and over. She also drew unevenly and the sputtering grated on his nerves, making it hard for him to maintain the merge with her.

I did it!

She had; the lights were off. And if this had been a battle, Nicole would already be dead. Dak needed to come up with some way to neutralize that damn amulet.

"I'll get better with practice."

"I know." But this had been an easy task requiring little energy. "Work with it some more—open the blinds, play with the lights, anything."

Nicole did increase her speed each time, but she wasn't quick enough, not by a longshot. Dak stopped her after half a dozen tries. Making sure their link was solid, he sent, *What you're pulling is what I used to strengthen your wards. I'm going to do the kind of draw I'd need to power up my arsenal in a fight. Feel the difference.*

He closed his eyes, something he'd never do in a real world situation, and gathered the energy. Since there was no way he was firing inside his home, Dak held it in his body for a few moments, enjoying the buzz it gave him, and then slowly allowed it to disperse.

Reluctantly, he let the last of it go and opened his eyes. Dak could sense how stunned Nicole was, and with a grimace, he rested his chin on the top of her head. "The amount I was able to call up isn't unusual; any strong demon can do it."

"Including me?"

"Yes." Dak hesitated, then added, "Vampires and demons can build an energy shield around themselves for protection. Battle usually means hitting their defenses over and over until they collapse."

"In quick succession while simultaneously carrying out a physical attack, right?"

He didn't have to say anything, she knew the answer. Nicole turned in his arms and leaned back far enough to meet his gaze. "This is what Mary Beth faced in the past during the demon wars."

"We call them the vampire wars, but yeah, probably."

With a sigh, she rested her cheek against his chest and Dak hugged her tight, one hand stroking her hair. Nicole wouldn't stay discouraged long—another thing he liked about her—but she needed to be aware of what kind of challenge they were up against. "I trained for five years to do my job and this was after using magic my entire life. You're not going to pick it up in a single afternoon no matter how stubborn you are."

"I prefer to use the word determined," Nicole said. "What is your job anyway?"

She could have delved in his head and gotten the information without asking, but she didn't. Dak smiled. Momentarily. His position was considered prestigious among demons, but Nicole had been raised human. How would she react?

He could probe her mind and try to come up with an answer, but she'd respected his privacy by not mining his brain and he'd do the same. Her emotions, though, could blast him if they were strong enough. Dak erected a mental barrier, and unwrapping Nicole's arms from around him, put physical distance between them as well.

When he was on the other side of the room, he rested his hands on his hips and measured her. He picked up curiosity, nothing more. With a shrug, he gave her the truth. "I'm an executioner."

Confusion came first, then she asked, "You kill vampires?"

"No, this is a first. Usually, I'm assigned to hunt demons who've been sentenced to death by our courts."

Nicole glanced down at the T-shirt she wore and her lips curved. "Rogue demon slayer, huh?"

Dak grimaced and ran a hand over the back of his neck. "That was a gift from my sister. My smart-ass sister. I've never worn it and I thought you'd be more comfortable in something new."

"Why are you—" She stopped short and became serious. "You're worried about my response to your job?" At his nod, she crossed to him. "I'm a vampire hunter. I'd have to be a pretty big hypocrite to toss stones at you."

Some of the tension leached from his muscles. "It's not going to be an issue between us?"

"No. Is my job going to be a problem?"

"Not once you learn how to use your powers." And that made him go taut again. "It's only a few hours until sunset."

"Yeah." Nicole stuck her hands in the back pockets of her jeans and rocked, a pensive expression on her face. "I know I've been the one who's been adamant about hunting Mary Beth, but it doesn't have to be tonight. In a couple of days, when I'm smoother with the power thing, then we can go out looking for her. I waited seventeen years to avenge my family; a few more days won't matter and we can lie low here until we're ready."

She didn't know. Dak thought she'd read that information from him already, that she understood his urgency. "We can't hide here, Nic. I didn't get it at first, but I thought about it all day. There's only one way the vampire could have found us as easily as she did last night."

"Because she knew where I lived."

"Maybe, but that's not how she zeroed in on us in the parking garage." He took a deep breath. "That amulet is tuned to my energy. She can use it like a fucking GPS to track me down. There's nowhere I can lie low."

Chapter Eleven

NICOLE GLANCED OUT THE FRONT window of the sports car, saw the sky had deepened to indigo, and looked back at Dak. He had a death grip on the steering wheel, but it was late enough that every vampire in the city was stirring by now.

Wanting to soothe him, she reached out and put her hand on his thigh. The muscles were tight there, too, and she ran her fingers up and down his inseam, hoping that would relax him.

His hand covered hers briefly before returning to the wheel. "There's time to drop you somewhere safe," he said.

She squeezed his leg. "Do you really want to have this argument again?"

"No, but I want you out of the line of fire, Nic."

The way he shortened her name, the tone of voice when he used it was intimate enough to make it an endearment. She liked that. And she liked how they'd become friends.

He'd gone from *demon males protect their mates* to *I want* you *safe, Nic.* Her, specifically, not her as his mate. It was a subtle difference and maybe she wouldn't have grasped the distinction if it wasn't for their mental connection. She wasn't sure anyone had really given a damn about her since her family had died, but Dak did.

"Mates stick together," she said and left it at that.

He grumbled, a sound barely short of a growl. "We should have left earlier."

Nicole ignored that. Leaving LA had been her idea, but it hadn't occurred to her until they'd brainstormed through quite a few other possibilities. "We could make better time on the freeway," she offered.

Dak shook his head. "I don't want to be going that speed if the vampire launches an aerial attack."

His leg muscles flexed under her palm as he braked for a traffic light. They were going through an industrial area and there were few people around. That wasn't bad because Mary Beth wouldn't worry about human bystanders, but Nicole would feel safer in a crowd.

"Do you think she'll do that?"

The light went green and Dak waited until they were through the intersection before answering. "It's one option, but that doesn't mean it's the action she'll take."

"Yeah." Nicole dropped her head back and let the motion of the car lull her. She wished the vampire was already dead and she and Dak were driving somewhere without any worries. In the past, she'd never been sure what she'd do once her vengeance was complete, but now dozens of tantalizing possibilities existed and a lot of them involved the male sitting beside her. She smiled.

Turning her head on the rest, she studied Dak's profile. He was gorgeous and sweet and he was hers. All hers. From the start he'd looked after her, he'd even wrapped her inside his energy cloak to keep her hidden—

Nicole sat up straight. It might work. Maybe.

"What? Did you pick up the vampire?" Dak asked.

"No. Sorry. I just had a thought." Nicole shifted, turning as much as she could toward Dak. "Mary Beth can't use the amulet against me or to track me because I'm only half demon."

"Yeah, so?"

"So what if I wrapped my energy around you the way you cloaked me last night? Would that protect you?"

Dak opened his mouth, closed it again, and his expression went thoughtful. She liked this about him, the way he didn't automatically dismiss her ideas. And if what she suggested wouldn't work, he explained why.

Damn, she had it bad for him if she was getting mushy over this.

"It might do the trick," he said quietly. "Can you hold the shield in place for an indefinite period over both of us?"

Nicole gave the question some thought. Dak needed her to be certain, not cocky. "I wasn't able to conceal myself from the vampire for the past two nights, so maybe not on the tracking, but I know I can keep you safe from the amulet."

Silence. She wasn't actively monitoring his thoughts, but she had no doubt he was calculating the risk to her. It was important to her that he be safe, too, and that never seemed to be part of his equation. Nicole hesitated, but maybe it was something he needed to hear. "You matter, Dak, and if you get yourself hurt, I'm going to be hugely pissed off at you. You better remember that."

His smile was slow, but it was real. He glanced over at her, winked, and then she got a grudging, "Okay, do it."

Without giving him a chance to change his mind, she put her wall around him. She'd expected it to be hard, but it wasn't. Dak fit as if he'd always been there.

He kept driving. Nicole had assumed he'd turn the car around now that he could fight the demon without worrying about the amulet, but he didn't. Unless he didn't trust her. Maybe he thought she'd let him down in the clutch.

"Why are we still heading out of town?"

Dak cut her another glance. "Because I want us to sit down and hammer out tactics and strategy without you needing to expend excess energy holding the shield up."

"Oh." And there he went, worrying about her again. The way he took care of her left her with this weird warm feeling. "We are going to work together then? You're not going to try to keep me safe, right?"

"I'd love to lock you away and take down the vampire on my own, but I won't. No demon with half a brain would do that to another who has a vendetta."

Good. Content with his answer, Nicole let her gaze wander. There was nothing around except derelict warehouses with chain-link fences around them. Dak thought *this* was safer than the freeway? Then she shrugged. For a demon with his power, maybe human crime wasn't a worry.

She could ask, but Nicole had something else on her mind. "I have another question."

"You always do." But Dak sounded amused, not irritated, and this time he was the one who reached over and squeezed her thigh.

When his hand returned to the wheel and she could think again, Nicole said, "The other night, you said your king assigned you to this job. Why does he want Mary Beth dead?"

"He doesn't. One of the vampire clan lords requested that we eliminate her for him. My understanding is that her violence is bringing too much heat to his people, but I didn't ask for details."

"Why doesn't he have his enforcers take her out?"

"Vampire politics." Dak sounded disgusted. "And politics are why our king agreed. It further cements the alliance between the vampire clans and the demons."

Our king? She wasn't sure how she felt about acquiring a monarch, but she did like the way Dak included her. That felt good. She had more questions, but she'd save them for later. Right now, she could simply be— at least for a while.

Nicole settled back in her seat, but she didn't have a chance to relax. Something strummed at her senses. She went rigid. "Dak." It would take too long to explain her disquiet with words, so she sent the whole thing to him. Immediately, he became more alert and he was plenty on edge before this.

She tried to pinpoint the sensation, tried to figure out what was causing it, but a heartbeat later, the engine went silent.

Dak maneuvered the car to the curb. Before he got there, his headlights picked up a figure standing in the street.

The vampire had found them.

Chapter Twelve

NICOLE STRUGGLED TO UNHOOK her seatbelt. Dak was already out of the car and she— There! She scrambled after him.

He and the vampire stood like two old-west gunslingers facing off. Mary Beth wore dark brown jeans, boots, and a brown-leather bomber jacket. With her blond hair pulled back in a ponytail, she looked so freaking normal it was criminal.

Nicole stopped beside Dak. The jacket he wore tonight was brown leather as well, but it was softer than the one he'd had on last night. She didn't know if it would hold up to the talons.

The vampire pulled out a disk suspended on a chain from beneath her shirt. There were rune characters engraved into the silver, and in the center, a small reddish-brown cabochon stone. Shaking her head with mock sadness, she said, "You are pathetically stupid."

And then Mary Beth let loose with the amulet's power.

A ripple went through Dak, Nicole could sense it, but that was the sum total of the medallion's impact on him. Satisfaction filled her. She'd done it, she'd protected her mate.

"Perhaps not so stupid after all," Dak drawled, and with a casual flick of his wrist, sent a lightning bolt at the vampire.

For an instant, Nicole simply gawked. Did he really expect her to be able to wield lightning? The shield around Mary Beth lit up, but it didn't fall and that seemed every bit as incredible as the weapon itself.

The vampire dropped the chain, letting the amulet fall to her chest, and her claws descended. "I loathe wizards," she said without heat.

As she started toward them, Dak released a torrent of lightning, one blast after another. Talk about feeling inadequate. Nicole was in over her head even after an afternoon of training. She pulled her wooden dagger and waited.

Mary Beth regrouped and started forward again. Nicole tried to draw power like she'd been taught, but the amount she was able to hang on to was minuscule compared to what Dak tossed out.

His barrage drove the vampire a few steps away, but instead of looking like someone who'd suffered a setback, she appeared angry. "This is tiresome."

"No shit," Nicole muttered. If the monster would cooperate and die, they could call it a night.

Dak shot her a look. *Just because Mary Beth couldn't use the amulet against me doesn't mean we're going to win. No.* He cut her off before she could argue. *Vampires killed demons in the wars—stop underestimating her.*

Nicole didn't think she was selling their enemy short, but how could anyone defeat Dak? He was throwing *lightning* for crying out loud.

Mary Beth, though, didn't look worried. Or impressed. Not even a little bit.

Nicole was the one gaping in awe.

And being completely useless. If she handled her job this way, she'd have died on her first assignment. She tried again to call up enough power to fire it.

It slipped away.

Grimly, Nicole pulled her other dagger. Maybe she couldn't fight like a demon, but she could fight like a vampire hunter.

Her charge forward was stopped with a sharp thought from Dak. Okay, so maybe she'd wait until he tired out the vampire, then drive the wooden dagger into the bitch's heart.

Mary Beth held both arms out at her sides.

What is she doing? Nicole asked Dak.

I don't know.

But he was paying rapt attention, trying to come up with an answer.

The vampire threw back her head and opened her mouth. A tone came out. It was high pitched and it nearly caused Nicole to drop her weapons. She tightened her grip on the hilts at the last instant, but what she wanted to do was cover her ears with both hands.

Dak's silent cursing jerked Nicole's attention to him. His lightning bolts were coming out like flashes from a strobe light at a nightclub.

What the—? She quickly sent her mind to the place she considered the pool of power. Instead of placidly waiting for them to draw from it, the water moved in angry waves. She couldn't gather anything and Dak only managed a fraction of what he'd been using.

The vampire lowered her arms and smiled. "There. That makes things more even."

This time as she started toward them, Dak extended his talons. *It's going to be hand-to-hand, Nic. I need you to cooperate with me.*

You got it. How long until the power settles?

I'm not sure. A while from the feel of it. I want you to stay behind me and—

Not a chance in hell, demon mine. We're stronger as a team, you know it as well as I do when your testosterone isn't overruling your brain.

Dak cut off mid-growl as the vampire charged. Nicole could actually feel how hard it was for him to put even a few feet between them to meet the enemy. She took a step forward and stopped.

The flurry of motion was nothing but a blur and she couldn't see anything.

Blinking hard, she tried to bring it into focus, but the two broke apart before she managed. Dak's brown leather jacket had a long scratch along the sleeve and blood ran from his scalp.

Mary Beth's ponytail wasn't as neat as it had been, but that was about it for damage.

Damn, they were in trouble. Nicole couldn't see the fight to join in and Dak wasn't accustomed to wielding his talons as weapons.

That was a glaring hole in the demon arsenal. How easy was it to become so dependent on lightning that other methods of fighting weren't honed?

As Dak and Mary Beth clashed again, Nicole struggled to slow it down. Then she tried speeding up her brain. She was used to attacking with knives. If she could only see what the hell was happening, she'd be able to help.

She cursed as a figure was thrown and Nicole identified Dak. He was on his feet the instant after he landed.

Nicole had to think. Why was she only getting a blur? Why?

Demon energy. She needed demon energy!

The pool kept roiling and she had a hard time siphoning off enough to fill her body, but a small amount was all she needed. She could see the fight now.

Dak had more gashes and some of the strikes had cut through the leather. Nicole growled, pissed as hell at what Mary Beth had done to her mate.

She launched herself into the fray, planning to attack the vampire from behind. Mary Beth sent her soaring backward with one blow. Nicole hit the ground hard enough to daze her.

A red haze coated her mind with fury. Dak's emotions. Damn, her getting knocked to the ground had pushed him out of control.

Leaping to her feet, Nicole sent him reassurances that she was fine. He had enough problems without his demon male instincts kicking into high gear.

Too late. He was furious, his self-command gone. Another blurred burst. Talons slicing, striking. The vampire sent him to the pavement and he didn't get up.

Dak wasn't dead. Nicole *knew* he wasn't because she could feel his essence inside her yet. But he was out cold and a sitting duck for the vampire. Nicole's own emotions threatened to swamp her.

As the vampire made a move toward Dak, Nicole clutched her knives harder. She'd be damned if anyone was going to hurt *her mate* while she had breath in her body. Nicole ran at Mary Beth.

She kicked the vampire's legs out from under her, sending her sprawling. Nicole launched herself at the other woman.

Still clutching the hilts of her daggers, she punched Mary Beth.

Blood spurted from her enemy's nose.

Before she could land a second blow, the vampire pushed her off with so much power, Nicole went flying. She landed on her feet, but staggered to catch her balance.

A set of talons came at her face and she ducked, kicking out as she spun out of the way.

Damn, she'd missed Mary Beth's knee, but she did catch her in the thigh. Not good enough. Coming around, Nicole stabbed out with the metal dagger.

The strike caught air, throwing her off balance and causing her to stagger.

That was all the vampire needed. Nicole cringed as she heard the talons rake over her already-battered leather jacket. They didn't reach her skin and she jumped away. Nicole fell over Dak, landing on her butt beside him. She didn't have time to make sure he was okay.

The vampire was coming.

Using the momentum of the fall, Nicole rolled to her feet. She wasn't letting Mary Beth near Dak and Nicole raced forward. Talons came at her. She ducked, slashing out with her blade.

It sank into the other woman's side, but before Nicole could swing the wooden dagger into her heart, she was flung off.

The language the vampire let loose with was archaic, but Nicole recognized swearing when she heard it. "Once a guttersnipe, always a guttersnipe, huh, Mabilia?"

Mary Beth made a hissing noise.

This time, the vampire's approach was more cautious. They circled each other, both looking for an opening. A weakness.

Fear rose up. Nicole scowled and shored up her protective shield. Damn vampires. "Mind control doesn't work on demons," she said.

"It almost did," Mary Beth countered. "You're more human than demon anyway. You know nothing of your father's people, nothing of their talents."

Two balls of fire streaked past her, slamming into the vampire hard enough to send her through the air. Dak reached her side and he looked okay. Not great, but better than she'd expected.

He paused just long enough to check her out and then he was past her, headed for Mary Beth. As he ran, he slung more fireballs at the enemy.

Before he reached her, the vampire let loose with that sound again, the one that had wrecked the pool of energy, and then she launched herself skyward.

Nicole waited for Dak to take to the air, too, but he didn't. *Get under the power lines,* he ordered.

She ran for the side of the street and stood near a power pole. Dak moved her direction, raking his talons upward as he went.

The vampire darted in and out, avoiding his strikes. She sliced Dak a few times.

"Can't you at least hover?" Nicole asked when he reached her side. She fought the urge to dab away the blood on his face. Now wasn't the time to tend injuries.

"My branch doesn't possess flight. She won't be able to stay up there—it requires too much energy."

He never looked away from Mary Beth. The power lines took away her ability to come at them from directly overhead, and the position of the fence behind them eliminated any strikes from the rear, but she could still attack from the front.

And she did. Flying in, slicing away at them, retreating over and over. To Nicole's surprise, her mate retracted his talons. Dak reached over, took the metal blade from her right hand, and hurled it. Forcefully.

Mary Beth came down with a thud, the knife buried in her left shoulder. "I told you she wouldn't be in the air for long."

As he headed for the vampire, he asked, *I'm taking the right flank, do you want the left?*

"Hell, yes!" Nicole couldn't manage to thank him, but she didn't need to. Dak knew how much she appreciated being included without her needing to say more.

The vampire pulled the dagger from her body. Blood gushed, but it wouldn't last. Her kind healed as fast as demons did.

With a snarl, Mary Beth threw the blade at Dak. He sidestepped it easily.

"You aren't going to shield your mate?" Mary Beth asked. She breathed heavily. "I thought demon males protected them with all their resources. Or maybe you don't care about yours? Perhaps you'd be happier without her?"

Nicole sensed his hesitation. *No! I know that's not the truth. I know you don't want anything to happen to me. I know it, Dak!*

He leaped back to evade those claws and then she felt him skim along her mind. Nicole opened for him, let him feel the truth of her words. Dak had tamped down his instincts for her, she wasn't going to let that vampire use it against him.

She'd never realized that someone could feel a smile, but while Dak's face remained expressionless, Nicole sensed his grin. *Let's take her down,* he sent.

The wooden dagger wasn't good for much, not unless she could stab it into the heart, but that was all she had. There wasn't even a rusted pop can around that she could use as a makeshift weapon, damn it.

Mary Beth swung toward her and Nicole kicked out, but before she could do more, Dak engaged the vampire.

Nicole held out her right hand, closed her eyes halfway, and imagined talons extending.

She squeaked when they shot out. *Holy—*

The vampire knocked Dak back a couple steps and came at her. Nicole hacked out with the talons, but she was incredibly awkward.

With a rumble low in her throat, Nicole charged. She brandished the claws, but they seemed to have a mind of their own, going different directions than her fingers were telling them. To hell with it, she decided, and pulling them in, she went in low.

Nicole's shoulder connected with Mary Beth's midsection and she took her down to the ground.

She punched her until the vampire tossed her off. Nicole rolled to her feet, but Dak was already there, taking over where she'd left off.

She wanted to be the one to defeat the vampire, but at least Mary Beth would die. At least Nicole's family would be avenged even if it wasn't by her hand.

Dak raised his head, his breathing harsh. "She's your kill."

Nicole met his gaze. He meant it. Dak was standing down for her. He moved away.

Mary Beth surged to her feet and ran. Nicole tackled her to the ground. The vampire writhed and cursed. A talon caught Nicole's arm and she nearly dropped the wooden dagger. Transferring the weapon to her right hand, Nicole swung it down in one, smooth motion, driving it into the heart.

For a long moment, she remained kneeling on the street next to the body. It was over. It was really over. Slowly, she climbed to her feet and slid the dagger back in its sheath. Looking into her mate's eyes, Nicole said, "Thanks."

"Do you have the peace you wanted?"

She took a long, hard look inside her heart. "My family's still gone. I still miss them. I'll still live the rest of my life without them." And she was still alone. Nicole shrugged. "But I have something. I finally have justice."

"Then killing the vampire was worth it."

"Yes, it was."

Dak slung an arm around her shoulders and tugged her against his side. "You're not alone, Nic—you have me. You'll always have me." He pressed a kiss to the top of her head and hugged her closer. "Let's take care of the vampire's body and go home."

Epilogue

NICOLE FELT THE EMPTINESS OF the condo as soon as she stepped inside. Damn, Dak wasn't home yet.

She locked the door behind her, hung her jacket in the closet, and shed her weapons. He worked less often than she did, but his job was more dangerous and she worried about him every assignment. It didn't help that he'd learned to block her when he was hunting. He wouldn't drop the shield until after he came down from the adrenaline.

"Stay safe," she whispered and turned on more lights.

After four months of living with Dak, it continued to take Nicole by surprise when she saw her things mixed with his. Her pink lamp looked ridiculous next to his tan leather sofas. His stone sculpture—a horse— seemed amused to be alongside her egg-shaped, acrylic curio cabinet. A cabinet she'd filled with things like a Rubik's Cube, sunglasses, and colorful miniature furniture.

The miracle was that Dak thought her cheap stuff looked fine with his elegant, expensive belongings. Nicole knew better, but she kind of liked it, too.

Unable to settle while he was gone, she went upstairs and changed into her pajamas. The drawstring pants rode low, the spaghetti-strap tank fit close and bared her midriff, but demons ran hot and she wouldn't be cold.

She was coming back down when the door opened. Nicole froze on the spiral staircase and studied Dak. He appeared weary and there was a definite pallor to his skin.

The urge to race down the stairs and demand to know if he was okay slammed into her and Nicole fought it. Instead, she concentrated on the fact he was alive, that he was moving without noticeable pain as he put his jacket away and walked into the living area.

With her self-command firmly in place, Nicole started down again. Dak stopped near the foot and waited. He reached for her as soon as she got to the bottom and she moved into his embrace.

"Rough night?" she asked, stroking his shoulders.

"There've been worse."

"And better, too?"

"Yeah." But he smiled slightly as he said it and that allowed Nicole to relax. She went up on her toes to kiss him and the rest of her tension seeped away. Her mate was home and safe.

Dak broke the kiss and put her an arm's length away. "You're okay?" he asked, checking her over.

That warm, mushy feeling swamped her again. "I'm fine."

"Good." Dak hesitated. "Things were closer tonight than I'm used to."

Her tension roared back and her fingers tightened on his. She took a deep breath to beat off the panic. "How close is closer than you're used to?"

"Not as bad as you're imagining. It got me thinking, though, about what matters. What doesn't."

Wariness kept her tense. "What did you come up with?"

"A couple things." Dak tugged her a step closer before she locked her muscles. "The first thing I realized was that I was damn glad you'd be here. This condo was just a place to sleep before you moved in, now it's a home."

Nicole gaped at him. She couldn't help it. This from the man who said he didn't want to be mated?

"I was wrong about that," Dak said. "Being mated to you is the best thing that ever happened to me. That's the other thing I realized. I love you, Nic."

He stopped blocking her, let her feel his emotions. She got his fear about the battle he'd been in earlier tonight. Nicole was tempted to find out what had happened, but Dak was also scared about her reaction to what he was saying. That amazed her. Didn't he already know how she felt about him?

But then she hadn't been aware his feelings for her either. Maybe he'd been as afraid to probe that direction as she'd been. "I love you, too," Nicole said, voice thick. "Always and forever."

This time when he tugged her closer, Nicole went.

"Always and forever," he promised. And then with a grin, he asked, "Why the hell did you make me wait twenty-nine years to find you?"

"You're lucky I didn't make you wait another thousand."

Dak laughed, then went serious, leaned in, and bit her shoulder. "Mine."

Nicole pushed his T-shirt collar aside and bit him in return. She didn't get a chance to make her own verbal claim. He bent down, swooped her over one shoulder, and headed up the stairs.

"You're not going to do me on the kitchen counter?"

"We'll save that for later." Dak put her down on the bed and covered her with his body.

As she looked up into the red glow of his eyes, Nicole ran her hand along the side of his face. She wasn't lost or alone any longer. This was where she really, truly belonged—with Dak.

ALSO AVAILABLE FROM MICHELE HAUF
AND SWELL CAT PRESS

Vampires, witches, and the Enlightenment.
Award-winning author, Michele Hauf, introduces a new
story in her world of Beautiful Creatures.

Available in print/digital format from most online retailers.

For more information about the stories in Michele's world visit:

MicheleHauf.com
blog.michelehauf.com
clubscarlet.michelehauf.com
Twitter: @michelehauf

RAVENOUS: the Dark Forgotten
One kiss is all it takes to lose your soul.
Holly Carver's grandma warns her that vampires are like a box of chocolate: they seem so tempting, but over-indulgence is a killer. That doesn't stop Holly from wanting her undead business partner, Alessandro. Unfortunately, an evil demon seems bent on dragging them into a supernatural war, and Holly's own magic holds the key to a hell dimension.

SCORCHED: the Dark Forgotten
Welcome to the Castle. The price of admission is your soul.
When they say ex-detective Conall Macmillan is hot, they have no idea. Now half-demon, he has ended up in the Castle, a supernatural prison. There he meets Constance, a strangely innocent vampire, who needs his help to find her kidnapped son. Will cracking this final case cost Mac his last scrap of humanity?

UNCHAINED: the Dark Forgotten

2011 RITA® WINNER, PARANORMAL ROMANCE

Been there, slain that.

Ashe Carver is one kick-ass monster killer, but a custody battle for her ten-year-old daughter has led Ashe to hang up her stakes and take a job at her local public library. Now supernatural prison guard Captain Reynard has only weeks to live if Ashe can't find the thief who stole his soul.

FROSTBOUND: the Dark Forgotten
Every dog might have his day, but the hellhound guards the night.
Someone's beheaded the wrong girl, and vampire-on-the lam Talia Rostova is the prime suspect in her own botched murder and the prisoner of her smoking-hot neighbor, Lore. He's the Alpha hellhound, bred to serve and protect. A good thing, because an ancient vampire is wreaking vengeance on the city—and on her—and Lore will have to go beyond a stake to put their enemy back in his grave.

www.SharonAshwood.com Excerpts. Videos. More.

Presenting-- TRUST ME

The first book in the new Vampire Hearts series by Lori Devoti

Dhamphir Harry Bisson has been hunting the female vampire
who turned his father for over a century. The vampire, who has been
building her power by feeding off her own family, thinks her bloodline
has run out, but Harry has found one last relative--Lindsey Dennis:
beautiful, trusting and the perfect bait.
With no knowledge of vampires, Lindsey thinks Harry is her savior and
the key to finding the family she has always dreamed of having.
Will Harry save her? Or will his thirst for revenge cause him to sacrifice
the only woman he could ever love?

www.loridevoti.com

From Patti O'Shea, stories set in the same world as **Enemy Embrace:**

Blood Feud – When a demon starts murdering vampires, a vampire enforcer and a demon prince are assigned to find the killer before war erupts. But Isobel and Seere have a past and that complicates their mission. (Short story)

Demon Kissed – Demon slayer Bree Molina has been tried for murder by the demons and sentenced to death. Andras has a plan to get her out of trouble, but he has secrets that will rock Bree's world. (Nocturne Bites)

Shadow's Caress – Former vampire hunter Cass Lanier didn't believe vampires could become ghosts, until the shade of the last one she killed shows up. Malachi James needs Cass to return him to his life, but other hunters have learned she can resurrect the vampires she killed and they plan to kill her first. (Nocturne Bites)

Other paranormal romances by Patti O'Shea

In the Midnight Hour – When a troubleshooter for a society of magic users rescues a private detective from a dark spell, she finds more than an ally as she faces down her former mentor. (2008 Booksellers Best Award Winner – Best Paranormal)

In Twilight's Shadow – Troubleshooter Creed Blackwood is trying to capture a demon hunting Maia Frasier's sister. But if Maia's suspicions about Creed's falling to dark magic are true, he might be a bigger danger than any demon could be. (2009 Write Touch Readers Choice Awards Finalist – Best Paranormal)

Edge of Dawn – Troubleshooter Logan Andrews has his loyalties torn between his people and the woman he's been assigned to protect. (2010 Aspen Gold Award Winner – Best Paranormal)

In the Darkest Night – Kel Andrews has spent the last year living with nightmares and flashbacks. He's withdrawn from his family and been removed him from his position as a troubleshooter. But when a woman asks him for protection from a demon, Kel reluctantly agrees to help—and finds himself facing an unexpected adversary, one he doesn't know how to fight. (2011 Beacon Award Winner – Best Paranormal)

www.pattioshea.com For excerpts, videos, and more

The authors would like to thank you for buying this book. We hope you enjoyed the stories within, as much as we enjoyed creating them!